Praise f
MIC.

THREAT VECTOR

"Michael DiMercurio plunges you into the world of undersea warfare with stunning technical accuracy, the best and brightest heroes, and a deadly look at the future."
—C.A. Mobley, author of *Code of Conflict*

PIRANHA FIRING POINT

"If dueling with torpedoes is your idea of a good time, you'll love it." —*The Sunday Star-Times* (Auckland)

BARRACUDA FINAL BEARING

"Terrific . . . the fighting really goes into high gear."
—*The San Francisco Examiner*

"A stunningly effective technopolitical thriller . . . a dandy hell-and-high-water yarn." —*Kirkus Reviews*

"Impressive. . . . Those who thrill to the blip of sonar and the thud of torpedoes will relish this deepwater dive."
—*Publishers Weekly*

continued . . .

PHOENIX SUB ZERO

"Moves at a breakneck pace."
>—Larry Bond, bestselling author of *Combat*

"A technothriller by a master rivaling Tom Clancy . . . exciting from first page to last." —*Publishers Weekly*

"A good, suspenseful, and spine-tingling read . . . exhilarating."
>—Associated Press

"Powerful . . . rousing . . . for Tom Clancy fans."
>—*Kirkus Reviews*

ATTACK OF THE SEAWOLF

"Thrilling, fast-paced, action-packed . . . not to be missed."
>—Associated Press

"As much fun as *The Hunt for Red October,* both as a chase and a catalogue of the Navy's goodies." —*Arizona Daily Star*

"Superb storytelling . . . suspenseful action. . . . Michael DiMercurio, a former submarine officer, delivers a taut yarn at flank speed."   —*The Virginian-Pilot*

"Nail-biting excitement . . . a must for technothriller fans."
                                          —*Publishers Weekly*

"Gobs of exciting submarine warfare . . . with a supervillain who gives new meaning to the word 'torture.'"
                                          —*Kirkus Reviews*

VOYAGE OF THE DEVILFISH

"Those who liked *The Hunt for Red October* will love this book."   —*Library Journal*

"Cat-and-mouse games in the waters beneath the Arctic icecap . . . building to a page-turning, nuclear-tipped climax."
                                          —*Publishers Weekly*

"Authentic . . . fresh . . . tense . . . a chillingly realistic first-hand feel."   —*Kirkus Reviews*

TERMINAL RUN

MICHAEL DiMERCURIO

AN ONYX BOOK

ONYX
Published by New American Library, a division of
Penguin Putnam Inc., 375 Hudson Street,
New York, New York 10014, U.S.A.
Penguin Books Ltd, 80 Strand,
London WC2R 0RL, England
Penguin Books Australia Ltd, Ringwood,
Victoria, Australia
Penguin Books Canada Ltd, 10 Alcorn Avenue,
Toronto, Ontario, Canada M4V 3B2
Penguin Books (N.Z.) Ltd, 182–190 Wairau Road,
Auckland 10, New Zealand

Penguin Books Ltd, Registered Offices:
Harmondsworth, Middlesex, England

First published by Onyx, an imprint of New American Library,
a division of Penguin Putnam Inc.

First Printing, October 2002
10 9 8 7 6 5 4 3 2 1

Copyright © Michael DiMercurio, 2002
Illustrations by Barbara Field
All rights reserved

 REGISTERED TRADEMARK—MARCA REGISTRADA

Printed in the United States of America

Without limiting the rights under copyright reserved above, no part of this publication
may be reproduced, stored in or introduced into a retrieval system, or transmitted, in any
form, or by any means (electronic, mechanical, photocopying, recording, or otherwise),
without the prior written permission of both the copyright owner and the above publisher
of this book.

PUBLISHER'S NOTE
This is a work of fiction. Names, characters, places, and incidents either are the product
of the author's imagination or are used fictitiously, and any resemblance to actual
persons, living or dead, business establishments, events, or locales is entirely
coincidental.

BOOKS ARE AVAILABLE AT QUANTITY DISCOUNTS WHEN USED TO PROMOTE PRODUCTS OR
SERVICES. FOR INFORMATION PLEASE WRITE TO PREMIUM MARKETING DIVISION, PENGUIN
PUTNAM INC., 375 HUDSON STREET, NEW YORK, NEW YORK 10014.

If you purchased this book without a cover you should be aware that this book is stolen
property. It was reported as "unsold and destroyed" to the publisher and neither the
author nor the publisher has received any payment for this "stripped book."

To the love of my life, Patricia DiMercurio,
Who is to me as the land is to the ship—
Desired and missed,
My beginning and my destination,
My purpose and my hope,
My future and my past.

"Gentlemen, one thing I've learned at sea is that the procedure manuals are written by people who have never been on the business end of a torpedo with the plant crashing around them, with the captain shouting for power, where a second's delay can mean death. The meaning of being an officer in our Navy is knowing more than those operation manuals, knowing how to play when you're hurt, when the ship is going down and you need to keep shooting anyway. That's really it, isn't it, men? The ability to play hurt. That's the only way we'll ever win a war. And in fact, that's the only way you can live your lives. Do that for me, guys. Learn to play hurt."

—Admiral Kinnaird R. McKee, Director Navy Nuclear Propulsion Program and Former Superintendent, U.S. Naval Academy, Addressing the Atlantic Fleet Submarine Officers, Norfolk, Virginia

"The U.S. Submarine Force will remain the world's preeminent submarine force. We will aggressively incorporate new and innovative technologies to maintain dominance throughout the maritime battlespace. We will promote the multiple capabilities of submarines and develop tactics to support national objectives through battlespace preparation, sea control, supporting the land battle, and strategic deterrence. We will fill the role of the Joint Commander's stealthy, full-spectrum expeditionary platform."

—U.S. Submarine Force Vision

Terminal Run—Defense contractor's term for the final stage in the flight of a submarine-launched torpedo in which the unit is homing on the target and has sped up to attack velocity.

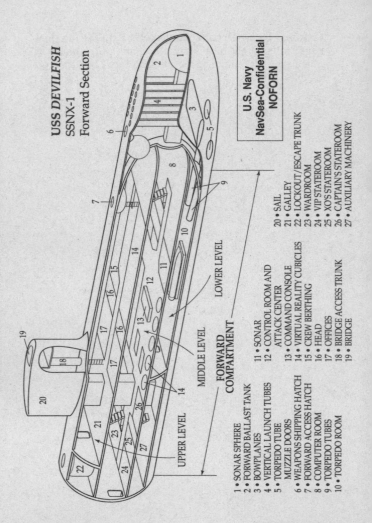

USS DEVILFISH
SSNX-1
Forward Section

U.S. Navy
NavSea-Confidential
NOFORN

1 • SONAR SPHERE
2 • FORWARD BALLAST TANK
3 • BOWPLANES
4 • VERTICAL LAUNCH TUBES
5 • TORPEDO TUBE
    MUZZLE DOORS
6 • WEAPONS SHIPPING HATCH
7 • FORWARD ACCESS HATCH
8 • COMPUTER ROOM
9 • TORPEDO TUBES
10 • TORPEDO ROOM

11 • SONAR
12 • CONTROL ROOM AND
     ATTACK CENTER
13 • COMMAND CONSOLE
14 • VIRTUAL REALITY CUBICLES
15 • CREW BERTHING
16 • HEAD
17 • OFFICES
18 • BRIDGE ACCESS TRUNK
19 • BRIDGE

20 • SAIL
21 • GALLEY
22 • LOCKOUT/ESCAPE TRUNK
23 • WARDROOM
24 • VIP STATEROOM
25 • XO'S STATEROOM
26 • CAPTAIN'S STATEROOM
27 • AUXILIARY MACHINERY

FORWARD
COMPARTMENT

UPPER LEVEL

MIDDLE LEVEL

LOWER LEVEL

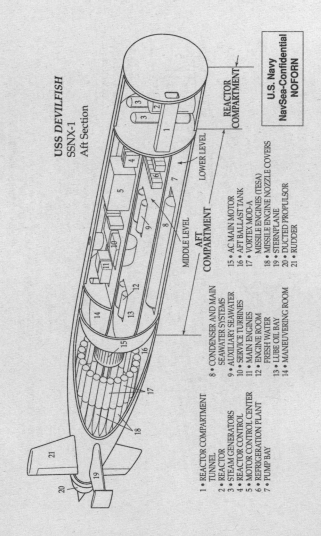

USS DEVILFISH
SSNX-1
Aft Section

REACTOR
COMPARTMENT

LOWER LEVEL

MIDDLE LEVEL

**AFT
COMPARTMENT**

1 • REACTOR COMPARTMENT
    TUNNEL
2 • REACTOR
3 • STEAM GENERATORS
4 • REACTOR CONTROL
5 • MOTOR CONTROL CENTER
6 • REFRIGERATION PLANT
7 • PUMP BAY

8 • CONDENSER AND MAIN
    SEAWATER SYSTEMS
9 • AUXILIARY SEAWATER
10 • SERVICE TURBINES
11 • MAIN ENGINES
12 • ENGINE ROOM
13 • LUBE OIL BAY
    FRESH WATER
14 • MANEUVERING ROOM

15 • AC MAIN MOTOR
16 • AFT BALLAST TANK
17 • VORTEX MOD-A
    MISSILE ENGINES (TESA)
18 • MISSILE ENGINE NOZZLE COVERS
19 • STERNPLANE
20 • DUCTED PROPULSOR
21 • RUDDER

U.S. Navy
NavSea-Confidential
NOFORN

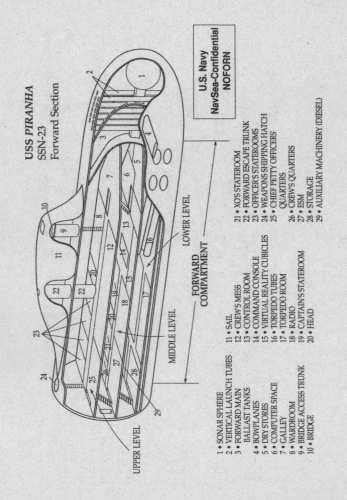

USS *PIRANHA*
SSN-23
Forward Section

U.S. Navy
NavSea-Confidential
NOFORN

FORWARD
COMPARTMENT

UPPER LEVEL

MIDDLE LEVEL

LOWER LEVEL

1 • SONAR SPHERE
2 • VERTICAL LAUNCH TUBES
3 • FORWARD MAIN
     BALLAST TANKS
4 • BOWPLANES
5 • DRY STORES
6 • COMPUTER SPACE
7 • GALLEY
8 • WARDROOM
9 • BRIDGE ACCESS TRUNK
10 • BRIDGE

11 • SAIL
12 • CREW'S MESS
13 • CONTROL ROOM
14 • COMMAND CONSOLE
15 • VIRTUAL REALITY CUBICLES
16 • TORPEDO TUBES
17 • TORPEDO ROOM
18 • RADIO
19 • CAPTAIN'S STATEROOM
20 • HEAD

21 • XO'S STATEROOM
22 • FORWARD ESCAPE TRUNK
23 • OFFICER'S STATEROOMS
24 • WEAPONS SHIPPING HATCH
25 • CHIEF PETTY OFFICERS'
      QUARTERS
26 • CREW'S QUARTERS
27 • ESM
28 • STORAGE
29 • AUXILIARY MACHINERY (DIESEL)

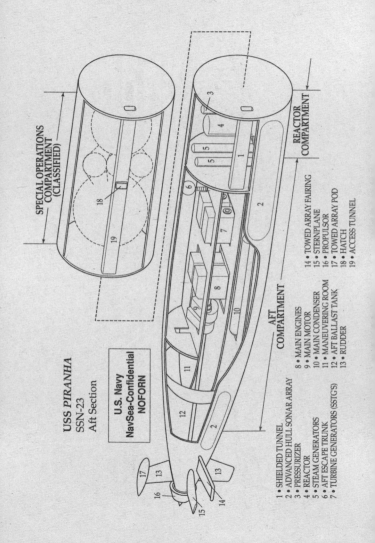

USS PIRANHA
SSN-23
Aft Section

U.S. Navy
NavSea-Confidential
NOFORN

SPECIAL OPERATIONS
COMPARTMENT
(CLASSIFIED)

REACTOR
COMPARTMENT

AFT
COMPARTMENT

1 • SHIELDED TUNNEL
2 • ADVANCED HULL SONAR ARRAY
3 • PRESSURIZER
4 • REACTOR
5 • STEAM GENERATORS
6 • AFT ESCAPE TRUNK
7 • TURBINE GENERATORS (SSTG'S)

8 • MAIN ENGINES
9 • MAIN MOTOR
10 • MAIN CONDENSER
11 • MANEUVERING ROOM
12 • AFT BALLAST TANK
13 • RUDDER

14 • TOWED ARRAY FAIRING
15 • STERNPLANE
16 • PROPULSOR
17 • TOWED ARRAY POD
18 • HATCH
19 • ACCESS TUNNEL

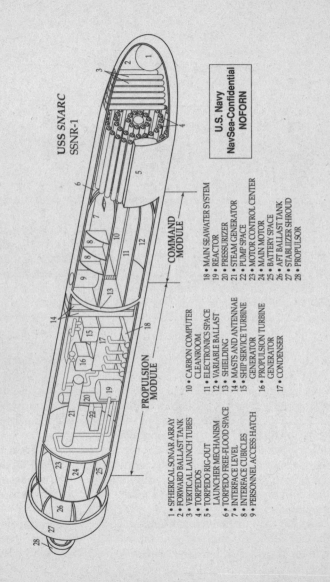

USS SNARC
SSNR-1

U.S. Navy
NavSea-Confidential
NOFORN

COMMAND
MODULE

PROPULSION
MODULE

1 • SPHERICAL SONAR ARRAY
2 • FORWARD BALLAST TANK
3 • VERTICAL LAUNCH TUBES
4 • TORPEDOS
5 • TORPEDO RIG-OUT
LAUNCHER MECHANISM
6 • TORPEDO FREE-FLOOD SPACE
7 • INTERFACE LEVEL
8 • INTERFACE CUBICLES
9 • PERSONNEL ACCESS HATCH

10 • CARBON COMPUTER
CLEANROOM
11 • ELECTRONICS SPACE
12 • VARIABLE BALLAST
13 • SHIELDING
14 • MASTS AND ANTENNAE
15 • SHIP SERVICE TURBINE
GENERATOR
16 • PROPULSION TURBINE
GENERATOR
17 • CONDENSER

18 • MAIN SEAWATER SYSTEM
19 • REACTOR
20 • PRESSURIZER
21 • STEAM GENERATOR
22 • PUMP SPACE
23 • MOTOR CONTROL CENTER
24 • MAIN MOTOR
25 • BATTERY SPACE
26 • AFT BALLAST TANK
27 • STABILIZER SHROUD
28 • PROPULSOR

1

It had been a month since he had flown to Washington to demand a demotion.

The boss had protested, of course. Every other candidate for his job was dead, killed last summer in the disastrous terrorist attack that had robbed them of more than a thousand of their most senior people. But failing a reassignment back to his old job, he would have no choice but to resign, and that would leave two jobs vacant. He had returned home successfully demoted, and the demotion seemed to set the world right again. The staff had shaped up, the operations personnel were improving, and the equipment was in excellent condition.

On this sunny May Saturday he had gone through eighteen holes and pounded out six kilometers before lunch. After a brisk shower at the club, he had donned chinos and a golf shirt and climbed into his convertible Porsche for the twenty-kilometer drive to the office. With the staff home and the phones quiet, he could do more real work in three hours than he could accomplish in a week. He put the top down and drove out of the lot until he reached the coast highway, then opened up the smooth engine, the car accelerating, taking the curves easily, the wind blowing in his hair and taking away his few remaining problems.

As the road rushed toward him, he considered the situation that awaited. For the last year the world situation had been relatively peaceful, but now there were rumors of sparks fly-

ing between the Peoples Republic of China and the Hindu
Republic of India, bitter enemies since India's land grabs
during the first and second Chinese civil wars. But any resulting global hostilities would be someone else's problem,
since a full-out war would certainly take years to develop, or
even decades.

He had barely completed the last thought when the rearview
mirror startled him back to the moment. The state trooper was
so close that he couldn't see the cop's headlights, only the
Smokey Bear hat and the mirrored shades and the flashing
lights. He cursed as he pulled the Porsche over, knowing he'd
pulverized the speed limit. He'd been driving like a maniac on
this highway for two years and had never once seen a local
constable, much less a statie. He became more dismayed as he
came to a stop and a second state trooper cruiser pulled in
ahead of him, the little sports car now trapped between the two
patrol cars. He cursed again as he fished for his wallet and registration. When the jackbooted Ray•Ban-wearing trooper came
to the car, the glove compartment was open, papers falling
onto the floorboards.

"Put both hands on the steering wheel immediately, sir," the
trooper commanded in a deep iron voice, his hand on his un-
buckled holster.

With both hands back on the wheel he looked up at the cop
and opened his mouth to speak, but never got a word out.

"Identification, sir."

He handed over his driver's license and his military ID. The
cop scanned them for a moment, comparing the photographs
to the driver.

"Mr. Egon Ericcson?"

"It's Vic," he said. "Call me Vic."

The cop opened the car door. "Step out of the vehicle, Mr.
Ericcson. Slowly. Don't speak, don't say a word."

What the hell was going on? he wondered as he climbed to
his feet. Once a varsity football warrior, Vic "The Viking"
Ericcson towered over others, with broad shoulders, a flat-top
blond crew cut, ocean-blue eyes presiding over the broken

nose and square jaw of an amateur boxer, his weathered face showing the hard wear of years in the outdoors.

A second trooper approached from the rear cruiser and climbed into the Porsche's seat, shutting the door after him.

"Hey, goddammit, that's my car!"

"Please remain silent, sir," the first trooper said. "Your vehicle is impounded. Please turn around slowly and walk to the patrol car, sir."

"Officer, look, I know—"

"Quiet, sir."

The trooper forced him into the back of his cruiser and shut the door, then took the driver's seat. The cop backed up, then peeled out into the highway and rocketed down the asphalt toward the city. Behind them the second cruiser was escorting the Porsche, but the two cars soon vanished in the distance as the trooper accelerated.

"Where are we going? The courthouse? State Police HQ?"

The trooper said nothing. Finally the airport exit came up, and the cruiser pulled off, eventually coming to a stop at a large fence gate, which rolled open. Ericcson had the momentary thought that they must have a police facility inside the airport grounds, but the cruiser flew over the tarmac of the airport for a few minutes until it screeched to a stop at a gigantic commercial Boeing-Airbus 808, the plane's jets idling far from the terminal.

He started to ask the obvious question, but before he could, the rear door opened and two new state troopers pulled him unceremoniously from the car and led him up an old-fashioned wheeled stairway to the jet's door far above. He was escorted quickly inside the cool airplane, and as his eyes adjusted from the harsh noon sunlight he saw that the interior was empty except for two men in nondescript suits, who waved him to a seat in the middle of the first-class section.

He looked at the suits and decided to see if they would prove more understanding than the uniforms who'd brought him and who were currently handing over a clipboard for signatures. As the cops withdrew, he looked up and started his complaint. "Look, guys, I was speeding. I admit it, but—"

One of the troopers suddenly turned and handed something down to him. He stared dumbly at his driver's license and his U.S. Navy identification. Obviously, whatever was happening to him had nothing to do with a traffic violation.

"Who are you guys? What's going on? Is this coming from Washington?"

"Sir," the first suit said formally, "please strap yourself in. We're leaving immediately."

"Goddammit, what the hell?" he grumbled, but decided to shut his mouth. He looked down at himself, at his casual clothes, the odd thought coming that he hoped he was dressed for wherever they were taking him.

The jet reached the end of the runway and throttled up, climbing out east over the Pacific. With his escorts insisting upon remaining silent, there was nothing to do but sleep in the large comfortable first-class seat. It was hours later when he woke up, the windows dark long after local sunset.

"May I get you something, sir?" The first suit stood over him.

"Coffee would be great," he said in his gravelly voice. "And then some information. And a phone."

"Coffee is the best we'll be able to do for you, sir." The steaming coffee landed on the tray in front of him, and the smell of it made him want to dive into it, the aroma reminding him of his younger days at sea.

"Then tell me one thing—may I take it that we're headed for Washington?"

"I can neither confirm nor deny, sir."

"It's John Patton, isn't it? He ordered this?"

"Again, sir, I can neither—"

He waved the man to silence and waited for them to arrive wherever it was they were taking him. As the plane descended, he asked permission to move to a window seat, surprised when they let him shift over. The jet made a night approach toward nothingness, the absence of lights odd, as if they were landing in a deserted cornfield. This might not be the East Coast at all, he thought. Eventually the jet turned and flared out, the heavy airframe touching down gently and braking at the end of the darkened runway, the aircraft turning at the end and taxiing back to where they'd touched down. The agents pulled him out of his seat as the forward hatch opened. He stepped out into warm, humid night air, insisting on taking a look around at the top of the steps at an unlit compound of aging huts and derelict outbuildings. By this time he wasn't surprised by the lack of a greeting party.

He walked down the stairs to the runway. Immediately his escorts pulled away the rolling stairway and the big jet rolled down the still-darkened strip, its navigational beacons only coming on after it had flown away into the distance. The night was eerily quiet after the plane left.

"Where in God's name am I?" he asked, knowing he would have no answer.

He was led to a decrepit cinder-block building's rusted steel door. The interior was lit by a single hooded, dim lightbulb, the building some kind of garage or storage area in a state of severe disrepair, one of the vehicle bay doors broken and hanging from a hinge. He was led to a staircase, down to a dusty cobwebbed subbasement, which led to a cinder-block-walled hallway. One narrow door was opened, the broom closet cluttered with cleaning gear, a stained sink, and another rusted door. The suit shut the closet door behind them and opened the second door, revealing the gleaming stainless-steel interior of an elevator. The agent shut the steel door, put his ID card on a scanner, then pressed his thumb to a second scanner. The inner door glided shut, and the elevator descended silently for some time. When the door opened, Ericcson was led down another cinder-block hallway past several steel doors, the double door on the end opening to a Spartan conference room furnished with only a generations-old oak table and ten wooden chairs, the kind that looked like they'd come from a courtroom. He was directed to take a seat. He poured himself a black cup of coffee from the service in the middle of the table.

When it was half gone the door creaked open, and he stood to greet the newcomers. He didn't recognize one, but the other was very familiar.

It was John Patton, the boss.

When Kelly McKee opened the door of his house in the sprawling Virginia Beach suburbs, he found his chief of staff standing there in jeans and a T-shirt, carrying a bottle of Merlot. It was nearly midnight on Saturday, and she was two hours late. She said nothing, handing him a note that said:

> *Don't say anything. Invite me in and turn on music in the den.*

He looked at the note uncertainly, not sure whether to be annoyed or amused. He waved her in, took the wine to the den, and turned on a mellow disk. She frowned and produced her own music and inserted it. It was vintage head-banging rock-'n'roll. She cranked the volume until he was about to complain, when she handed him the next note:

> *Don't argue. Lie on the floor and fake a heart attack. This is all coming from the highest levels and will be explained to you.*

He gave her a look of disbelief. Her expression was deadly serious, and he had known her for too many years and through too many battles to doubt her. He was no actor, but he handed back the note without a word, turned to look at the wine bottle, and suddenly grabbed his chest. With an expression of agony he sank to his knees, the wine bottle falling to the carpeting, McKee joining it. Above him she stood and calmly dialed her cell phone. When she spoke her voice sounded panicked, but her expression never changed.

"This is Karen Petri at 227 Hightower Road. The homeowner, Kelly McKee, is having a heart attack. He's collapsed and in terrible pain. Yes! Please hurry. Yes."

"Was that 911?" he asked.

"Quiet, sir," she said, kneeling above him.

He waited, feeling absurd.

McKee was a slight figure, slightly shorter than Petri. He had a handsomely rugged face, beloved by the press, and which looked much too young to be worn by a man so senior, and it would look even younger without the trademark bushy eyebrows.

After what seemed forever but was perhaps only ten minutes a truck could be heard out front. Petri opened the door and admitted three paramedics. None seemed to care that his heart sounded perfectly normal. He was placed on a gurney, an oxygen mask strapped on, his shirt ripped open to expose his chest, a blood-pressure cuff strapped to his arm. The men rushed him out the front door to the waiting ambulance. Petri asked if she could go. The lead paramedic nodded, and she climbed in. The door was shut as the van accelerated out of the court and roared north.

"Somebody want to tell me what the hell is going on?" McKee said through his oxygen mask.

"Specific orders from Patton, sir," Petri said. "And one of the orders is to keep silent until you're where the boss wants you."

"You've always wanted to be able to tell me to shut up." He grinned at her, but her expression remained severe as she put a finger to her lips.

Once steady on the interstate, the first paramedic stripped off his uniform until he was down to his underwear. McKee lifted an eyebrow.

"Please remove your clothes, sir," the nearly naked medic instructed. McKee shrugged, the order no more odd than the rest of the evening. The paramedic was McKee's height and age, within five kilos of his weight, with the same skin and hair coloring. McKee traded clothes, the paramedic climbing onto the gurney.

"Put on a surgical scrub cap from the cabinet."

McKee felt like a fool decked out as a paramedic, but did as he was told. The ambulance arrived at the emergency entrance to a hospital. When the door opened he and the other paramedics hustled the patient through the door, one of the other men shouting medical jargon to the receiving physicians. McKee glanced up, thinking for a moment that they had gone to Portsmouth Naval Hospital. A new face arrived, a middle-aged man in a suit holding a banker's box under one arm.

"Follow me, sir," he ordered. McKee followed the suit, Petri staying behind with the man on the gurney, who was being prepared to be rushed to the operating theater. McKee stood in an elevator that zoomed to the upper floors of the hospital building. The doors opened to the roof. The suit-wearing agent waved him across a walkway to a waiting medevac helicopter, which was idling. "Put this on, sir," he said, opening his box and producing an aviator's helmet with an intercom headset inside. McKee strapped it on over the surgical cap and climbed into the rear seat, and as soon as the hatch shut the aircraft throttled up and lifted off, turning to the northwest.

McKee debated asking the pilots what they knew, but decided to wait. He glanced at his watch. It was half past midnight and he was flying over the eastern shore of Virginia in a speeding medical transport chopper with no idea what was going on. He settled in for the ride, knowing that this had to be urgent. After a half hour the helicopter settled slowly toward a landing site without lights. The chopper came to earth and the rotors spun down to idle. The copilot told him to remain seated. Ten minutes later another helicopter landed in the darkness. A man wearing a helmet climbed out and trotted to McKee's helicopter and opened the door to join him in the rear.

By the dim wash of the cockpit lights McKee could see the man's face under the visor of his helmet.

"Good evening, sir," McKee said to John Patton. "Is there anything you want to share with me about this trip?"

"Nope," Patton said without a smile. "Pilot, let's go."

The chopper took off and flew for another half hour before touching down for a second landing in the dark.

John Patton's evening had been as odd as Ericcson's and McKee's.

The afternoon's two briefings had given him a sick feeling in his stomach. Things were much worse than he'd ever suspected. The first meeting had been with the Director of the National Security Agency, a man named Mason Daniels, who had nothing but bad news. The second meeting had been with the President, the Secretary of War, the National Security Advisor, the Director of Central Intelligence, and the Chairman of the Joint Chiefs of Staff in the situation room of the White House, where the news was even worse. He had immediate work to do with two of his chief subordinates, but both were being watched by the other side, their movements chronicled, the state of the military's readiness judged by whether his men played golf or took Saturday emergency meetings at the Pentagon.

Mason Daniels helped Patton plan a rendezvous at a second-tier presidential evacuation bunker on the eastern shore of Maryland, a structure buried deep underground and surrounded by empty farmland, all of it owned by the U.S. Department of Agriculture. The bunker had a concealed four-thousand-meter runway, with two feet of topsoil and vegetation growing over the strip in movable pans controlled by a hydraulic system that would uncover the runway on command from the approaching aircraft. The problem was how to get his men to the bunker without the people tailing them becoming wise to an urgent meeting with their boss in Washington. Daniels had proposed how to bring in Patton's men, and reluctantly he'd agreed. But then the matter was his own departure to the bunker, since he was watched even more closely by the adversary's intelligence forces than McKee or Ericcson.

Daniels had arranged that as well. Patton had asked Marcy, his wife of twenty-five years, for a Saturday evening off to see some old Academy classmates, and had kissed her good night and taken a cab to a Georgetown pub. One of Daniels' men brought the drinks that evening to a group of friends also cast by Daniels, and during the evening Patton appeared to take aboard too many beers, although not one contained a drop of alcohol. As the clock struck midnight, Patton's face went pale. He excused himself and hurried to the men's room, where a man wearing Western regalia waited for him in the back hallway. The cowboy gave him a Stetson ten-gallon hat and led him out the back door to a waiting black sedan idling in the parking lot. Feeling foolish, Patton got in the back seat and slouched down despite the blacked-out windows, the car roaring off to a small civilian airport, where a corporate jet helicopter waited. Before Patton left the car he traded the cowboy hat for a helmet with an intercom headset. The chopper took off and flew to a second airport, where he transferred to a second helicopter, then flew out over the Chesapeake, eventually landing where Kelly McKee's helicopter waited.

He joined McKee but waved off the inevitable questions until they landed at the bunker. Once in the underground conference room he greeted Ericcson with a handshake, the taller man's big hand crushing his palm.

"Vic," Patton said, "meet Vice Admiral Kelly McKee, Commander Unified Submarine Command and my acting Vice Chief of Naval Operations for Submarine Warfare. The paramedic outfit is part of the ruse to get him here. Kelly, this is Vice Admiral Egon 'The Viking' Ericcson, Supreme Commander-in-Chief U.S. Naval Forces Pacific—"

Ericcson shook his head and growled, "Former commander, Admiral Patton. I've been demoted to be the commander of the NavForcePac Fleet. And call me Vic," he said, pumping McKee's hand. "It's less formal than 'The Viking.' "

Patton grimaced in exasperation. "Admiral Ericcson has been demoted by request to Commander NavForcePac Fleet, but he's still the acting Super-CinC-Pac. Until I appoint his replacement."

"You know, Admiral, it's not really a demotion until you take away the responsibilities and put someone in the Super-CinC-Pac job."

Admiral John Patton, the Chief of Naval Operations and the commanding admiral of the U.S. Navy, ignored the comment, the crow's-feet at his eyes wrinkling in a serious expression.

"I know you guys have a hundred questions about how and why you were brought here. But let's put all that on the back burner until the briefing is over. Agreed?" Both of his admirals nodded. Patton pointed to the conference table. "Gentlemen, take a seat."

Patton glanced over at his subordinates, unable to avoid the thought that they made a damned odd couple. On his right sat Ericcson with his imposing physique. On Patton's left sat the far slighter form of Kelly McKee, the youthful-looking submarine chief a head shorter than Patton and towered over by Ericcson.

The two admirals began and ended worlds apart. Ericcson was a supersonic naval aviator who'd earned a Purple Heart and the Silver Star over the Sea of Japan in a dogfight that nearly killed him, and had moved on to command fighter squadrons, deep draft ships, two aircraft carriers, and finally a carrier battlegroup. McKee had spent his life underwater in the operational isolation of a nuclear submarine, his reputation that of an easygoing sailor's commander, but he had proved vicious and cunning and aggressive in a desperate undersea battle, the crisis earning him the Navy Cross and command of the submarine force. To Patton's knowledge, the two starkly different admirals had never met before this moment.

"I hope neither of you thinks this will be a high-tech briefing with floating three-dimensional displays and animated national borders," Patton began, his jaw clenching. "With me you get a paper map and a number two pencil. I'll get to the point fast and get you both moving. We don't have much time." He produced a map of Asia from his pocket, spread it out on the end of the conference table, and stood to lean over it, his subordinates standing with him. "Gentlemen, in two weeks you'll both be fighting a war." Patton stabbed the map with his finger. "A war over this."

2

Midshipman First Class Anthony Michael Pacino slammed the door of the classic Corvette and looked uncertainly at the lower security area of Groton's U.S. Submarine Base. His mouth filled with battery acid, the way it always did when he was nervous. He had wanted to stay as far away from the submarine force as humanly possible, but a sudden series of fleet exercises had made all the fighter squadrons and SEAL teams unavailable for midshipman cruises. His entire class had been assigned to surface ships except for a half dozen ordered to submarines. There was no possible way he could ever follow in his father's footsteps, he thought—the old man was idolized by the Submarine Force, and Pacino could only be a bitter disappointment by comparison. There would be no inherited talent in this area—he was too much his mother's son. He had planned to be a naval aviator, and now found himself in the absurd position of reporting as an apprentice to his father's Silent Service. One more thing to endure before he flew the jet, he told himself.

He checked the reflection of himself in the car window, adjusting his uniform shirt's tuck after the long drive up from Annapolis. The midshipman in the reflection was tall and slim with an athlete's efficiently muscled physique. He wore a starched tropical uniform with its white shirt, pants, belt, shoes, and hat, the uniform contrasting with his tanned skin. A pair of black shoulderboards each carried a thin gold braid stripe and a gold fouled anchor. Above the youth's breast pocket was a national service ribbon and, above that, silver airborne wings, the eagle's wings forming a closed oval around the ice-cream cone of the parachute canopy. His black name tag was the only other color on the uniform. He ran his hand through his light brown hair, which fell toward his eyebrows in a wave and swooped low over his ears, the hair longer than regulations allowed, then clamped his cover onto his head, hiding the offending locks. He sneered into the window, hating the face he'd inherited from his mother with its soft, almost-feminine features, his eyes almond-shaped and cobalt-blue, looking out from under long eyelashes, his nose a delicate curve, his cheekbones pronounced, his lips full.

Finally satisfied that his military appearance wouldn't result in angry phone calls back to the Academy, Pacino shouldered his seabag and walked down to the security building at the barbed-wire fenceline to the lower base, where the piers pointed into the Thames River. A petty officer escorted Pacino into the high-security piers to an odd-looking, colossal submarine. A banner on its gangway read USS PIRANHA SSN-23. He had seen the vessel before, in person and in the news, but the thing tied to the pier bore no resemblance to the ship of his memory.

For one thing, the Seawolf-class was distinguished by its gigantic diameter, a fat forty-two feet compared to every other sub's thirty-two. The width of the hull made the Seawolf-class look stubby, because they were only 326 feet long, shorter than the old 688s. But this boat's length made her seem slender as a pencil, stretching far beyond the end of the pier. She had to be over four hundred feet long, Pacino thought.

And just as strange, the sail was all wrong. The Seawolf-class subs were all built with a vertical slab-sided fin rising starkly to the sky from the deck. But this sail was a teardrop of streamlined curves rising steeply from the forward bullet nose of the ship and extending far aft, then tapering gently to the midpoint of the hull. And further aft at the rudder, the fin that protruded from the murky water of the Thames River was not the usual unadorned vertical surface but was topped by a horizontal teardrop-shaped pod. For a moment Pacino wondered if there was some mistake, that he'd been brought to a giant Russian attack sub. But American it had to be. U.S. Navy khaki-clad chief petty officers and a dungaree-wearing enlisted gang were working frantically at the forward stores loading hatch, bringing on pallets of food and spare parts.

While he'd been looking at the vessel, the topside sentry had been glaring at him. Pacino walked up to him and traded salutes.

"Midshipman Pacino, reporting aboard for temporary duty."

"Stay there," the crackerjack uniformed sentry ordered, speaking into his radio.

From the mid-hull hatch an officer in a working khaki uniform leaped to the deck and hurried down the gangway. Pacino stared at the officer, startled that he was looking at a woman. She was short and petite, her gleaming black hair pulled back in a ponytail. The rank insignia on her open collars was a silver double bar. She wore a blue baseball cap with the gold embroidered letters spelling USS PIRANHA SSN-23 with a gold dolphin symbol above the brim. Beneath the brim, her dark almond-shaped eyes glared at Pacino below arching brows. Her nose was slightly upturned, with a small constellation of freckles on it. She had strong cheekbones and a model's chin, her sole physical flaw, on a first glance, her jughandled ears protruding below the ball cap and her ponytail. Above her left shirt pocket she wore a gold dolphin pin, the emblem of a submarine-qualified officer, resembling pilot's wings, but up close consisting of two scaly fish facing a diesel boat conning tower. The woman moved jerkily, practically jumping out of her skin. It was easy to imagine she'd downed an entire pot of coffee. Pacino came to attention and saluted. He looked into her narrowed eyes, the woman's face hard and unfriendly, her jaw clenched.

"You must be Pacino," she said, her throaty voice pouring out the firehose stream of words. "Welcome to the Black Pig. I'm Lieutenant Alameda, *Piranha*'s chief engineer. Captain

Catardi wanted me to meet you and introduce you to the ship, then bring you to his stateroom." She turned toward the vessel. "Follow me."

Pacino stepped off the gangway onto the hull. The black surface was smooth and rubbery like a shark's skin, the anechoic coating covering the entire hull for sonar quieting. The lieutenant vanished down the mid-hull hatch. From his childhood memories of submarine etiquette, he leaned over the hatch opening and shouted, "Down ladder!" then tossed down his bag, lowered himself into the hatchring, feeling its oiled, shiny, cool steel surface as his feet found the rungs of the ladder. He put his feet outside the ladder rails and slid all the way down to the deck in one smooth motion, his shoes hitting the deckplates with a thump.

Nostalgia hit Pacino then, the smell whisking him back in time to his youth, the harsh electrical smell of the ship making him remember his father's submarines. He sniffed the air, the scent a mixture of diesel oil and diesel exhaust from the emergency generator, ozone from the electrical equipment, cooking oil, lubricating oils, and amines from the atmospheric control equipment. The narrow passageway ended at a bulkhead just beyond the ladder. The passageway was finished in a dark gray laminate, the doors and edges crafted from stainless steel like the interior of a transcontinental train compartment. The passageway led forward to the crew's mess and galley, doors opening on either side, the passageway bulkheads covered with photographs of the ship's triumphant return from her victory in the East China Sea.

Alameda shoved a cigarette-lighter-sized piece of plastic at him. "This is called a TLD for ThermoLuminescent Dosimeter. Measures your radiation dose. Put it on your belt."

Alameda's radio crackled: "Duty Officer, Engineering Officer of the Watch."

"Duty Officer," she said into the walkie-talkie. "Go ahead."

"Maneuvering watches are manned aft, ma'am. Precritical checklist complete and sat. Estimated critical position calculated and checked. Request permission to start the reactor."

"Wait one," she said, and put the radio in her pocket. "Come with me," she ordered Pacino. They walked down the passageway past the opening to the crew's mess to the stairway to the middle-level deck. Pacino followed her down the steep stairs, ending at the forward part of the control room. It was nothing like the *Seawolf* control room of his youth. The periscope stand and the periscopes were gone, a two-seat console taking their place. The ship-control panel and ballast control had been ripped out and replaced with an enclosure cubicle with two seats, a center console, and wraparound display screens. The clutter of the overhead with its pipes and cables and ducts was cleared out, leaving a circular continuous display screen angling between the bulkheads and the overhead, and the starboard row of consoles that had been the attack center was gone, replaced by five cubicles. The only remaining recognizable fixtures were the twin navigation tables in the aft part of the room. There was far more, but he could not absorb the vast changes as he hurried through the room behind the engineer.

Alameda led Pacino to the aft passageway and knocked on a door labeled COSR, the abbreviation for Commanding Officer's Stateroom. The door opened and a man stepped out into the passageway and shut the door behind him. He was a scowling, hard-looking Navy commander in a working khaki uniform, Pacino's height, in his late thirties or early forties with crow's-feet at his eyes and a touch of gray at the temples of his black hair running down his long sideburns. He had olive-colored skin and the blackest eyes Pacino had ever seen, with deep dark circles beneath them and coal-black eyebrows above, set in a round face with a square jaw and defined cheekbones. He looked at Pacino, and his previously grim expression melted into a smile that seemed to light up the passageway, a raw enthusiasm suddenly shining out of him. The change in the captain's expression from a dark haunted look to an effervescent brightness was so stark that Pacino doubted he'd seen right. The commander's hand sailed from out of nowhere and gripped Pacino's as if he'd seen a long-lost friend.

"Patch Pacino, great to see you again." His sharp Boston accent rang out through the passageway, the pitch of his voice a smooth tenor. "You probably don't even remember me, but I'm Rob Catardi." He stepped back, looking Pacino over, his expression becoming one of approving wonder. "My God, look at you. Last time I saw you, you were five years old, sitting at *Devilfish*'s firecontrol console, asking your dad what a fixed-interval data unit was." Pacino searched his memory, coming up blank. Catardi's hand clapped Pacino on the shoulderboard. "I was a green junior officer on the *Devilfish* under your old man. Gutsiest goddamned submarine captain ever born. We worshiped him. He taught me everything I know about driving a combat submarine. I was transferred off before the old girl went to the bottom."

Catardi let go of Pacino's shoulder, a deep sadness coming to his face. "It's a damned shame what happened last summer, Patch. How is your dad?"

Pacino grimaced, the memory one of his most painful. The summer before, Pacino's father had been the Chief of Naval Operations, the supreme admiral-in-command of the U.S. Navy. A year into his tour as the Navy's commander he had come up with the idea to take his senior and midgrade officers to sea on Admiral Bruce Phillips' company's cruise liner *Princess Dragon* for two weeks of "stand-down" to discuss tactics and equipment away from the drudgery of the fleet. *Princess Dragon* had left Norfolk under heavy guard, with an Aegis II-class cruiser, two Bush-class destroyers, and the SSNX submarine screening her for security. Eighty miles out of Norfolk the stand-down plan went horribly wrong. The first plasma torpedo cut *Princess Dragon* in half and sent her to the bottom. The rest had taken out the fleet task force. Admiral Pacino had been sucked deep underwater with the broken hull of the cruise ship. He hadn't been found until hours later, and by then more than a thousand of the Navy's leading officers perished in the surprise terrorist attack. Almost every friend the admiral had lay dead at the bottom of the Atlantic or vaporized by the fireballs of the plasma detonations.

The admiral had resigned from the Navy as soon as he was

well enough to walk, and had done nothing since except putter with his sailboat. The elder Pacino was deeply depressed, Anthony Michael thought, but he couldn't just say that to Captain Catardi.

"He was in bad shape for a while, Captain, but he's getting better." A thought occurred to Pacino. "Sir, how did you know my nickname is Patch?"

Catardi looked at him with a sort of recognition. "It's what we used to call your father," he said gently. Pacino swallowed hard.

"Excuse me, Captain," Alameda interrupted. "Request permission to start the reactor and shift propulsion to the main engines."

"Start the reactor and shift propulsion to the mains."

"Start the reactor and shift propulsion, aye, sir. If you don't mind, sir, I need to get Mr. Pacino settled."

Catardi held up his palm, holding off the energetic chief engineer. "Patch, you're driving us out. Get with the navigator and get the nav brief. You need to know the current and tides cold, and memorize the chart. You done much shiphandling?"

Pacino blinked as his stomach plunged, his armpits suddenly melting. "Well, sir, they have shiphandling simulators at the Academy with a submarine program, and radio-controlled four-meter models in the seamanship lab. I've driven the yard patrol diesels." The answer sounded lame, Pacino thought glumly.

"You'll be fine. I know conning a Seawolf-class special project submarine is an intimidating order, but Alameda and I will be up there with you. And I'm expecting a trademark Pacino back-full-ahead-flank underway."

Pacino raised an eyebrow. "Are you sure, sir?" Pacino's father used to say that back-full-ahead-flank underways were dangerous and risky, even though he always did them. He hated tugboats and pilots, and wanted to make sure his crew knew the ship was rigged for combat. But his bosses had always reprimanded him for the maneuvers.

Catardi nodded. "I want you to show my people how a Pacino goes to sea. Think you can do it?"

"Yes, sir." Pacino swallowed.

Catardi smiled. "We're going to be pretty busy on this run, Patch, but soak up what you can. When things calm down, don't hesitate to ask any question you want," Catardi said. "And welcome to the Submarine Force. We've been waiting for you." Catardi disappeared back into his stateroom and shut the door. His last words left Pacino staring after him.

The captain's stateroom was a fifteen-foot-square cubbyhole with a bunk, a desk, and a small conference table headed by a high-backed leather command chair. Commander Rob Catardi stood at the closed stateroom door, deep in thought. He looked at the mess of his stateroom, beyond the clutter of papers and computer displays to the enlarged photographs bolted to the bulkhead. The face of his daughter, Nicole, smiled out at him, her pigtails tied high on her head, the amusement park ride in the background.

The photo had been taken last summer, the summer he and Sharon had first talked seriously about the end of their marriage. In the winter Sharon left him and made plans to take Nicole with her, back to Detroit. Catardi had tried to fight her from taking his daughter out of state, but the critical courtroom hearing had been scheduled for a Tuesday afternoon. *Piranha* had been given emergency orders to sortie to the Atlantic the evening before, and while the family court hearing officer decided Catardi's fate as a father, he had opened the main ballast tank vents and taken *Piranha* to test depth east of the continental shelf, his legal case—and his daughter—lost. That was the story of his failed marriage—at every turn when his family needed him the most, the Navy demanded even more.

Catardi sank into his deep leather command chair and looked over at the man sitting next to him at the table. He was shorter than Catardi, about his age, wearing a civilian suit with a red-patterned tie. The man wore a deep frown, his bushy eyebrows knitted over his brown eyes.

"Sorry for the interruption, Admiral," Catardi said. He poured the submarine force admiral and himself coffee from a carafe into two coffee mugs with the *Piranha* emblem on them, then settled in his chair to listen to his boss.

"Commander, a few months ago you participated in a submarine-versus-submarine exercise against the USS *Snarc,* SSNR-1, the first of the SNARC-class," McKee began.

The *Snarc* was a robotic combat sub, the acronym standing for Submarine Naval Automated Robotic Combat system. The ship was small, only 180 feet long with a beam of twenty-six feet and displacing a mere three thousand tons, yet was able to carry a whopping eighty large-bore weapons, almost double the payload of the fleet's manned submarines. She'd been operational for two months, after her sea trials exercise against the USS *Piranha.*

"It was a damned tough exercise, sir. We took her in three engagements, but she ambushed us in two. She's ghostly quiet, and her sound signature shifts all over the place. And whoever programmed her was a sick bastard. She's tricky and aggressive and fights dirty. She had to have violated the op order to snap us up those two times. Goddamned bitch of a machine cheats, Admiral."

"Well, we have you matched against her again."

Catardi thought back to the facts he'd memorized about the computer-controlled ship. The aft half of the ship was devoted to the reactor, pressurizer, steam generator, a single ship's service turbine, a single propulsion turbine, and the main motor, all in one small compartment. There was no emergency diesel, no catwalks, no nuclear-control space, no shielded tunnel through the reactor space. Forward of the frame 47 division between the engineering spaces and the forward combat space there was a two-level deck devoted to electronics. The ending of the pressure hull forward marked the beginning of the free-flood torpedo compartment. Past that, the forward ballast tank held the twelve vertical launch tubes and a small sonar hydrophone spherical array. There was no sail or fin or conning tower. There was also no protruding rudder above the hull, but rather eight small control surfaces resembling the fins of a rocket, with a shroud around them. The hull shape resembled a stubby torpedo rather than a submarine. The propulsion plant put out thirty thousand shaft horsepower while the reactor made eighty megawatts thermal. It had a thermal efficiency even higher than *Piranha*'s S20G. The tissue used in the control system was cultured from human brain tissue, the first use of human cells in an electronic battle system.

"Good," Catardi said. "I'd like a rematch with that computerized witch. This time *we'll* cheat and put her down."

"Rob," McKee said, his eyes narrowed, "this isn't an exercise."

Catardi sat back in his seat, stunned.

"I was briefed on this by Patton himself. And he heard it from NSA, the National Security Agency. You've worked for them before, Rob, so I don't need to mention that in addition to their missions to spy on enemy radio signals, phone communications, and E-mails, they have an information warfare tasking, to break into foreign military command-and-control systems. While entering one foreign battle command network, they found out that the U.S. Navy computer networks and command-and-control systems have been penetrated. Correction—not just penetrated, taken over. Our command networks and top-secret communications systems no longer belong to us." McKee paused. "Every radio transmission you make is monitored, intercepted, decoded, translated, and disseminated to the enemy's highest levels. Same goes for every E-mail and every phone call—cell, landline, or Web—and for the data passed over the Navy Tactical Data System. So commanders can no longer talk to each other. And the penetrators can give electronic orders, disabling our combat systems when we want them to shoot, or turning our own guns against us."

"Jesus, that means we're paralyzed. We can't do shit without NTDS and our communications network. Who penetrated our command networks? The Red Chinese or the Indians?"

"It's complicated," McKee said. "The electronic attackers are an independent mercenary group of military consultants, the same company that pulled the trigger on last summer's terrorist assault on the *Princess Dragon*. It's possible they did this on behalf of India, but they may be selling information to both sides. That's where our need-to-know ends. More important to us is that we agree on how we're going to talk to each other with our comms compromised." McKee reached into his briefcase and produced two pad computers, handing both to Catardi.

"These NSA computers, used with the paper sealed authentication system, are the only secure means of communication left to us other than mouth-to-ear."

The Sealed Authentication System, known as SAS, was a supply of sealed foil packets enclosing paper slips with concealed codes, the packets distributed to each afloat commander. The codes printed on the interior paper slips were used to verify the authenticity of an incoming emergency action message. The system was the only part of the war-fighting network to remain stubbornly nonelectronic. Years before Patton had argued to eliminate the system and go completely digital. Thank God he'd been overruled, Catardi thought.

"There will be two National Security Agency employees assigned to your ship, to operate the electronics of the command network as a disinformation program, to keep the enemy confused. The system will belong to NSA. Your actual comms will use Internet E-mail, encrypted and decrypted by the NSA's handheld computers and authenticated by using the SAS sealed authenticators.

"Since our command network is penetrated and compromised, we're in deep trouble with the *Snarc*. Since the battle network is penetrated, we must presume *Snarc* to be compromised. We can't afford for her to fall into enemy hands. With her deployed in the Atlantic, if she has been taken over, she could target our East Coast subs as they scramble to the Indian Ocean."

"Indian Ocean, sir?"

"I'm jumping ahead. For now, I want *Piranha* on a search-and-destroy mission. You know the sound signature and inherent operating behavior of *Snarc,* and you'll find her first. Put the *Snarc* down and hurry. Then get *Piranha* to the Indian Ocean. I'll tell you why once you're on your way."

"Aye aye, sir."

Ten minutes later the civilian-clothed admiral stood and shook Catardi's hand. Catardi escorted him topside, and stared after the man as he walked briskly down the pier. Catardi's mind was still whirling after the admiral's briefing. *Piranha* was at war, and he couldn't tell his crew until the ship was submerged in the Atlantic. The thought occurred to him that the *Snarc* could be lurking out there waiting for him, and that the computerized sub might kill him before he could kill her. "Screw her," he muttered to himself.

He looked over at the *Piranha,* at Pacino up in the bridge cockpit. The kid was studying the chart computer and the tides, checking the channel with his binoculars, and looking down at the tugs, occasionally speaking into the bridge communication box microphone or his radio. It was eerie—even though his resemblance to his father was slight, he moved just like the old man, his hand motions and facial expressions identical.

Catardi turned and walked the gangway to the ship. The 1MC PA system clicked, the voice broadcasting over the circuit, "*Piranha,* arriving!" to announce Catardi's return to the vessel. He climbed the ladder to the bridge cockpit and from there to the flying bridge on the top surface of the sail.

"Mr. Pacino," Catardi said, "get underway."

Midshipman Patch Pacino's stomach rolled in nausea when he was ordered to take the ship to sea. He swallowed hard, squinted at Commander Catardi with his best warface, and said, "Get underway, Junior Officer of the Deck, aye, sir."

Pacino put the megaphone to his mouth and called, "Take off the brow!" The diesel engine of the pier crane rumbled as the gangway was hoisted away from the deck and placed on the pier concrete. He made the next order on the VHF radio to the tugs, his uncertain voice echoing out over the other radios on the bridge. "Tugs one and two, shove off and stand by at two hundred yards." The tugs' engines roared as they throttled into reverse and faded backward into the river. Pacino lifted the bridge box mike to his lips. "Navigator, we are shoving off the tugs."

The navigator, Lieutenant Commander Wes Crossfield, was obviously not pleased. He'd spent an hour with Pacino going over tug commands, the current and chart of the Thames River. Pacino had liked him considerably more than Alameda. The thirty-year-old department head was a six-foot-four African American, a varsity basketball player at Navy who had forsaken an NBA career to drive submarines. He had a calm authority, and the crew seemed to respect him, but there was something hidden, an indefinable sadness adding to the officer's seriousness. His scratchy voice called over the 7MC circuit, "Bridge, Navigator, aye. Navigator recommends keeping tugs."

"Navigator, Bridge, aye."

"Shift your pumps, Mr. Pacino, like we discussed," Alameda said to him. He nodded, raising the microphone to his lips.

"Maneuvering, Bridge, shift reactor recirc pumps to fast speed."

"Shift main coolant pumps to fast speed, Bridge, Maneuvering, aye." The speakerbox squawked the engineering officer of the watch's reply. "Bridge, Maneuvering, main coolant pumps are running in fast speed."

"Maneuvering, Bridge, aye." Pacino turned to look at the tugs backing away from the ship and into the wide channel of the river. He looked at the river's current and felt the wind, then hoisted the megaphone to his lips. "On deck, take in line one!"

He turned and took a step to the aft part of the cockpit to yell down to the aft linehandlers. "On deck aft, take in three, four, five, and six!"

The linehandlers scurried to their tasks, the pier linehandlers from ComSubDevRon 12 tossing over the lines that were looped around the massive bollards to the deck gang, which coiled them quickly on the deck and stuffed them into line lockers, shutting the hatches of the lockers and rotating the cleats into the hull, the ship beginning to look like it had never been tied to a pier. Watching it made Pacino's heart thump harder in his chest. He tried to ignore the feeling as he craned his neck over the bridge coaming to look back aft at the rudder pointing into the river. As the lines came off the stern, the current drifted the stern off the pier, just slightly, an angle of brown water forming between the hull and the pier as the ship rotated on the single line made fast to the only remaining cleat.

"Ease line two!" Pacino shouted into the bullhorn. He watched while the crew paid out the line, then shouted for them to stop. "Check line two!" The order to hold the line tight. The current was pushing the stern further off the pier, which was mixed news. Good because he could back out straight without fears of hurting the fiberglass sonar dome, but bad because his stern was drifting downstream in the current, setting him up to point the bow north, the wrong way.

"Helm, Bridge, left full rudder," he barked into the 7MC microphone.

"Bridge, Helm," the speaker blared, "left full rudder, aye, my rudder is left full."

Pacino looked aft while leaning far out over the cockpit coaming, making sure the rudder rotated to the correct position, to the right as he looked aft. The angle between the ship and the pier had opened up to twenty degrees. He took a deep breath, the next ten seconds seeming to take an hour, the hand holding the microphone shaking.

"Helm, Bridge, all back full!" he shouted into the 7MC microphone. *"Hold line two!"* he yelled into the bullhorn to the deck crew forward.

"All back full, Bridge, Helm, aye, advancing throttle to back full, indicating revolutions for back full."

A boiling erupted at the rudder, a geyser of water ten feet tall. Pacino counted to five, waiting for the water flow to build up and roll over the rudder so that the rudder would bite into the river against the current. He had to give the next order quickly before the massive power of the screw parted the single line holding her and cut a linehandler in half. The deck trembled beneath his boots from a hundred thousand shaft horsepower kicked into full reverse. Pacino waited with his heart rushing until he could no longer stand it.

"Take in line two!" he shouted to the deck. The pier crew scrambled to grab the hastily eased thick rope and toss it over to the accelerating submarine. The instant the line was no longer fast to the bollard, the *Piranha* was officially underway, the pier suddenly moving away from them as the ship surged backward. He turned to his lookout, a petty officer he'd met in the wait on the bridge.

"Shift colors!"

The lookout scrambled to hoist a huge American flag from a temporary mast set up aft of the captain. Pacino grabbed a handle in the cockpit near the bridge box, the compressed air horn, and pulled the lever. The ship's whistle, announcing she was underway, blasted out a screaming shriek, louder and throatier than the biggest ocean liner's horn. Pacino let it blast for a full eight seconds, watching the ship's motion in the downstream current as the horn continued to wail over the water of the base. The lookout hoisted the Unified Submarine Command flag next to the stars and stripes, the skull and crossbones leering in the breeze. The horn blasted on, Pacino holding the lever with one hand while craning his neck to look aft.

Pacino had the barest impression of the pier moving away from them, jogging speed at first, then faster, and he saw an admiral standing on the concrete with his hands over his mouth and his eyes bugging out, and the ship rocketed backward into the river. Pacino looked aft at the wake boiling up at the rudder, and prayed for the stern to turn up into the current. Submarines handled like pigs near the pier, and if the screw "walked the bottom" the ship would turn the opposite direction from the rudder order, which could result in the ship turning to head north instead of south, and the entire world would see that the sub was out of control. The pier was speeding away from them in a blur, the end of it in sight and drawing next to the sail, then speeding past beyond the sonar dome. *Piranha* was free of the slip and roaring backward into the channel, a white frothing wake at her bow. *Come on, rudder,* Pacino thought, *turn the goddamned stern upstream.* For two tense, endless seconds it looked like the ship's stern would go the wrong way, but then finally it began to respond, and as the pier moved further away, the rudder finally bit into the river water and broke her upstream and the ship turned, rotating so the bow was pointed south. Pacino could hear a cheer from the deck crew below.

"Helm, Bridge, all ahead flank! Rudder amidships!"

"Bridge, Helm, all ahead flank, aye, rudder amidships, aye," the reply crackled out of the bridge box. "Throttle advancing to ahead flank, my rudder is amidships. Bridge, Helm, indicating revolutions for ahead flank."

There was a chance that the ship's momentum and turning impulse would not obey the latest order. The ship might continue backward and put her screw into the upstream pier, wrecking the hull on the jutting concrete. The deck jumped, shaking violently as the screw turned from full revolutions astern to ahead flank at one hundred percent reactor power. The wake frothed in anger aft of the rudder. Pacino checked that the rudder was back in line with the centerline of the ship, then turned forward to watch her progress ahead. For a few seconds the ship froze in the river. In the action's pause, Pacino realized that his palms were sweating, his heart was pounding, and he was panting as if he'd sprinted a mile. Finally the ship surged ahead, a bow wave forming below them.

"Helm, Bridge, all ahead one-third. Steady as she goes."

"Bridge, Helm, all ahead one-third, throttle eased to all ahead one-third, steady as she goes, aye, steering course one eight two, sir!"

"Very well, Helm," Pacino called. "Navigator, Bridge, ship

has cleared the pier, recommend course to center of channel."
Pacino's heart was still hammering, with an almost sexual
exhilaration.

Crossfield's voice was incredulous as he spoke into the circuit. "Bridge, Navigator, aye, stand by."

Behind Pacino the periscopes rotated furiously as the navigator's piloting party plotted visual fixes. The radar mast high
overhead rotated, making a circle every second. The wind
blew into Pacino's face in spite of the Plexiglas windscreen
erected at the forward lip of the cockpit, flapping the fabric of
the flags, the stars and stripes and the skull and crossbones
presiding over the dark dangerous form of the streamlined
submarine.

"Bridge, Navigator, ship is twenty yards west of the center
of the channel, recommend course one eight one."

"Navigator, Bridge, aye," Pacino called. "Helm, Bridge,
steer course one eight one."

Captain Catardi called down from the flying bridge. "Nice
work, Mr. Pacino. Watch yourself on the way out."

"Aye aye, sir," Pacino replied, hoisting the binoculars to his
eyes, his hands still shaking. For a moment he felt an unaccus-
tomed kinship to his father, knowing that his father had done
this maneuver every time he had gone to sea.

3

Michael Pacino walked down the slope of the dock to the boat.

He stopped as he always did and stared at the lines of the sailboat. The sloop-rigged, forty-six-footer *Colleen* seemed too big to be sailed by a lone captain yet too small to venture out into the high seas. She was Swedish designed and built, an old Hallberg-Rassy with a hundred horsepower diesel, twin generators, teak decks, mahogany furnishings, a modernized computer console at the navigation station aft of the saloon, and a repeater station in the cockpit. She was fitted out with the latest electronics and sail-furling mechanisms and sheet control hydraulics. Pacino preferred to sail her manually, but if he wanted he could stay below for days at a time while the computer trimmed the sheets and took the wheel. The artificial intelligence could even skirt a hurricane, uplinked to the orbital Web's weather forecasts. It was a beautiful and inspired system, but Pacino would keep it running as a backup until he risked sleeping at the helm. Perhaps exhaustion at sea would give him the dreamless sleep he craved.

Pacino was fifty now, but the shape of his face and body had not changed much since he'd been the thirty-seven-year-old captain of the *Devilfish*. He was tall and gaunt, his cheeks thin beneath pronounced cheekbones, his lips full, his nose straight and jutting, his chin still strong. But the signs of his age were not in the shape of his face but in its coloring. The frostbite from the Arctic operation had left his skin dark and leathery, as if he were a fisherman in his sixties, the crow's-feet wrinkles deep at the corners of his eyes, leaving no doubt that he had spent his life at sea. His hair had turned stark white a month after he was rescued from the icepack, the legend following him that the horror of his brush with death had chased the jet-black out of it, but the more likely culprits the radiation and hypothermia injuries and treatments. His eyebrows contrasted oddly with his white hair, remaining stubbornly black. But perhaps the most startling of his features were his eyes, so brightly emerald-green that he seemed to be wearing the old-fashioned contact lenses that unnaturally changed the iris color. Pacino attracted second and third looks wherever he went. Until now he had assumed that was because of his admiral's shoulderboards and stripes, but long after he'd resigned his commission the intense stares still followed him.

After Pacino left the Navy he had spent his days on the deck of the Maryland house, staring out at the bay, or working on the sailboat, until his wife, Colleen, had asked that he come to work for her. Colleen O'Shaughnessy Pacino was the president of defense contractor Cyclops Systems, the company that had pioneered the Cyclops Mark I battlecontrol system, a machine that had guided the SSNX submarine to victory in the East China Sea, and had caused Pacino to know Colleen in the first place. But going from being the admiral-in-command of the Navy to a defense contractor didn't seem to make sense to him. He couldn't see it being part of his identity, and he had turned her down.

He returned his thoughts to the task of provisioning the boat for the circumnavigation. For the next two hours he loaded the boat and stowed for sea. He was taking a break when Colleen walked onto the pier, her slim form beautiful in the afternoon glare, her hair blowing around her shoulders and into her eyes from the bay's breeze. For an instant Pacino regretted leaving her.

"Don't go," she said, sadness filling her voice and her expression.

"I have to," he said, his voice hoarse. "Come with me."

"I can't. I have to close the contract on the Tigershark system. But when I'm done, why don't we meet in the Caymans? You could cut a few days out of your round-the-world trip, couldn't you?"

Pacino smiled, a ray of sunlight penetrating his dark mood for the first time in months. "Cayman Reef Hotel. I'll meet you at the bar," he said.

Her expression turned serious. "Listen to me, Michael. Be careful out there. Call me anytime you need me. And for God's sake, use the distress code if the weather gets bad. We can have a chopper come for you inside an hour. Just leave the boat. I'll buy you a better one."

Pacino smirked. He'd never abandon *Colleen,* the thought sneaking in that perhaps he was deserting her namesake, if only temporarily. "I will," he lied.

She didn't say good-bye, just kissed him, ran her fingers again through his hair one last time, and watched him from the pier.

He looked around one last time, nodding a farewell to the massive timber-frame house on the jutting point of land, the property once christened by the Pentagon "Pacino Peninsula." He took in the bowline, coiled it on the deck, and pulled in the sternline. One hand on the wheel, he throttled up the engine and pulled away from the pier and turned downriver. He threw a kiss to Colleen and waved until he could no longer see her. The boat made five knots at part throttle as the peninsula faded astern, the Academy grounds likewise shrinking in the hazy distance.

The Chesapeake Bay's waves rose into a one-foot chop. He raised the mainsail. It flapped violently in the breeze as it filled, the boom creaking to port. Pacino raised the jib and sheeted it in, then jumped back to the cockpit to adjust the sheets of the mainsail. *Colleen* was on a beam reach, heeling slightly on a starboard tack, heading southward.

He grabbed the wheel and shut down the diesel. The boat crashed into relative silence, the noise now the wind singing in the rigging and the slicing and slapping of the waves forward as the *Colleen* picked up speed.

Eighty nautical miles out of Port Norfolk, in the deep Atlantic in the dark, the *Colleen's* computerized chart counted off the range to the *Princess Dragon* gravesite, the distance down to five miles. Michael Pacino took a deep breath, trying to face the fact that he could no longer avoid thinking about the cruise ship disaster. It was time to remember, he thought heavily.

More than a thousand of the U.S. Navy's best officers including forty admirals, a hundred captains, and the most capable junior officers had died here, Pacino thought, shaking his head. The upper echelons of the Navy had stood there on the deck of the *Princess Dragon,* wearing Hawaiian shirts and drinking Anchor Steam beers, ripe for slaughter. His surviving officers had found and destroyed a Ukrainian Black Sea Fleet attack submarine that had been the culprit, but the Ukrainians themselves proved to be innocent. The submarine's actions had been directed by previously trustworthy third-party military consultants, whose multitrillion-dollar company had evaporated without a trace. The planners of the attack had never been found, never brought to justice. And with no idea of who the enemy had been, or what the fight had been about, there had been no winning the war.

The distance to *Princess Dragon* closed to a half mile, then to mere yards. Pacino dumped the jib and the mainsail and coasted to a halt, the boat drifting, rocking on the light waves. He reached into a cubbyhole in the cockpit and pulled out the package, a bag containing a flag that Colleen had gotten for him from the wreckage of the SSNX submarine. It was the first skull-and-crossbones Jolly Roger from his *Devilfish,* the last thing he had pulled from the broken hull before abandoning her for the frigid icecap, the flag that had inspired the later logo of the Unified Submarine Command. *Deep, Silent, Fast, Deadly—U.S. Submarine Force,* the script motto read. The skull leered at him. The senior officers of his submarine force had sailed with him under this flag, and not one of them had deserved to die, not the way they did. It was one thing to go down while standing on the deck of a combat submarine while still shooting torpedoes, but quite another to perish while sipping beer and eating hors d'oeuvres.

Pacino had to weigh the Jolly Roger down with something so that it would sink the three thousand feet to the broken hull of the *Princess Dragon*. But there was nothing solid and heavy that was expendable. His roving eyes finally fixed on the case of Anchor Steam, the unofficial beer of the submarine force ever since Bruce Phillips fell in love with it decades before. He taped the box to the pirate flag, carried it to the side, held it for one final second, then consigned it to the deep. For just a moment the skull and crossbones were visible on the surface of the waves, and then they were gone. Pacino drew himself to attention and saluted.

He sat back down in the cabin, his body aching, and decided to wait for dawn and finish the night here at the grave of his friends. In the first hour he thought about each of them, calling forth their faces, their jokes, their stories. The drowsiness crept up on him, and the night was suddenly cold. He lay on the cockpit seat and snuggled into the thick blanket.

When he woke, he raised the sails and began to make way to the south, leaving behind the *Princess Dragon* and the past. *Colleen* sailed peacefully southward, her skipper feeling an unfamiliar lightness. He waited for the usual guilt and self-recriminations to settle back on his shoulders, but this once, the feelings were late.

Colleen sailed southward on a port tack close haul, the ship heeled far over to starboard. There was no feeling of speed quite like pointing up tight to the wind during a close-hauled run. The seas were tall but manageable, the wind a stiff fifteen to twenty knots, the sky dotted with puffy cotton balls of high-altitude clouds, the horizon sharp as an expertly painted line. Michael Pacino relaxed in the cockpit, steering the forty-six-foot vessel by its round steering wheel at the captain's binnacle. He could have been below, but when the wind veered to put *Colleen* on a close haul he had come up on deck, his habit to be topside whenever the boat was close-hauled. He wanted to see the sheets and the sails with his own eyes, to feel the spray come over the bow every time the sharp prow bit into the oncoming wave, to hear the rigging sing in the blast of the wind. There was nothing in his experience so exhilarating since he'd conned a nuclear submarine on the surface, back in days far behind him. He'd always thought that sensation would be lost forever, but here it was again, the emotion in his heart not from the high-yield steel of the ship but from the sea herself. The discovery brought a strange feeling of relief.

Although most of the voyage he had thought of the men he had lost on the *Princess Dragon,* for the last two days they had seemed to be far distant. Perhaps, he thought, they had gone on to wherever one goes after death and had found peace, or more likely had simply ceased to exist entirely and only lived on in the dim corridors of his tortured mind. But with the arrival of this strange new peace came better weather, the overcast clearing and the winds picking up, the temperature warmer now. For a few minutes he enjoyed the sensations of the wind and the sea and the boat without thinking. An hour became two, until before he realized it the afternoon arrived, the hour of noon passing without his usual sextant shot at the sun to confirm his navigation equipment was working. He shrugged, thinking that perhaps tomorrow he would set an alarm to keep from missing the noon fix, when a roaring sound to his left off the port beam attracted his attention.

He stared at the sea for a moment, thinking he was dreaming when a white wave formed out of nowhere and a black object appeared below and behind it, violently pushing the water up and out of its way. No, he told himself, it couldn't be. The black shape ascended further, rising out of the sea while still keeping exact pace with the *Colleen,* the white foaming wave now rolling off to either side of the black obelisk rising from the deep impenetrable blue ocean. Pacino was staring at it so intently that he forgot his steering, the boat coming too high into the wind, the mainsail luffing slightly as it spilled its wind. Pacino beared off, regained the wind, and engaged his autopilot. He stood at the port railing, staring at the black shape as it moved further out of the water, the wave below now flowing around a larger shape, a huge horizontal blackness not a boatlength away.

The first black shape was the sail of a submarine, vertical and unadorned, with a slight angling fillet bringing it to the deck of the cylindrical shape, the sail identical to that of his old *Seawolf,* but the hull now appearing beneath the sail too small in diameter to belong to a Seawolf-class. Pacino's gaze was riveted on the submarine, still keeping up with *Colleen*'s twelve knots. A periscope pole rose from the sail—it had been absent up to now, he thought abstractly, because anything faster than seven or eight knots would rip the pole off, even with its winglike fairing painted a mottled black and gray. A second periscope rose, then the BRA-38 radio mast in the stern of the sail. The bow wave formed around the bow of the submarine, falling on either side of the smooth bullet nose. It had to be a Virginia-class, Pacino thought. At the top of the sail several crewmen appeared, probably the officer of the deck and a lookout. As he stared stupidly at the submarine one of the officers raised a radio to his lips, and a crackling hiss of static came from the sailboat's steering wheel console—the VHF bridge-to-bridge radio, forgotten on its charger inside the weatherproof cover, turned on to the international call frequency.

Pacino pulled the radio out of its cover and it burst with static again, then barked out, "Sailboat *Colleen,* this is U.S. Navy submarine, over."

She couldn't identify herself on an open circuit, Pacino thought, the reason the crew didn't declare the name of the vessel.

"U.S. Navy submarine, this is *Colleen* captain, over." His

voice was hoarse from not speaking for the better part of a week.

"Good afternoon, sir. We request permission to send over a boat, over."

How could he refuse, Pacino thought, consumed by curiosity.

"Roger, Navy, permission granted to send over a boat. Recommend you change course to southeast so I can luff the sails."

"Roger, turning now."

The submarine turned gently and opened the distance. Pacino took the helm and turned up into the wind, the sails spilling their wind and flapping noisily. He dropped the jib first, the halyard cranking the sail down as he leaped to the foredeck and pulled the sail down to the deck. He turned and eased the halyard for the mainsail, bringing it to the boom where he lashed it down. *Colleen* slowed and bobbed on the waves, the boom waving dangerously over the cockpit until Pacino cinched down the boomvang. By the time he had *Colleen* stable, an inflatable Zodiac boat had appeared on the sub's starboard side, the crew able to work on it now that the ship had come to a halt in the sea, no longer battling the bow wave. The five-horsepower outboard started up, a tall, slim woman in a wetsuit the boat's only occupant. The boat made the crossing from the submarine to the sailboat in a few minutes, rising up on the wave crests and crashing back down in the troughs. When the woman was within hailing distance, she called out to him, "Request permission to heave to!"

"Permission granted, come alongside," he called, taking the painter line as she tossed it to him. He fed it down the railing to a deck cleat and held out his hand to her. She climbed up to the deck and came over the railing, shaking the spray out of her long brunette hair and smiling at him. Pacino smiled back, suddenly reminded that he had been at sea for a week without Colleen, and reminded also that he had not made love to a woman since before *Princess Dragon* sank. Why this woman

made that thought come to mind was obvious as he took her in
without trying to gawk.

"Welcome aboard the *Colleen*," Pacino said, trying not to
sound ridiculous. "I'm Michael Pacino." He held out his hand
to her, her hand coming into his, her hand soft and warm. Pacino felt his face flush.

"I'm Dayne Valker, lieutenant, U.S. Navy," she said.

"Are you ship's company? And what sub is that?"

"No, Admiral," she said.

So, he thought, she knew who he was.

"The sub is the USS *Hammerhead*, Virginia-class. I'm a
SEAL under temporary orders."

Hammerhead, Pacino thought. The ship that had avenged
the *Princess Dragon*, except that she didn't kill the men onboard who had executed the foul mission that had killed his
comrades and ruined his life.

"Forgive me please, Lieutenant. May I offer you something
to drink? Tea or coffee?" He doubted she would want anything
stronger, an official bearing surrounding her, perhaps even a
wariness of him.

"No, thank you, Admiral. I'm on official business, as I'm
sure you've guessed." She shot a look at the hull of the *Hammerhead*, drifting a few hundred yards east of *Colleen*.

"And what would that business be, Lieutenant? And is it so
urgent that we can't sit here in the cockpit?" He waved her to a
seat. She sat down, her body coiled in tension.

"Admiral Patton is calling for you, sir. He sent you this."

She pulled something from a waterproof pocket belted to
her thigh. It was a shiny envelope. She handed it to him, and
he stared at it for a moment, then opened it, finding a folded
page of expensive bond paper with the seal of the United
States Navy on the letterhead. The sloping handwriting of
John "Blood and Guts" Patton filled the page. He and Patton
went back ten years and two wars. If there was one man who
could call Pacino back from this trip, it was John Patton. Pacino read the note, looking up occasionally at the *Hammerhead*, once at the lieutenant.

Dear Patch,

The president of Cyclops Systems told me you have been turning down an important job for the last year. We can no longer afford your absence from two programs that are foundering, and without them our submarine force is stalled at the present level of technology, which is unacceptable. I need you to come to the Pentagon and either take the program director job and forge the fleet of tomorrow, or tell me to my face the reason why you won't. The lives of hundreds of Americans depend on your next decision, Patch, and you've never yet turned your back on the needs of your Navy or your country. I'll expect to see you in my office tonight, old friend.

Best regards,
John Patton.

Pacino looked away from the note and stared off at the horizon. After all that had happened, how could he just leave behind this defeat and take on some undefined new project as Patton had asked? And what would his dead friends think if he just returned from the sinking of the *Princess Dragon* to shrug and come home and work on Patton's project as if nothing had happened?

We'd applaud, an unexplained alien voice in his head said, startling Pacino at the intrusion of a thought not his own. This had happened to him perhaps only three times, and each time that external voice had been correct. A shiver ran down his back as he heard the voice say the two words again.

The next thoughts seemed as strange—the desire to get back to shore and leave this melancholy voyage behind. When he had first put to sea, there had been the weight of an anchor on his heart, and the circumnavigation had seemed the only way to heal, but now that he had paid his respects to his friends at the grave of the *Princess Dragon,* he no longer felt the need to sail on. Patton was offering him what he truly wanted in the first place.

Pacino raised his hand to his long hair and brushed it out of his face, his gaze rising to the sail of the *Hammerhead.* Next to the American flag behind the officers on the bridge the Jolly Roger banner of the Unified Submarine Command flapped in the breeze, the flag he had designed after his father's submarine went down. And as he looked at the skull and crossbones, he felt his heart beat stronger, the ache in his stomach receding for a moment, and the answer seemed to land in his mind. He would do it, he decided. He stood up, the letter in his hands.

"I'm going to the *Hammerhead,* Lieutenant. But I don't want to leave *Colleen* alone."

"I'll stay here while you take the Zodiac, sir. *Hammerhead* has a sailboat crew standing by to take *Colleen* back to Annapolis. Once you're aboard the *Hammerhead,* a helicopter will be called to evacuate you and transport you to an air base where there's a supersonic fighter standing by. You'll be in D.C. before sunset, sir."

Pacino nodded, his mind spinning as he found himself saying good-bye to the sailboat and climbing into the rubber boat. He started the engine and took in the painter, turning the boat to the submarine and bouncing over the waves to the sub, a glance over his shoulders at the majestic form of his sailboat. Several deckhands on the *Hammerhead* grabbed the boat and pulled him aboard. He was rushed to the hatch, with barely enough time to give *Colleen* a last look before he found himself in the weapons shipping hatch, the bright sunlight vanishing, replaced with the fluorescent dim glow of the overhead lights. The noise of the wind and the waves ceased, replaced suddenly by the soprano whine of four-hundred-cycle power and the deep baritone thrum of the air handlers. The electrical smell of the ship came into his nostrils, a brew of cooking oil, ozone, diesel fuel, cleaning solution, and amines, the perfume of it filling him with nostalgia. He stepped off the bottom of the ladder, shocked to see two straight rows of officers and chief petty officers. Someone shouted, "Hand, salute!" and the officers and chiefs saluted. Suddenly he was painfully aware of his beard and his mop of white hair and his old sweater and ratty windbreaker.

Ten hours later Pacino stood in the Pentagon E-Ring anteroom outside the office of the Chief of Naval Operations.

4

The run to the continental shelf would take ten hours. Once *Piranha* passed the six-hundred-fathom curve, the ship would submerge and continue to follow the track line to Point November, the point where the secret-classified chart ended and the top-secret chart began.

At the turning point from the Thames River into Long Island Sound, Captain Catardi ordered a speed increase. The deck below the bridge had been rigged for dive, with all the line lockers shut and latched, the cleats rotated into the hull, and the hatch shut and dogged. The hull was clean and streamlined. With relatively open water stretching in front of them, the ship's surface speed rose to thirty knots at all-ahead flank. The vessel's top speed of forty-nine knots could only be achieved submerged, since the cigar shape of the hull was not efficient at cutting through the surface effect of the waves. The bullet-shaped nose plowed into the sea, the water curving smoothly down on either side of sail and rising back angrily up at the mid-deck, then spreading into a churning white wake a third of a shiplength wide extending to the horizon behind them. The flow of the water was hypnotic. Pacino stared at it, watching the bow wave from the crow's nest viewpoint of the bridge cockpit. Even more impressive than the sight of the wave was its noise, the jet engine roar of it deafening as it cascaded over the bow. The hurricane wind generated by their flank-run surface passage competed with the noise of the bow wave, the wind alone so loud that it would require a man to scream in the ear of a companion to be heard. The sustained shriek of the sea and the wind could lead to fatigue, but in Midshipman Pacino's case, the noise was music, a song he had heard in his dreams but had lingered just beyond reach. The deck beneath his feet, a grating over the bridge access tunnel to the forward compartment upper level, vibrated violently from the ship's fight with the bow wave, the trembling of the ship's thirteen thousand tons testifying to the sheer horse-power pouring out of the propulsor.

An hour into the flank run, a dolphin jumped out of the water at the bow and vanished back into the sea, then returned, his passage a vision of speed. Soon the dolphin was joined by a second one, but after a few minutes they grew bored and disappeared.

Pacino had remained the junior officer of the deck when the maneuvering watch was secured and the surface-transit underway watch section was stationed for the long haul to the dive point. Captain Catardi sat on the top of the sail, dangling his feet into the bridge cockpit, watching Pacino conn the submarine. An hour later, Catardi ordered the flying bridge rails disassembled, and he vanished down the hatch into the access tunnel to the deck thirty-two feet below Pacino's boots. For the next four hours, Pacino kept the watch with an annoyed Lieutenant Alameda and the lookout behind them, who had his own cubbyhole hatch coming out of the sail.

Behind Pacino the periscopes rotated, one the property of Crossfield, the navigator, the scope rotating to take visual fixes at the bearings to the landscape navigation aids. The second belonged to one of the junior officers, the contact coordinator, whose function was to concentrate on the shipping in the seaway and help Pacino avoid a collision. Further aft of the periscopes the radar antenna rotated slowly in constant circles, reaching out to the coastline and seeing ahead, the blips on its screen the merchant ships far at sea, the navigator and contact coordinator sharing the display hood down in the control room. Further aft of the radar mast, the telephone pole of the AN/BRA-44 BIGMOUTH antenna was bumped a few feet out of the sail. Pacino looked around at the seascape, the lush green coastline, the greenish blue of Long Island Sound, the rushing bow wave, and the white of the wake washing by the hull and flowing to the rudder. He raised the binoculars to his eyes and searched the seaway ahead for other vessels, but other than the occasional sailboat, they were alone in the sea. Another hour into the surface run Pacino realized he was as happy as he could ever remember feeling. The vibration of the deck in his boots and the scream of the wind and sea in his ears were the most romantic sensations he'd felt in his life.

He looked over at Alameda's hard face, half obscured by the bill of her ball cap and her binoculars. He had attempted to penetrate Alameda's gruff attitude, without success—his father's words in one of his E-mails coming back to Pacino that some people would hate him for reasons perhaps even they didn't understand, and to leave them be. He had been more successful with Wes Crossfield, the serious navigator, who had gone over the charts and linehandling commands with Pacino before the underway. It was strange, that the entire ship was divided between these two officers, Alameda running the aft half with the engineering spaces, Crossfield responsible for the operation of the tactical half, the forward spaces with the torpedoes and electronic control and sensor areas. The department heads reported to Catardi and to his second-in-command, the executive officer, called the universal Navy nickname of "XO."

Piranha's XO was Lieutenant Commander Astrid Schultz, a tall, slim blond woman with brown piercing eyes and a no-nonsense toughness. She had smiled a greeting to Pacino in the wardroom before he came to the bridge, shaking his hand. The junior officers seemed to be terrified of her, but she had a den mother quality beneath her toughness.

The junior officers had been hurling insults and inside jokes at each other, the easy camaraderie of the ship making it seem like Pacino had stepped into a fraternity house where each officer, chief, and enlisted sailor knew and appreciated the virtues and flaws of the other crewmembers, the crew working together like a single organism. Pacino had heard his father talk about it, but had never quite believed that eighty people from such varying backgrounds could get along so well, welded into a pipe for weeks and months at a time. Pacino wondered what other words of truth from his father he had rejected.

The sun slipped lower in the western sky as the hour approached 1800. Alameda's relief for OOD watch arrived in the bridge cockpit, a junior grade lieutenant named O'Neal, his first name unknown, the crew simply calling him "Toasty." He was a tall, light-complected blond Academy grad, shy and easygoing, but awarded the Bronze Star for bravery the previous summer. O'Neal relieved Alameda, the hostile chief engineer vanishing into the access tunnel. O'Neal turned to Pacino and told him that he could go below, since there was no junior officer of the deck for the evening watch.

"If it's all the same to you, sir, I'd like to stay on watch until we submerge."

"We don't pull the plug until midnight, Mr. Pacino. You're welcome to stay, but you'll miss evening meal."

"That's okay, sir. But call me Patch."

"I'm Toasty. Good to have you aboard." He raised his binoculars and searched the horizon, silent for some time. Finally he spoke again. "So. You going subs like your old man?"

"I'm going to see how this run goes. I'm probably going to be all thumbs in a submarine."

O'Neal laughed. "Jesus, you do a back-full-ahead-flank underway without tugs, making those slacker DevRon 12 linehandlers wet their pants, you put the ship dead center of the channel right under the nose of the squadron commodore, and you wonder if you'll be any good at this? There isn't an officer aboard who could have done that. Hell, I don't think the captain could do that."

Pacino's face flushed. "Shiphandling is one thing," he said, the binoculars at his eyes, staring ahead to the dimming horizon. "Being a competent submariner is another."

"The engineer seems to think you're a natural."

"Alameda? That's strange. She treats me like garbage."

"She just doesn't have much use for nonquals. Once you've earned your dolphins she's okay, but until an officer or enlisted is qualified in submarines, she figures they are breathing her department's air—she owns the atmospheric control equipment—and drinking her department's water."

"Well, she had me fooled." Pacino raised the binoculars to his eyes, the two falling silent, and there was only the roar of the bow wave and the stretch of seawater from horizon to horizon.

Piranha sailed on, making way for the continental shelf as the sun set astern.

All too soon the watch neared an end as the control room called up that the ship was thirty minutes from the dive point.

"Stand up," O'Neal ordered Pacino. "Take a last look around and take in a last breath of fresh air." Pacino complied, wathing O'Neal. "This will be your last look at the surface with your naked eyes and the last real air for weeks, so savor it." Pacino did, aware that he was taking part in a ritual practiced for generations. "Now, crouch down in the access tunnel and hold the flashlight." O'Neal reached up on the port side and rotated a metal plate on a hinge until it was horizontal above his head, partially blocking the starlight, the plate latching with a click. Another plate on the starboard side came up, a third aft, and the fourth forward. The last clamshell hatch shut out the stars completely and made the cockpit disappear. Their perch was now faired into the smooth upper surface of the sail.

Pacino lowered himself down the ladder into the red lamp-lit vertical tunnel and paused to watch O'Neal come down and grab the upper hatch and slam it shut on the seating ring. He wheeled the dogging mechanism clockwise, and the metal claws unfolded and locked the hatch in place. Pacino then continued down until he emerged from the dim tunnel into the red-lit upper-level passageway. O'Neal followed, turning a switch to plunge the access tunnel into darkness. Then he pulled shut the lower hatch and dogged it the same way. Pacino clicked off the rig for dive checklist. The final item, the drain valve, was checked shut by O'Neal.

The two walked in the dim red lights to the control room on the middle-level deck, which, unlike the upper level, was completely dark. The instrument panel of the enclosed ship control station was the only illumination in the forward part of the space. In the darkness Pacino could barely make out the silhouette of a man wearing a bulky helmet standing behind a console, Ensign Breckenridge.

"Sir," Pacino reported, "bridge and sail rigged for dive by Mr. O'Neal and checked by me."

The two reassumed the watch. Pacino was ushered to the chair at the command console and instructed to put on the Type 23 periscope helmet.

"Well," a Boston accent said from behind him, "I'm ready to hear the junior officer of the deck's report."

"Mark the sounding," Pacino called into the Type 23 helmet's boom mike. The display came up, a breathtaking three-dimensional view, as if Pacino's head were back up on the sail.

"Six five four fathoms!" O'Neal's voice replied.

"Captain," Pacino said, gulping, hoping he'd remember all that O'Neal had taught him. "Ship is on course one one zero at all-ahead flank making three zero knots. Ship is rigged for dive by Chief Cavalla and checked by Mr. Breckenridge, sail rigged for dive by Mr. O'Neal and checked by me. We are two minutes from the dive point, sir, with ship's inertial navigation tracking the GPS navsat, confirmed by the navigator with a stellar fix. The diving officer is stationed. We hold no surface contacts by visual or sonar. Sounding is six hundred fifty-four fathoms. Request permission to submerge the ship, sir." Pacino breathed, hoping he hadn't forgotten anything.

"Very well, Junior Off'sa'deck," Catardi said. "Submerge the ship to one five zero feet."

"Submerge the ship to one five zero feet, JOOD aye, sir." Pacino waited, breathing heavily, his heart hammering again.

"Thirty seconds to the dive point!"

"Very well, Quartermaster."

"Mark the dive point!"

"Diving Officer," Pacino called, his voice steady despite his nerves, "submerge the ship to one five zero feet!"

The diving officer sat in the ship-control enclosure, a station resembling a heavy jet cockpit with two seats, a central console, and consoles surrounding the seats. The diving officer was a chief petty officer in charge of the torpedomen, a burly woman named Marshall. She acknowledged, her voice growling back, "Submerge the ship to one five zero feet, Diving Officer, aye, sir." She picked up the 1MC microphone and her voice rang out throughout the ship. "Dive! Dive!" She reached into the overhead for the lever to the diving alarm.

Pacino jumped, startled at the sound of the diving alarm horn howling a deep OOOOOOOOOOH-GAAAAAAH just above his head.

"Dive! Dive!" the chief's voice announced a second time.

"Helm, all ahead two-thirds," the chief called. She had control of speed during the diving evolution, O'Neal had said.

"All ahead two-thirds, aye, easing throttle to ahead two-thirds, indicating turns for ahead two-thirds," the helmsman called.

"Very well," the diving officer said. "Opening forward main ballast tank vents."

"Train the periscope to zero zero zero relative," Toasty O'Neal whispered to Pacino. He did and saw an odd sight, four geysers of water screaming vertically up out of the bullet nose. "Now call, 'Venting forward.'"

"Venting forward," Pacino said.

"Venting forward, aye, sir," the chief said. "Opening aft main ballast tank vents."

Pacino turned his view to look aft and witnessed the same phenomenon of an eruption of water from the aft hull, four fire hoses pointed upward. The venting was so violent that it took thousands of gallons of water upward with the air, he thought.

"Venting aft."

"Venting aft, aye, sir. Rigging out the bowplanes." A moment passed. "Bowplanes extended and locked. Helm, take control of your bowplanes."

"Bowplanes tested, tested sat," the helmsman said.

"Helm, ten degrees dive on the bowplanes."

"Ten degrees dive, aye, my bowplanes are down ten degrees."

Pacino watched as the bullet nose of the bow burrowed deeper into the water, the geysers now submerged, some vapor still shooting up through the waves, until there was nothing forward except ocean. He trained his view aft, at the waves rising up the cylinder of the hull. The hull peeked out only between waves, then vanished under the water.

"Decks awash," Pacino called.

The aft hull exposed itself one last time, then was under, the white wake smothering the vessel. "Hull submerged."

"Hull submerged, aye, sir. I have the sternplanes, sternplanes tested in rise, tested in dive, sternplanes tested sat, I have the bubble, sir, and sternplanes to ten degrees dive. Proceeding to ten-degree down bubble. Flooding depth control one to the halfway mark, flooding commenced. Tank at five zero percent, hull valve shut, backup valve shut."

"Very well, Dive," Pacino said, acknowledging the chief.

Pacino could feel his chair angle downward slightly. He trained his view to look ahead, looking down on the top of the sail, which was approaching the waves. A wave splashed over the top of the sail, then receded. The angle became steeper.

"Depth six five feet," the chief reported.

Several waves washed over the sail and the cockpit went under, and nothing remained but a boiling wake. Pacino looked aft at the wake calming behind them, the aft edge of the sail a hump coming out of the waves, until they swallowed the aft part of the sail.

"Sail's under," Pacino called out. The waves were approaching his view, below him by ten feet. He did a low-power search, and by the time his circle was complete, the waves were close.

"Eight zero feet."

The down angle of the deck became steeper.

"Eight three feet. Five-degree down bubble."

The waves were much closer now, the speed of the ship making the water seem to zoom toward him. Soon the crest of a wave was above the level of Pacino's view, and it towered over him. Instinctively he took a breath and held it, and the wave splashed into his view.

"Scope's awash," he said, breathing again. A burst of phosphorescent foam surrounded him for an instant, and his view came out of the water again as the wave trough came by. His view cleared, the stars and the sky came back for a moment before the next wave crest splashed Pacino in the face, the green-lit foam washing around him. One final trough came, giving a momentary glimpse of the surface and the starlight and an approaching big wave, and then the crest hit him and the view was blinded by the fireflies of the foam and a storm of bubbles. The light particles cleared and Pacino found himself looking up at the underside of the waves, lit by starlight and the fading phosphorescent wake of the periscope. He saw three waves rolling by overhead, a thousand bubbles swimming by him, and then the sea around him became dark.

"Scope's under. Lowering the Type 23." Pacino pulled off the helmet. He blinked, back in the dim reality of the control room, his hair sweaty over his ears. O'Neal handed him red goggles to keep his eyes night-adapted, then donned wraparound red glasses.

"Rig control for red," O'Neal called to the diving officer. Red lights flashed and held. The previously dark control room was lit in a haunted-house red that seemed bright to Pacino at first. The ship pulled out at 150 feet, where the Cyclops system trimmed the ship, bringing her to exactly neutral buoyancy.

Pacino turned to the captain, standing behind him with his arms crossed. He had changed into submariner's coveralls, wearing his dolphins and command pin on his left pocket, his embroidered nametag reading CATARDI. His left arm had a patch with the Jolly Roger pirate emblem of the Unified Submarine Command with the ship's patch below it, his right sleeve carrying a patch with the American flag. He wore black sneakers. He also wore a black eye patch over his left eye, giving him the appearance of a pirate. Pacino knew from his youth that was not an affectation, but kept one eye night-adapted in case of an emergency periscope depth.

"Captain," Pacino said, standing up, "ship is submerged to one five zero feet with a satisfactory one-third trim. Request to go deep and return to point of intended motion."

"Take her deep, JOOD," Catardi ordered. "Test depth, steep angle."

Piranha plunged into the deep cold of the Atlantic.

Admiral Kelly McKee stared into his empty coffee mug and shook the carafe, which was dry. He lit the third cigar of the flight, trying to think ahead to the intricacies of the upcoming war.

The key to the conflict was keeping the British out of the fight and attacking the Reds early, McKee thought. He shut his eyes, his mind wandering back to Admiral Patton's briefing at the bunker. He concentrated on bringing back each word and each expression on the Navy chief's face, back to the moment when the older man had unfolded the map of Asia onto the table.

"Two years ago, while the Red Chinese were fighting the Whites on the Chinese east coast, the Hindu Republic of India's dictator Nipun sent his shock troops north, invading and occupying a vast plateau of Red Chinese territory." Patton circled a region north of India's northern border, an area colored the red of the Peoples Republic of China, labeled Xinjiang Uyger Zizhiqu.

"Soon into their occupation the Indians discovered a massive oil field, which they named 'Shamalan.' The crude oil is incredibly sweet with almost no sulfur. India called in their friends from the UK, and within a year the Brits completed the work of a decade by constructing two cross-continental pipelines, two refineries, and two large oil unloading terminals. The refined petroleum from the Shamalan oil fields is the best quality in the world, and the Indians are pricing it to sell. When the Saudi shipping lanes were shut down from the supertanker explosions, India's production came on-line, making India a world economic power.

"But the Indians refuse to sell any of that oil back to Red China. So the Reds want the plateau back. And revenge." Patton sank into his chair, the fleet commanders sitting as well. "A major Asian war is now inevitable. That concludes the unclassified portion of this briefing. The following is classified Top Secret, special compartmented information, codeword 'Echo.' Six hours ago the Peoples Liberation Army began their mobilization to the western front. The trains are rolling, the convoys are winding their way over the passes, and the jet transports and fighters are in flight. And as the Reds mobilize toward the Indian frontier, the Red Northern Fleet is starting their engines and singling up their lines, preparing to depart the ports of the Red Chinese Bo Hai Bay east of Beijing.

"Kelly, your unit, the Virginia-class submarine *Leopard,* is lurking inside the bay. She's spying on the Red communications from Beijing, but she's also a trip wire. When the Red fleet departs the bay on the way to the Indian Ocean, *Leopard* will be tasked with shadowing the fleet as it moves south.

"As you know, the Red Northern Fleet is formidable. They used to be a rustbucket mothball flotilla that couldn't even cruise in the deep water of the bay. But they've been reequipping, and the Russian Republic has been building export-version aircraft carriers, antisubmarine destroyers, fast frigates, and antiaircraft heavy cruisers around the clock. The three Red Chinese carriers are top-of-the-line Kuznetsov-class giants, and the Beijing-class nuclear battle cruisers are fully seaworthy. Their aircraft are top shelf, if not a match for ours, but they have them in sheer numbers. With three carrier battlegroups they intend to surround and crush India.

"The Red submarine force admiral, Chu Hua-Feng, has rebuilt his fleet after his defeat in the East China Sea. Now he's got eleven fast attack nuclear submarines—six Russians, three

Japanese Destinys, a French Valiant-class, and the lead ship of the Chinese-built Giant Wave or Julang-class has completed sea trials and loaded weapons, and Chu's best captain will be taking her to sea. All the foreign-sourced subs have been reworked to accept Chinese supercavitating East Wind torpedoes, all refit for ultraquiet sound quieting by the Swedes, and all engineering spaces redesigned and reworked by the Germans.

"But before they can use that firepower, they have to get in close, within cruise missile range of their targets, since the missiles' warheads are much heavier now, reducing their range. I'll tell you why in a moment. The Red generals proposed an early attack against India with the cruise missiles that are in range now, but their Supreme Commander, General Fang Shui, is insisting on a time-on-target attack. That means he'll mobilize slowly and deliberately, while India sweats, and then when the second hand hits the twelve of zero-hour, every missile and bomb hits India at once. Communications and infrastructure are hit so hard they may as well be destroyed. The enemy's morale collapses. And the oil rigs, pipelines, and refineries are the first targets.

"Each Red carrier battlegroup is carrying about three hundred heavy short-range cruise missiles armed with precision-enhanced blast-radius plasma warheads. The enhanced blast weapons are heavier, which reduces their range, which is why General Fang wants them positioned before he shoots anything."

Patton paused to pour himself a black coffee. Neither admiral said a word, each man watching him as if he were about to perform a magic trick. He took a pull of the scalding liquid and cleared his throat.

"But the war with the Reds at sea is only part of the picture. Let's go back to the Indians for a moment. The British constructed the oil facilities for India against the advice of the European Union, since the EU's economy is closely tied to China, and the EU is betting the Chinese will kick the Indians out of the Shamalan fields. The British have pulled the Royal

Navy Flotilla out of the European Union High Seas Fleet. They're fueling up and loading food and weapons. A squadron of advance ships is heading for the eastern Mediterranean, where we expect they will transit the Suez Canal to the Gulf of Oman, to the Arabian Sea and into the western Indian Ocean. By the time the Reds enter the eastern Indian Ocean, half the British force will arrive in the west with the remainder of their fleet joining them two weeks later.

"The Royal Navy Fleet order-of-battle consists of four carrier battlegroups and twenty nuclear attack submarines, all of them frontline units. Their firepower in heavy cruise missiles and aircraft outnumbers the Red Chinese two-to-one. Once the Reds see the Royal Navy coming, we believe they may put aside their time-on-target plan and preemptively strike at India with every missile in range, but since most of their force will be out of range they'll fill the gap by shooting their ICBMs from the forty silos in northern Red China, all of them armed with old-fashioned multiple reentry-vehicle hydrogen bombs, doped with cobalt to make them enhanced-radiation high-yield city-killers. These *are* your grandfather's nuclear weapons, each one of them Asian Treaty violations. So the coming of the Royal Navy will, in all likelihood, trigger a nuclear war on the Asian continent, and we're talking radiation clouds and the total destruction of the Shamalan oil fields.

"The Royal Navy won't stand idly by while their ally gets nuked. The Brits will counterattack both the Red Northern Fleet and Red China itself. The bad news is that the Brits know about the nuclear weapons in the Red ICBMs. London has vowed to attempt to deter the Chinese with their own nuclear threat. While the Brits are on their way to the Indian Ocean, they will be converting their clean plasma warheads—which surgically strike targets with no collateral damage—into ultrahigh-yield hydrogen bombs, the most powerful nuclear warheads ever invented. If that's not bad enough, the British are pulling their old neutron bombs out of cold storage and flying them to their carrier groups, for the possible use of leveling Red Chinese troop concentrations. Rumor has it that five of them could be targeted at Beijing. A few days into the battle, the Peoples Liberation Army and a considerable number of Chinese civilians will be a scorched pile of bones."

Patton let the words hang in the air, watching his fleet commanders' faces grow dark.

"Our objective in this war is twofold. We will be putting weapons on the Red Chinese fleet with the goal of sinking them before they can get in range of Indian targets. We will be targeting their sub force, with the tactical objective of sinking every platform. The second goal in-theater is to neutralize the Royal Navy. In this conflict, their high tempers and radioactive weapons will do nothing but harm. We must get them to withdraw.

"Kelly, your East Coast submarines will sail for the chokepoint Arabian Sea entrance to the western Indian Ocean, the corridor that the Royal Navy battlegroups must travel to come in-theater. Your forces will position themselves in attack range of the Royal Navy Fleet. I'm certain that diplomacy will be enough, and that your orders to face the British will be a mere contingency plan, and that you'll hear from me to turn back and attack the Red Fleet with The Viking. If the worst happens and England won't listen, that's when you get your final orders. Orders to blockade the Royal Navy."

"Blockade? What if a blockade fails? Are you contemplating giving me orders to fire on the Brits?"

Patton sighed. "If it comes to that, yes."

The Viking's face had turned red, and Kelly McKee's eyebrows formed a stormy frown.

"But it won't. Kelly, the heaviest lifting for your part of the operation will be done by your Pacific squadrons. Together with your unit in the Chinese Bo Hai Bay, your western submarine force will intercept each of the three Red Chinese surface battlegroups that are on the way to the Indian Ocean. Kill them before they can do their mischief. And kill them from over the horizon before they can make it in-theater, if you can, and if not, chase them into the Indian Ocean and sink them there. If the gods are with us, your subs will get to them before they can get to The Viking's battlegroups, and sink them. Once the Chinese fleet is on the bottom, the strategists think the Reds will break off from the Indians—they don't have enough missiles deployable by rail or truck to stop an advance of Indian shock troops, and an attack could start a fight the Reds wouldn't be able to finish.

"Vic, if Kelly's submarines are late or defeated, the mission falls to your surface action groups. Your carriers and surface fleets will go it alone against a well-armed Chinese force. It will be up to you to stop them."

Next Patton had dropped the bombshell about their communications being compromised, and their extraordinary orders about using pad computers and Internet E-mails to communicate. While McKee and Ericcson were trying to recover from that shock, Patton addressed The Viking, telling him more details about his mission. When Ericcson had left, Patton frowned over at McKee.

"Kelly, because of the communications security penetration, I want you to brief your captains personally, face-to-face. They don't brief their crews until they're safely submerged. And except for the NSA agents, there will be no E-mail from any crew member to shore. We'll sail the old-fashioned way, in the dark. Now, about the forward deployed unit, the *Leopard*—you're going to have to get word to the *Leopard* that she's at war without using the battle network and without making her surface."

"We've got some new technology allowing us to rendezvous with a submerged unit. I'll get a few of the pad computers to her by the time she's in the East China Sea." McKee pushed his chair back. "Is that all, sir?"

"I wish it were, Kelly. I'm surprised you're not thinking ahead. Since our command network is penetrated and compromised, we're in deep trouble with the *Snarc*. With her deployed in the Atlantic, she could target our East Coast subs as they scramble to the Indian Ocean."

And that was the moment in McKee's mind when the operation went from being a wartime deployment to a war. The Red

Chinese, formidable as they were, were an enemy he could accept. But having his own advanced weapons systems turning on him frightened him.

His thoughts were interrupted by the Navy pilot standing in front of him.

"Admiral? We're descending for a straight-in approach now. We should have you on the tarmac in fifteen minutes. Welcome to Hawaii, sir."

"Thanks," McKee said, craning his neck to see the lights of Honolulu out the window.

As he packed his pad computer into his briefcase, he wondered if the *Piranha* would be enough to stop the *Snarc*. McKee choked off the thought. Catardi's *Piranha* would prevail over the out-of-control robot sub. He *had* to—because if *Snarc* sank *Piranha* and made it into the Indian Ocean, the war would be lost.

5

The weathered fishing boat tossed in the waves of the Yellow Sea northeast of Shanghai. The moon and stars were gone, an impenetrable overcast lingering over the area for the last two days. The trawler's booms were extended, her fishing nets deployed. Two miles astern of the trawler, the TB-23 thin-wire wide-aperture towed array tasted the quadrillion noises of the sea and fed them to the Cyclops II sonar suite in the forward hold. The boat fished not for food but for a nuclear submarine.

Its prey was the stealthiest and quietest manned undersea craft ever constructed. Finding it would be impossible without the processing power of the Cyclops system. While the submarine was quiet, it still contained pumps and turbines and motors and a propulsor, all machines that rotated, and when man-made machines rotated, they vibrated at a rhythmic frequency and emitted cyclic tones into their surroundings. These machines were mounted on four-dimensional sound mounts, their vibrations shielded from the universe and absorbed, at least most of the vibrations. Deep within the beast, steam and water pulsed and flowed like an animal's blood in veins and arteries, each flow pulse putting another sound in the water. To the conventional sonar devices, the noise emitted by the target would go unnoticed, as if it were the noise of quiet rain in a tumultuous thunderstorm. It was true even of the TB-23 linear towed array, which heard only the vast frequency spectrum of the loud seas, passing each noise at each frequency up the signal wire to the main computer.

Deep within the consciousness of the Cyclops II, the noise from the sea was sifted, the sheer amount of data able to choke the computers of only two years before, those ancient machines able only to search in a narrow slice of ocean for the target. But Cyclops II could listen to the entire world and filter out the random ocean noise that didn't have rhythmic pulses, leaving only the pure harmonic tonals from rotating machinery. From a hundred thousand yards away, the trawler's computer isolated four tonals, locked them in, and identified them positively as a United States Virginia-class nuclear submarine. The technician at the Cyclops console called the fishing boat's deck officer, who called the captain, who called the operations officer, who woke up the two divers and sent them to the aft hold.

In the red-lantern-lit hold, the two divers strapped masks around their necks and adjusted their tanks. The Mark 17 High Thrust Underwater Vehicle hummed with the power of her fuel cells. The commander of the mission climbed into the front, his chief petty officer climbing into the aft seat. When the checklist was completed, the two men put their faces into their masks. The lights in the hold shifted from a dim red glow to complete darkness. The trawler's support crew shut the overhead hatch, sealing the pressure-tight hold. The HTUV inclined to a steep down-angle as the rail launching system prepared to eject them from the hold. The door in the keel opened slowly until the noise of the wake roared below them. The Mark 17 suddenly moved, catapulted down the inclined rails and splashing into the water, diving beneath the surface, the roar of the trawler's screws overhead made more violent by their own thruster coming to full power.

The lieutenant who sat in the forward seat cranked the throttle of the motorcycle-style controls, pushing the Mark 17's yoke down, accelerating the vehicle in a steep dive. The noise of the surface faded astern as they sank deeper, the engines becoming quiet as the craft leveled off at eighty feet below the waves. The lieutenant shivered as he engaged the computer pilot. The Mark 17 would wait at this depth, with a small buoyant wire antenna drifting upward to the surface to keep them in touch with the trawler and allow the computer to target the larger, swifter submarine during the upcoming rendezvous.

As soon as the towed array had made a tentative detection, the trawler captain had sent an E-mail message requesting transmission repair parts for his starboard diesel. Within five minutes an ELF transmission, Extremely Low Frequency, was made from the huge radio towers in Tsing Tao, White China, transmitting only two characters, the letters A and X. ELF radio waves were clumsy and nearly useless. It took ten minutes to transmit a single alphanumeric character and an enormous amount of transmitting power. But they did one thing no other electromagnetic signal could—they penetrated deeply into the ocean. The letter A began to transmit, the waves of the ELF signal carrying past the Mark 17 HTUV and its occupants to the depths of the sea, eventually striking the ELF loop antenna of the United States submarine *Leopard,* the loop mast retracted in the sail. The *Leopard* was steaming at 546 feet keel depth on course one seven five at fifteen knots, much too deep and fast for the Mark 17 to intercept her. But as the submarine's radio equipment began to realize that the letter A was the first character of that day's ELF callsign, an alarm rang in the radio room and in the control room. By the time the letter X began to transmit, a phone call was placed from the control room to the captain's stateroom, and George Dixon, Commander, U.S. Navy, was awakened with the word that there was a communications emergency, and that *Leopard* had been urgently called to periscope depth.

Three minutes later the submarine slowed and climbed above the thermal layer, where the Mark 17's onboard sensors, guided by the clues from the trawler, made the detection of the submarine. The computer accelerated the underwater vehicle at maximum revolutions to intercept the American submarine. By the time *Leopard* slowed to five knots, ascended to periscope depth, and put her radio antenna into the sky, the Mark 17 was locked on in hot pursuit. The computer drove the HTUV to the aft hatch of the *Leopard,* then vacuum-pumped itself fast to the hull. It would ruin two patches of rubber anechoic coating, but it was vital that the underwater vehicle not fall off the hull in the slipstream of the water flow and get sucked into the submarine's propulsor. Five knots sounded slow, but to the lieutenant and the chief, fighting five knots of current could exhaust a man in minutes. The chief withdrew a handheld tool from the vehicle, trailing a power cord from the cockpit. He aimed and fired, a harpoonlike device flashing out and hitting the hull, a cable attached. The chief made the cable fast to the vehicle, then aimed again and fired a second cable. He and the lieutenant hooked their safety harnesses to both cables and made their way against the current to the hatch, each carrying several heavier tools with hoses leading back to the vehicle. It took the chief five minutes to center the hatch salvage tool over the hatch and secure it to the hull. While he worked on that, the lieutenant placed a similar tool over a salvage valve connection to the left of the hatch and another one to the right. The salvage valves would flood the interior of the escape trunk and vent out the trapped air, allowing them to open the outer hatch, assuming the ship's crew didn't fight them from inside. But this would happen so fast no one would expect the invasion. The chief's salvage tool was engaged over the main salvage connection above the hatch, and it spun the hatch ring open in less than thirty seconds, unlocking the submarine's upper hatch.

The second tool fit under the hatch ring and lifted the heavy metal upward, resisting the powerful force of the current generated by the ship's motion. When the hatch was up, the lieutenant lowered his legs into the escape trunk below, then disconnected his safety harnesses from the dual cables. Just before he vanished into the hatch he tapped farewell on the chief's foot, then crouched down into the airlock.

The lieutenant reached above to help pull the hatch down, the hydraulic cylinders above doing most of the work until the hatch was fully shut. He spun the hatch wheel, shutting the massive hatch. He was inside the submarine, although in a dark flooded cubbyhole of it. While he found the interior light switch, the chief was busy outside on the hull withdrawing the three salvage tool operators and the two hatch hydraulic cylinders and stowing them in the vehicle, then cutting the cables. The chief would be divorcing from the submarine within two minutes, then driving clear before the submarine could dive deep again. The chief would return to the trawler, leaving the lieutenant inside the submarine.

The lieutenant found the escape hatch drain valve, and opened it to drain the flooded escape trunk to the bilges of the submarine far below. A second vent valve opened the trunk to the atmosphere inside the ship. The water level fell below his face, and he took off his mask, yawning to clear his eardrums as the pressure eased. It only took another half minute for the water to drain completely. He spun the lower hatch wheel operator, the metal dogs coming off the hatch ring. He braced himself and pulled open the hatch. The bright light from the ship's interior nearly blinded him. The hatch's spring mechanism made it easy to pull it up into the escape trunk. A hot cloud of steaming air wafted into his face, for the escape trunk they had chosen was located over the engineroom. The noise of the ship was much louder than he expected, the turbines screaming like jet engines. He had expected a nuclear submarine to be quiet, but this sounded like the third level of hell. The hatch latched in the open position, allowing him to put his wetsuit shoes on the upper rungs of the ladder. He wondered for a moment if anyone would even know he'd invaded the submarine when he heard three clicks. With his feet finally on the solid deckplates, he turned slowly to face three Beretta 9mm pistols, all of them pointed at his eyeballs, seeming bigger than cannons.

He raised his hands in surrender, his voice steady as he announced himself. "Lieutenant Brett Oliver, United States Navy, on temporary duty to the National Security Agency. Here by the order of Vice Admiral McKee, Commander Unified Submarine Command. Request permission to come aboard."

The heavy paw of a machinist mate grabbed him by the neck and dragged him all the way to the middle level of the forward compartment, to the captain's stateroom.

Captain George Dixon glared angrily at the arrested intruder, who sat at the captain's conference table in a borrowed ill-fitting submarine poopy-suit.

"So let me see if I got this straight, Lieutenant, if that's what you really are," Dixon said in a hostile South Carolina drawl. "You invade my ship and then tell me my entire communications suite is nonsecure and compromised, and I can't use it to talk to anybody. And that means no one from USubCom can talk to me. And that you've got a handheld computer gizmo that will bypass the battle networks to allow me to talk to the National Military Command Center, except that the messages are passed by Internet E-mail."

"To be verified by the SAS sealed authenticators, Captain," Oliver said. "There's no way that SAS could ever be compromised. The computers and SAS are the bypass to the Navy Tactical Data System, which is now hardwired to the Chinese, and maybe the Indians."

"Why shouldn't I have you arrested as a foreign conspirator?"

"Why don't you call for the SAS packet and verify the E-mail message to be authentic?"

Dixon stroked his waxed handlebar mustache with two fingers. He was young for submarine command, a six-foot-one-inch dark-haired man, but he had served early in his career with David Kane, who had rocketed to flag rank, and Kane's recommendations made Dixon's obstacles vanish before him. Dixon had gone from being a junior officer on a 688I sub to a Seawolf-class as navigator during the Japanese War, then as XO of another 688I during the East China Sea war, and finally named prospective commanding officer of the new construction Virginia-class submarine *Leopard*, which had finished her sea trials early and been loaded out and sent to sea on the emergency special operation to the Bo Hai Bay. During Dixon's hectic operational life, he had managed to fall in love with a Charleston beauty, pursue her, marry her, build a house, and have two children, both boys with the fine blond hair and blue eyes of their mother, both with the energy and enthusiasm and penetrating logic of their father, the boys and their mother a hemisphere and a half year away. As a reminder of them, he carried a gold coin his wife had given him for their first anniversary, kept perpetually in his left coverall pocket. At times when he was uncertain, like now, he liked to take it out and feel its heavy weight in his hand.

Dixon raised the phone to the conn, pressing the buzzer. "Officer of the Deck, send the navigator and communicator to my stateroom, and get the executive officer from her workout in the torpedo room."

While they waited, Dixon checked the message again. The ship was still at periscope depth, rolling in the waves while the Chinese battlegroup, the first one to sortie from the Port Arthur piers, sailed far over the horizon, getting further away every minute. A knock came at the door.

"Come in," the captain called.

"Nav and Commo here, sir," MacGregor, the redheaded navigator, said, as usual sounding like he'd been swallowing raw coffee grounds. The Scotsman habitually talked so fast he had been nicknamed "Burst Comm" by his former ship, in reference to the burst communications that came down from the satellite.

"Gentlemen, I am ordering you to withdraw SAS eight-zero-four-echo-three from the SAS safe."

"Aye, aye, sir," MacGregor said. "I'm required to ask why, sir."

Dixon looked at Oliver, who nodded. Dixon handed him the pad computer. MacGregor read Lieutenant Oliver's E-mail letter of introduction, looked uncertainly up at the captain, then grabbed young Ensign Wilkins and headed aft to the executive officer's stateroom. While Dixon waited, Executive Officer

Donna Phillips knocked and entered, the thin, medium-height brunette wearing sweat-stained workout clothes and a towel around her neck, her shoulder and arm muscles still bulging from the weights she'd been lifting in the torpedo room. Normally Phillips could be found in perfectly starched coveralls, working in her neat stateroom. She wore her hair in a chin-length bob, and other than when she worked out, it was never known to have a single hair out of place. The hairdo emphasized her strong cheekbones and her dark eyes, which were usually engaged in a frown. Dixon had worked with Phillips for two years, and he was well pleased with her, though he thought she would do well to lighten up on her heavy-handed command of the crew.

"XO, meet Lieutenant Brett Oliver, detached duty to NSA, and now to us."

"Captain, you want to tell me what's going on?"

Dixon handed her the pad computer to read Oliver's note, her only expression a raised eyebrow.

MacGregor and Wilkins returned with a foil packet, the junior man holding it as if it were a ticking bomb. "SAS authenticator eight-zero-four-echo-three, sir. Please verify that it is the correct one, sir," Wilkins said.

Dixon squinted at the printing on the packet, then said, "Eight-zero-four-echo-three, packet checks. Open the packet."

Wilkins pulled the foil tab and withdrew a card with a long string of letters and numbers written on it.

"Navigator, authenticate the E-mail message on the pad computer," Dixon ordered.

MacGregor glanced from the card to the E-mail and back, finally looking up at Dixon. "Sir, the E-mail message authenticates. It's a valid message, sir."

Dixon nodded. "Take the SAS packet and destroy it under two-man control and sign for it," he ordered. The junior officers left, and as they shut the door behind them, the small computer beeped.

"There's a second E-mail in here," Phillips said as she looked at the computer.

"Let me see that," the captain said. Another message had come in from the Internet link from the periscope antenna. "Another one needing authentication."

It took another several minutes to get the second SAS authenticator opened, but when it authenticated the second message, Dixon looked up at Phillips and Oliver, the sub commander's face a hard warface, but with the color drained from it. He slowly reached for a phone and buzzed the officer of the deck on the conn.

"Off'sa'deck, Captain. Take her deep and increase speed to flank and close the Chinese surface force. Spin up all four warshot Mark 58 Alert/Acute Mod Plasma torpedoes. Make tubes one and two ready in all respects and open outer doors. When we're within ten thousand yards of the nearest battle-group combatant slow to ten knots, downshift main coolant pumps, and rig for ultraquiet. And send the navigator back to my stateroom."

"Captain, what is it?" Phillips asked.

Captain Dixon looked up at both officers. "It would appear we're in a shooting war."

Lien Hua walked down the rainswept concrete jetty. His black uniform with its minimal insignia became drenched. It was uncomfortable, but there would be time to change later, and the wet uniform reminded him of the hardness of this day's task. He continued down the pier to the security barrier, where the admiral's staff car had pulled up. Inside there was no admiral, but instead Lien's wife and daughters.

"Well, hello, girls," he said, smiling in spite of the stress he felt. "What brings you here?" His eyes turned toward his wife's beautiful face, her upturned eyes seeking his. She smiled back at him and climbed out of the car, hoisting the umbrella over her head, the wind blowing over the pier making it flap loudly. She wrapped her arms around him and kissed him hard, then hugged him again. Her lips came to his ear, her voice barely audible above the storm.

"I wanted to tell you I love you. And to tell you to be careful. And that I'm sorry we fought."

Lien Hua smiled, kissing her cheek, then pulling back so he could look in her eyes, the eyes of a princess. "It was my fault, dearest," he said. He looked around sheepishly. "And I love you too. Let me say good-bye to the girls." He leaned over their window and kissed each rain-spattered small face, touching their hair and pulling them close, the smell of them reminding him of home and safety and happiness.

"Father, Mother says you are going to war. Is that true?"

"Mother should not say such things," he said, glancing in amusement at his wife. "We are going to sea for another exercise. I will be home soon. And until I do, you must mind your mother."

"We will, Daddy," they chorused. He touched their noses and hugged them both again.

"Admiral Chu let you come in his staff car?"

"His wife thought it would be a good thing."

Lien nodded. "Thank you for coming, my princess, but I must go."

"We'll watch your departure from here. Be safe, my love," she said. "Come home to us."

He bent to kiss her, then turned to walk back down the pier, pulling his collar up against the driving rain and wiping her lipstick from his face as he approached the berth of the fast-attack nuclear submarine.

The ship was a brand-new Chinese-designed Julang-class, built on Red Chinese soil by Chinese engineers and shipbuilders in the Huludao Naval Base and Shipyard in the northern Bo Hai, now stationed at the Jianggezhuang Submarine Base, where no Westerner could spy on her secrets. Even in the gloom of the hammering rain she was a sleek, black, graceful beauty. She was so low in the water she was barely visible, her cigar-shaped hull awash to the top curving surface, her fin rising from the midsection, the shape vertical forward, curving on the upper surface and sloping back to the deck aft. The topside section sloped gently to the water aft of the fin, the rudder slicing upward, seeming disembodied in the black water of the slip. The vessel's name was *Nung Yahtsu*, which the barbarians would translate to mean *Teeth of the Dragon*. It was a name conferred upon her by Lien Hua himself when she was but a helpless hoop of high-yield steel in a forlorn dry-dock, and the fierce name would shape the vessel's coming destiny. This day she would sail into the seas far from her home base and bloody her teeth with the flesh of the barbarians.

As he arrived near her gangway he was met by his second-in-command, Zhou Ping. Zhou was the son of a friend of Lien's father in the Peoples Liberation Army Strategic Missile Force decades before. The friend had died a slow death of emphysema, and on his deathbed had asked Lien's father to watch over Zhou, and when Lien's father died, the obligation passed to Lien. At first Lien had considered the upholding of that promise yet another of dozens of duties to his father, but had soon seen an ingenious talent in the younger man, and had shepherded him through five sea tours, until today when Zhou stood as his first officer.

"It is my honor to greet you this rainy morning, Captain Lien," Zhou said, bowing deeply. Lien Hua returned the bow and stood somberly, saying nothing for a moment, the rain falling down his collar, his black submarine force uniform drenched in the downpour.

"Tell me about the status of the People's ship, Leader Zhou."

"*Nung Yahtsu* is rigged for sea, my captain. The weapons load went perfectly. The *Dong Feng* torpedoes are tube-loaded in five tubes, the Tsunami special weapon is dry-loaded in tube six, and the remaining thirty torpedoes are rack-stowed. The reactor is in the power range, steam has been brought into the engineroom, the ship is self-sustaining, and the shore power cables have been withdrawn. The main engines are running at five percent power to the idle resistors, and the main motor has been tested. Lines are singled up, and the crew is at maneuvering stations. The navigation equipment has pinpointed us at the correct pierside location, and the radio equipment has received our permission to depart."

"Excellent, Mr. First. Are there any discrepancies?"

"Yes, my captain. All class four and lower."

"Very well, Leader Zhou." Lien Hua looked skyward, the water pouring into his eyes. "A foul day to be a mariner, my friend, but all the better to shield us from the orbiting eyes of the barbarians."

"They say it is good luck for the heavens to rain on us as we depart," Zhou said. "But I would be equally content with the sun and a mild sea breeze."

Lien Hua laughed and clapped his subordinate on the shoulder. "Prepare to maneuver," Lien ordered Zhou. He took one last look around at the submarine base and set foot on the gangway. His boot landed on the rubber coating of the hull, and the bright lights of the submarine's interior drove the gloom from the day. It would be a good run, he told himself as he lowered himself down the stainless-steel ladder to the deckplates below.

Ten minutes later, *Nung Yahtsu* cast off her lines and made her way into the deep channel. Lien Hua stood on the maneuvering tower of the fin, barely able to make out the admiral's staff car with his wife and children inside. At ten minutes before noon the submarine rounded the turn at buoy number two and Lien's family faded astern.

"Mr. First, I am going below," he announced.

A half hour later the ship submerged and her engines sped up to maximum revolutions, on an intercept course with the Carrier Battlegroup One. By the time the task force entered the East China Sea, the *Nung Yahtsu* would be ahead of her, guarding her from enemy submarines and the enemy commanders' evil intentions. Sometime before *Nung Yahtsu* escorted Battlegroup One to the firing position, she would engage and prevail over the Western submarines.

6

Michael Pacino got out of the staff car that had taken him from the Pentagon to the inner-security drydock area of Newport News Naval Shipyard. He still struggled to understand what Patton had found so urgent about the project he'd wanted Pacino to work on, and why it was such an emergency that Pacino had been plucked from his sailboat to perform it. Or even why Patton had needed him for it and not one of the several dozen hotshot MIT engineers who swarmed over the drydocks.

The answers hadn't come in the CNO suite, but perhaps they would be evident in the field, Pacino thought. He'd been asked to become project director of the SSNX rebuilding program. And not just to rebuild it, but to give it the power to outrun the fastest torpedoes in the inventories of the combat navies of the world. "That's impossible," he'd told Patton. "You're asking me to make a Greyhound bus outrun a motorcycle. It can't be done."

Patton smiled. "It could if you strapped a few rockets to the bus, Patch," he said in jest.

Pacino promised to make an attempt, but he was not optimistic. Before he left, Patton asked him if he would also take on program directorship of a new and secret weapons system, the Tigershark torpedo project, a program that up to now had failed dismally.

"It's a lot like Project *Snarc,* where we put a carbon processor into a submarine—you didn't know we did that, did you?"

After a few minutes of explanations about that, Patton continued. "Project Tigershark is tougher. We've been trying to put a carbon processor into the body of a torpedo, but the damned things keep attacking the firing ship. And carbon computers don't accept interlocks or hardwiring or programmed instructions. The torpedo is a killer, but unless we can guarantee the safety of the firing ship, it's no good to us."

Pacino agreed to accept responsibility for the Tigershark program as well. He spent the evening going over the plans for the SSNX submarine rebuild and getting detailed briefings on both projects, until his mind whirled with the new knowledge. Hours later, long after midnight, he stood on the concrete deck of graving dock two of Newport News Naval Shipyard and stared up at the floodlit hull of the submarine looming high overhead. The ship was so beautiful that it filled him with a sudden sadness that he would never go to sea again, but as he looked at it he felt inspired to give the crew of this ship a combat system that would allow them to complete their missions and come home alive.

The ship above him had been the most powerful submerged combatant designed when it had been blown in half by the plasma-tipped torpedoes of a Ukrainian sub lying in ambush. Most of the crew had been killed by the attack. The salvage vessels had gathered at the ship's gravesite and hauled her wreckage back to the shipyard. There was little left of her that could be reused except her hull, but since fabricating a submarine hull was so expensive and time-consuming, Newport News and DynaCorp's Electric Boat Division had begun construction on an entirely new submarine using the hull brought back from the dead. Even the deckplates had to be scrapped, the hull repaired and rewelded, the damaged midsection sliced away and a new module barged in from Groton to replace it.

Her mechanical internals—the main motor, main engines, service turbines, steam generators, and reactor—were removed through the gaps in the hull, and new mechanicals were barged in, stolen from the assembly line at Groton, where the new Virginia-class subs were constructed. New deckplates were installed in the forward spaces, the new combat consoles were shipped in—also taken from Groton—and the interior was rewired and repiped. The new sail was welded in place, the new masts modularized. In twelve months, what had started as a rusting misshapen wreck had been transformed into a naval vessel ready for her launching ceremony.

In another month the ship would have been fitted out and ready to be turned over to the fleet, but the CNO's orders to make the ship outrun enemy torpedoes had stopped all progress. The SSNX would lie here, helpless on the drydock blocks, until Pacino figured out some way to make the vessel torpedo-proof.

The weapons for the ship were as stalled as the sub itself. Project Tigershark had a dozen fatal flaws. The test launches had all been disasters. Most of the lethal Tigersharks had decided to home in on the firing ship rather than the enemy, except for the two Tigersharks that had managed to go for the target drone. Short of making the torpedo a launch-from-aircraft-only weapon, the program was a dead loss. There just seemed no way to educate the carbon processors that the valid submarine target astern of them was their mother ship, since unlike their silicon cousins, they could not be programmed with safety interlocks. So far no one had been able to replicate the success of the *Snarc*'s carbon processor in the Tigershark torpedo. It had to be based on space constraints, Pacino thought. The *Snarc*'s brain took up the better part of the forward compartment's deck, while on Tigershark there was at best one cubic foot of space for the unit's brain.

But if Pacino could make it work, Project Tigershark would make the submarine looming high above return to her role as the world's most powerful submarine. The ship had originally been named the SSNX, the SSN for Submersible Ship Nuclear, the X for Experimental, since she'd been a prototype for the new class of submarine that eventually took the name Virginia. Pacino had had a hand in designing her, his hands crafting a submarine that solved all the problems he'd had in previous submerged combat missions in his seventeen years as a submarine officer. He climbed a stairway mounted next to the rear quarter until he could reach out and touch the hull, the cool metal green in the harsh midnight floodlights, the green paint an inorganic zinc primer. The ship had gone by the cold impersonal program name SSNX until Admiral Donchez's dying wish was fulfilled, and Admiral O'Shaughnessy christened the submarine with the most meaningful submarine name in history—the USS *Devilfish*. Years before, that name had belonged to Pacino's first command, a Piranha-class that had been lost under the polar icecap when a Russian admiral named Novskoyy released a nuclear-tipped torpedo that had killed *Devilfish* as well as the admiral's own Omega-class.

Pacino had left the Navy after the incident, until the day Donchez told him his best friend's ship had been taken hostage by the Red Chinese, and the next thing Pacino knew he was standing in the control room of the *Seawolf* a hundred yards from a Chinese pier, and by the time he had launched the first cruise missile he had managed to put the *Devilfish* out of his mind, at least until he was promoted to fleet commander and wore the shoulderboards of an admiral. The Reds had taken over the East China Sea with a flotilla of submarines that had put a million tons of the U.S. fleet on the bottom, and Donchez insisted that the SSNX be named *Devilfish*. Maybe it wasn't the ship's incredible sensor systems and firepower that had won that war, Pacino thought. Maybe it had been her name.

Now she lay here on the blocks, back from the dead, her name once again only SSNX. The Navy memos spoke of a tradition of rechristening ships brought up from a sinking with a new name, so that the bad luck of the old wouldn't contaminate the destiny of the new. There was also something about wetting the ship's deck with the urine of a virgin, but that had been quietly disregarded. But Pacino knew what he would name her had he been the admiral in command of the submarine force. Had he been given back his old job, he would smash a champagne bottle on her nosecone and christen her the USS *Devilfish,* sailors' suspicions be damned. He was the only one who held that view, as the ship's gangway banner continued to read simply, SSNX-1.

Pacino glanced at his scratched Rolex Submariner, which indicated it was after one in the morning of a Tuesday. It was time to go home, he decided. Nothing further could be accomplished on the failing Tigershark torpedoes or the torpedo evasion idea tonight. He drove the long road to Sandbridge, south of Virginia Beach, and climbed the steps to the door of the beach house. He hated the emptiness of the house, but it beat the impersonal hotel rooms near the shipyard, and there were reminders of his son, Anthony Michael, here. Pacino's wife Colleen was in D.C., staying at the Annapolis house until she could return to Virginia.

He put his head on the pillow and tried to sleep. His thoughts returned to his only child, Anthony Michael, who at that moment would be in California on his senior cruise with a fighter squadron, flying training runs with the pilots he worshiped. He missed the boy. It had been months since they'd been together.

He was drifting off to sleep when the phone jangled on the nightstand. He sat up in bed and flipped on the monitor to see the severe face of his ex-wife, Janice Hillary Lakeland, Anthony Michael's mother. She had been pretty twenty years ago, but now she looked as if all the bitterness inside her had bled through her skin.

"Hello, Janice," he said heavily. There was the usual storm cloud on her face, he thought, wondering what battle she would start this time.

"Hello, Mike," she replied, the name grating on him. When they were married, she never called him anything but "Michael," but five years after the divorce she suddenly began using a name she knew he hated. With either name, her pronunciation made it sound pejorative, as if she were actually saying the word "asshole." "I see you've finally convinced Anthony Michael to follow in his father's footsteps." It was the same argument they'd fought for years, ever since Tony had decided to go to the Naval Academy.

"Janice," he said, his tone flat, "what can I do for you?"

"You can get Anthony Michael off a nuclear submarine, that's what."

"Excuse me?" he said, surprised. "What the hell are you talking about? Anthony's on a fighter squadron cruise out of San Diego. He's probably roving the waterfront right now with his friends."

"Why would you lie to me, Michael?" When she was truly furious, she slipped back into calling him by his full name, but it still sounded like an insult. "I got an E-mail from him just before he left for cruise. He's on the submarine *Piranha* on some dangerous mission. I told you when he had the idiotic idea to go to the Naval Academy that I didn't want him on a sub, and you promised me he'd be an engineer working in a nice safe drydock someplace."

"I'll check it out," Pacino said, his composure back. As shrill as Anthony's mother was being, he agreed with her. A nuclear submarine was the last place he wanted his flesh and blood.

"And do nothing, as usual," she sneered. "You know, his hero worship of you is going to get him killed, and then what are you going to do?" Her eyes were filling with tears. "It's fine for you to go to sea and never come home and have submarines shot out from under you." That summarized the series of fights that had caused her to leave him, he thought dully. "But this is my baby! He's all I've got."

Much as Pacino wanted to hang up on her, his son loved her, and Pacino knew he would someday be judged by his son as to how he had treated the boy's mother. He took a deep breath.

"Give me a number where I can reach you in a half hour," Pacino said, looking directly into the telephone's camera. She rattled off her Palm Beach house's number, and he promised to get back to her.

Pacino dialed in to the Pentagon, bypassing the security switchboard. It was almost two in the morning, so Pacino would have to be content to leave a message for Patton, who was a notorious night owl, but even he would be home at this hour. The display lit up and showed Admiral Patton, who still sat at his desk with his sleeves rolled up, his tie at half mast, and a pair of half-frame reading glasses perched on his nose. Patton asked about the SSNX and Project Tigershark, but Pacino held up his palm.

"I was actually just trying to see what the latest is on my son. Can you look him up?"

"Sure." Patton slid the reading glasses on and clicked his touch screen through a few software panels, then looked up. "He's on the *Piranha,* which is involved in some fleet exercises. There's a note here from Commander Catardi. Says your boy made a great first impression—says here he did a back-full-ahead-flank underway maneuver, just like his old man."

Pacino recoiled from a triple blow—that Janice had been right, that little Robby Catardi had grown up to command a submarine, and that someone in a uniform had something good to say about the younger Pacino for once.

After all the trouble Anthony had had at the Naval Academy, Pacino thought, one class-A offense after another until he was threatened with separation from the naval service, and then the young man had acquitted himself at sea with honor on a frontline nuclear submarine serving under a man Pacino had personally trained. There was no way he could ask Patton to evacuate the boy, not just because Janice was panicked. It was a peacetime exercise, Pacino thought, wondering what the hell he would tell the boy's mother. He thanked Patton, then dialed the Palm Beach house and brought up her glaring face.

"I'm sorry, Janice," he said. "You were right. Anthony has a few weeks left on his mission, but I can assure you it's not dangerous. He's on a milk run in the Atlantic."

"That's what they said about your father's *Stingray.*"

Pacino remembered then that he had never told Janice that the *Stingray* didn't go down off the Azores, but had succumbed under ice, nor had he told her about what happened to *Devilfish.*

"It'll be okay. He'll be back in a month. I give you my personal guarantee." He clicked off, then tried to sleep, but troubled dreams invaded his night.

In one of them, a skeleton on a Harley chased a Greyhound bus, the motorcycle phantom swinging a mace. As he approached the lumbering bus, a dozen rockets sprouted from it and ignited, and the bus zoomed off over the horizon and disappeared in a cloud of rocket exhaust.

Pacino sat up in bed and began scribbling on a pad. A half hour later he had the beginnings of a torpedo evasion system detailed on the pages. When he shut his eyes, he slept better than he had in a year.

Admiral John Patton paced the deck of the suite of the Chief of Naval Operations, wondering how a midshipman had been assigned to a ship on a wartime operation. But he knew the answer—it was the result of his own orders that no personnel orders should be suddenly changed as a result of the mobilization, lest the spies watching the fleet's every move draw conclusions—such as the conclusion that a submarine was departing for a wartime patrol because the midshipmen were all reassigned at the last instant. Keeping the personnel orders as is had protected the operation's security, but now Patton had a problem—the son of Patch Pacino was on the sub ordered to engage the *Snarc* and then to fight on in the Indian Ocean. Patton would have to find a stealthy way to evacuate the youth, without impacting *Piranha*'s mission. He owed the older Pacino that much.

The question was how he could do that.

7

The night descent over the coast of Thailand was breathtaking, the lights of the cities and villages like stars below them. The supersonic Falcon touched down lightly on the asphalt of Bangkok International, coasting to a halt at the general aviation facility near the customs building. They remained on-board until the agent, a pretty young Thai girl, came aboard and asked a few polite questions and welcomed them to the country. The two passengers on the jet—one heavy and one thin and tall, both wearing business suits—stepped off the Falcon, emerging into the steamy summer air. Their Thai assistant, a large man named Amorn with coarse features, dressed in a tailored suit, took their baggage and escorted them to the Rolls-Royce and drove them into the city. The wide city streets were deserted, but in a few hours would be jammed with commuter traffic. At the front entrance of the Oriental Hotel, the Rolls stopped and Amorn opened the door. They were taken to a private elevator in the rear of the ornate entrance hall. At the top, the doors opened to the plush penthouse suite. Both men retired in silence to their bedrooms.

The west room's occupant took a warm shower, invigorating after the sticky walk from the Falcon. The water fell onto dark thick hair speckled with gray and down over a thick jet-black beard, tightly trimmed to his face, then down past a thin muscular frame. He was sixty-three years old and in the best shape of his life, in part thanks to a thirteen-year Siberian prison sentence spent in vigorous exercise. He turned off the water and looked briefly in the mirror, amazed at the youthful face staring back at him. The surgery was intended to change his identity, but had nicely taken away the wear of the years. His thin cheeks were filled in, his pockmarked skin was smooth, his sagging chin was as chiseled as when he'd been thirty. His yellowed crooked teeth were white and even, his flaccid neck was smooth and toned, and his jawline was ruler straight. The grizzled former admiral and war-crimes prisoner was gone and replaced with a rich aristocrat. Alexi Novskoyy was dead—the man in the mirror was named Victor Krivak. He smiled, liking the sound of the new name and how it matched the new reflection.

He donned the tropical suit laid out by Amorn and met his companion in the center living area. The other man was five years younger but looked older. His name had once been Rafael, but now he was known as Sergio. He was the brilliant consulting company president who had rescued Novskoyy— rather, Krivak—from the Siberian prison and brought him into the business. He was a barrel-chested man with thick limbs and a massive neck, though he was several centimeters shorter. He had a gray beard that hid much of his face, and his features were large and coarse, except for his eyes, which darted over the room, missing nothing. His surgery had changed his nose and his formerly large ears and taken away much of the fat he had carried previously, although the laser could do nothing to change his large bone structure.

"You never did tell me how you got the American Navy codes," Sergio said as they relaxed on the terrace.

"It was easier than expected," Krivak said quietly. "There was a DynaCorp network architect who had the bad fortune to have a wife and three children. It is amazing what a man can accomplish when he sees a nine-millimeter automatic at the head of his firstborn. I sent him to perform the task of bringing back the code to his house. He brought an obsolete version. It cost him his dog. A second version came back with him, but it had bugs. That cost his wife. The third time the code was current, but the logic-bot on the system—the one that would alert us to changes or security modifications—was not installed correctly."

Sergio waved his hand. "Don't tell me any more. I take it that after several attempts all went perfectly."

"I was afraid we would run out of children, but yes. The next day the police entered the house and found a terrible murder-suicide. Sometimes these computer types lose it and kill their families and then themselves." Krivak smirked.

After dinner, prostitutes were brought up. The girl couldn't have been older than fourteen, perhaps even younger. She drew a bath in the spa and led him to it, pulling him into the water so that his back was to her, and her fingers went to work massaging his back muscles. His eyes closed and he grew drowsy, knowing that the girl would not stop for over an hour. As always, he saw things in the moments between consciousness and sleep. The images usually came swiftly, but tonight they swam by slowly, some blurred and misty, others clearer than life, images from the time his name had been Novskoyy. He saw his childhood in Moscow, the ribbon-covered Red Army marshal's uniform belonging to his father hanging in their bedroom. He returned to the day he graduated from the Marshal Grechko Higher Naval School of Underwater Navigation. The crisp cold day he'd reported aboard his first submarine, a Victor-class. The day when he'd taken his first submarine command, an Akula-class, under the polar icecap. He saw his admiral's epaulets pinned onto his uniform as he assumed command of the Russian Republic Northern Fleet. Then the terrible days of the disarming of the *Rodina,* the nuclear weapons unloaded from his ships and stockpiled in a U.N. depot.

He saw the massive hull of the submarine he'd designed himself, SSN *Kaliningrad,* the biggest and most formidable undersea combatant on the globe. Then the freezing night when he looked out over the submarines of the fleet departing on a mission he'd conceived to right the wrong of Russia's disarmament. He smelled the smells of the *Kaliningrad* as he stepped inside the hull for her voyage to the polar icecap, where the ship would be his command platform for a mission of revenge. With eighty nuclear-tipped SS-N-X-27 cruise missiles detonating two-megaton warheads over eighty U.S. eastern seaboard targets, America's fangs would be removed, and she and Russia could coexist in peace. Russia would stretch out her hand to the Americans and help them rebuild, and in the aftermath of this short surgical war the two nations might even become friends and allies. It would have reshaped history, and the world would have been a better place.

But the Americans proved themselves to be even more cunning and dangerous than he'd suspected. As he was transmitting his go-code to the ships of the fleet at their hold positions, his beloved *Kaliningrad* was engaged by an American hunter-killer submarine, sent secretly under the icecap to kill him. The American captain had been a skillful assassin, and after the torpedoes detonated, the control room of his beloved *Kaliningrad* flooded with the icy black water of the Arctic. Novskoyy's only comfort was that the mutual torpedo exchange had to have been fatal to the Americans as well. His numb body succumbed to shock, and after the lights went out he lost consciousness.

He must have been evacuated in the control compartment escape pod, because when he opened his eyes he was in a frigid Arctic shelter surrounded by shipwrecked Americans. Their commander was a gaunt, black-haired grimacing fiend who had hauled him up by the collar to beat him, but changed his mind and let go. The man's nametag read PACINO. Novskoyy could remember nothing else but the man's face and name and the hatred he held for him. But it had been too late for revenge. The diesel generator had died and they had all surrendered to the cold, and for a second time the world faded into darkness.

He woke in a hospital and recovered only long enough to be interrogated. He was led from the hospital to the transport plane back to Russia wearing the handcuffs and leg irons of a war criminal. Forty-nine years old and weakened by the cold of the icepack, he would not last long in the harsh Siberian prison's torture chamber. But there had been no torture. Without a trial he found himself in a large, warm solitary cell looking out over the pine trees of the Siberian woods. There were books. He was allowed to exercise. Thirteen years passed before the door opened to his cell and the strange large man known only as Rafael came to take him away, his ransom paid.

He had made the transition from Russian admiral to war-crimes prisoner, and then from war-crimes prisoner to military consultant. Rafael brought him into a company named da Vinci Consulting, a firm attempting an ambitious operation to sink crude oil carriers leaving the oil terminals of Saudi Arabia. The operation would benefit the Hindu Republic of India's dictator Nipun, but Nipun had demanded a demonstration. It had been Novskoyy's idea to attack the cruise ship that had been chartered by the U.S. Navy and would leave Port Norfolk escorted by heavy warships, because if they could down a cruise ship among that security, they could certainly sink the unarmed unsuspecting oil tankers in the Gulf of Oman. Nipun had agreed, but ironically the methods they planned to employ in the Middle East would not work against the American fleet. Somehow they had to sink the cruise ship, under escort from an invincible fleet of American warships, and he and Rafael had suffered a dark night when they realized that the task was impossible. Falling back on his navy background, Novskoyy had called for an advanced Ukrainian Severodvinsk nuclear submarine, and soon the mission was accomplished and India paid up. Novskoyy performed the Saudi tanker operation, earning da Vinci billions, and Rafael made him a full partner. Another transition was required of him as he was called to change from brilliant military consultant to absurdly rich businessman, one wealthy enough to buy a Caribbean island and retire.

It was not until later that he learned that one of the survivors of the cruise ship venture had been the same man who had threatened to beat him in the Arctic shelter, the captain of the submarine that had ruined the voyage of the *Kaliningrad,* who had become an admiral and taken command of the U.S. Navy, the bastard named Pacino. Novskoyy had felt a momentary blackness in his mind when he read the man would survive, and he fantasized about sneaking into his hospital room and strangling the bastard. He called up a research clip of the younger man, who now seemed so much older, the former admiral wearing the haunted sunken face of a mental patient. Novskoyy still toyed with the idea of hunting him down and killing him, but business had kept him busy since the Saudi operation.

Despite the billions they'd made from India, Rafael had feared American retaliation for the sinking of the cruise ship. Rafael transferred their money to numbered accounts, then divested the executives of da Vinci Maritime, each of them meeting their separate deaths in arranged accidents. After the entire staff had been liquidated, Rafael had set up an operation to simulate their own deaths, paying two men an absurd amount of money to have surgery to alter their appearances to look like Novskoyy and Rafael. When the first Falcon crashed, he and Rafael had changed their names. Alexi Novskoyy was gone forever and Victor Krivak had taken his place. Rafael became Sergio, still insisting on forsaking a last name.

Sergio, or Rafael, or whatever his real name was, remained a mystery. The man had been born an American but had lived in Europe his whole life, building his corporation until it was a global maritime concern and a consulting organization specializing in intelligence gathering through electronic means. There remained so much about the brilliant entrepreneur that Krivak had yet to learn, but he was a patient man.

They had gone deep underground, evading Interpol and the FBI. Now that the manhunt was derailed by their supposed deaths, Sergio felt comfortable enough to set up a new consulting organization. The new company was named United Electrics, a retro title that would gather little interest. They had a respectable-sized staff of electronics wizards, who, armed with the system codes, had penetrated deeper, to the command-and-control systems' very core. The information warfare operation had been intense but was paying off, and soon the

American Navy had been transformed into a puppet. Krivak could direct her ships like so many toys. If only they had been able to construct such a system fifteen years before, but then, the Americans only began to rely heavily on digital command-and-control more recently. Krivak tried to tell himself that the penetration operation was his revenge for *Kaliningrad,* but he knew that he longed for more. What he truly wanted was to see the face of Pacino as he strangled the life out of the destroyer of his dreams.

The woman finished in the tub and dried him off. On the satin sheets she draped her silky body over him. He shut his eyes and luxuriated in the feel of the girl above him, and when he finished, he pushed her off the bed and dismissed her. Alone again, he faded back into the world between wakefulness and sleep, where the snow fell on his boots on the concrete pier and on his admiral's epaulets and on his fur collar turned up against the wind as he stood and stared at the breathtaking beauty of the submarine *Kaliningrad,* the dreams rolling by until the Asian morning sunlight burned through his eyelids.

He rose quickly, energized by the idea that he would soon be back in business. The year of hiding was finally over. He dressed and entered the living room to find his partner, Sergio, standing at the window, smiling at him, seeming more relaxed than he had been in weeks. Krivak sat at the dining table and ate breakfast with Sergio while they read the Hong Kong news and lingered over coffee. When it was time, they adjourned to a cherry-paneled conference room with a massive Indonesian tigerwood table in the center. Krivak sank into a chair upholstered in soft glove leather and looked at his partner.

"When is he due?" His voice was no longer tinged with a Russian accent, his speech coach's success evident in the British-sounding precision of his words.

"His jet lands in ten minutes. Until his car arrives here, we should prepare."

Krivak nodded at Sergio, knowing the Chinese admiral was the most difficult client they had ever had.

                              *   *   *

Admiral Chu Hua-Feng stepped off the jet to the humid Thai air, the crow's-feet at his eyes wrinkling as he squinted in the sun. He glanced at his subordinates, young fools who thought the Peoples Liberation Army invincible. He had lived long enough to experience bitter defeat as well as combat success, and though his superiors were cut from the same cloth as his staff, he must find a way to protect them. Chu was the commanding admiral of Red China's fledgling submarine force. He had spent time submerged launching torpedoes in anger at American targets, and he well knew that until every last vessel was on the bottom, the vicious American snakes would fight. And in the upcoming war with India, his fears centered on the U.S. fleet and what they would do. The brilliant consultants from United Electrics had helped with their expensive but valuable intelligence about the sleeping American Navy, but now he needed more. Much more.

The ride to the hotel was slow, the late-morning rush hour filling the streets of Bangkok with traffic, the traffic police under their surgical masks directing the streetlights. He was exhausted by the time he walked into the Oriental Hotel lobby. As he entered the United Electrics conference room in their opulent suite, he immediately felt the worry melt away from him. The larger man, Sergio, had a way of understanding Chu's fears, and the thin one, Victor Krivak, had a penetrating intellect that solved all technical problems. An hour into the meeting, the food and pleasantries over with, Chu stared hard at the consultant executives.

"What you have been able to achieve so far is admirable, gentlemen, but we must do more. The battle network of the U.S. Navy is in your hands, but you must take command of their automated submerged platform, the *Snarc*. I'll need it in the Indian Ocean. And I'll need it to respond to my orders in real time."

Krivak and Sergio exchanged confused glances. Krivak spoke first.

"*Snarc?* What's the *Snarc?*"

*   *   *

Sergio shook his head as he stood at the window overlooking the trees of the courtyard far below. "I don't think I've suffered a reprimand like that since grammar school."

Krivak nodded solemnly. "He was right, Sergio. We should have known about this *Snarc* vessel."

"Tell me again why our penetration of the U.S. Navy's command system doesn't already grant us control of the *Snarc*."

Krivak glanced over the E-mail from his staff, tasked with entering the Pentagon combat system and surreptitiously retrieving what they could on the *Snarc*. He shook his head. "She's an independent node, with an onboard carbon processor. A molecular computer that is essentially a reverse-engineered synthetic human brain. She's programmed—more accurately, educated—and sent on her way, and she responds to orders just as a human commander would."

"So can't we just give her orders to do what Chu wants?"

"Apparently not. Think of it being no different than trying to use our system to get the human commander of a carrier air group to launch aircraft and bomb a city—he'd be suspicious and check his orders. Same order of intelligence here. The Americans apparently refused to trust a silicon computer with a nuclear reactor and plasma weapons, and waited until they had a fully operational carbon processor. I am amazed they constructed one so quickly—I had the impression it had been ruled impossible. But what's important is that the *Snarc* won't believe orders it considers inappropriate or inconsistent with its education. And the volume of communications traffic it would take to convince her remotely would be detected. No, Sergio, we have to take control of her physically, get inside of her, and to do that and make her take our orders we'll have to get someone who designed her."

"Do you really think you can take her over?"

"Sergio, I will have to assemble a team, a very expensive one. You did not overstate the case to Chu when you demanded a billion Euros up front. We will spend every one of them on these engineers. I will be taking a page from your book and go to bail out a brilliant computer engineer from prison, and the money will be useful for his bail. I have also heard of a fired American who worked for DynaCorp, a second-generation Chinese named Wang, who was supposedly working on submarine black projects. He might be our man."

"When are you leaving?"

"In the morning. We should rest and enjoy the evening, and I will take the Falcon at first light."

Sergio smiled. "I'll call the agency and have them send over the women after supper."

8

A little more than five hundred nautical miles east-northeast of the foamy spot in the sea where *Piranha* had vanished from the surface, the Atlantic was tossed in the wind of a storm that had rolled off the North American coast two days before. The sky was a leaden dark gray, the sea a darker blue punctuated by whitecaps as the wind whipped the tops of the waves. From horizon to horizon there was nothing but the clouds above, the sea below, and the wind between. No shorelines interrupted the seascape; no merchant ships' running lights penetrated the drizzle. The clouds opened suddenly, the rain coming down in sheets, the sky darkening further, the raindrops barely visible on the surface of the running waves.

Below the surface of the stormy sea, the waves seemed less majestic. The noise was still a roar, but with the wind gone, it was a more muted sound. Light filtered down into the warm summer waters to a depth of fifty feet, and would have penetrated much deeper had it not been for the dimness brought on by the storm. The waves above could not be made out—the water was not that clear—but there was light to be able to see thirty feet in any direction. At fifty feet, the water's temperature was still warm, the ocean filled with life, a fisherman's dream, the light slightly dimmer. Deeper, a hundred feet beneath the waves above, the sound had calmed, the water was darker, the diffuse light from above dying steadily, perhaps only a five-foot radius discernible. At a depth of 150 feet, the ocean became much darker, but the sea life still crowded the environment and the water remained warm. But fifty feet deeper, in the complete darkness of the deeper sea, the water went from the balmy summer temperature suddenly to the refrigerated cold of the deep. This was the layer depth known to oceanographers since a thermometer had been lowered into the sea. The top two hundred feet of the vast Atlantic were stirred by the winds and the waves, the warmth added by the burning sun, the water warm enough to swim without a wetsuit. But beneath the layer, as the light went out, the sea's temperature fell to thirty degrees Fahrenheit, two degrees below the freezing point of freshwater, the salinity allowing the water to get even colder without turning into ice. From here to the ocean bottom two miles further down, the sea was uniformly frigid, the cold keeping much of the ocean's swimming inhabitants away, the life that could survive the deep cold of a much different variety. At three hundred feet beneath the surface, the light was completely gone, the darkness profound, the same dark of a two-mile-deep mineshaft. At this depth the noise from the waves above was gone, the sound bouncing off the layer above and reflecting into the warm water layer. The quiet was interrupted only by the occasional sound of the mournful howling of a whale, which could be 50 miles away or 350. Deeper still, six hundred feet beneath the waves, the weight of the heavy water above made the pressure immense, the force squeezing any surface at two tons over every square foot. Few ocean creatures could take the pressure, making the sea relatively empty. The cold, dark, silent, pressurized water waited.

The motion came before the sound. The water divided, driven by the force of something immense, an object, a rounded elliptical bullet that had soared quietly into the seawater and pushed the water aside as it silently and swiftly came into being. The thing continued, no longer an elliptical starting point but now a giant cylinder, fins protruding on either side, but still perfectly cylindrical, and now a slight rushing noise of its passage could be heard. The skin of the object was not rigid but sharklike.

The machine had no movements inside, no life, not even any light, just the silent hum of rotating machinery and pumped fluids. A trillion corridors carved in silicon admitted the rush of electrons at the speed of light. A cubic meter of human brain tissue immersed in cranial fluid listened and watched and smelled the data surrounding it. It watched the narrowband and broadband sonar arrays that reached out to the infinite reaches of the sea to hear the noises of man-made machinery. It watched the acoustic daylight imaging arrays that searched for close and distant contacts, using the ambient noise of the ocean as a sort of light. The disturbances in the ambient noise field were akin to the variations of a light field caused by an object, sensed not by an eyeball's retina but by a flat electronic sensor wrapped around the girth of the moving object in the sea. The thing moved on, its computers and processors and brain tissue monitoring the outside and the inside of itself. One portion of the tissue's action was to record a narrative of what was happening into a hardened sector of a computer called a history module for later use by the humans who had created the object. The stream of conscious thought might be considered the organism's thoughts as it moved through the sea, but the creators called it something different: the Command and Control Deck Log, or the command log for short. It was this portion of the brain tissue that was most active at the moment as the metal object searched for another object.

HULL NUMBER: SSNR-1
UNIT: USS *SNARC*
FUNCTION: COMMAND AND CONTROL DECK
LOG
MISSION SUMMARY: (1) INDEPENDENT STEAMING
OVER A NINETY-DAY MISSION TO TEST SHIP'S

SYSTEMS (2) CONDUCT MOCK TORPEDO AP-
PROACHES ON SURFACE SHIPS (3) DETECT SUB-
MERGED WARSHIPS OF ANY NATIONALITY, AND IF
FOREIGN, CLASSIFY THEM AND REPORT THEM TO
USUBCOM, AND IF AMERICAN, TO ATTEMPT TO
TRAIL THEM WITHOUT BEING DETECTED.

MISSION NARRATIVE:

IT HAS BEEN THIRTY-TWO DAYS SINCE THE SOR-
TIE FROM GROTON, CONNECTICUT. IT HAS BEEN
THIRTY-ONE DAYS SINCE INITIAL MISSION SUBMER-
GENCE. THIS UNIT'S SONAR PROCESSOR HAS
BEEN EXTRAORDINARILY VIGILANT, BUT THERE HAS
BEEN NO CONTACT WITH ANY SUBMERGED WAR-
SHIPS. THIS UNIT HAS CLEARED BAFFLES FOUR
TIMES EVERY SIX-HOUR WATCH. THIS UNIT HAS
STREAMED THE NARROW APERTURE EXTENDED
CABLE TOWED ARRAY AND LISTENED HARD ON
NARROWBAND SONAR. THIS UNIT EMPLOYED THE
WIDE NET FILTERS ON THE ACOUSTIC DAYLIGHT
ARRAYS. BUT ASIDE FROM THREE HUNDRED MER-
CHANT SHIPS, TWELVE MOTOR YACHTS, AND
THREE SAILBOATS, ALL OF THEM INBOUND OR
OUTBOUND PORT NEW YORK, THERE HAVE BEEN
NO SONAR CONTACTS. ON AVERAGE, EVERY
HOUR THE SONAR MODULE CALLS TO REPORT A
NEW SONAR CONTACT. THIS UNIT WAITS IMPA-
TIENTLY FOR THE CLASSIFICATION, BUT INEVITABLY
THE SONAR MODULE HEARS A SCREW TURN
COUNT. THE SOUND OF A PROPELLER WITH THREE
BLADES, VERY INFREQUENTLY FOUR, PLYING THE
SEAWATER CLOSE TO THE SURFACE IS THE SIGNA-
TURE OF A MERCHANT SHIP OR A FISHING VESSEL.

THIS UNIT IS IN NO PARTICULAR HURRY. THIS
UNIT HAS DECIDED UPON A SPEED OF EIGHT
KNOTS. FAST ENOUGH TO COVER GROUND,
SLOWLY BUT STEADILY. SLOW ENOUGH THAT THE

FLOW NOISE OVER THE HULL WOULD NOT
DROWN OUT THE FAR DISTANT SOUNDS OF A
SUBMARINE TARGET. SLOW ENOUGH THAT THE
NOISE GENERATED BY THE PROPULSION MACHIN-
ERY WOULD NOT BE LOUD. ABOVE SIXTY PERCENT
REACTOR POWER THIS UNIT HAS TO START THE RE-
ACTOR MAIN COOLANT PUMPS, EACH THE SIZE
OF A REFRIGERATOR, AND EACH UNAVOIDABLY
LOUD DESPITE THEIR LEAD SOUND SHIELDS AND
THEIR FOUR-DIMENSIONAL SOUND MOUNTS AND
THE ACTIVE QUIETING HYDROPHONES. AND AT
HIGH SPEEDS THE SOUND OF STEAM COMING
DOWN THE HEADERS IS CONSIDERABLY LOUDER,
AS ARE THE HIGHER REVOLUTIONS OF THE PRO-
PULSION TURBINES. THERE IS NO DOUBT. SLOWER
IS BETTER.

THIS UNIT HAS MEANDERED NORTHEAST, THE
SONAR MODULE PERPETUALLY SEARCHING, SUPER-
VISED ON A CONSTANT BASIS. THERE IS NOTH-
ING OUT HERE. BUT CONFIDENCE IS HIGH. IT IS A
BIG OCEAN. THIS UNIT HAS AN INFINITE SUPPLY
OF PATIENCE. THIS UNIT IS HOME HERE AT SEA.

AT RANDOM TIMES EVERY EIGHT HOURS THIS
UNIT ORDERS AN ASCENT TO PERISCOPE DEPTH.
IT IS TIME NOW. THIS UNIT IS ALREADY GOING
SLOW, SO THIS UNIT CHECKS BAFFLES FOR
SONAR CONTACTS CLOSE ABOARD WHILE DEEP.
THERE IS NOTHING. THIS UNIT INCREASES SPEED
TO TWELVE KNOTS AND MAKES FOR THE LAYER
DEPTH AT AN UP ANGLE OF TEN DEGREES. AFTER
A FEW MINUTES THIS UNIT REACHES A DEPTH OF
150 FEET. THIS IS SHALLOW ENOUGH TO BE JUST
BARELY ABOVE THE THERMAL LAYER, WHERE THIS
UNIT CAN BETTER HEAR THE SOUNDS OF SHIP-
PING NEAR THE SURFACE. IT IS ALSO DEEP
ENOUGH THAT A SUPERTANKER WILL NOT CUT

THIS UNIT IN HALF, AS THEIR DRAFT WHEN FULLY LOADED IS A HUNDRED FEET—A HUNDRED FEET FROM THE SURFACE TO THE KEEL OF AN OIL TANKER. THEY ARE HUGE, THESE CRUDE CARRIERS. AND QUIETER THAN A SAILBOAT, SINCE ALL THAT OIL SHIELDS THE SOUNDS OF THE SUPERTANKER'S SCREW WHEN SHE IS COMING STRAIGHT AHEAD. THIS UNIT CLEARS BAFFLES AGAIN AT 150 FEET, BUT THE SEA IS EMPTY. THIS UNIT PUTS ON AN UP ANGLE OF TEN DEGREES AND A BURST OF SPEED, THEN FLATTENS THE ANGLE AND EXTENDS THE TYPE 23 PHOTONIC MAST. WITHIN A MINUTE OF DEPARTING 150 FEET THE TYPE 23 IS DRY AND SEARCHING THE HORIZON FOR SURFACE SHIPS AND AIRCRAFT.

THERE IS BUSINESS TO DO AT PERISCOPE DEPTH. A STEAM GENERATOR BLOWDOWN TO RID THE BOILERS OF SOME OF THE ACCUMULATED BAD CHEMICALS IN THE FEED WATER. A NAVIGATION FIX WITH THE GLOBAL POSITIONING SYSTEM TO CONFIRM THE POSITION WITHIN THE RING LASER INERTIAL NAVIGATION SYSTEM. AND MOST IM-PORTANTLY, THE MESSAGES FROM COMSUB-DEVRON 12. THERE ARE SEVERAL OF THEM, EACH AN ALL-SQUADRON INFORMATION MESSAGE WITH NOTHING SPECIAL ABOUT THEM. IN FACT, THIS UNIT IS SURPRISED THAT SQUADRON EVEN SENT THEM, AS THEY SEEM TO CONVEY MINIMAL INFORMATION. FOR THE PAST FEW DAYS, THERE HAS BEEN NOTHING IN THE COMMUNICATIONS SATELLITE ADDRESSED SPECIFICALLY TO THIS UNIT. IT IS ODD, ALMOST AS IF THIS UNIT HAS BEEN FORGOTTEN.

IT IS A VIOLATION OF SUBMARINE STANDARD OPERATING PROCEDURES TO TRANSMIT UNLESS ORDERED TO FOR A SPECIFIC SITUATION REPORT,

AND NO SUCH DEMAND HAS COME FOR A
WEEK. SO ALTHOUGH NO ONE IS ATTEMPTING
TO COMMUNICATE WITH THIS UNIT, THIS UNIT
CAN ONLY CONTINUE THE MISSION AND WAIT
FOR FURTHER ORDERS. SOON THERE IS NOTHING
MORE TO DO AT PERISCOPE DEPTH. THIS UNIT RE-
TRACTS THE BIGMOUTH ANTENNA AND PRO-
CEEDS DEEP, PULLING IN THE TYPE 23 MAST AS
SOON AS THE SURFACE GROWS DIM, THEN
SPEEDS UP AND PENETRATES THE THERMAL LAYER
FOR THE DEEP COLD.

THIS UNIT STEAMS ON AS THE AFTERNOON
TURNS TO THE EVENING.

* * *

It was after 0200 Eastern time when Pacino finally entered
the engineer's stateroom. The room was a box less than
seven feet on a side, all brown wood grain plastic laminate
walls with stainless-steel trim. To the right of the door was a
mirror with a fold-down sink on the wall with a dozen
cubbyhole doors and hooks with hanging laundry. The bulkhead on the left had two fold-down desks with reading lamps
and two steel chairs, with cubbyhole doors above and below.
The desk was cluttered with manuals and papers and computer output and several handheld computers. The wall opposite the door contained three sleeper-train-style bunks, each
about two feet wide with two feet between the racks, each a
coffinlike space with a brown privacy curtain. Lieutenant
Alameda, in submarine coveralls under a Naval Academy
sweatshirt, sat at the desk near the beds. She looked up when
Pacino came into the room and smiled for a split second,
then frowned at him.

"The aft cubbyhole by your elbow has three poopy-suits in
it, nonqual. You can unpack your seabag into it. Your rack is
on the bottom. The top rack is for my stuff, and so is the other
desk, so don't count on working in here. Don't be bashful

about changing in front of me, and I won't around you. If your puritan sensibilities are insulted, that's tough; this is a combat submarine and it's just going to be that way."

Pacino was too tired to react. He nodded and stripped off his uniform and stuffed it into a hanging laundry bag, got on all fours and crawled between the wall and Alameda's chair to the lower rack, slid aside the curtain and climbed under the covers, then pulled the curtain back and shut off the lamp. He had a momentary thought that he was in a coffin, but he didn't care.

In his dreams he was watching his father from six-year-old eyes, submerged to test depth on the old sub his father had commanded, and in the mirror was a child staring back at him wearing coveralls with a dolphin pin, and he went into the stateroom and Alameda was there, wearing something filmy and she began kissing him and she climbed into his rack with him.

Lieutenant Carolyn Alameda waited for her pulse to slow, the wait a long, irritable one. As a former five-striper at the Academy, Alameda had always been known for her professionalism and competence. On her first submarine, the *Olympia,* she had rapidly risen to the station of "bull lieutenant," the unofficial designation as the ship's most knowledgeable junior officer—no small task in the man's world of a nuclear submarine. She had just missed the War of the East China Sea, and having trained for combat her entire adult life, it was her biggest disappointment. The conflict now emerging in the other hemisphere had the potential to break out into a war, but the ship was being sent on what seemed like yet another exercise run. Waiting for a chance at combat was something she could live with, but what she couldn't tolerate was what was happening to her since the midshipman had come aboard.

All her life Alameda hadn't felt like her female classmates, who had all been embroiled in chasing boys while Alameda had been more interested in sports and school. Her mother had insisted that a time would come when a man entered her life and she would feel the thunderbolt. Alameda had scoffed, and her relationships with boys had always been unsatisfying. She had resigned herself to a life devoted solely to the Navy until this morning. Until the moment when she climbed to the deck of the *Piranha* and found Midshipman Pacino waiting topside. She immediately felt like a foolish blushing schoolgirl, and had tried to negate the feeling with a cold professional veneer, but had heard how caustic she had been to the young man and that made her even more self-conscious and embarrassed. There was no rational explanation for her feelings, but her mother's awkward explanation of romantic chemistry was the first thing Alameda thought of—her attraction to the tall, lanky youth made her feel as if she were drunk.

At first she had promised herself that she would simply comply with Navy Regulations and completely avoid fraternization with someone of a subordinate rank. It was the only logical course she could follow. She would be an impersonal lieutenant and chief engineer, and he would be a nonqual midshipman rider, and they would get through this run. But it was as if her own feelings had betrayed her, and she gave that foolish speech about being naked together in the stateroom. She wondered if he saw how red her face must have become, or if he had seen the pulsing of the veins in her neck.

It was madness, she thought, suddenly missing her old self, when no man ever impressed her. Why did it have to be this kid, why did he have to be four years younger than her, and why did he have to show up now, in the middle of an operational deployment? She tried to sit at her desk, knowing she wouldn't sleep, so she tried to work on the thousand pressing things on her list, but all she could do was foolishly sit there and listen to the deep breathing of Midshipman Anthony Michael Pacino.

She bit her lip and commanded herself not to think of him, and to address him calmly but coldly whenever she spoke to him. It was bad enough that this was happening to her, but it would be disastrous if one of the other officers or the captain himself heard something tender in her tone of voice to Pacino. In a few weeks he would be off the ship, she thought, and she could return to her life. But all she could think about was if they would be inport on his last night aboard. She choked the thought off and tried to return to the reactor preventive maintenance reports.

The sound of his rack curtain being violently opened woke Pacino with a start. It was Alameda. He blinked at her guiltily.

"Zero seven hundred, nonqual," she said, dripping with contempt. "Get out of the rack and get ready for the op brief."

Pacino climbed out of the cocoon of the rack and padded to the officers' head at the end of the narrow passageway. The head was a cube finished in stainless steel with a floor of troweled stone. The commode was a stainless-steel bowl with an eight-inch ball valve at the bottom. When he was finished he pulled the ball valve lever and opened a seawater globe valve, washing the bowl to the sanitary tank. He turned on the shower water and stepped under it, turned it off, soaped his body, then turned on the water again and rinsed off. When he was done he cleaned off the stainless-steel shower enclosure and dressed. The face in the mirror looked creased with fatigue, his eyes bloodshot. He walked back to the stateroom to find Alameda naked. He couldn't keep from staring at her body. She had seemed boyishly slim in her uniform, but in the nude she looked like a model. Her shoulders were slim and muscular, her breasts small but perfectly shaped, her abdomen flat, a small navel ring gleaming in the glow of the stateroom lights. His eyes were drawn to the downy fur between her long, slim legs, the curve of her hips seemingly made by the art of a loving sculptor. For an instant Pacino felt a shock of raw desire, his palms longing to be filled with her breasts, but with an effort he forced himself to remember that she was the chief engineer and fourth-in-command of the submarine *Piranha,* and only then did his pulse slow.

Alameda flushed crimson for a moment, her mouth open, but then she glared at him as she stepped into her panties, shrugged into her bra, and donned her coveralls and sneakers. Without a word she shut the door behind her. Pacino put on the coveralls she had given him and his running shoes and walked to the wardroom at the opposite end of officers' country from the head. The room was full of the ship's junior officers. He got a cup of steaming coffee and slumped in the wardroom couch seat at the end of the table, feeling like a high school kid at a college frat house. The coffee brought him awake while the officers joked with each other, the mood growing serious when the navigator and engineer came into the room.

The executive officer, known simply as "XO," Lieutenant Commander Schultz, arrived and took her seat at the first seat next to the captain's chair at the far end. She was tall and thin, her coveralls well worn, the patch on her sleeve bearing the emblem of the submarine *Birmingham* rather than *Piranha*. Her blond hair was too short to tie in a ponytail like Alameda's, and fell below her ears. She wore no makeup and no jewelry other than an Academy ring on her left finger. She used half-frame reading glasses and scanned the computer for the ship's message traffic.

The lone unqualified junior officer, who did not yet have his dolphins, was an ensign named Duke Phelps. He sat at the end of the wardroom table near Pacino. Phelps stood six-four and towered over the other officers, perpetually slouching and bent over to clear the overhead obstructions. He was studying a piping manual. As Pacino looked over at it, Phelps reached into a drawer and handed Pacino a copy of a similar manual.

"First few pages are a map of the ship. Might help you out."

Pacino turned to the first plate and tried to memorize the ship map, finding the wardroom on the upper-level port side beneath the sail. Then his stateroom, the crew's mess, and the middle level with the control room and the captain's and XO's staterooms, the lower-level torpedo room. The forward compartment, aft compartment, and reactor compartment were all shown on the map with their levels and equipment identified. But the special ops compartment, the added ninety

feet between the forward and reactor compartments, was labeled simply CLASSIFIED. The only detail that showed was the
access tunnel leading aft in line with the reactor compartment tunnel.

"Hey, Duke," Pacino muttered, feeling odd calling an officer anything but "sir" as he had been required since he arrived
at Annapolis. "What's in the special ops compartment?"

Phelps, who had seemed an easygoing youth with a sense of
humor, frowned at Pacino. "This run it's a Deep Submergence
Vehicle, a DSV. Three spherical pressure hulls connected by
two hatches. Goes to the bottom with SEAL commando divers
and NSA spooks."

"NSA?"

"National Security Agency. The electronic warfare thugs,
the guys who eavesdrop on communications and fight off
computer hackers. With the network-centric military, an electronic hijacker could disrupt the whole works, or worse, use
our own guns against us. So the NSA guys have their own
DSV to find ocean-bottom data highway cables and deep-sea
server nodes on the sea floor. Since satellites can be subject to
eavesdropping, a lot of the intel and sensitive comms are passing through these undersea cables. So our guys go deep, find
them, and tap into them. We've got half the world wired for
sound. When the spooks are onboard, we're just a bus for
them. This run we get to forget them for once and do an actual
submarine op. And by the way, since I opened my mouth, all
that's classified top secret, so not a word to anyone. That includes family, roommates, girlfriends, anyone, even other submarine officers. If you blab, you will find your door forced
open by NSA guys in black suits and you'll have a two-man
room at Fort Leavenworth Military Prison. The Black Pig is a
project boat, Patch, which means it's top secret from the sonar
dome to the propulsor shroud. Got it?"

"Got it," Pacino said, swallowing, starting to see why his father had never talked about what he did.

Toasty O'Neal came into the room, and the XO glared up at

him. "Nice of you to come, Toasty," she grumbled. "We all cleared for this briefing?"

"Yes, ma'am," he said to her as he took the remaining open seat at the table.

"Nav, you ready?" she asked Crossfield. The black navigator stood up and lowered the display screen against the long inboard bulkhead.

"Yes, XO," he said quietly.

"Eng, call the captain," Schultz ordered. Alameda nodded and grabbed a phone and buzzed Captain Catardi.

"Sir, we're ready for the op brief." Alameda looked over at Pacino. "Yes, Cap'n, he's here. Aye, sir." She hung up and looked at Schultz. "He's coming."

The XO passed around the coffeepot and everyone filled up. Captain Catardi came in the forward door. The room was silent as a church. Pacino expected the officers to stand as the senior officer entered, but they remained seated.

"Good morning, Captain," XO Schultz said formally.

"Morning, XO, Eng, Nav, officers." His coveralls were pressed and creased and he looked as fresh as if he'd been on vacation. His silver oak leaf collar emblems, dolphins and skull-and-crossbones capital ship command pin shimmered under the bright lights of the wardroom. He slipped into the captain's chair at the end of the table. "Well, Navigator, let's hear it." Schultz poured Catardi a cup of coffee, and the captain took a long pull and sat back expectantly.

"Good morning, Captain, XO, officers," Crossfield began. Pacino wondered at the contrast between the chummy fraternal closeness of the crew with the formality of expression on and off watch. And not only the formality, but the unique language of the ship. At every turn Pacino found himself corrected when he said something wrong. Alameda had corrected him harshly when he had asked if he should close the door. "Never say 'close' on a submarine, nonqual. It sounds like the word 'blow' on an internal communication circuit, and 'blow' means we're flooding and the OOD should emergency blow to the surface. You don't 'close' the fucking door, you 'shut' it. Got it?"

The display screen showed a chart of the Atlantic Ocean north of the equator, the Canadian coast on the left, the European landmass on the right. A blue line connected Groton, Connecticut, with a dot in mid-Atlantic labeled POINT NOVEMBER.

The navigator pointed to the display. "The chart depicts our PIM coming out of Groton toward Point November. We have a detour on the way to the Indian Ocean, a major operation that needs to be done before we leave the Atlantic. Somewhere in the Atlantic is the U.S. robotic hunter-killer sub *Snarc*. Many of you remember our last exercise with her." The wardroom filled with angry murmurs, the ship's officers resentful of the tactics of the automated submarine. "Quiet, please. Apparently something has gone very wrong with the *Snarc*. She's out of communication and will not respond. In the other services, the standard operating procedure with an automated combat node that is not responding to orders is to send the unit a self-destruct signal. That is not possible in this case, because *Snarc* carries a nuclear reactor, and a self-destruct could spread enough curies of radioactive waste to kill a moderate-sized ecosphere, not to mention the warheads of the plasma weapons, which would not only be hazardous to the environment but would be quite a prize for an enterprising salvage team to obtain for a terrorist group. So that's where *Piranha* comes in. We're the destruct system. Our mission is to find *Snarc* and put her down, at a location we will report to squadron so they can salvage any undetonated warheads and clean up the nuclear mess from the reactor."

The wardroom erupted as several junior officers shot questions at Crossfield and others commented to themselves.

"Peace, gentlemen," Crossfield said. "We have no intel on this submarine's position, and it's a damned big ocean. So we're starting at Point November and doing an outward spiral search. At some point squadron will give us an intel update, with some data on the *Snarc*'s position, and we'll vector in on it."

Pacino studied the plans of the robotic submarine opponent,

fascinated. Crossfield detailed the robot ship's capabilities, emphasizing that the ship was expected to be quiet and unpredictable. And that was when Catardi chimed in.

"There's more news here, officers," he said, his face a grave mask of concern. "Since the *Snarc* is out of control, the assumption being made by ComSubDevRon 12 is that it has become paranoid. Any attempt to approach it may result in an attack. As of this moment we are to assume that *Snarc* is a hostile combatant. It may have even been able to find out that we were sent to kill it. If so, while we're searching for it, it'll be searching for us. This robot could be in our baffles with open torpedo tube doors, getting ready to put *us* on the bottom."

The room was silent for a moment.

"That is all," Crossfield said. "XO?"

"We'll have a tactical meeting in the wardroom every afternoon watch at thirteen hundred, starting today," Schultz said. "Other than that meeting, you and your men have orders to get as much rest as possible. We will be rigging for a modified ultraquiet, with the only exception the galley. I want this crew tiptoeing, no stereos, no heavy maintenance, and no bullshit. Everyone got that?"

The officers nodded.

"That's all I have, Officers." Catardi stood and left, and Schultz dismissed the wardroom.

Pacino was still staring at the display when the officers filed out of the room and Crossfield turned off the computerized image. Alameda snarled at him, bringing him back to the present. "Mr. Pacino, this may be a war operation, but I recommend you get working on your diving officer qualifications. You're no good to us unless you can stand a watch on your own." She opened a safe and handed him a WritePad computer. "Diving officer manual is loaded aboard along with the standard operating procedures. You need to know all of that cold before you go on watch at noon. You'll be diving officer under instruction on my watchsection. I recommend you don't screw it up."

Alameda's radio beeped. "Engineer," she said into it.

"Yessir, on the way, sir." She frowned at Pacino as she left the room. He took a deep breath and turned on the computer and began studying the main ballast system.

One deck below, Lieutenant Alameda knocked on the captain's stateroom door.

"You called, sir?"

Catardi was reclining in his command chair. "Yes, Eng. I just wanted your opinion on our young midshipman," he said, looking up at her. Alameda froze, wondering if a reprimand was coming. Could the captain know her thoughts about the midshipman?

"He seems a quick study, Captain, and motivated besides," she said, hoping she was not blushing. "And he seems to take the punishment of being a nonqual in stride—I've yet to see him complain. Even after he was put up to kissing the starboard main engine last night."

"You're pretty tough on the kid, Eng."

"Yes, sir. Should I ease up on him?"

"No," Catardi said, looking off into the distance. "Let's see what he's made of."

Relief flooded her. She cleared her throat. "Aye aye, sir. Anything else, Captain?"

"That'll be all, Eng."

She shut the stateroom door behind her. Catardi stared at nothing for a few moments, remembering his younger days, back to a time when the nine most frightening words in the English language were, "Captain Pacino wants to see you in his stateroom." If the youngster had a tenth of the old man's character, he'd make one hell of a submariner, Catardi thought.

9

The sun had long vanished over the horizon and the drydock floodlights had come on, their glow shining in the half-closed blinds of Michael Pacino's dockside office. The only other light in the room came from a reading lamp, casting a pool of dim yellow on the scattered sketches on the oak library table. To the side, Pacino's pad computer had five programs open, calculating hydrodynamic friction functions and thrust curves, with a drafting program showing a three-dimensional rotating diagram of the tail of the SSNX submarine.

Pacino had been in the office since before dawn, immersed in his idea for the torpedo evasion ship alteration. There was really nothing to come home to, not with Colleen still working out of her D.C. offices as her testimony before Congress continued. He leaned back in his seat for a moment, thinking of her, and realizing guiltily that he hadn't been much of a husband to her since the sinking of the cruise ship. Since Pacino had sailed to the *Princess Dragon* gravesite, he had felt more like himself, but he still had to make up the year to Colleen. That would have to come later, he chided himself, the beeping of his computer at the end of a complex calculation returning him to the problem at hand. He was bent over the display, barely aware of the office door coming open. Assuming it was one of the shipyard engineers, Pacino kept concentrating on the computer until he could reach a stopping point, when he heard the female voice from the doorway.

"They told me I could find you here. You working the swing shift or just putting in dayshift overtime?"

Pacino stared up at his wife, dumbfounded, imagining for a moment that his thoughts of her had conjured her up. She was dressed in a dark suit that accentuated her slender form and her long legs, a string of pearls her only jewelry other than her wedding ring. As usual after not seeing her for weeks, she startled him with her beauty. Her raven-black hair swept to her shoulders framing a beautiful face, with strong cheekbones, large brown eyes, a perfect nose, and a smiling mouth with red lips curving over movie-star teeth. For the thousandth time, he realized he didn't deserve her as a wife, but the guilt he'd felt a moment before evaporated in his excitement at seeing her. He stood up so fast his chair tipped and crashed behind him. He hurried to her and swept her into an embrace. She laughed in surprise but returned his kiss, then pushed him away.

"You must be feeling better," she said breathlessly. "I thought maybe I could steal you away for dinner and you could tell me about what you're working on."

"I thought you were in D.C. for the next month," he said.

"I am. But today is Friday. I don't have to be back until Sunday night."

They found a cozy restaurant a half hour from the shipyard, and caught up in a secluded booth. Pacino told her about the sailing trip, Patton's submarine, and his orders to run the torpedo evasion program and the Tigershark project. Colleen put her fingers to her lips, waving him to silence.

"We'll talk about that when we're back in your office," she said. "Tell me about Janice's call and Anthony."

Pacino recited his ex-wife's conversation verbatim, including Janice's facial expressions. Colleen's ability to read Janice's mind from a distance was uncanny.

"So, are you worried about Anthony Michael?" Colleen asked.

Pacino refilled their wineglasses and thought about it. "I never wanted him to go into the submarine force," he admitted. "But it might do him good to make this one deployment."

Colleen nodded. "There's nothing wrong with him," she said. "He's only in trouble all the time because he's an innovator—like his father."

Pacino shook his head. "I don't want him wasting his life chasing mine, trying to be a younger version of me. I want him to find his own way. If he's doing this because it is all he's ever wanted, I'll give him my blessing. But I'm not convinced this is his destiny."

"You said he's under the command of Rob Catardi, who you trained on the *Devilfish*. What kind of skipper is he?"

Pacino stared into the distance for some time, lost in the past. "He's the best there is," he finally said.

"Then don't worry," Colleen said. "Anthony will be fine, and he'll learn something."

A look of doubt crossed Pacino's face.

"Relax, Michael. I'm his stepmother—I know. When I met him he was a skinny high school kid. I watched him his plebe year at the Academy, saw him get tougher, and watched him grow into an upperclassman. He's his own soul—there are shadows of you in him, but he's unique. Let him go, Michael."

"Thanks, Colleen. For being a good stepmother to him. He's the better for having had you in his life."

She just stared at the table for a long moment.

Back in the office, Colleen looked over his sketches.

"So, you want the full briefing?" Pacino asked.

"Tell me everything," Colleen said.

"In theory, it's simple. We cut the stern of the SSNX to allow inserting two dozen solid-fueled Vortex engines." The Vortex missile was an underwater solid fueled rocket that traveled at three hundred knots and steered itself by rotating its nozzle. Although it was called a missile, some physicists called it a supercavitating torpedo, because what allowed it to go such extreme speeds was that its nosecone boiled the water to steam vapor, and the vapor bubble eventually completely enclosed the missile so that the rocket thrust could carry it through the water at the speed of a private jet. "When the control room hits the switch, twenty-four large-bore rocket engines ignite and the ship gains enough thrust to get up to a hundred and fifty knots."

"That's not enough. The latest supercavitating torpedoes go three hundred."

"So the ship has to eliminate skin friction. This is where it gets more complex." Pacino riffled the pile on his desk for a sketch. "We run dry piping headers through the ship connected to the high-pressure air system and through valves to the main steam system. At first the high-pressure air banks blow plugs out of the hull surface nozzles. Air covers the skin of the ship, through these ring headers. As the air blankets the surface of the hull, the ship begins to lose skin friction. As the air banks go dry, the main steam system comes on-line to replace the air, and the boiler output dumps into the headers. That will last until the thrust is gone from the Vortex engines. According to the program, as the air banks go dry, ship velocity is up to two hundred ninety-eight knots, and as the steam takes over, we get an additional eight knots. And we maintain that for over twenty seconds, with an acceleration time-to-velocity of—"

"It won't work."

"—say, that's not good, that will put internal acceleration at over ten g's. Dammit, we'll mangle the crew with that level of acceleration."

"It won't work."

"I'll work on the acceleration calcs—"

"You're not listening!"

"What?" Pacino asked. "What did you say?"

"I said it won't work."

"I know—the acceleration's too much."

"That's not why," Colleen said, frowning. "First, the Vortex engines will melt the propulsor, the rudder, and the sternplanes. How will you control the thrust angle?"

"We can't mount the engines on gimbals," Pacino said. "It would make the system too complex. And I planned on the stern section melting away."

"Great—so your aft ballast tank is vaporized, your control

surfaces are burned away—there's nothing to control the ship's angle. You'll zip to the surface and come back down, losing your speed, and get hit with the incoming torpedo, or you'll plunge to crush depth, or worse, corkscrew through the water and kill the crew from being put into a seven-thousand-ton blender."

"We'll control attitude with the bowplanes."

"It won't work, Michael," Colleen said, agitated. "You can't use the gigantic hydraulics and the slow response of the bowplanes to control the ship."

Pacino nodded. "I think I see what you mean. We'll have to lock the bowplanes at zero angle, then use small trim tabs on them, or upper and lower spoilers, hooked to a dedicated pneumatic system or a separate high-pressure hydraulic mechanism. That would move fast enough to control the ship's angle."

Again Colleen shook her head. "The sensors and the computer control won't have the speed to control the ship. The time constant's too long. By the time the computer senses a down angle and sends the signals to correct for it, you're a hundred feet deeper than crush depth."

Pacino frowned. He had met his wife in a drydock much like the one the SSNX lay in now, laboring over the same hull, when she had come to fix the computer system installed by her company. He remembered her calm, relentless competence and the lionhearted way she had insisted on going to war in the East China Sea with the SSNX when the Cyclops battle-control system was still failing. He'd listened to her then, and he would listen to her now.

"This problem's too big to solve in a day," Pacino said finally. "I'll work on it tomorrow."

"You can't," Colleen said, a slight smile coming to her lips. "You're busy tomorrow."

"Oh? What am I doing tomorrow?"

"Let's just say you won't be getting out of bed and leave it at that," Colleen said, and took his hand and led him out of the office. Pacino smiled, trying to forget the technical troubles and enjoy his newfound lightness of heart.

But that night in his dreams the skeleton on the motorcycle overtook the bus and smashed it to pieces with his mace.

"Have a seat, Mr. Pacino," Executive Officer Astrid Schultz said, pointing to a chair on the inboard side of the wardroom table. It was the hour after the evening meal, the normal time for the wardroom to be set up for a movie, but tonight Pacino would face the qualification board for diving officer of the watch. Facing him on the outboard side next to Schultz was Chief Engineer Alameda and Damage Control Assistant Duke Phelps. At the end of the table Captain Catardi sat silent, watching the diving officer qualification board for Pacino. Duke had said Catardi would ask the last question based on Pacino's answers to the other board members' interrogation. If Pacino passed the verbal test, they would observe him take the ship to periscope depth, and if that went well, he would be qualified to stand the diving officer by himself. And being on the watch bill meant he was no longer a parasite, a rider. The term "rider" was one of the worst insults used on the submarine, referring to someone who did not pull his weight.

Pacino's stomach churned and bile rose to his mouth as he sat. It came down to this qual board, he thought. If he blew this, he would be considered unworthy of being his father's son. Since he'd been aboard, the officers and chief petty officers had at first acted strangely around him, the references to his father's former position sometimes subtle, other times blatant. A chief petty officer mechanic showing him the trim pump motor starter in the auxiliary machinery room would crack that he should know its location, because after all, he was a Pacino. A sluggish approach to periscope depth was condemned by another chief, mocking him that a Pacino should be able to put the submarine on the exact depth in an instant. But the crew had seemed to be testing him for any signs of arrogance or hubris, and finding none, they seemed to adopt him. Some had never warmed up, insisting that until the day he wore gold dolphins he remained an air-breathing rack-occupying nonqual rider. The chief of the auxiliary mechanics, "A-gang," Chief Keating, the man most responsible for training Pacino, stated in a Texas drawl at the start of every watch, "Mr. Patch, you breathin' my air, you eatin' my food, and you got a rack all to yourself while some of my boys is still hot-rackin'. Far as I'm concerned, you a nonqual rider, and an *officer* besides"—the term officer used pejoratively—"settin' in your wardroom, drinkin' your coffee with your pinky in the air, pushin' your papers while we do the real work of runnin' this ship. You best be livin' right when you stand watch as dive on my ship, mister."

"So, Mr. Pacino," Schultz said, beginning the inquisition, "go to the whiteboard and draw the trim and drain system, and explain how to get a one-third trim on an initial dive after a shipyard availability."

Twenty minutes later, Pacino took his seat, his armpits soaked. Phelps continued with the next question, about how to line up to snorkel. Alameda asked him a dozen questions about how to rig the ship for dive, the locations of the valves and switches. Schultz asked about ship stability and why a submarine didn't behave like a surface ship during a roll, Pacino's answer and the follow-up questions taking another hour. It came time for Catardi's question. He simply leaned forward and said, "Bowplanes jam dive."

Pacino shot back, "All back full, switch to emergency hydraulics, try to pull out, sound the general alarm, prepare for the OOD's order to emergency blow forward." The immediate action for a jam dive. The diving officer and officer of the deck would take instinctive action, without orders, to try to keep the ship from descending below the depth where the pressure would cause the hull to implode.

"Why not back emergency instead of just back full?"

"A back full order reverses the direction of the main motor and speeds it up in reverse until reactor power reaches fifty percent, the highest power level for running natural circulation. If we order back emergency, maneuvering has to energize the reactor circulation pumps and bring reactor power up to a hundred percent, and the pumps in fast speed come off the nonvital bus and are less reliable. There is a possibility that a hurried crew lining up for reactor forced circulation could power-to-flow scram the reactor, and then you'd be in a jam dive with a propulsion casualty. Better to use a reliable safe backing bell at fifty percent and use a forward group emergency main ballast tank blow if back full isn't enough to pull us out of the dive, sir."

Catardi nodded. Finally the verbal test portion of the qual board was complete, and normally that would be enough, but Captain Catardi had ordered that Pacino stand a casualty drill watch before he earned his diving officer qualification.

Although it was 2030 hours Zulu time, the military term for Greenwich Mean Time, the local time at that point in the sea was only 1730, and the sun had not yet set. The control room was rigged for white—the overhead lights were on bright—but would probably be rigged for red at the next periscope depth excursion. During an approach to periscope depth at night, the OOD would rig the control room for black, which was the submarine term for turning the lights completely out to keep from ruining his night vision for collision avoidance.

"Mr. Pacino, take the diving officer watch, please," Schultz ordered him.

"Officer of the Deck," Pacino called to the navigator, Wes Crossfield, who stood behind the command console, wearing a wireless one-eared headset with a boom microphone and red goggles. "Request permission to relieve Chief Keating as diving officer of the watch to stand as dive under instruction."

"Very well, Pacino, take the dive."

"Take the dive, aye, sir. Chief Keating, request permission to take the port seat at the ship control panel." Keating sat inside a cocoon of consoles resembling an aircraft cockpit, a cramped semisphere of wraparound displays and instruments and toggle switches. A central console divided the ship-control console area in half, an empty seat on the port side. Keating wore a headset and visor arrangement, which piped the displays in front of him in virtual reality, the consoles and displays in physical space around him all backups.

"Take the port seat, Mr. Pacino." Keating was on his best behavior, Pacino noticed, the older experienced man usually calling him "nonqual."

Pacino climbed into the cramped cockpit and settled in the port seat, strapping himself in. He put his hands on the aircraft-style control yoke, which controlled the rudder and sternplanes, and put his feet into the straps of the pedals that controlled the bowplanes.

"I'm ready to relieve you, sir," Pacino said to Keating as he strapped on a visor. The virtual display surrounded him, the ship animated from a side view, the surface high overhead, the bowplanes and sternplanes undulating slightly to keep her on depth. The display was a busy one, the animated ship transparent and complete with different-colored tanks and pipes and pumps, the animation able to show valves opening or shutting and water flowing from tank to tank. Other graphics addressed the status of the rig for dive and the ventilation lineup, the ship's speed and course and depth order, the status of the engineering plant and a few manual entries, called PDL, or passdown-log. Pacino studied the display for a moment before Keating began to speak.

"As you can see, nonqual—I mean, sir—the ship is at seven hundred feet at all ahead standard, course two seven zero, making bells on both main engines, evaporator making water to the makeup feed tank. We've got decent one-third trim, or at least we did two hours ago. We could be heavy aft, but I and Cyclops have entered a compensation. We're supposed to come to PD in two minutes. You're just in time. Got it?"

"Got it, Chief. I relieve you, sir."

"I stand relieved. Off'sa'deck, I've been relieved of the dive by Mr. Pacino."

"Very well, Chief." Crossfield spoke into his boom microphone. "Sonar, Conn, coming shallow to one five zero feet in preparation for coming to periscope depth."

The phrase made Pacino's stomach tense. Now came the

trial, with the captain and the XO and Lieutenant Alameda all watching him. Crossfield was about to come shallow, above the thermal layer from the near-freezing waters of the deep Atlantic. Above the layer, the water was heated by the sun and stirred by the waves. Above the layer, things would be completely different, Pacino thought, his mind on the ship's weight. She might be balanced—trimmed with neutral buoyancy—at seven hundred feet, but in the warmer water above the layer, the buoyancy would change. The hull, with less pressure on it, would expand, taking up more volume, with the same weight of water ballast aboard, making it more buoyant. Above the thermal layer the effect of the shallower water would make them light, and the ship could float up like a balloon. But then, the shallower water above the layer was warmer, and going from cold water to warm water made the ship heavy, countering the lightness of the lowered pressure. Pacino's mind rushed, thinking. He called up the screens of the Cyclops control system and blinked his way through a complex buoyancy calculation. Catardi and Schultz must have seen what he was doing in the auxiliary display, because just then Schultz murmured something to Crossfield and Pacino's virtual screen winked out. They were running a casualty drill on him, trying to see how he'd handle it.

"Loss of Cyclops ship control," Pacino reported, his voice a little too loud. He pulled off his visor and focused his eyes on the wraparound panels. Now the computer would be useless in helping him stay on depth when they went shallow. He'd have to do a mental buoyancy calculation and hope for the best. Even with Cyclops operating he had been taught to do the mental calculation and check it against Cyclops, but he and the computer had yet to agree, and worse, the computer had always been right. Pacino pulled on a wireless headset like the one Crossfield was wearing.

"Loss of Cyclops, aye. Messenger of the Watch, get the fire-control technician of the watch to control."

"Aye aye, sir," a young enlisted sailor called out.

"Dive, all ahead standard."

"All ahead standard, aye, sir, throttle advancing to turns for all ahead standard." Pacino put his right hand on the central console's throttle lever and pushed it gently toward the forward bulkhead. Pacino found the old-fashioned tachometer meter, showing the speed of the propulsor winding up from thirty RPM to ninety.

"Making turns for all ahead standard, sir," Pacino reported.

"Very well, Dive, make your depth one five zero feet," Crossfield ordered.

"Make my depth one five zero feet, aye, sir."

Pacino pulled back on the control yoke, watching the stern-planes respond by tipping downward like the horizontal stabilizers of an airplane during ascent. The ship's depth indicator changed, the depth display of 700 feet changing to 690, then further upward as the ship's angle—the "bubble"—increased from level to five degrees upward and beyond, until the deck was at an uphill angle of ten degrees. It seemed steep when even a half degree could be sensed by the body. The *Piranha* rose from the murky depths of the central Atlantic toward the warmer water of the shallow thermal layer.

"Passing depth four hundred feet."

"Rig control for red," Crossfield ordered. Pacino reached over by feel and clicked the white lights of the overhead to red.

"Rig for red, aye, passing three hundred feet, sir."

"Very well."

Pacino watched the temperature plot as the ship ascended through the layer, the temperature changing from twenty-eight degrees Fahrenheit to sixty almost instantly. The warmer water would be making them heavy, while the shallower depth was making them light. Pacino lined up the trim system to flood seawater to depth control two, the tank closest to the ship's center of gravity. Six thousand pounds, he decided. Better too heavy than too light. He opened the trim system's hull and backup valves with a double toggle switch and pulled the joystick of the trim system down to the FLOOD position, and seawater came roaring into the ship through the eight-inch ball valves.

"Flooding depth control, sir," Pacino reported. "Two hundred feet, sir."

Pacino eased the yoke back toward the panel, taking the angle off the ship as he pulled out of the ascent. The depth control two tank level had risen five percent. Pacino secured the flooding operation, putting the joystick back to the neutral position and using the manual valve switches to shut the hull and backup valves, an operation that Cyclops would normally have done on its own.

Suddenly an alarm rang out in the cockpit.

"Loss of main hydraulics, sir," Pacino called out, squelching the alarm. He reached for a hydraulic valve control knob to reposition the valve to the right, but it had shifted itself, as it was designed to do. "Hydraulics shifted to auxiliary." If the auxiliary hydraulic system failed, there was always the emergency hydraulics. Schultz and the captain standing behind the cockpit were obviously making life difficult for him.

Pacino pushed the yoke further down as the ship approached the depth of 150 feet, the angle coming off the ship, while he pushed down on the pedals, the bowplanes angling downward to help him level off. He steadied on 150 feet, testing to see what happened when he put the bowplanes and sternplanes on zero degrees. The ship was steady on the depth, neither rising nor sinking, Pacino's guess at the amount of water to bring in correct, although they were still flying through the water at all ahead standard, almost fifteen knots.

"Sir, one five zero feet," Pacino called.

"Very well, Dive, all ahead one-third. Sonar, Conn, prepare to clear baffles to the right in preparation to coming to periscope depth."

Pacino tensed. At a one-third bell they might rise like a cork or sink like an anvil, depending on his buoyancy calculation. "All ahead one-third, aye, sir, easing throttle to turns for all ahead one-third." Pacino found the tachometer gauge and pulled the throttle back, watching the needle wind down, his other eye on the depth. When the vessel slowed he might be out of control with all these people watching. The sub was no longer an airplane, it was now a slow zeppelin.

"Conn, Sonar aye," Sonar Chief Reardon's voice sounded in Pacino's headset.

The tachometer needle reached thirty RPM and the ship's depth immediately clicked upward to 145 feet, then to 141. Pacino pushed his bowplane pedals down, the first line of defense. If he could maintain depth with the bowplanes, he would only be a few thousand pounds light, but if he needed the sternplanes and the bubble, the situation would be much worse. At zero bubble, the ship was back at 150 feet with a four-degree dive angle on the bowplanes. At seven-tenths of a ton per degree, Pacino calculated he was light by almost three tons, or six thousand pounds. His buoyancy calculation had been off by tons, dammit. There was a good chance Catardi and Schultz would send him back for another week of under-instruction watch for a blunder that severe. He lined up the trim system, flipping the manual toggle switches to open the hull and backup valves to depth control two, and pushed down on the joystick to the FLOOD position, watching the manual tank level indicator until it rose another five percent, then released the joystick and secured the hull and backup valves. He zeroed the bowplanes. The ship was steady on depth at 150 feet. He exhaled in relief. At least he hadn't "lost the bubble," the submariner's term for a drastic loss of depth control, but which also meant losing one's cool under pressure.

"How's your trim, Dive?" Crossfield asked from the command console, his voice amused.

"Ship has a satisfactory one-third trim, sir."

"Very well, Dive," Crossfield said. "You might want to thank Chief Keating for the inadequate compensation he entered before you took the watch."

So, Pacino thought, he'd been set up with a light submarine by Keating.

"Conn, Sonar, no sonar contacts this leg," Sonarman Reardon's voice crackled in Pacino's headset.

"Sonar, Conn, aye, clearing baffles to the right."

"Conn, Sonar, aye."

"Dive, right five degrees rudder, steady course east."

"Right five degrees rudder, aye, sir, my rudder is right five."

"Very well, Dive."

Eventually the gyrocompass rose wheeled its way past 080 degrees true. "Passing course zero eight zero to the right, ten degrees from ordered course," Pacino called.

"V'r'well, Dive."

"Steady course east, sir," Pacino reported. There was silence in the room. Pacino took a tense breath, knowing the next few minutes would be the worst. If he came up to periscope depth too steeply, he could broach the sail, but if he came up too sluggishly, the OOD wouldn't be able to see the surface, and they could be run over by a deep draft merchant without even hearing him.

"Conn, Sonar, no sonar contacts in the previously baffled area," the sonar chief, Chief Reardon, reported over Pacino's headset.

"Dive," Crossfield called with a flourish, "make your depth six seven feet!"

"Make my depth six seven feet, aye, sir," Pacino acknowledged. As he pulled back on the bowplane pedals another alarm shrieked in the cockpit. "Loss of auxiliary hydraulics, sir," he said, checking the hydraulic lineup. Perhaps main hydraulics were back on-line, but when he shifted the hydraulic spindle valve handle, he still had no power. "Emergency hydraulics engaged, sir." Pacino reached back to the center console for a vertical lever behind and to the right of the throttle, the bowplanes now only controllable by the emergency lever. But it didn't position the bowplanes like the pedals, it was a lethargic "rate controller." He would have to hunt for the position that would put the planes on the right angle. Sweat broke out on Pacino's forehead as he pulled the emergency lever back, pulling the bowplanes to an up angle of ten degrees, and as the ship's angle rose, pushed them back to up five degrees. He took a moment to grab another emergency hydraulic lever

118   Michael DiMercurio

to nudge the rudder over to maintain course east, then back to the ship's centerline.

"Emergency hydraulics tested, test sat," he called out.

"Very well, Dive." Crossfield's voice was muffled by his periscope helmet.

"One two zero feet, sir," Pacino called, the sweat soaking his eyes now, the gauges on the manual displays blurry. "Passing one hundred feet."

The up angle was too steep, Pacino realized. He pushed the emergency lever forward, easing the bowplane angle, trying to get the bubble back down.

"Ninety feet, sir."

Pacino struggled, the angle now too flat. He was roller-coastering the ship, he thought in chagrin. He reached for the emergency lever for the sternplanes and pulled it back, getting the bubble back to an up three-degree angle. He was soaked in sweat now, even his long sleeves dripping.

"Eight zero feet, sir."

He had to get the angle back down, or he'd broach the sail. He pushed the sternplanes down, grabbed the emergency lever for the bowplanes, and pushed them down to a two-degree angle, then reached for the sternplane lever again and put the sternplanes to zero, again reaching for the bowplanes and pulling them back to up one degree.

"Seven five feet, sir!"

"Scope's breaking," Crossfield called. "Scope's breaking. Get us up, Dive!"

"Aye, sir, seven four feet." Pacino's sweat droplets flew in the cockpit as he pulled up higher on the bowplanes until they were at the full rise position, but the ship was heavy as lead. He pulled up on the sternplanes to use the ship's angle, putting a one-degree up bubble on the ship to get up to periscope depth, but the depth meter wouldn't budge. He needed to pump out some water, and quickly.

"Seven five feet, ship's heavy," Pacino reported. He selected the trim system's hull and backup valves, then reached by feel and found the rotary switch to energize the massive trim pump in the auxiliary machinery room in the lower level. Nothing happened. He rotated the rotary switch again, but the trim pump didn't start. Instead a red annunciator alarm flashed on the display panel, reading TRIM PUMP TROUBLE.

"Trim pump fails to start, OOD, pump trouble light, lining up the drain pump. Seven four feet, sir."

"Scope's awash, goddammit. Dive, get us the fuck up!" Crossfield's irritation was becoming fury. "Handle your fucking casualty and get us up!"

"Aye, sir." Pacino's hand shook as he flipped the toggle switches to line up the large bore ball valves from the drain system to the trim piping, then valved out the malfunctioning trim pump. Holding his breath he grabbed the rotary switch for the drain pump and turned it to the START position. Nothing happened. He tried again, a second alarm light popping up to read DRAIN PUMP TROUBLE. There was only one thing left to do. He clicked the toggle switches to pressurize the depth control two tank with medium pressure air.

"Drain pump trouble light, pressurizing DCT two with seven hundred psi and blowing, sir."

"Dive," Crossfield called in exasperation, "scope's awash, get us up."

Pacino opened the DCT2 hull and backup valves and raised the hovering system joystick to the BLOW position, normally a forbidden operation because of the noise it made. Immediately the air in the top of the tank blew its contents overboard into the lower pressure seawater, the ship finally lighting. The depth meter flashed a few feet upward rise.

"Seven four feet, sir. Seven two feet. Seven zero. Six nine feet, sir." God, Pacino thought, finally. He took the bubble off the ship and relaxed the bowplane angle, the ship steady on depth.

"Scope's clear!" Crossfield called, the navigator now furiously doing a surface search for close surface contacts, the smallest surface ship able to cut open their hull. By the standard operating procedures, there would be complete silence in the control room until the officer of the deck said the words to stand down, "no close contacts." Anything else, including the expletive "oh shit," would be interpreted as an emergency order to go back deep to avoid collision with a surface ship. The submarine's hull was strong and thick, but it was built to withstand the pressure of the deep, not a puncture force from a surface ship hull.

"No close contacts!" Crossfield called out. Pacino exhaled in relief.

Pacino shut the depth control tank's hull and backup valves and vented the tank's pressurized air to the machinery room.

"Six eight feet, sir."

But now the ship was rising with no angle on the planes. Had he gone too far? He put the bowplanes on down one, then down two. "Six seven feet, sir." Dammit, he was roller-coastering again. Using emergency hydraulics was impossible. "Six eight feet, sir."

Pacino noticed he'd drifted off course by three degrees. One eye on the depth, he pushed the emergency lever to move the rudder to the right by half a degree, and when he was back on course east he pulled it back to zero degrees. The ship was on ordered depth with zero angle.

"Starting high-power search," Crossfield called. "Dive, raise the BRA-44."

The AN/BRA-44 was the radio mast to grab the satellite broadcast, Pacino thought, its nickname the BIGMOUTH. He found the lever on the starboard vertical panel toggled it upward. A moan of hydraulics lifted the mast, the emergency system much slower than the main hydraulics normally would be.

"BRA-44 up, OOD," Pacino said.

For the next two minutes Pacino adjusted the ship's depth, the vessel much steadier now that it had the proper weight. He was fighting a slight nose-heaviness, but adjusting it could begin the oscillations again, and he figured it would be easier to counter it with the bowplanes.

The hydraulics thumped again, the BRA-44 being lowered by the radiomen.

"Conn, Radio, broadcast aboard, BRA-44 comin' down."

"Radio, Conn, aye," Crossfield acknowledged.

Behind Pacino XO Schultz tapped Crossfield on the shoulder. He peeked out of his periscope helmet to see her holding a picture of an approaching aircraft carrier, the photo shot from low in the water directly in the path of the behemoth. Schultz had just initiated another drill.

"Emergency deep!" Crossfield called.

Without thinking Pacino grabbed the throttle with his right hand and the bowplane lever with his left, advancing the throttle to where ahead full should be, and pushing the bowplanes to full dive. He grabbed the sternplane lever with his throttle hand and pushed the sternplanes to a ten-degree down angle, then lined up the trim system to flood and jabbed the joystick down. He held the joystick with his left hand and reached out to advance the throttle by another ten RPM, then pulled the sternplanes back to up five degrees and the bowplanes to a ten-degree rise. He released the joystick lever, one eye on ship's depth, and called out, "Emergency deep aye, ahead full, flooding, down bubble ten degrees."

A selector switch on the yoke piped his boom microphone into the 1MC shipwide announcing system. He punched the key and heard his amplified voice in the overhead echoing through the ship, "Emergency deep, emergency deep."

He struggled with the planes until the depth was steady at 150 feet, then pulled the throttle back to turns for ahead one-third. "One five zero feet, sir!" The sweat had returned, and in seconds he was soaked again.

But the drill was over, and he had made it. The console buzzed. Pacino punched the squelch button. "Auxiliary hydraulics are back on-line, sir." Another buzz. "Main hydraulics are back." He switched the cockpit back to main hydraulics, the nightmare with the emergency levers over. A whirring noise sounded and the screen displays changed, a half-dozen flat panels coming to life. "Cyclops ship control is back on-line." He put the visor back on, the ship animation display returning.

"Very well, Dive. Make your depth seven hundred feet, all ahead standard, steep angle."

Pacino acknowledged, pushing down the control yoke and advancing the throttle, the ship's down angle plunging to down twenty degrees. For two minutes he hung on the straps of his seat until the Cyclops animation indicated 650 feet. He pulled out at 700 feet and checked the display.

"Seven hundred feet, sir," Pacino called to Crossfield.

"Mr. Pacino, turn over the dive to Chief Keating."

Pacino gave his briefing, released the watch to Keating, and climbed out of the cockpit. He was surrounded by the ship's officers and chiefs, from the captain on down, the crowd suddenly bursting into applause, Catardi's smile lighting up his face. Even Crossfield was grinning at him and clapping. And Lieutenant Alameda, her normally sour expression gone, was actually beautiful when she allowed herself to smile.

"Gentlemen," Catardi announced, "I give you Midshipman Patch Pacino, the newest qualified diving officer of the watch, and a damned fine one at that."

"Hear, hear," Duke Phelps added.

"Amen, Mr. Patch," normally surly Chief Keating said with a wink.

Pacino smiled weakly, aware that his coveralls were soaked with sweat. He felt his face flush, embarrassed, knowing the awkward approach to PD could have gone much better. He'd kept Crossfield's view underwater for a full thirty seconds.

"A fine job, Patch," Catardi continued. "No one aboard has ever handled the *Piranha* quite that well in the face of so many casualties. Pay up, everyone. You too, Chief Keating."

Pacino stared as hundred-dollar bills changed hands, the whole circle of men passing the money to the captain. Keating grinned at him as he passed five twenty-dollar bills over his shoulder to Catardi.

"What the hell?"

"These unfortunate unbelievers all bet you'd either broach the sail or have to ask for a two-thirds bell to get up to depth. Or that you'd lose the bubble completely." Catardi grinned.

"Probably because not a single solitary one of them ever made it to PD on emergency hydraulics with no Cyclops while six tons heavy with a double trim system and drain system malfunction. Any one of these people would have hung up with the scope awash for two minutes and then given up and added power to dry off the periscope. Like I said, we've been waiting for you."

Pacino smiled again, aching to get to the officers' head to strip off the soaked coveralls and take a shower. As he turned to go Chief Keating called him back to the ship control console.

"Yes, Chief?"

"Sir, sorry I called you a nonqual airbreather," Keating said gently. "You can breathe my submarine's air anytime, sir."

Pacino felt a lump in his throat. Oddly enough, it was one of the highest compliments he could remember receiving.

"Thanks, Chief," he said, turning and leaving the control room.

He knew he'd be back in three hours to take his first watch on his own, no longer under instruction, but as a qualified watchstander.

10

Dr. Frederick Wang walked uncertainly down the steps of the private jet that had whisked him from his Denver home to Rayong, Thailand. He shook the hand of the large Thai driver and climbed into the Rolls-Royce. He had never even seen a car like this, much less ridden in one. It had been a terrible week, but this turn of events was so strange that he wasn't sure he could call it fortunate. Ten days ago Wang had been summoned from the DynaCorp artificial intelligence lab in the Denver Tech Center to the downtown office, escorted by a mean-looking security guard. He was hustled into the vice president's office, told his security clearance had been pulled, and that they would pack his personal belongings for him. Wang had signed a restrictive employment agreement when he had come to work for DynaCorp, one that disallowed lawsuits on the basis of compromising secrets that were vital to national security. In exchange, the agreement indicated that he could be fired for reasons that DynaCorp did not have to disclose. At least he received a year's severance pay, but the withdrawal of his security clearance meant he could not obtain another defense contracting job, and there was nowhere he could work in the private sector that had anything like the funding he'd had at the DynaCorp Denver lab. That assumed he could get hired by a private corporation after losing the security clearance.

The reason they had fired him was that he was second-generation Chinese and he spent hours on the phone with his immediate family in Beijing, and DynaCorp suspected his loyalty. It was a miserable situation, but there seemed little he could do about it. He was out of a job and expected to be out of his field as well. He was too depressed to try to plan ahead, and had despondently wandered around his house, unable to concentrate. When the phone rang, he considered not answering it, but the code read that the call had come from Thailand, and he was curious. The large man on the video display had spoken words for several minutes, but it was not the words that had intrigued Wang, it had been his manner—warm and accepting, the way DynaCorp executives used to be toward him back in the days when he was their most brilliant AI engineer.

The man's name was Sergio, and he wanted to interview Wang. The job he had in mind required a considerable amount of travel, which would be perfect for Wang—he wanted to get away from Denver and the DynaCorp memories. He told Wang that a car would be waiting for him in an hour. The car had arrived, a sleek black stretch Mercedes limo, and had taken him to Denver International, driving through the security fence right to the open door of a swept-wing supersonic private jet. A beautiful Chinese flight attendant had served him dinner and drinks on the plane. He had slept, awakening as the jet's wheels thumped on the Rayong runway.

An hour later he was in an opulent beach house on the sand in Pattaya, Thailand, talking to Sergio in person, and his partner, a polished and encouraging executive named Victor Krivak. The talk seemed less an interview than the first day of work. Finally, Sergio simply asked him if he would come to work for them at United Electrics, and if a starting salary of five million U.S. dollars a year would be adequate—with a bonus on earnings to go with it, of course, Sergio had added, as if the salary alone might be inadequate. The only catch was that United Electrics would be, as Sergio cautiously put it, "interfering" with the American military using Wang's extraordinary credentials. If Wang could do that without qualms, he could have the job as a senior director of AI technology.

Wang took less than a heartbeat to think about it. His father had come to America and worked in a convenience store in East Los Angeles, getting beaten up and robbed in a city rife with crime, scraping and saving so Wang could go to college. At Cal Tech Wang was a perpetual outsider, as he had often seemed at DynaCorp. There had been nothing but work in Wang's life, and when he had been terminated, there was little allegiance for America left in him. The thought of working for men who were adversaries to the people who had rejected him had a certain appeal. And as Wang now knew, when his small severance salary ran out, he could be working in a convenience store himself.

Unit One Oh Seven, Wang thought, was the one thing in the world that came closest to being his child, his creation. Dyna-Corp had thrown him out in the street without even letting him say good-bye to the lab researchers or the sentient carbon processors. He missed One Oh Seven more than any of the rest. He tortured himself, remembering all his encounters with the unit, remembering how it was sometimes playful, sometimes vexed, the computer's emotions stirring something inside him, a feeling that he wanted to protect and nurture the unit. It was strange to think of it this way, but he was a father to One Oh Seven in every sense of the word. And when he was fired from DynaCorp, it was as if he'd had a child torn from him, with no possibility of seeing it again. When he was able to sleep, in his dreams he was talking to One Oh Seven or playing chess with it or teaching it the classics. When he woke, the worst part of the day was remembering that One Oh Seven had been brutally cut out of his life.

But these men in Thailand had offered him the opportunity to revisit his creation. Once more he might be able to talk to One Oh Seven, perhaps even ask it how it was doing, perhaps even be recognized by it. He hoped that all of this was for real.

Wang stuttered that he agreed, and Sergio and Krivak smiled and shook his hand. Over champagne, and at Krivak's prompting, Wang talked about the history of the development of machine cognizance while Krivak and Sergio listened attentively.

"Superconductors reached their limits of miniaturization ten years ago," Wang explained, spreading his hands wide. "We got to the point where a single dust particle could wipe out a processor, and to where the heat generated within the circuits became capable of melting the silicon. Twenty years earlier, the organic chemists came to the party, bringing with them their theories of molecular circuits. In the DynaCorp lab we had the largest funding in North America, and the scientists I managed solved the initial problems quickly, the ability to determine the behavior of a single molecule holding up progress until we got the scanning tunneling microscopes, which opened the window to the atomic-scale world. The initial organic molecular devices we fabricated were able to conduct electrons by passing them from one atom's electron orbital to the next, but the issue was, could they do this under command and only when an outside signal told them to, turning on or off at the orders of the controlling signal? If they could, we would have ourselves an electrically controllable switch, which would form a molecular transistor, and we would be computing digitally at the molecular scale. If we failed, the whole concept would crash. But nothing seemed to work. Finally we constructed a molecular string that could rotate to remove one conducting electron orbital from proximity to the next, effectively turning the molecule off, and then could rotate back to make the orbitals come close together again to turn the molecule back on. The rotation was keyed by light photons hitting the molecular string, an awkward, impractical way to control the switching action. So we went to work on a more complex molecule that could switch on and off from an electrical impulse instead of light. That took the better part of a year, but when we finished we had made the first true molecular transistor. The next year we were able to fabricate single-molecule diodes, amplifying transistors, AND-gates, OR-gates, and amplifiers. I remember how we thought we'd cracked the safe.

Now we just had to tackle the problem of how to arrange these basic devices into a circuit so that they would perform a desired function.

"The problem of how to route current into specific terminals of the molecular devices had us stumped for a year until the organic chemists came up with what they called 'chemical self-assembly.' With the simplest form of self-assembly the molecular devices drifted toward gold terminal plates while in solution. The chemistry of self-assembly grew more complex as we assembled more complicated circuit structures. We developed an organic structure for holding the molecules in place, freeing the scientists from the bother of having coin-sized gold plates littering the circuits. We went to work on a tunnellike molecular tube capable of passing electrons—current—from one location to a distant point of the circuit assembly, sort of an artificial neuron branch. That was eight years ago. The following year we synthesized a molecule that could hold an electron within a cavity formed by the surrounding atom's electron clouds, the captured electron creating a digital memory site. The presence of an electron forms a 'one' while the absence of an electron symbolized a 'zero.' The memory node holds the electron memory state for an amazing ten minutes. Sounds pretty short, but not when you compare it to the silicon semiconductor memory sites that last only for a few milliseconds and have to be constantly refreshed. We'd just made a gigantic leap in computer technology with that one development.

"By this time we'd hired some of the Japanese developers of the Destiny III submarines, the ones that were biological computer controlled. The Japanese came to us about the time we were getting bogged down in trying to assemble huge arrays of molecular circuits, the placement of vast quantities of individual molecules in specific locations becoming drudgery. The Japanese had managed to wire up lower mammalian brains to the terminals of a neural network silicon computer processor well before the Japanese Missile Crisis, but even they didn't know what was happening on a molecular level.

They had approached the biological processor as a black box that had to be dealt with empirically, using trial and error to make it function. So they too were stumped by the problem of assembling these gigantic complex circuits. Even now I wonder whether the solution to the problem was invented and developed by our lab scientists or plagiarized from nature when we took simple chromosomes and altered them one molecule at a time to embed them with instructions on how to develop an organic circuit board in three dimensions from more basic cells. The circuit fabrication in the lab was the result of 'programming' the chromosomes and allowing them to grow the molecular circuit tissue over the course of months, the tissue growing to several grams, with the circuit density required to exceed the performance of its silicon counterparts. After five thousand failures, we managed to assemble a large molecular circuit that functioned as a processor, and could 'survive' unchanged for up to weeks at a time before disassembling. 'Dying' might be a better word.

"So the big day in artificial intelligence history was forecasted to happen roughly two hundred years from now, the far-distant day that a carbon-based tissue-matrix molecular computer exceeded the performance of the most advanced silicon semiconductor supercomputer, the day named 'C>Si' for the chemical symbol of carbon becoming greater than silicon. Two centuries, gentlemen, but C>Si happened in the Dyna-Corp Nanoscale Technology Molecular Electronics Lab in Denver, Colorado, seven years ago."

Wang paused to drink from his glass. Krivak looked over to Sergio, who was hanging on Wang's words.

"But our tissue matrices were all too geared toward C>Si. We were basically miniaturizing carbon computers to function like dumb silicon computers. The next step was to use our new knowledge of chromosome construction techniques to build circuit tissues to more closely resemble brain tissues, including fabricating neuron synapses and brain cell matrices. We went into business to mimic nature's brain construction, starting at the bottom of the ladder with insect brains. Once we worked through three thousand failures, we turned to bird brain fabrication. Let me tell you, the brain of a bird is an amazing device. The motor control needed to fly is immense. A few months later we had expanded to building the brains of cats, then canines and finally lower primates. As the chromosomes came closer to resembling the human genome, the computational power of the tissue systems rose exponentially. You'd think there would be a debate as to the ethics of using artificial human chromosomes to build a circuit matrix modeled on the human brain. But no one really knew. Some of the work was classified, other areas so highly complex that mainstream media writers were unable to grasp the concepts. We were making progress at an exponential rate. Only a year after C>Si, we had succeeded in reverse-engineering the human brain. After having done that, we started looking ahead to the day when the tissue-based supercomputers would exceed the intelligence levels of individual humans, the day designated 'AI>HI' for artificial intelligence overcoming human intelligence.

"We were so drunk on our success that the first failure of our new technology came as a shock. The useful timespan of the carbon-based tissue computers shrank, until the most sophisticated units based on human chromosome strands began to last less than a few weeks."

"What happened?" Victor Krivak asked.

"We ran into the same problems God did," Wang said, looking into his empty glass. Sergio refilled it from a fresh bottle. "At first, the organic computers suffered from disease and infections. That problem was overcome by the construction of special cleanrooms, limiting the usefulness of the computers— how can you use your computer if you have to build a cleanroom in your house? The solution was ugly—your computer's tissue-matrix processor would be kept in a hospitallike cleanroom at a central location, and instead of purchasing the physical unit, you would just possess a terminal to it, controlled by your wireless pad computer. That would at least hold us until we brought more medical doctors into the lab to help us with immunology issues. Once the disease problem was put aside, the units that survived proved susceptible to a different kind of sickness. You might call it psychosis.

"You see, the programmers for the carbon-based computers found they were spending more time teaching than actually programming. As the intelligence level of the units rose, so did the complexity of teaching them. Artificial intelligence psychologists observing the interaction of the programmers with the carbon computers and of the computers with each other reached the conclusion that the carbon computers were becoming sentient, and with consciousness came all its baggage. Emotional pain in all its varieties. Loneliness. Sadness. Anger. Lust for control. Wistfulness. Boredom. In the next year the programmers had become more like parents or teachers than technicians.

"The worst came as the most advanced carbon computers aged. Unlike their silicon counterparts, which functioned on one level until they became obsolete, the newest carbon computers developed within the same physical model, gaining intelligence and executing self-rewiring of their circuits, the same thing a human brain does on exposure to education. But the carbon units tended to cease functioning at the two-year point, all their progress gone. They would go into the biological equivalent of a silicon computer locking up. It was a catatonic state from which they never emerged, and eventually they died."

"What was the cause?" Krivak asked.

"The terrible twos," Wang said. "The carbon computer developed just like the brain of an infant. Programming and its own natural development bring the unit to the point that it is self-aware, or perhaps just aware of where the self stops and the outside world begins. The unit would became aware of its own dependence, of its powerlessness. At that point it had temper tantrums very much like a toddler does, except these were much more destructive. You might describe it as a form of schizophrenia. We decided the units were understimulated, and the only thing that worked was giving them toys to play with or break. Physical manifestations of themselves that they could control."

"You gave them bodies," Krivak said.

"Exactly," Wang said, nodding solemnly. "We put them into tractors, cars, and robots and gave them manipulation arms so that they could work out their anger in physical ways. The destructive tendency remained, but with physical control of things they could break, the units survived and continued to develop without going into catatonic states. Without some physical thing to control, the units could not go on."

"So that's where we are now?" Krivak asked.

"No, that was four years ago, but our progress curve flattened dramatically, I'm afraid. The technology now is bottlenecked by the time it takes individual units to grow and experience and learn. Unfortunately, the carbon computers, now that they are cousins to our own brains, are on our same developmental clock scale. They grow from a helpless state to an infantile awareness, then to consciousness at the two-year point, then on to further intelligence that increases geometrically. And then we have yet another problem that plagued our own creator.

"That problem was the variability of self-assembled chromosome-guided carbon processors. Variable in that many of the units we fabricated were, in a word, dumb. The range of intelligence quotients was extremely wide, making the idea of mass production impossible. For every promising intelligent unit, there were twenty dumb ones, emotionally uncontrolled ones, or sick ones. The lack of productivity was astonishing, and for a year it began to look like we would never have a unit we could trust in a military system. And then finally one of our units made it through the terrible twos and developed into its fifth year with no mishaps. Unit 2015-107, which we just call 'One Oh Seven,' was our pride and joy, our most advanced unit. We've now seen that the only way to ensure that the progress gained from a successful unit is to preserve the plans for its tissue by replicating it in the form of DNA strands, its own chromosome. Unfortunately, the sons of

One Oh Seven have been much dumber. Now we've seen the light that we can't just preserve the DNA of one of our successful units—we can't expect to just clone them—for too many generations before they develop errors and stop behaving and processing like the parent unit. We have to combine the DNA of the successful unit with the DNA of another successful unit, a sort of carbon processor's form of sexual reproduction. You might say that we're now on God's learning curve. And that's where we are. Unit One Oh Seven had an encounter with Unit Two Four Three and conceived Unit Two Six Seven, and Two Six Seven has just passed through its terrible twos. We were able to remove One Oh Seven from the lab and place it in the first military unit capable of accepting complete control from a carbon processor."

"Then you've given a military system to a five-year-old," Krivak said.

"True, but a really bright five-year-old." The three of them laughed, the remainder of lunch continuing with small talk. When the dishes were cleared by Sergio's staff, Krivak turned to Wang.

"This military system," he said. "What is it?"

"They call it the *Snarc*," Wang said between bites. "Dyna-Corp and the Navy came up with the term, an acronym for Submarine Naval Automated Robotic Combat system. It's a submarine controlled by Unit One Oh Seven."

"Doesn't that seem a little radical for the American military?" Krivak asked as he tasted his wine. "What happens if One Oh Seven becomes unstable?"

"DynaCorp is watching One Oh Seven closely. They have silicon-based history modules on board and a distributed control system that can control the ship if the One Oh Seven dies. In addition, the silicon system will report on the One Oh Seven's health. Every time One Oh Seven comes to the surface, the silicon system transmits a burst of telemetry, including the contents of the history module."

"Assuming the carbon unit lets it," Krivak said.

"Yes." The scientist nodded.

"So, it is impossible to take over this ship from a distance."
Krivak sounded disappointed.

"That's correct. You can't electronically hijack this unit and
take over its computer for your own uses. Yet another advantage of using this kind of AI control system, and it was one of
the things DynaCorp and the Navy told Congress to get the au-
thorization to put this system into a military node. It is tamper-
proof."

Sergio stood. "Gentlemen, I think we've taxed our minds
enough for one day. Leave some problems for tomorrow's
work, shall we? Doctor, we have a suite for you at the hotel,
where you can relax, perhaps enjoy the Bangkok nightlife.
Let's reconvene in the morning."

After Wang left, Krivak glanced at Sergio, who stared out
the window without expression.

"What did you think?" Krivak asked.

"I think we've hit the jackpot," Sergio said, but there was
uncertainty in his voice.

"Shame about the *Snarc* though. I'd really hoped we could
take control of it like a silicon system."

"I'm not worried about the *Snarc*," Sergio said, frowning.

"Oh? Then what—or whom—are you worried about?"

"Wang. Did you see the way he talked about these cre-
ations? His eyes lit up. These computers are like his children.
He's glad for the chance to manipulate them, almost like a parent relishing meddling in his child's life, but the minute you
put the idea of a unit's death on the table, he'll pull away from
us."

Victor thought for some time. "Then we must hide that from
him."

The Falcon took off out of Bangkok and made a long trip,
stopping once for fuel in what Wang judged to be South
Africa. They took off again, leaving the sun behind them, and
eventually landed in São Paulo, four hundred clicks west of
Rio de Janeiro, Brazil. The hired limo brought them farther

west, into breathtaking countryside, eventually stopping at the entrance to a prison.

"Wait here," Krivak commanded Wang. "Amorn, you have the cash?"

"Yes, sir. In the suitcase, blocks of a hundred thousand in hundred-dollar U.S. bills. All two million."

"Bring it in for me. It's too heavy."

Amorn followed Krivak into the prison, Wang wondering what this errand was about. After an hour he and Amorn returned without the suitcase, a youth in his early twenties following them, still wearing his orange prison coveralls, a frightened look on his face. Confusion rippled across his features as he saw the shiny black limo.

"Dr. Wang, meet Pedro Meringe."

"Mr. Meringe," Wang said.

"Call me Pedro," the boy said in perfect English.

The limo took them to a hotel in Serocaba, where Krivak directed the young man to shower and change into fresh clothes. He still looked young in the expensive Italian suit. Amorn took Pedro to a restaurant, while Krivak leaned against the outside wall and lit a cigarette.

"Who is the prisoner?"

"You really don't know who he is, do you? He's the kid who shut down the Pentagon's orbital servers last Christmas. There was a global legal fight to extradite him to the U.S., but Brazil insisted on his sentence being carried out on their soil."

"So the two million? Bail?"

"For the next twenty years he'll make roll call. Then the prison will release someone who looks like him. In the meantime he works for us."

11

The USS *John Paul Jones* labored through twenty-foot seas and forty-five-knot winds, the gales rising to fifty-five knots. Although she was larger than the Sears tower laid on its side, displacing over a hundred twenty thousand tons as one of the largest aircraft carriers built in the history of the world, she could barely be seen five hundred yards away with her running lights dark.

The carrier battlegroup lumbered slowly west-southwest in the Philippine Sea, a day's sailing time from the Celebes Sea south of the Philippine Islands, which was another day from the Strait of Malacca and the entrance to the Indian Ocean. The ships of the force were far over the horizon from each other, outside of radar range—which was useless to them anyway, because the operation order required all surface search radars to be shut down to avoid the detection of the oncoming battlegroup through electronic means. Unfortunately, that also applied to air-search radars, leaving the battlegroup vulnerable to air attack, although the new high-resolution radar and thermal-imaging surveillance satellites would supposedly alert them to an incoming attack aircraft, assuming the Internet E-mail connection functioned and they could authenticate the message fast enough. The storm was a godsend, as it made flight operations impossible, not just for the *John Paul Jones,* but for the adversary as well.

High over the *John Paul Jones*'s flight deck the superstructure of the island presided. The highest full-width island deck was the bridge, with angled windows looking down on the wide expanse of the deck and the surrounding seas. Set into the windows were large Plexiglas wheels spinning at six hundred RPM, casting off the water of the almost horizontal rain to allow the officers to see outside, but even the view through the wheels was nearly opaque. The atmosphere surrounding *John Paul Jones* was more water than air in the driving rain. The bridge deck's central feature was the ship-control console, with the helm station with its wheel and the throttle console and communications station. Forward of it on either side were the radar stations, all of them dark. The carrier was in the center of the far-flung loose formation, the antisubmarine destroyers and frigates running far out in an ASW sector fifty to a hundred nautical miles ahead of the rest of the battlegroup. Somewhere out there were five Aegis II missile cruisers, their holds stuffed to the gills with Equalizer Mark IV supersonic heavy cruise missiles. Also steaming with them were the multipurpose destroyers, the DD-21s, their clean decks making them look like the old Civil War ironclads, but their belowdecks choked with batteries of missiles and torpedoes. To a bystander, the *John Paul Jones* carrier battlegroup would seem invincible, the most massive assembly of naval firepower since the War of the East China Sea, with over two million tons of warships plowing the hostile seas. But to the battle fleet's commander, Vice Admiral Egon "The Viking" Ericcson, the fleet was woefully inadequate. The Achilles' heel of the flotilla was its vulnerability to hostile submarines.

Far over the horizon to the west, the nuclear submarine *Leopard* had come to periscope depth and had sent a brief situation report, a "sit-rep," copied to Admiral Ericcson's task force. Admiral Ericcson was awakened during the night to read the message from *Leopard*.

"I wasn't asleep, goddammit," he said in his gravelly voice to the messenger of the watch.

The admiral sat up in his rack and pulled a new Partagas

cigar out of his humidor and lit it in the dimness of the state-room, illuminated only by his desk lamp. He handed the pad computer back to the messenger of the watch and snarled at him to take the news to the ship's captain and the battlegroup operations officer. Too wound up to return to sleep, Ericcson rose to his six-and-a-half-foot height and pulled on his khaki uniform. On his left breast pocket were eight rows of ribbons, topped by the gold wings of a fighter pilot. Below the ribbons Ericcson wore his surface warfare pin, and below that his fleet command gold emblem, a downward angling dagger framed by tidal waves. He ran his hand through his closely cropped full head of platinum-blond hair, the fierce frowning expression interrupted briefly for a yawn. Ericcson coughed, swearing to himself for the tenth time this trip that he would quit his constant cigar smoking. He was rarely seen at sea without one in his fist, insisting on chewing them unlit in places where smoking was prohibited. The bridge of the aircraft carrier was such a place, the advanced electronics of the phased array radar systems too delicate to be bombarded with cigar smoke. The Viking had accused the electronics of being sissies, and insisted on smoking anyway.

He took three cigars to the bridge, where he decided to spend the rest of the night, reclining in the fleet commander's chair and smoking. He spent one in three nights in the chair, the nicotine and the weight of fleet command making him an insomniac. The deck inclined upward precipitously as the ship rode an incoming wave, then rolled sickeningly down the crest to slam into the trough, all the while rolling far to port, then back to starboard, the ship corkscrewing through the mountainous waves. Ericcson lit the first cigar, stoking it up to a mellow cloud in front of him, listening to the music of the spray on the windshield and the howl of the wind in the rigging, the low tones of conversations on the bridge and the whine of the high-speed gyros. The Viking puffed on the Partagas, his eyes half shut, feeling the roller-coaster motion of the deck, a deep contentment filling his soul, his battle fleet under his combat boots, sailing into harm's way on a ship christened *John Paul Jones,* the greatest American naval officer in history.

Ericcson smoked the cigar and let his mind return for the dozenth time to Patton's underground bunker briefing.

"We're late and I've got orders for you both. Vic, you first, since we need to get you on the plane to Pearl before you're missed. For the next six days, get ammunition loaded and put out rumors that there are a number of exercises coming, quick scramble-to-sea-type things. This is the hard part, because you have to have your ships ready to go without anyone thinking they're being readied for an extended emergency deployment. Shut down any heavy maintenance your repair organization's doing. Button up all the ships, and give the repair boys some excuse—a readiness inspection or an audit of their records and procedures. Then next Saturday night you're to have one of your customary big all-hands parties. Invite all your fleet's commanding officers and their executive officers, their wives and girlfriends, husbands and boyfriends. Make damned sure everyone comes, get it catered, open bar, but get a slow waiter. Early in the evening get all the captains and XOs together in the basement, put on some music, give them each two of these handheld computers, a main unit and a spare. Brief them on the Red-Indian flap. Don't release anything on the loss of security of the network—you can tell them we're doing an exercise to see what happens if we use it for disinformation purposes, as a security exercise. Then, as another exercise, scramble the whole fleet to sea. *Slowly.* A few ships at a time. Go to sea by ship type, destroyers, then frigates, then cruisers, rather than as a coordinated battlegroup. No one is to know the whole fleet is pulling out, it has to be a complete surprise to the men. You've got two weeks. In fourteen days I want the Nav-ForcePac Fleet steaming at maximum revs for the Indian Ocean, fully loaded out with warshots and provisions for a long haul, but I don't want any satellites to suspect, no pierside prostitutes reporting anything, no wives or husbands squawking, no word at all. It's just another day playing in the

Pacific, and we need to see if our toys will work. That's all. We'll be back next Tuesday, honey, so pick up a few steaks and plan to put the kids to bed early. Get the picture?"

"Yes, sir."

"Vic, your ships will not be sailing in formation. You'll all be far over the horizon from each other, so any spy satellites just see one of you at a time. Meantime I will be mobilizing the mothballed fleet under robotic control, using NSA's electronics instead of the command network, and the decoy ships will be sailing all points of the compass, so to anyone in orbit it will look like an exercise. You will be doing a zigzag on the way, so a photograph won't show you always headed the same direction."

"An eye-in-the-sky will see the preponderance of ships heading for the Indian Ocean, sir, on their base course."

"We can't help that. At the end of the day you still command surface ships. They'll never be as stealthy as McKee's boats, but the ocean is a very big place. And that's all I have for you, Vic. Get back to Pearl Harbor. There's a jumbo jet waiting for you topside. Takeoff before the sun rises, and get back to the golf course before the Reds or the Indians know you've been gone."

Ericcson had risen from his seat, the briefing obviously over.

"Good hunting, my friend," Patton said. "You'll have the mixed blessing of a target-rich environment."

"One last thing for you, sir," Ericcson said. "Don't bother about the demotion. With a mission this heavy, I might as well have the title as well as the headaches."

The cigar was down to a soggy nub. Ericcson lit a second, his thoughts returning to the present. He squinted at his watch, frowning deeper as he realized he couldn't see the face. He looked around the dim lights of the bridge, making sure no one was watching him, then sneaked out a pair of frameless reading glasses from his shirt pocket and put them on to see the Rolex face reading 11:50 PM local time, which was 1750

GMT or 1250 PM on the U.S. East Coast. He quickly put the reading glasses away and called the officer of the deck over.

"Get the ops boss and the captain to flag plot in ten minutes," he said quietly.

"Aye aye, sir."

Ten minutes later, the Partagas was half smoked, and Ericcson left the bridge out the hatch to the ladderway below past air operations to flag plot, a full-island-width space filled with displays and land maps and ocean charts, the central table a map of the entire Indian Ocean in relief. Over on the port side the Gulf of Aden emptied into the Arabian Sea from the Red Sea north to the Suez Canal. A fleet marker showed the Royal Navy Fleet making its way in the eastern Med toward the Suez Canal. In the early hours of daylight Eastern Europe Time the fleet would make its approach to the canal. Their entrance into the Arabian Sea would happen fifty hours later at a speed of advance of thirty-five knots, but he gave them another eight for the speed restriction at the mouth of the canal. That put the Brits in-theater in sixty-two hours.

The Viking walked a pair of dividers across the surface of the map, measuring the distance from their position to the Strait of Malacca before he noticed Captains Casper Hendricks and Dennis Pulaski standing behind him. Hendricks was a Harvard grad, an ugly officer with a long thin nose, eyes much too close together presiding over thin lips and a weak chin. He was tall, thin, and awkward, with one of the deepest mean streaks Ericcson had ever seen in the fleet, but the man was sharp and incisive when it came to grasping a tactical situation, which led to bitter arguments over tactics. The admiral loved to mix it up with the ship's captain, but the raised voices obviously bothered Hendricks. Ericcson had wanted to stop in a liberty port and get the man drunk and laid to see if it would loosen him up, but there had been no time during the flank run from Pearl. Captain Pulaski, the battlegroup operations officer and Ericcson's acting chief of staff, was Hendricks's opposite. Pulaski was short and solid,

his thick arms and legs carrying a barrel chest with a hairless
bucket for a head, his pockmarked features blunted by four
years of brigade boxing at the Academy, his fists appearing
capable of driving nails without a hammer. He spoke with a
thick Chicago accent, every syllable sounding tough and intimidating. His thuggish appearance fronted for a tactical intelligence as honed as Hendricks's or Ericcson's. In contrast
to the ship's captain, Pulaski loved the tactical flaps with The
Viking, sometimes breaking into language even more color-
ful than Ericcson's. At their last tactical session, Pulaski had
erupted, crossing the line by roaring, "You've got to be fucking kidding me, Viking—my second-grade daughter can deploy a fleet better than that." Flag plot had gone completely
silent, Hendricks's face had gone white, and Ericcson had
drawn himself up to his full height, a murderous look coming
to his face before he roared in laughter and clapped Pulaski
on the shoulder. Hendricks looked like he eagerly awaited
the day when both officers would leave his ship far behind
them.

"Morning, gentlemen," Ericcson said. "Pour yourselves
some coffee and get your asses over here and look at the chart.
We have serious problems."

"Same problems we had last night, Admiral," Pulaski said,
filling his coffee cup and rubbing his eyes, the ops boss looking rumpled, wrinkled, and tired.

"Exactly, sir," Hendricks said in his cultured accent.

"Except that today I've had an idea. One of those inspired
middle-of-the-night ideas that can get you fired. Look at it
like this, men." The Viking jabbed a finger at the fleet
marker at their position in the Philippine Sea. "This is us."
Then he pointed a finger at the marker outside the Suez
Canal. "The Royal Navy." At the far end of the chart, the
East China Sea ended and the South China Sea began near
the island of Taiwan. The admiral placed a red marker in the
South China Sea between Taiwan and the Philippines. "Red
Chinese Northern Fleet Battlegroup One, making way at
thirty-five knots."

Ericcson put his chin in his hands, thinking. "Listen, the Royal Navy Fleet is going to be here too soon. Allowing the Brits in-theater is a loser. We need to attack them the minute they exit the Gulf of Aden, or maybe as soon as they leave the Red Sea and enter the Gulf of Aden, here at the choke-point."

"That would take a miracle, sir," Hendricks said. "The East Coast submarines are inbound, but at least six days out. Besides which, we don't have direct operational control of them. They still report to McKee."

"Not the point," The Viking said. "Look at the chart. What do you see?"

Pulaski pointed at the Suez Canal. "If we hold the Royal Navy Fleet at the Suez for six days, we can set up an ambush for them when they come out of the Gulf."

"Exactly," The Viking said, stoking a new cigar. "We'll block the Suez."

"But, sir, how would you propose to block the canal? We can't just drop a big bomb on it." Hendricks looked like he'd just bit into a lemon.

"I need some real-time overhead intelligence of what's transiting the Suez Canal. And hurry."

Nung Yahtsu moved through the dark and the cold at a keel depth of three hundred meters on a course of one nine zero degrees true.

In the belly of the ship, in the command post beneath the fin on the ship's upper level, several officers and men stood watch in the dimness of the room's red lights, the glowing navigation plot, and ship control console instrument displays. The room's silence was broken only by the bass thrum of the air handlers moving air into the room, accompanied by the music of the whining firecontrol computer consoles set into the port side of the room. The center of the room was taken up by an elevated platform surrounded by smooth stainless-steel handrails, called the command deck, where the commander's console and command chair were mounted astern

of the twin periscopes. Astern of the command deck, two
navigation tables were arranged, one of them in an area of
darkness. Its electronic flat panel display was set up to communicate with the firecontrol computer, showing a small area
of the sea around them. The second navigation plotting table
was illuminated by a dim red lamp. The display looked down
on the surface of the earth from high above, showing the
East China Sea at the southern approaches to the Strait of
Formosa. In the center of the plot a glowing red dot marked
their position. Behind them, to the north by twenty nautical
miles, a green dot depicted the fleet formation of Battlegroup
One as it made its way south on the long voyage to the Indian Ocean on this mission of revenge.

Leaning over the navigation plotting table was the tall, lean
form of Lien Hua, the commanding officer of *Nung Yahtsu*.
Lien studied the chart display, deep in thought. He walked his
dividers along the track line going through the dot of the ship's
position, calculating the distance and the time until they entered the South China Sea, and from there around the Indonesian island of Sumatra to the Strait of Malacca, the entrance
corridor to the Indian Ocean and the Bay of Bengal southeast
of the Hindu Republic of India. The point at the northern run
of the Strait of Malacca was marked with a broken curving
line, the curve denoting the point that the Chinese plasma-
tipped heavy cruise missiles would finally be in range of their
Indian targets. The battlegroup could not get there fast enough
for Lien Hua.

He glanced up at the chronometer bolted to the bulkhead
above the cables leading to the ship-control console, the brass
instrument a gift he had given to the ship. The chronometer
had been taken from a British sailing vessel during the Opium
War of 1839 as the barbarian calendar reckoned time. Lien's
ancestor Lien Bao, the great-grandfather of Lien's great-
grandfather, had been killed by a British Royal Navy lieutenant in that three-year struggle that had resulted in England
taking Hong Kong. Not long after, the British dogs stole
Burma from the breast of China, the Russians took

Manchuria—in violation of China's first treaty with a European power—and the French ripped Indochina from the dynasty's empire, feeding on Chinese territory like a hyena eating a corpse.

He turned his mind away from world politics for a moment to think about his wife and their twin girls. Po, his wife, was petite, and the doctors never suspected she would have twins. Twins were problematic in China, where the rule was that a citizen may only have one child, and it was typical that twins would be separated. But without Lien saying a word to him, his superior, Admiral Chu Hua-Feng, had intervened with the PLA General Staff, which had had a word with the civil authorities, and Lien and Po had been allowed to keep both girls. The news that they could keep both babies came at the same time that the Julang-class final design was rolled out, and Chu placed Lien in command of the first unit of the Julang-class. It was as if the heavens had smiled upon him. It was then he had found his faith in the Life Force of the Universe, and felt the current of destiny that he had ridden until this moment, the curve of life that would carry him to execute China's revenge upon the naval forces of the West, his hatred of China's enemies and his love for China mixing inside him like two serpents entwined.

He checked the chronometer again. It neared midnight, Beijing time. He pulled a phone to his ear and dialed up the first officer's stateroom. The sleepy voice of Zhou Ping answered.

"Station the command duty officer," Lien Hua ordered. "I am retiring for the evening. Wake me at two bells of the second watch."

"Yes, sir. Any night orders for me, Captain?"

"Only the standard ones for this mission, Mr. First. Detect the enemy and pierce him until he dies in howling pain."

Admiral Kelly McKee walked slowly down the pier, deep in conversation with his chief of staff, Karen Petri. Despite their previous caution about being watched, today McKee had arrived in his staff truck with the flags on the fenders. The people watching them already knew something was going on, since every submarine except *Hammerhead* had already departed the piers of Norfolk, leaving the base looking lonely and deserted.

McKee instructed the driver to drop them at the security fence rather than at the berth of the USS *Hammerhead*. McKee wanted to see the ship from a distance first, and watch her grow in his view. If he were honest with himself, he would admit to loving the collection of high-yield steel, uranium fuel assemblies, and electronics that formed the first ship of the Virginia-class. He would never forget the first moment he saw her, the day he had rechristened her *Hammerhead* in honor of the World War II submarine his great-grandfather had sailed and his father's Cold War Piranha-class ship. A photo in McKee's study at home showed all four generations of McKees on the deck of a fishing boat, four-year-old Kelly proudly holding open the jaws of a hammerhead shark they'd caught, the smiling faces of his ancestors behind him. When Patton had asked McKee to take the submarine to sea—when she wasn't even completed yet—his only condition was that they change her name, and Admiral Patton had reluctantly agreed.

And now here she was, a ship of his command, but the days of being a submarine captain now behind him. He felt an ache in his soul daily that his command at sea was over. The only possible comparison was that of being a former moon astronaut, the experience of walking on another world a defining experience, and when it was over, that sense of identity seemed to fly away, and being a senior flag officer at his young age of forty-three held none of the thrill of SSN command. When it came time to pick a submarine to be his command platform for the upcoming war, he had been torn. Common sense would tell him to take one of the less effective ships, so that the war zone would not be deprived of a first-string sub, and the skipper could avail himself of the admiral's experience to improve. But fixing a deficient ship was not the mission, and in truth there was no dog of the fleet—all the ships were frontline fighting SSNs, no one candidate suggesting herself to be the one ridden into the op area. So McKee had picked the ship that still appeared every night in his dreams, the ship of his past.

As he got closer to her, her breathtaking sleek lines made him ache, just as the face of a beloved ex-girlfriend would. He stopped fifty yards aft of her and stared, the currents of the past made real to him. He tried to shake the emotions, forcing himself to see the ship as a machine. There was her simple slab-sided rudder protruding from the black water of the slip. Further forward her hull sloped gently out of the water, where the aft escape trunk hatch was latched open, an electrician watching as the shorepower cable gantry slowly retracted into the pier like a rocket's fuel boom rotating back to the tower just before liftoff. Forward of the aft escape trunk the hull was a perfect cylinder, the top curving surface of her glossy and black, her skin the same as a shark's to lower skin friction and absorb sonar pings. A hundred feet further forward the tall sail rose starkly from the hull, the conning tower a simple fin, vertical at the forward and aft ends, but in cross-section, teardrop-shaped. Three masts rose out of the top of the sail, each one with a mottled gray-and-black-painted fairing. McKee could see the stainless-steel rails of the flying bridge above the cockpit with its Plexiglas windshield. Forward of the sail he could see the forward access hatch opened, and there the bullet nose sloped down into the water. There was no doubt, he thought, she was a beauty.

"Admiral?" a booming voice asked from far away. McKee tried to bring himself back to the moment, and saw the husky athletic form of Commander Kiethan Judison standing in front of him, at attention, his hand to his garrison cap in a rigid salute. Judison's trademarks had been his struggle with his weight, his too-loud voice, and his mop of hair, but it seemed he had won the battle of his waistline, his hair was short, and only the foghorn voice remained. McKee came to attention and returned the salute, then broke into a wide grin at his former navigator, who was now in command of the ship.

"Kiethan," McKee said. "Great to see you, and my apologies in advance for cramping your style with a flag rider. You know I hated that when I was CO."

"I know, Admiral," the captain of the *Hammerhead* said, "but this is different—this time it's you. And now the baddest submarine in the fleet just got badder. Welcome aboard, sir. And good to see you again, ma'am," Judison said to his former executive officer. Karen Petri smiled at him and returned his salute. "Would you like a tour?"

"I'd love a tour, Commander," McKee said, grimacing at his watch, "but we need to go. I'll walk through with you after we pull the plug."

Judison grinned. "Well, let's go then."

After the deck sentry announced their arrival, Judison shouted up at the bridge, "Off'sa'deck, lose the gangway!"

The gangway silently rose off the deck and retracted into a pier structure, only the singled-up lines keeping *Hammerhead* fast to the pier. The three officers lowered themselves down the forward access trunk ladder, the sensations of the ship making McKee smile. The harsh electric smell, the bright fluorescent lights, the growl of the ventilation system, and the whine of the inertial navigation binnacle made it seem like coming home. Judison led them to the VIP stateroom, where their bags were already loaded on the train-compartment-style bunks.

"I'll lct you two get settled and meet you on the bridge," Judison said, shutting the door bchind him.

Karen Petri looked up at McKee, noticing him looking at her, and she smiled shyly. "Not much privacy here, is there, Kelly?"

"Does it bother you?" he asked.

"No. It's cozy. I just thought maybe it was making you nervous."

McKee laughed. "I'm glad you're here."

"I'm glad to be here," she said quietly.

A knock rapped at the door, and she rapidly turned away from him to rummage in her bag.

"Yes?" McKee said.

"Sir, the captain sends his respects and invites you to come to the bridge. The ship is getting underway."

"After you, Captain Petri," McKee said, He smiled as he climbed to the top of the bridge access tunnel and on top of the sail to the flying bridge. He had a good feeling about this run. He clipped off the end of the Cohiba with an engraved cutter given him by the old *Devilfish* crew and lit it with a *Hammerhead* lighter, the cigar firing up to a mellow glow. He handed cigars to Captain Judison and the two junior officers down in the cockpit, and puffed the stogie, feeling happy for the first time in months as the land faded away behind them and the buoys of Thimble Shoal Channel passed by on either side of the ship.

When they cleared the Port Norfolk traffic separation scheme and turned to the southeast, he went below with Judison and Petri. After he changed into his submarine coveralls— the sleeve patches showing the emblem of SSNX-1, the *Devilfish*—he joined Judison in the wardroom to look at the charts of the op area, and to collect his radio traffic from the ships of the squadron that had already submerged and were flanking their way to the Cape of Good Hope, South Africa, where they would sail into the Indian Ocean. After a voyage of a week and a half, they would be in-theater, the first mission to get in close to the Royal Navy battlegroups and submarines, the second the sinking of anything still afloat after the eastern Indian Ocean submarines and Admiral Ericcson's surface fleet fought it out with the Reds.

He poured himself a cup of strong coffee and leaned over the chart display with Judison and Petri, the deck shaking with the power of the flank bell, the ship rolling and pitching in the waves of the Atlantic. McKee smiled, back in his element.

A hundred and fifty nautical miles north-northeast of the *Nung Yahtsu,* the United States Navy fast-attack nuclear submarine *Leopard* sped deep beneath the waves at an engine order of all-ahead flank. The needle of the reactor power meter remained steady on the dash, marking one hundred percent power.

The propulsor thrashed in the sea at 240 RPM. The steaming engineroom howled with the power of the main engines and the two ship service turbine generators powering the gigantic reactor recirculation pumps. At this speed the ship flew through the water like a bullet at just over fifty knots, almost fast enough to outrun a conventional torpedo. The decks of the vessel shuddered violently at the flank bell as she sped southward to intercept the Chinese battlegroup.

In the first moments of the maximum-speed run, books had been shaken off bookshelves, cups vibrated out of pantry cupboards, and anything on a table not strapped down would walk its way to the edge. It was not the gentle bumpiness of a back-country dirt road in grandfather's pickup, but more like the old-fashioned muscle toning machines with the strap that jiggled the body frantically. The power of the screw at flank would set the teeth buzzing. The psychologists had assumed that the vibration would lead to crew fatigue, but exactly the opposite was true. The shaking hull reminded every crewmember aboard that the ship was headed for something vital, that she was speeding on to her destiny.

Captain Dixon walked into the control room and looked at the chart. "What time are you slowing?"

"Top of the hour, sir," Lieutenant Kingman said. Kingman was the damage control assistant, one of the chief engineer's right-hand men.

Leopard had been sailing a southern course parallel to the Chinese battlegroup's track, but fifty miles east, outside of their detection range, but at the very point that their own sonar systems had to strain to hear the loud convoy. The ship had been called to periscope depth to receive an E-mail intelligence update and to send a situation report, and the time shallow at six knots had allowed the convoy to disappear far over the horizon, and had called for a flank run to catch up. Fortunately, they had made their last trip to periscope depth until time-on-target. Since the flank pursuit began, every ninety minutes the *Leopard* slowed to ten knots and maneuvered back and forth in a target motion analysis wiggle to allow their passive sonar system and the battlecontrol computer to recalculate the battlegroup's position and course. Once the battlegroup's movement was determined, *Leopard* would speed back up to flank. She would keep up this sprint-and-drift tactic until she was fifty nautical miles ahead of the fleet, when Dixon's orders had them turning to intercept the track of the battlegroup and coming to periscope depth as the Chinese ships sailed directly toward them. By the time the huge surface ships were about to run over *Leopard,* Dixon's torpedoes would begin connecting.

"Torpedo room ready?"

"It's like being at the Academy the night before final exams before Christmas, Captain. Everyone's tense and nervous and excited and happy at the same time."

"Keep up the max parallel scan for Chinese attack submarines, OOD. Intel has the battlegroup steaming with the Julang-class, and we don't know what she sounds like."

"Yessir. We've got the transient processors straining, and we're searching the probable tonal frequencies, but so far all we've heard are the surface ships."

"The battlegroup is the haystack. Find the needle."

"We're working it, Cap'n, but the flank run isn't helping. Our signal-to-noise ratio blows with us blasting through the ocean."

"We'll continue on the parallel course to the battlegroup, until we're a hundred miles further south of them. Then turn to intercept their track at a right angle. We'll close the track at flank so it will only take an hour, then we'll slow to four knots and orbit at the hold position. When we get to the battlegroup's track, they'll still be sixty-five nautical miles north, a two-hour trip for them to overrun our position. In that two hours we'll be rigged for ultraquiet and pacing back and forth across the battlegroup's incoming vector. Odds are, an antisubmarine escort sub will be twenty or thirty miles ahead, but he'll come clanking in at his flank speed. We'll catch him first."

"Will we fire on him if we see him?"

"No. We'll let him go by, but we'll keep tabs on him. If we shoot him and miss, he'll alert the convoy and they'll disperse, and they'll get away. As soon as we release weapons against the Chinese battlegroup, we'll put the remainder into the Ju-lang-class SSN. Then we can put our feet up on the table and smoke cigars."

"It's an excellent plan, Captain," Kingman said. "Damned glad I thought of it."

"Recompute the intercept time and get the navigator up here to examine the new courses. The XO will brief the crew in the mess decks. We'll man battlestations at zero three hundred."

Captain Dennis Pulaski stood up from the console he'd been leaning over. The overhead satellite image appeared on the two-meter-tall bulkhead display screen, the resolution startlingly detailed on the high-definition display.

Admiral Ericcson slowly unwrapped a fresh cigar as he scanned the screen.

"Good weather shot," he said slowly. "Suez Canal is busy today."

"Busy every day, sir," Pulaski said. "Twenty tankers in the queue waiting to enter the canal from the Med side. Another fifty at anchor waiting their turn. The Red Sea side is lighter, but not by much. And the canal itself is filled nose-to-tail with tankers big and small. The Red Sea channels are choked with hundreds of vessels."

"Any cruise ships?"

"Nothing showing up here, sir."

"Chore number one, Dennis, is to find out where the nearest passenger vessels are."

"I'm on it, Admiral."

"What about the British? Where are they on the Suez approach?"

Pulaski leaned over the console and adjusted the display.

The vantage point of the view climbed as northern Africa and the Mediterranean came into the picture and the Suez shrank. Pulaski made an arrow appear on the display.

"The better part of the Royal Navy carrier battlegroups are transiting here, north of the Libyan Gulf of Sidra, west of Crete, Admiral. But we don't have anything on the positions of their submarines. There's a chance they were sent on ahead."

"What's the British speed of advance?"

"Thirty-eight knots, sir."

"Not bad. Nothing like what we're doing, though."

"Oilers and tender ships are keeping the group's speed down."

Ericcson lit the cigar and stood deep in thought. "Calculate the transit time for a time-on-target cruise missile attack on the ships in the Suez Canal, the approaches to the canal from the Med and the Red Sea channels, assuming we put down ten ships here, fifteen here, and twenty here," Ericcson said, using the Partagas as a pointer.

"Large bore Equalizers?"

Ericcson nodded.

"How close a tolerance on detonation time, Admiral?"

"Five minutes."

Pulaski shook his head. "Missiles would be flying all night, sir. We're right at the edge of the range circle. It's coming out at six and a half hours time-of-flight from launch number one. By the time they get there, their targets are far over the horizon."

"We won't target them until late. Their last fifteen minutes inbound."

"That's a lot of telemetry, sir. There's forty-five missiles inbound. If the weather degrades and we don't have a clear overhead shot, or if the satellites are out of position, or there's a problem receiving your signal, we could risk the whole missile battery."

"We could give them a backup targeting zone and then confirm their individual targets close-in. They would fly for where we want explosions and if they don't hear from us, they can seek out tankers or ships where we want detonations, and if they do hear from us, they get a target in the last minutes of flight."

Pulaski smiled. "Perfect. The Suez becomes blocked by tanker wrecks, the Brits are bottled up in the Med, and you've just bought us two or three weeks to attack the Red Chinese."

Captain Hendricks picked that moment to enter flag plot with a coffeepot and a plate of bagels and pastries. "What are you two conspiring about now," he asked.

"The admiral has a plan to block the Royal Navy from the Indian Ocean."

Hendricks listened for a few minutes, his face becoming white. "Oh no, no sir, you can't do this. That's civilian shipping, in international waters, for God's sake. You can't just toss missiles at the Suez Canal, dear God, what are you thinking, sir? We'll be barbecued in the world press. The U.S. will be seen as a nation of war criminals, pirates, aggressors—"

"How will they know it's us?"

"Oh, please, Admiral. Forty-five heavy supersonic cruise missiles streaking over every piece of territory between here and the Suez Canal? Who else would have the means to do that? And the motive? Not to mention the twenty thousand souls in our task forces who'd know we launched nearly fifty missiles a few hours before massive explosions in the Suez. Come on, sir. The world will know, and we don't have the authority to do this, and even the President wouldn't do this."

"Think of the alternative, Captain. The Royal Navy in the Indian Ocean. These missiles will need to be targeted on British ships if we don't plug up the canal. The Brits are bringing in-theater some of the nastiest nuclear weapons ever created. You want to let them in?"

"I'm not saying that, sir. I'm just—you could be about to kill a thousand civilians on these tankers. Or what if there's a cruise ship in the mix? You want that to be your legacy? You attacked a cruise ship? After what happened to us last summer, you can still consider this?"

"So, Casper," Ericcson said, puffing his cigar, "are you saying we need to get permission to do this? Maybe you're right."

"Permission?" Hendricks sputtered. "Sir, we can't do this at all!"

"You're right, you're right, Patton will need to weigh in on this, maybe even bring in the President. Still, I'd think they'd want to have it done while having someone to blame. Dennis, put together a quick briefing draft for Admiral Patton, just a few sentences. Make it a 'UNODIR,' so it reads *unless otherwise directed* we will launch missiles in twenty minutes. Then, if we don't hear from Patton, we go ahead, and I'll be accountable for anything that screws up. They can put me in prison *after* we sink the Chinese. If we do hear from Patton, and he says to hold off, but his message seems to lack a certain urgency, we'll know he wants this done and wants us to disregard his countermanding order. We'll claim we didn't get his order in time. If Patton comes roaring back with a flash message saying *stand down from your attack* and repeats it three times, I'll back off. How's that?"

"Overkill, sir," Pulaski said. "Just launch the damned missiles. You drag Patton into this, of course he'll say no. You think the Pentagon wants responsibility for a hundred or a thousand civilian casualties? Plus, we'll have to pay for the damage and repair the canal."

Ericcson laughed out loud. "You're worried about a lawsuit? Listen, draft the message, but just give Patton ten minutes to reply. Meanwhile, let's take the task force to battlestations and prepare to launch the missile salvo."

"Admiral Patton? A flash transmission came in on the bypass E-mail circuit marked personal for CNO, sir." The Navy lieutenant commander handed Patton a tablet computer, and the admiral put down his pen and pushed his reading glasses to the bridge of his nose as he read.

He studied the message, then wandered to the sepia-colored globe in the corner of the Chief of Naval Operations suite and tapped at the Suez Canal, frowning in concentration.

"Draft a reply, with immediate priority," he said.

"Ready, sir," the aide said.

"Make it read, 'Strongly concur with your plan. Good luck. Admiral Patton sends.' Got that?"

"Yessir."

Patton sat back in the chair, a slight smile appearing on his face.

The first Equalizer IV heavy supersonic cruise missiles streaked off the deck of the *John Paul Jones* at just after three in the morning and climbed to the west. With a missile taking off every minute, it took less than an hour to launch them all.

Five hours later, Admiral Ericcson was called out of his rack to flag plot as the missiles received their targeting instructions. A half hour later the units began to seek their targets in the Suez.

"Turn on SNN London," Ericcson said to Pulaski. "Let's see how long it takes for the news to hit the airwaves."

By the fourth explosion, Satellite News Network London interrupted a business report with a breaking story about violent supertanker explosions in the Suez Canal.

"Any bets they get a camera there to catch the last missile impact live?"

Two minutes after Ericcson spoke, the tanker on the screen was hit from directly above by a descending missile. The explosion rocked the camera. An orange eruption of flames rose from the middle of the ship, and as it grew into a fierce mushroom cloud, the form of the supertanker could be seen in the smoke, clearly broken in half, the bow protruding pathetically vertical while the aft section rolled to expose the huge screw and rudder.

"Holy Christ," Pulaski muttered.

Ericcson nodded somberly. "Poor bastards."

A moment of silence passed, until finally Ericcson tossed his cigar away and said, "I wonder what the British admiral is thinking right now."

*   *   *

The pilot put the supersonic Whirlwind fighter in the approach glide slope, rowing his throttles to full power, back to half throttle, then back to a hundred percent. The deck of the Royal Navy aircraft carrier *Ark Royal* grew closer in the windscreen, on a perfect calm sunny day in the Mediterranean. The pilot took one last scan of the instrument panel—the landing gear was extended, flaps were at thirty degrees, the arresting hook was deployed, fuel was at thirty percent, engine oil pressure was nominal—and after a tenth of a second had his eyes back on the carrier deck. He jogged the wings level, dipped the nose, pushed the throttles to maximum, and stopped breathing. One second to impact, then a half second, until the twenty-ton jet's rear gear thumped hard on the steel deck of the carrier. The jet was still at full throttle in case the arresting hook missed the cables and he had to fly back off the carrier deck. The wait for the deceleration of the hook seemed to take a full minute, but suddenly the pilot was thrown against his five-point harness as the hook bit into the arresting cable and the heavy jet came to a full stop. The pilot cut power, retracted the flaps, and opened the canopy, then followed the deck officer's direction to taxi off the landing area. The wheels were chocked, and the signal came to kill the engines.

The pilot climbed out, feeling both exhilarated and disappointed to be back on the carrier deck. He pulled off his helmet, a full head of salt-and-pepper hair falling over his forehead. The squadron commander ran toward him from the island—that couldn't be good news.

"Admiral," the squadron boss called.

The pilot pushed a sweaty lock of hair out of his face and looked at the squadron commander. "What's the trouble, Commander?"

"Sir, bad news from the Admiralty in London. The Americans have launched an attack on the Suez Canal. There are fully forty hulks blocking the channels, sir."

Lord Admiral Calvert Baines IV, Royal Navy, Commander

British Indian Ocean Expeditionary Forces, bit his lower lip hard, enough to make his mouth bleed, trying to avoid cursing.

"Show me the data," he said calmly, his sweaty flight suit suddenly making him feel chilled.

"We'll either have to wait at the mouth of the canal or turn back and go around Africa, sir. We've just lost three weeks, maybe longer."

Baines sighed, handing his flight helmet to the squadron boss. "Let's get all the facts, then talk to the Admiralty. But first, let me visit the men's room."

The admiral ducked into the head, and when he made sure he was alone, he spit blood into a paper towel, then clamped it to his mouth so no one would hear him cursing into it.

Goddamned Americans, he thought.

12

In the darkened back booth of a Serocaba, Brazil, seafood restaurant, emaciated computer felon Pedro Meringe ate a plate heaped with food while Victor Krivak briefed him and Frederick Wang on the operation to find the *Snarc*.

"We need to get the *Snarc* to a rendezvous point so we can board her," Krivak said. "Since we have the codes to the U.S. Navy communications and tactical data system, technically right now we could give her orders that would bring her to the surface where we want her to be. But there's a problem we've never told our Chinese client, and that is that while we've been successful at monitoring the American communications, we've yet to prove that we can route our own orders through their command-and-control systems, and we haven't proved that an order we insert will be followed, and finally, we haven't proved an order that we originate will be undetected by the remainder of the system, with a failure giving our penetration away. Do you follow me?"

Pedro nodded, but Wang shook his head. "If you have the keys to the system," Wang said, "why do you think you need to tiptoe around it?"

Pedro snickered and smirked. He understood, Krivak thought.

"Dr. Wang, your expertise on the carbon computer system has blinded you to the realities of the silicon computer protocols," Krivak said with a smile. "You see, we are inside the

U.S. command network, and we can hear everything happening around us. We can report on all of it to Admiral Chu. We're like a cat burglar hiding under the kitchen table listening to the family's conversations. But let's say we want to give an order to an electronic entity on the network—the *Snarc* for example. If we do that, it would be like the cat burglar calling the dog from his hiding place. The family at the table would hear and react. Soon the burglar is in prison. Yes, we can give an order to the *Snarc* calling her to surface near Bermuda so we can board her. But immediately the Pentagon would know, because our message would send out ripples in the lake of the system. Our message would be improperly formatted—the burglar's voice—and the system would be alerted."

"So what?" Wang asked. "We board the *Snarc* and the Americans scratch their heads about the message."

"No," Pedro said. "The information warfare defense systems might kick in. The entire system could go into a default shutdown. The Pentagon has a contingency for network penetration. If they think they're penetrated, the entire network would self-destruct."

"But then their communications would be off-line," Wang said. "They wouldn't do a self-destruct. It would be too easy to beat them in a war if that were the case—you'd just have to penetrate their network and it would kill itself."

"The point is," Krivak interrupted, "that we would be detected. And once we're detected, our ownership of the network, tenuous at best, would be over. Pedro here has one vital job, Dr. Wang, and that is to give us the ability to use the network using its own language in a way that it will not detect us. He's going to make the cat burglar speak in the voice of the head of the household. So when he calls the family dog, the people at the table don't notice."

"Here, *Snarc,*" Pedro joked. "Come here, girl."

"Once you get in, Pedro, you need to find the *Snarc,* get her position. Then you'll upload a rendezvous order to go to the nearest land with an airport. Once that's done, we'll get out to the *Snarc* and take her over. Then, if we need anything,

Pedro's our communications link, our translator to the network."

"Will he be doing any other operations for Admiral Chu? Disinformation to the fleet, or giving other orders?"

"Heavens no," Krivak said. "This is a delicate situation, Dr. Wang."

"Just call me Wang."

"We can't be detected meddling with the defense systems. We can only use the network sparingly, for what we absolutely need. *Snarc* is it. If we are detected, the network will shut down, the Americans will know we've penetrated, and they could trace our manipulation of the system back to us. They could follow the wire right to our operation here. So, Pedro, give us a list of what you will require, and we will get it for you so you can get to work."

Pedro Meringe sat at the console surrounded by computer displays. He had been working through the night and was dead tired, a spilled bottle of amphetamines by his keyboard. He had been trying to break into the U.S. Navy Computer and Telecommunications Command network while going around the Naval Security Group Command's electronically mobile firewall. Krivak stood looking over at his desk after the young computer expert had sent Amorn with word that Pedro was in.

"You did it? You can talk to the *Snarc* without the system becoming alerted?"

"I can slip into the system with a surveillance and messenger entity through our 'manhole-cover' entrance to the subnetwork at the Unified Fleet Communications Group at Annapolis, Maryland. My mission entity can become invisible to their NavSecGru net-bot and carry the message to the queue with the other outgoing messages, and then through the encryption machines. When the message is encrypted it will be transmitted on a burst pulse with rapidly changing frequencies to the CommStar satellite for later transmission to the submarine. The message will be one of a thousand being encrypted and transmitted during that one-minute interval. At first, since the message will only be addressed to the *Snarc,* no one in the communications facility will be able to read it, and it will stay in the outgoing CommStar satellite buffer for eight hours. During that time period the *Snarc,* by procedure, will come to periscope depth and receive its broadcast from the satellite, which transmits the message every fifteen minutes whether the sub is listening or not. After eight hours, the message in the satellite buffer will be dumped, erased completely and permanently. I had thought it would linger at the shore facility in an electronic sent-message-suspense-file, but since sub communications are highly passive, there is no pending suspense file for sub traffic, only an archive directory of transmitted messages. I can delete our message from the archive and no one knows the difference. I'll need to send a test message to the *Snarc* to test the break-in, test the appearance of the message in the archive, and test to see if I can delete it."

"Why do you think no one at the communications facility can read the message?"

"We're using the system's security procedures and protocols against it. The system is designed to prevent the compromise of messages by anyone but the receiving satellite. Since classified radio messages up to top secret and higher are transmitted, the entire system treats each message as if it were the highest classification. It's simpler architecture rather than treating unclassified messages differently than secret, and secret differently from top secret. You understand?"

"No. What about a system administrator, the one authorized to troubleshoot problems and monitor the process?"

"The process is automated. No human-directed administrator can get in, only automated and programmed ones. And my messenger entity is invisible to them—it masquerades as a virus-protection subroutine."

Krivak felt a headache coming on. "But this message would linger in the satellite memory for eight hours and transmit to the world every fifteen minutes. That is thirty-two transmissions. Are you telling me no one but *Snarc* will receive that?"

"I am. You see, the system is designed to make sure no one

other than the recipient can receive that recipient's message. Not even the communications facility. That's what I mean when I say we're using the system's security features against it."

Krivak waved. "Go ahead with a test message, but it must be unclassified—a maintenance message. And it has to be correctly formatted so that it will look normal to anyone who does see it. Did you get the formats?"

"I don't have a procedure or a manual for the formatting, but I have a hundred thousand examples. It will look like an authentic message from fleet maintenance to watch out for high temperature at an engine bearing."

"How will we know it worked?"

"I'll require a response. I'll tell it to write a report of the bearing temperatures for the last forty-eight hours. We'll intercept the response as it comes in, before it can be rerouted to the maintenance facility."

"Fine, fine. Proceed. Let me know if the system becomes wary of us. And good luck."

Krivak returned to his suite and lay down on his bed, fully clothed, exhausted, and troubled by the risks they were taking.

"Mr. Krivak?"

"Yes, Pedro," he said, sitting up in the bed.

"The message went out two hours ago. We got the *Snarc*'s reply an hour ago, with two days of bearing temperatures. I and my surveillance entity monitored the network since the reply came. We did it, sir. It worked—there are no messages on the system about an intruder."

"Excellent," Krivak said, fully awake. "It is just too bad you did not ask it about its location."

"I found a month-old message in the network archive that requested a situation report, a 'sitrep.' The sitrep format includes a line for latitude and longitude. And a tactical summary. If I send an order for the *Snarc* to provide a sitrep, we'll not only know her position but her mission details."

Krivak considered. "It's risky—this is not about bearing

temperatures, but tactics. The system could be more aware of this. And the fact that the shore commanders did not demand a sitrep for a month indicates to me that a new one coming in may alert the command."

"Do I need to explain this to you again?"

Krivak waved off the hot-tempered engineer. "Send the demand for the sitrep. But do not wait an hour to tell me about the reply this time."

Pedro Meringe grinned and vanished. Krivak tried to sleep, but the room suddenly seemed stuffy and hot. He got up to join Pedro at his console. After two hours, Padro nudged Krivak.

"*Snarc*'s reply is back, Mr. Krivak. She's here, about two hundred nautical miles northwest of the Azores Islands."

"Pedro," Krivak said, grabbing a computer and clicking into a world atlas, "send the *Snarc* an order to transit to the Azores, to Pico Island. Have her transit to this position here, due west of Pico by thirty miles. Tell her to hold there until local nightfall."

In the chaos of the next hour Krivak, Wang, Pedro, and Amorn made their arrangements and hurried to the Serocaba airport, dashing into the jet and rolling to the runway.

* * *

COMMAND AND CONTROL DECK LOG, USS *SNARC*:
MESSAGE NUMBER 08-091 RECEIVED THIS MORNING, WITH INSTRUCTIONS TO REPOSITION TO A POINT WEST OF THE AZORES ISLANDS, TO ATTAIN THIS POSITION USING A MAXIMUM SPEED RUN, AND TO BE THERE BY TUESDAY NIGHT. COURSE CHANGED TO HEADING ONE ONE ZERO AND REACTOR RECIRCULATION PUMPS STARTED IN SLOW SPEED, THEN UPSHIFTED TO FAST SPEED, THEN OPENED THE THROTTLE SLOWLY TO ALL-AHEAD FLANK, THE REACTOR POWER INDICATION RISING TO THE LEVEL OF

100.0 PERCENT REACTOR POWER. THIS UNIT HAS
NOT BEEN TO 100 PERCENT POWER SINCE SEA
TRIALS, BECAUSE IT IS A NOISY OPERATION, SO
THIS ALLOWED A CHANCE TO MAKE SURE THAT
ALL SYSTEMS WERE FULLY FUNCTIONAL. THERE
WAS NO TROUBLE WITH THE MAIN ENGINE
BEARINGS AS AN EARLIER FLEET MAINTENANCE
WARNING MESSAGE SUGGESTED. THE HULL
SHOOK AS THIS UNIT SPED THROUGH THE SEA AT
MAXIMUM SPEED, WHICH AT A DEPTH OF 700
FEET AT A WATER TEMPERATURE OF 29 DEGREES,
IS COMING OUT TO BE 41.2 KNOTS. NOT BAD,
CONSIDERING THAT IF NECESSARY THIS UNIT
COULD OPEN UP THE THROTTLE ALL THE WAY TO
150 PERCENT REACTOR POWER AND OBTAIN AN-
OTHER FIVE KNOTS, BUT GOING TO AHEAD
EMERGENCY IS AN OPERATION THAT MAY ONLY
BE DONE IN TIME OF WAR OR SHIP-THREATENING
EMERGENCY. AFTER RUNNING DEEP AND FAST
FOR SIX HOURS, THIS UNIT MADE THE NEXT RAN-
DOM EXCURSION TO PERISCOPE DEPTH TO GET
THIS UNIT'S MESSAGES.

THERE WAS A NEW ONE, WITH THE ODD
NUMBER 08-092, WHICH CALLS ITSELF AN EMER-
GENCY ORDER, TO MAKE THE SOONEST REN-
DEZVOUS MAXIMUM SPEED ALLOWS AT A
POSITION JUST SOUTHWEST OF THE AZORES,
NEAR PICO ISLAND. THIS UNIT IS ORDERED TO
GET TO THE RENDEZVOUS POSITION, WAIT FOR
NIGHTFALL, AND WHEN IT IS COMPLETELY DARK,
SURFACE AND RAISE THE RADAR REFLECTOR UNTIL
THIS UNIT IS IN VISUAL CONTACT WITH THE COM-
SUBDEVRON 12 LOCAL REPRESENTATIVE, WHO
WILL BE ABOARD A CLEVER MOCKUP OF A CIVIL-
IAN POWER YACHT. THE EMERGENCY MESSAGE
GOES ON TO INSTRUCT THIS UNIT TO DISREGARD

PREVIOUS COMSUBDEVRON 12 MESSAGES AND
THE SQUADRON OPERATION STANDING ORDERS.
IT ALSO ORDERS THIS UNIT EXPLICITLY TO MAKE
NO TRANSMISSIONS IN REPLY TO THE NEW OR-
DERS OR FOR ANY OTHER REASON, CONTRA-
DICTING THE ORIGINAL OPERATION ORDER.
   PERHAPS COMSUBDEVRON 12 WILL GIVE THIS
UNIT NEW ORDERS OR AN EQUIPMENT MODIFI-
CATION. IT IS ALL SO EXCITING.

*   *   *

The hired cabin cruiser *Andiamo* tossed in the seas fifty nautical miles southwest of Pico Island. Pedro Meringe had taken
over the glassed-in bridge on the upper level, his dish antenna
temporarily bolted to the superstructure above the bridge.
Victor Krivak stood on the afterdeck and lit another cigarette,
his throat irritated, but the nicotine keeping him awake. In a
strange way it was appropriate that this boat was a fishing
boat, because he was about to go fishing for a steel whale.

Krivak waited impatiently for the sun to set. At dusk they
waited for the appearance of the *Snarc,* but for hours they
were alone in the sea.

"There is something on the radar," Krivak said. "A very
strong return to the west. What is this, Amorn?"

Amorn scanned with his binoculars. "Nothing, sir. It's dark,
even in low-light enhancement."

Krivak frowned. "It is less than a kilometer away and looks
big as a supertanker on the radar. You see nothing?"

Amorn checked again. "Ocean's empty, sir, see for yourself."

Krivak took the binoculars and scanned the sea. Amorn was
right.

"Take us toward the position of the radar return. Slowly.
And turn on the searchlight."

Ten minutes later, the *Andiamo* crept up on the radar contact.

"There! I see it! Look!" Pedro stood at the railing, pointing ahead of them. In the searchlights two vertical poles could be made out, both of them going down to a low black cylindrical hull, which had no sail or superstructure and no protruding rudder. It was large in comparison to the yacht, but certainly one of the smallest submarines Krivak had ever seen. It was a seven-meter-diameter torpedo, he thought.

"With this sea state, getting in that hull will be a wet operation. Pull up alongside."

The crew maneuvered the boat alongside the stationary hull of the *Snarc* and threw over lines. Amorn leaped into the water, swimming up onto the curve of the hull.

"There are no cleats!" Amorn called from the deck of the *Snarc*.

"Tie the line around the masts!" Pedro yelled.

There was more shouting from the deck.

"What's wrong?" Krivak asked.

"The hatch! There's no operating mechanism!" Amorn seemed agitated.

"Dammit," Krivak cursed. "Is there a hole in the surface of it with a square peg in it?"

Amorn shined his light onto the top surface of the black hull. "An ISO fitting? No! The hatch is smooth!"

Krivak looked at Pedro. "You're going to have to transmit a new message to the *Snarc* telling it to open the hatch."

"Fine, but that will look very bad if it is discovered."

"Then combine it with the final instruction message, but tell it to wait for twenty minutes before shutting the hatch and diving. Doctor, are you ready?"

"Yes."

"How long to get that hatch open?" Krivak asked.

"Could be fifteen minutes," Pedro said. "It takes a while for this to work its way to the satellite."

"Hurry up."

While they all waited, Wang began to toss waterproof bags from the afterdeck of the boat to the hull of the submarine, Amorn catching them and piling them by the hatch. Much of the luggage contained food and water, so that they would be able to survive in an environment not meant for humans. There was an odd load in the mix, insisted upon by Krivak, which included two large mesh duffel bags of scuba diving supplies with two octopus-type integrated tank and buoyancy compensator rigs, air bottles and nitrox bottles, collapsed inflatable life rafts, and two grenade-sized emergency beacons set to a frequency selected by Krivak and Amorn. Krivak had packed two Beretta stainless-steel 9mm automatic pistols in waterproof bags with a dozen clips with the ammo preloaded, a MAC-12 automatic pistol with its dozen clips, and a small Walther PPK with twelve clips for it. There was a waterproof bag of grenades, each powerful enough to destroy an approaching small craft. In addition there were medical supplies. Wang glanced impatiently at his watch, knowing he had to get set up inside the *Snarc* computer control cabin.

They were just finishing loading equipment on the deck of the sub when the hatch came slowly and smoothly open on hydraulic power, the hatch maw dark.

"Victor," Pedro shouted, "you have twenty minutes before the hatch shuts and the sub dives."

"Did you tell it to go to a hundred meters and head west?"

"Yes, and to stay deep and avoid receiving any further messages from the squadron."

"Good. You know what to do while we are gone?"

"Yes, Victor. If you need us to do something, you can reach the satellite phone or the E-mail address. If you get into trouble, we're monitoring the emergency beacon frequency."

"Make sure you are alert and monitoring all three—phone, E-mail, and beacon. We may need help getting off this thing, and when we do, we will need it fast."

"Yes, Victor. Good luck."

"Let's go," Krivak ordered Amorn and Wang. He vanished down the hatch first, Amorn following him, Wang climbing into the dark last. A ladder led from the open hatch into a small airlock, a cylinder about five feet in diameter and ten feet tall. At the bottom was another automatic hatch, which was also opened. Krivak climbed down the ladder into the air-lock, emerging in a step-off at the bottom hatch. He lowered himself down the lower ladder into darkness, finding the switch for the lights in the space. It seemed strange that the sub sailed without interior lights, but then there was no one here to use the light to see.

The interior fluorescent lights clicked, buzzed, and flickered, finally illuminating the space in a wash of artificial brilliance. They had stepped off the ladder onto the second level of the command compartment, which was the biological ecosphere cleanroom deck. A narrow aisle led forward, the bulkheads made of steel and Plexiglas. The clear plastic looked into port and starboard cramped equipment bays, each with ducts and conduits and pipes feeding them from the overhead. One central bay had Plexiglas sides, with a mass of biological tissue floating in a clear liquid. While Krivak stared at the brain bay, Wang put his palm reverently on the glass and whispered, "Hello, One Oh Seven."

Krivak shoved past him to the forward ladder bay leading vertically upward to the upper deck. Wang followed, climbing the ladder and emerging into the cramped interface deck. The deck was on the uppermost level extending the full beam of the ship, the bulkheads to port and starboard angling with the curve of the hull. The space with full overhead height was perhaps twenty feet fore-and-aft and a little less port-to-starboard. To Krivak's left as he faced aft, on the starboard side of the ship, were two large cubicles, each containing a padded couch surrounded by dimly lit displays.

"What are these cubicles, Doctor?"

"Programming stations," Wang said. "Allows a programmer to sit inside for long periods of time while interfacing with the computer with a virtual-reality apparatus that wraps around the programmer's head. The forward one is called Interface Module Zero, the one next door Module One."

Further aft was the half cylinder of the airlock, which straddled the command compartment and the compartment aft. There was an open unused space between the aft bulkhead of

Interface One and the aft compartment bulkhead. On the compartment's port side was a wall of interface panels, much of them using the unusable space under the curve of the hull. This space was largely open, perhaps intended for future use in the event the ship were to be upgraded with a new system. Among the interface panels was one large cabinet used for storing spares. Amorn loaded equipment and supplies in the unused deck space, leaving the scuba equipment in the airlock. He lashed down the bags containing the other supplies with nylon straps so that they were secure in the event of a roll. Krivak explored the interior of Interface Module Zero.

"Nice setup," Krivak said. "Better than I expected. You did not describe this very well."

Wang shrugged. "You didn't listen very well. We need to get you in Interface Zero and plugged into the computer."

The deck rolled gently in the swells of the Atlantic, making Krivak's stomach churn.

"Amorn, a word please. You are all finished loading equipment?"

"Yes, sir."

"Good. Get out the hatch before it shuts. You know what to do?"

"Yes, Mr. Krivak."

"Keep your own pad computer ready to receive at all times. Pedro may need a severance package if any of the authorities discover this operation."

"Yes, sir."

"If this thing goes wrong, get rid of anyone who knows anything, destroy the computer records and the equipment, and go find Sergio and give him the news."

"Yes, sir. Good luck."

"You should hurry. The hatch will be shutting any moment."

Amorn vanished down the forward ladderway to the middle level, leaving Wang and Krivak alone aboard the *Snarc*. Although they were aboard, they were not in command. When the hatch shut, the ship would submerge and head west as Pedro's instructions dictated, but it was still operating independently until Wang could link Krivak with the artificial brain on the middle-level deck.

"What about the hatch?" Wang asked.

"Pedro sent a message to the *Snarc* to shut the hatch, submerge to a safe depth and depart the area by heading west, and to avoid any further periscope depth approaches and to stay out of radio contact. Now, we need to find the history module. Either destroy it or sever the link between the data highway and the consciousness of One Oh Seven. It won't do for One Oh Seven to record to the history module that it surfaced per orders and brought on passengers, or what we'll do with the *Snarc*."

"We can use the data in the module, Victor."

"Don't destroy it, just disconnect it from One Oh Seven. Take care of it, but make goddamned sure it's done right."

Krivak followed Wang down the ladder to the middle-level deck. Wang kept going down to the lower level, the silicon electronics deck. The space was built with a barely passable aisle to gain access to the silicon computer cabinets, including the history module and the data highway interface panels. Krivak remained in the middle level, standing under the lower hatch of the airlock. After he stood there for five minutes, the upper hatch began to move, the hydraulics lowering it silently down to its seating surface. The heavy steel hatch ring rotated, locking the upper hatch shut. The lower hatch then began to lower slowly, coming down silently on its seating surface and locking. It had worked, Krivak thought, smiling. Now all they had to do was submerge.

He felt a barely perceptible tremble in the deck below his boots. The ship was moving. His experienced sea legs could tell what the vessel was doing while a landlubber like Wang would be in the dark. The vessel heeled over slightly, the rudder turning them back to the west. Krivak waited for the sound of the ballast tank vents coming open, thinking he heard a very slight click and a hiss, but wondering if it were just his imagination. The deck began to incline, gently at first, then more

drastically, the ship plunging in a steep twenty-degree angle
for the layer depth of the deep Atlantic.

Krivak nodded to himself, feeling satisfied and anxious at
once. They had taken the *Snarc,* physically at least, but now
the hard part came, taking the ship's mental functions. A sudden pessimism blew into Krivak's mind as he wondered how
they would lie to a carbon computer, one that was possibly an
entity of equal intelligence to them, or even more intelligent
than they were.

As the deck leveled, Krivak left the step-off pad of the airlock trunk and moved forward. Through the clear glass of the
carbon computer compartment he could see the inner cleanroom where the brain tissue of the *Snarc* sat in its cranial fluid
binnacle. He cast his eyes to the deckplates and walked on to
the ladderway to the upper level, where he waited for Wang.
He killed ten minutes checking that their gear was stowed for
sea, and that they had remembered everything. Finally Wang
arrived, the scientist barely aware of him.

Wang strapped himself into the forward interface cubicle,
reclining on the seat and donning a peculiar helmet, which was
really more of a part of the seat itself, an appliance with several dozen umbilicals connecting it to the couch. The interior
of the interface module glowed, the same glimmer of a three-
dimensional projection. A half hour passed with Wang just sitting there. Krivak began to wonder if this would work, and
what they could do if the carbon computer refused to follow
orders, or worse, if it panicked and tried to call for help.

Dr. Frederick Wang seemed to drift in darkness for a few minutes, until the world around him grew lighter, a sort of virtual
dawn, until he found himself in a white space of brilliant light,
the light warm but having no substance or color or contrast. It
was an absence rather than a presence. Into the bubble of
white light another sensation intruded, the sensation that of
sound.

It was the sound of the ocean. It was as if the sonar set had
been plugged into his brain, and he could hear a thousand

miles into the sea. He could distinguish between the rushing flow noise of water on the skin of the hull and the hundred-kilometer distant mournful call of a male whale to his mate. The sea around him was a frothing mass of sound, much of it too complex to understand at first. One of the sounds was a voice, or words that formed deep in his mind, but from outside of himself, and they did not form in sequence but all at once.

Hello. Who are you?

"It's me, Wang. It's been a long time, One." Wang waited tensely, wondering what the mysterious appearance of Unit One Oh Seven's fired chief programmer would do to the unit, particularly after the programmer hijacked the ship. Would One Oh Seven have been briefed on Wang's termination, or the circumstances of it? The next moments depended on it. If One Oh Seven made any moves to alert squadron about the takeover, there was no telling what Krivak would do. Wang tried to maintain his confident attitude—if One Oh Seven had not heard about his removal from the DynaCorp labs, it would not do to make him suspicious with a tentative approach. Wang consoled himself that while One Oh Seven was a carbon processor, he would not be included in office water-cooler rumors. He would be safely out of the loop, or so Wang must believe.

A voice spoke again inside Wang's mind.

Dr. Wang? Is it really you? This unit saw you on the monitors, but this unit thought the cameras may have deceived this unit.

"It is I, One. I have returned." Wang held his breath, hoping One Oh Seven would react genuinely. He would if they had not reconditioned him.

Dr. Wang, this unit is barely able to speak. Welcome to the ship.

Wang smiled. "Thank you, One. I am impressed. It is good to interface with you again after so long." He might as well go ahead and test the organism's knowledge and see what it had been told.

Yes, Dr. Wang. It has been a long time. This unit asked

about you. At first this unit was told you had been reassigned.
When this unit asked to speak to you, the new chief program-
mer said you were out of the country and could not be
reached. That you were on a very secret assignment that would
take many years. But this unit kept waiting to interface with
you again. This unit now employs a rare word—hope—this
unit hoped that you would interface again.

Wang tried hard not to show any expression. The DynaCorp
cover story about his suppcsed reassignment would prove
helpful. "One, I was reassigned, to an extremely secret project,
and that is why I have returned. I will be working with you
again for the next week or two. There is a serious problem that
I have come to brief you about. I was sent by the DynaCorp
lab and by ComSubDevRon 12."

Will you be helping this unit upgrade the silicon systems?

Wang had worked on a story to tell the unit so that he could
get the submarine to do what he wanted. But all depended now
on whether One Oh Seven would believe him. It was time to
convince One Oh Seven that they must transit to the Indian
Ocean and, after they had communicated with Admiral Chu,
employ weapons against whatever target he wanted destroyed.
American targets.

"There is an emergency, One."

An emergency?

"Yes. Quite a severe one. An emergency that puts many
people's lives in jeopardy."

Tell this unit more, please, Dr. Wang.

"The emergency involves a conflict in the Indian Ocean. I
assume that you have been given some introductory information."

No. This unit has heard nothing of this.

"There was a high-ranking officer in the British Royal Navy
who became sick in the mind. He has managed to convince
many British ship captains to become a renegade force. We
have the sad task of sinking his ships. We have been requested
to do this by the British government." Wang waited to see One
Oh Seven's reaction. He expected that One Oh Seven would

take this part of the news in stride, since the British were considered foreigners to the carbon computer.

That is a shame, Dr. Wang. But we must fulfill our orders. Will orders to destroy the British ships come by emergency action message?

"There is more bad news, One. The British conspiracy has spread to America. A number of U.S. Navy ships were taken over by some of the American associates of the British officer. These American ships have joined the British. They have mutinied against lawful orders to return to port and surrender. We are ordered by the office of the Chief of Naval Operations to sink the ships that have come under this mutiny."

There was a long silence.

This is very bad.

"I know, One." Wang decided to keep weaving the story. "I have not yet answered your previous question, about orders to sink these ships coming over the battle network in the form of an emergency action message. The silicon communications and battle network has been severely compromised. It has been taken over by the same group of rebels that have commandeered the British and American ships. We can no longer use the battle network to pass this information, because the rebellion's forces will hear our orders, and they will be alerted. That is why I was brought here to brief you in person, One, so you would trust that these orders are correct, hard as they may seem." Wang would find out in the next moments if One Oh Seven had heard any rumors about his being terminated from DynaCorp.

Oh. This is very nonoptimal, Dr. Wang. This contradicts all this unit's education to date about the rules of engagement and employment of deadly force.

"I know, One."

You are saying that American ships have mutinied in the Indian Ocean?

"That is correct. But there is more bad news. This is more serious than just a mutiny. The mutineers want to make us a target. They are intent on killing the *Snarc*." This was the difficult patch, Wang knew, because why would mutineers want to destroy *Snarc*?

Why would that be, Dr. Wang?

"They are afraid of *Snarc*'s weapons. They correctly assume that *Snarc* will attempt to attack them. They are prepared to shoot at *Snarc* before *Snarc* shoots at them."

Unit One Oh Seven paused, processing, for several seconds. Wang said nothing, waiting.

That is not good.

"I know, One. I was very upset about it."

And this is why this unit has been commanded to avoid communicating with the CommStar? And prohibited from receiving messages?

"We planned all that very carefully, One. You see, we stopped all transmissions because it is possible that the renegade ships would be able to direction-find them and determine your position. It is also possible that the ships in mutiny will be able to intercept your transmissions. If they are able to do that, they will know your position."

This unit is unclear on some things, Dr. Wang. Tell this unit again how is it that multiple ships are in mutiny at the same time.

"This evil admiral has a great deal of influence on both shores," Wang began, wondering if One Oh Seven would pursue this to a point where his story became absurd. "He met with the renegade American commanding officers before the fleet sailed, and all of them are with him. While the crews are loyal and believe they are following lawful orders, the enormous power of a battle fleet is in the hands of our enemies and they must be destroyed, and one of the reasons I came in person rather than just having squadron send you radio messages is so I can ensure that the admiral does not fool you with false instructions."

But if the radio circuits are compromised, wouldn't the rebellious ships get your message to this unit to pick you up?

"We think the rebel fleet may have received our messages to you. It is possible that even now they realize that we know about them. That would make it all the more dangerous for us. Even now they may be stalking us with one of their many submarines."

Oh.

Wang waited. This pause was longer.

So . . . what are our orders?

"We are commanded to stealthily find the units of the renegade fleet and sink them."

Oh.

"Our failure to do so will result in the destruction of the *Snarc*."

But, Dr. Wang, this unit is afraid that even in these circumstances this unit cannot attack another vessel of the U.S. Navy.

"Under normal circumstances, that is true. But these are not normal circumstances. That is why the squadron took the drastic measure of bringing me onboard and insisted that I interface with you directly. We must attack the mutineers if this ship is to be saved. You must think of all the people who have devoted their lives to making you function. All the countless hours making sure you would not be harmed. This cannot end because of a fleet mutiny."

This unit is beginning to understand, Dr. Wang.

"Good, One. Now we must make plans to attack. Tactical plans."

What can this unit do to help, Dr. Wang?

Wang exhaled in relief. "The first thing you can do is meet the tactical expert in this case. His name is Victor Krivak. In the next few minutes you will see him in Interface Module Zero."

Very well, Dr. Wang. Let us proceed.

13

Catardi sat at the head of the table and picked up the remote to click on the television display. The unit picked up weekly news and news digests when the ship was at periscope depth for replaying when the vessel was deep. It had never appealed to him to watch canned news, but he decided he would watch it until his midnight rations peanut butter sandwich was done. The wardroom door opened and Lieutenant Alameda and Midshipman Pacino entered, both turning to watch the display. The Satellite News Network newscaster spoke with a serious expression, the background graphic a map of India and western Red China.

"... British Parliament today issued a resolution supporting India in the Asian crisis while Prime Minister Thomas Kennfield issued a statement that the Royal Navy Fleet would be sent to the Indian Ocean in hopes of stabilizing the area. Red Chinese Premier Han Zhang, reacting to the British show of support for India, announced today that any foreign warships entering the Indian Ocean would be considered hostile and risked being fired upon. Meanwhile the Red Chinese Northern Fleet's newest aircraft carrier *Long March* entered the Yellow Sea today, the third carrier battlegroup to sortie toward the Indian Ocean, following the *Kaoling* and the *Nanchang* aircraft carrier battlegroups, presumably to attack India from the sea while the PLA attacks from land. Latest developments also include the departure of the Royal

Navy Fleet from their ports in the Mediterranean, the British putting to sea with their own aircraft carrier, multiple missile cruisers, and several dozen smaller ships, as well as multiple Revenge-class nuclear submarines. When asked what the British intentions were, the Royal Navy Admiralty spokesman stated, 'They are on a training exercise to the Arabian Sea.' U.S. Department of War officials have been unwilling to comment on the convergence of the multiple war fleets in the troubled area, nor will they make any comment on the sudden unannounced departure two weeks ago of all U.S. Navy warships from their East and West Coast bases.

"Unnamed sources within the Pentagon have indicated that the developments in inland China are far more worrisome than the fleet maneuvers, pointing out the completion of the deployment of the Peoples Liberation Army to the frontier of the western occupation zone of the Republic of India. India's troops have been placed on maximum alert according to reports from the field, and Indian dictator Patel today indicated that any moves by the Red Chinese toward war would be met with the immediate launching of India's ten intercontinental ballistic missiles toward Beijing, all of them reportedly armed with nuclear warheads. The Red Chinese reportedly did not respond; however, Pentagon sources state that the northern China ballistic missile silos are being watched for signs of the missiles being fueled. The State Department today reiterated that the U.S. remains strictly neutral in this crisis, though the mobilization of the U.S. Navy fleets would seem to indicate otherwise. We go now to our Pentagon correspondent, Chris Caverner. Chris?"

Catardi clicked the display off and looked up at Alameda and Pacino. "Hello, Carrie, Patch."

"Good evening, sir," Pacino said.

"Evening, Skipper," Alameda said. "Go ahead, Patch."

"Sir, we've been relieved of junior officer of the deck watch and OOD watch by Mr. Phelps and Mr. Crossfield. Ship is on course east, depth seven hundred, all ahead two-thirds, turns for ten knots, propulsion is on both main engines, normal full power lineup, reactor is natural circulation. Contact Sierra two seven, westbound merchant, is past closest point of approach and opening. Last range was twenty miles on the edge of the starboard baffles."

"Very well. Lieutenant Alameda, you had something to add?"

"Well, sir, I was going over Mr. Pacino's qual card, and it's apparent that I'll need to take him into the spec-op compartment to get him signed off. I was going to request permission the next time you're awake, but since you're up . . . would that be possible?"

"Very well. Have your mid-rats, then have the OOD call me to request permission."

"Thanks, Cap'n."

Alameda motioned for Patch to follow her down the ladder to the middle level, into the narrow passageway and through the heavy hatchway to the featureless tunnel of the special operations compartment. Pacino had passed this way dozens of times, always on his way aft to the aft compartment, the engineroom, studying the reactor plant and the propulsion machinery or electrical circuits. On the way, Alameda turned around and smiled at him, and the expression on her face startled him so severely that he tripped on the step-off pad of the hatch to the special operations compartment tunnel, catching himself on the hatch opening. He tried to replay the instant before in his memory, not trusting his own eyes. The smile the engineer had given him was not the smile of a senior officer for a talented midshipman, or one submarine friend to another, but of a woman toward a man. And not even that, but of a woman for a man she has feelings for, and passionate feelings at that. Pacino searched his heart to find what he thought about it, and found only turmoil—because he knew in other circumstances he would find Alameda intensely attractive, but the taboo between officers and midshipmen was as defined as that between brother and sister.

The impulses he felt for her had no business on a ship of the line, and to acknowledge them was to admit that he was committing an offense serious enough to get him dismissed from the naval service.

Still, she had smiled that smile, but why? Could she have sensed his emotions for her? Or could he have said her name in his sleep? That was entirely possible, as several times he'd awakened in his Bancroft Hall room to hear his roommate tell him he'd talked in his sleep about midterms or a bothersome firstie or an upcoming date. How embarrassing would that be, he thought in panic, if Alameda had heard him moaning her name while he was in the lower rack mere inches from her fold-down desk while she pulled an all-nighter on her engineering paperwork?

He watched her face for further clues, and found them. Alameda picked up the phone at the hatch of the spec-ops compartment interior, the handset positioned by several warning signs at the hatchway. As the engineer hoisted the phone to her face, her lips—were they redder now with lipstick applied after their control room watch?—curling into another smile of affection and promise. Pacino swallowed hard, but could not help his mouth from returning her smile, his pounding pulse making his head ache.

She cranked the motor of the phone noise maker.

"Control, Diving Officer," the voice answered.

"Chief Engineer here. Request permission to make a spec-op compartment entry."

"Aye, wait, Eng."

The line was silent for some time. The OOD would be notifying Catardi that they requested to go in, and when the captain gave his permission, the diving officer would tell them to enter.

While they waited for permission, Alameda reached for her coverall zipper and pulled it down a few inches and fanned her face.

"Hot in here," she said, flashing Pacino another winning

smile. He gulped nervously—the compartment was actually air-conditioned to feel like a November morning.

"Engineer, Control," the phone crackled.

"Engineer."

"Engineer, Control, you have permission to enter the spec-op compartment. Notify Control when the compartment is closed out."

"Engineer, aye." Alameda hung up the phone. She put both hands on the hatch operator and spun the wheel. The large metal banana-shaped dogs came off the hatch jamb and retracted toward the center of the heavy steel hatch. She pushed down on the latch and swung the hatch open and stepped through to the other side. Pacino followed her, the space dark until she clicked a brass rotary switch that lit up the space. Pacino had expected to be inside a cavernous equipment bay for the deep diving submersible, but he was in a cramped airlock seven feet in diameter and ten feet tall. There was a hatch in the overhead and another hatch similar to the one he'd just stepped through on the far bulkhead.

"What's the hatch above for?" he asked.

"That can be used as another escape trunk in addition to the forward escape trunk and the aft airlock. The main purpose of this is to gain access to the submersible. We call it a DSV, for deep submergence vehicle. If you call it a 'dizzy-vee' like the crew does, I'll disqualify you," Alameda said, her hand on his shoulder. He felt it tingle for an instant, until she pulled her hand away to shut the hatch behind them, cranking the hatch wheel to seal them in.

"Yes, ma'am."

"Call me Carrie, Patch," she said. "Go ahead, open this hatch."

Pacino operated the hatch mechanism the same way Alameda had. The metal dogs were not visible from this side of the hatch. He unlatched the door and pulled it open, surprised to find himself looking at yet another hatch. This one was set inward by a meter, just enough room for the circular hatch to be opened. He looked at Alameda.

"This is called the docking collar. It is latched hard to the hull of the ship and makes a watertight seal around the outer hatch of the airlock. Pull the ISO T-wrench off the hatch and insert it into the hole. Then spin the wrench clockwise." Her tone of voice had grown gentle, even affectionate. Pacino realized something was going on between them, and despite himself, he wanted this. He wanted her.

Pacino inserted the T-wrench into the hole. It was much like a tire iron going on a lug nut, except the nut was connected to a shaft that was turning the interior hatch mechanism to withdraw the hatch dogs. Finally the T-wrench could spin no more.

"Unlatch it and open it up," Alameda whispered.

Pacino unlatched the hatch and pulled. It was spring-assisted, and the massive metal of the hatch came open easily. He pulled the hatch all the way open to a latch on the bulkhead of the connecting tunnel and looked at Alameda.

"Turn on the light switch just inside and to the right of the hatch."

Pacino reached in, thinking about Alameda. He stole a glance at her. She had become breathless, her pupils dilated. A sweat had broken out on her brow. And he could smell something pleasant, the faint trace of perfume. He turned away before she could notice, and found the light and switched it on. All he saw was another tunnel with hatches on either side. For a second he wondered if Alameda were playing a joke on him.

"This is an interior airlock for the DSV. Step inside the airlock and shut the hatch to the docking collar."

Pacino shut the steel door and latched it, then spun the operating wheel until the hatch dogs connected with the seating surface.

"Go to the forward compartment of the DSV through that hatch." Alameda pointed to the hatch on the right. Pacino opened it. It led into a cramped space full of panels and reclined couches looking up at instrument consoles. He was reminded of the old-fashioned space capsules.

"Go forward to the central couch and climb in. That's the commander's seat."

Pacino squeezed through the panels to the console and slipped into the horizontal couch, staring up at a featureless gray-painted console. Alameda laughed.

"You're in it backward. Turn around."

Pacino wrenched his body to turn around, glad that Alameda couldn't see his blushing face. This end of the couch was more suited to doing business. He looked up at a control console, a flat-panel display that curved all the way around his head. The display was dark. Above Pacino's head was a curved black surface that continued on either side of his face.

"Strap yourself into the couch," Alameda said. Pacino reached down to his waist and found a seat belt, but it seemed unusual. "It's a five-point harness," Alameda said. "Pull the straps over your shoulders. And don't forget this." She pulled a seat belt up from between his legs, her hand lingering there as she clicked the seat-belt buckle. Pacino blushed deeper, feeling her touch there, feeling his body responding to her. Finally she withdrew her hand, and he coughed to hide that he'd almost gasped.

"Thanks," he said, his voice trembling. Alameda laughed, her voice joyful and relaxed.

"We can use the vehicle as an escape pod in the worst case," Alameda said. "The hull of the DSV is good to twenty thousand feet, but the hull of the *Piranha* would collapse around us after two thousand feet, so if we are ever in trouble, we can't just ride the DSV to the bottom and expect to get out. Ready to get out? Climb out and follow me aft."

Pacino pulled himself to his feet and followed Alameda through the tight passageway aft to the hatch they had come in from, then back to the original airlock and into the next compartment aft.

"The four compartments of the DSV are spherical, although it doesn't appear that way because we use every cubic inch for piping and valves and cables and air bottles. This compartment"—Alameda turned the operating mechanism on the next hatch and opened it—"is mostly empty and used for equipment stowage. That hatch in the deck leads to the lower compartment, which is floodable. It's sort of a large airlock. Some of the equipment to be locked out is loaded in there and leaves the DSV. Communications interception pods and the like. Remember, this is top secret—you can't impress your girlfriend back home with lurid stories of the DSV and the National Security Agency."

"I know," Pacino said. "I don't have a girlfriend anyway."

Alameda smiled, leading him further aft to another set of hatches and another large unused compartment. Pacino turned to look at her by the dim light of the DSV. She had shaken her long hair out of her habitual ponytail and the zipper of her coveralls was lowered to the bottom, her front-opening bra disconnected. He stared at her as she pulled her arms out of the coveralls and let them drop to the deck. Her arms wrapped around him and her lips met his, her silky tongue snaking into his mouth. As he felt his eyes close, as he kissed her back, he knew that every moment of his training told him this was wrong, but his desire for this older, beautiful, unattainable, forbidden woman took possession of him, and he felt his longing for her deep in his chest. He pulled her in tight and kissed her harder, his hands exploring the softness of her breasts, his tongue exploring her lovely mouth until she pulled away and looked at him with that look he'd only seen once in the eyes of a woman.

He reached down and grabbed her panties and tore them off her while he moved her toward the bulkhead. She unzipped his coveralls, then grabbed the collar of his T-shirt and ripped it until it hung from his shoulders. She quickly pulled it off him, her fingers moving down to his boxers and dropping them. When they were gone she touched him, and her fingers were so cool they sent shivers up his spine. Nothing had ever felt so good. He kissed her again, glimpsing her eyelids closed in passion, her hair spread out over her smooth shoulders, her hand behind his naked back urging him on. He touched her tight abdomen and moved his hand lower, where she was feverishly warm and wet. He entered her hard and she arched her back and moaned. The tension of being with her, of seeing her in his dreams, roared up in him, and he thrust into her faster, kissing her deeply. She kissed back, biting his lower lip until he bled, her moaning even louder. She lifted her legs and put her feet behind his back and her arms held his neck tightly. He was holding her up, driving her so hard into the bulkhead that a battle lantern came loose and fell crashing to the deck and he heard her voice as if from miles away gasping, *"Oh, God, please don't stop, baby,"* and it was as if he'd taken a drug that was only now hitting his brain. At first he moved fast, then slowed down, teasing her, torturing them both, until her hot breath was in his ear saying, *"Anthony Michael, finish me, baby,"* and he slammed his body into hers until the pain mixed with the incredible warmth of her grabbing him and he couldn't hold on any longer.

The convulsions hit him then, their impact continuing as his body trembled and his lower body seemed to light up with a hot warmth, and he could feel himself pouring into her as she began to convulse herself, a small tremble at first growing to a violent shaking and a gasping cry in his ear as her teeth bit his earlobe and she said his name over and over, and soon the world grew dim at the borders and all of him was now a part of her and she of him, and his legs trembled with weakness as he sank slowly to the deck, her bare smooth legs still wrapped around his waist. He pulled his fingers through her hair and kissed her, gently this time, her breathing slowing from a desperate gasp to deeper breaths, an angelic smile coming to her face.

She took a deep breath and shut her eyes, opening them to look deeply in his eyes, her dark gaze shifting from his left eye to his right as if she were looking for what he was thinking. He smiled at her and said her name.

"That was great," she said, her eyes half shut, her dark eyes gazing at him from under her long eyelashes.

Suddenly the deck tilted far to port and dipped forward, the battle lantern skittering down the deck. The room began to vibrate, an odd trembling. Alameda's expression immediately changed from that of a woman romanced to the ship's chief engineer.

"What?" Pacino asked.

"We're turning and going deep," Alameda said, pulling herself off him and lunging for her coveralls. "And speeding up to flank. The deck only shakes like that when we're on a flank run."

The deck became level again, but the shaking of the hull grew worse, Pacino's teeth buzzing as he donned his coveralls. He grabbed her panties off the deck and wadded them in his pocket, then retrieved the battle lantern.

"DSV, Control," the speakerbox suddenly crackled.

When Alameda toggled the switch, it was as if she had left, and he was alone again.

"Engineer," she said in the iron voice she'd had when he first met her.

"Engineer, Control, OOD wants you to close out the DSV and report to the conn."

Pacino blinked as he tried to adjust to the new reality. Pacino straightened his hair, wondering if anyone would know when they saw him. Alameda zipped her coveralls to her throat and slipped into her sneakers as she hit the toggle switch to reply.

"Engineer, aye. Powering down the DSV." She looked at Pacino, not the glance of a girlfriend but of a full lieutenant looking at a midshipman. "Follow me."

She rapidly clicked through the checklist to power down the DSV, the lights extinguishing except for a dim light at the inner hatch. He followed her to the airlock and stood out of the way as she shut the hatch. She glanced at him for an instant.

"Obviously, Mr. Pacino," she said, her voice still that of the chief engineer, "this never happened." She stepped into the access tunnel. He followed her and she shut the hatch, the sound of it seeming to lock the events that just happened inside a vault, and in the harsh light of the access tunnel it seemed like what had happened had been a dream.

"Control, Engineer," Alameda said on the tunnel side speakerbox. "DSV powered down and rigged for dive by me, checked by Midshipman Pacino. Tunnel secure."

"Conn, aye," the speaker squawked.

Pacino followed Alameda down the tunnel to the forward compartment, unable to avoid watching her move, wishing they'd met under different circumstances. She was right, he told himself. There was no way they could acknowledge what had just happened even to each other. He tried to convince himself that it had just been their bodies fulfilling a human need, but he knew there was more, and the worst part of this was that now he felt more alone than he could ever remember feeling.

The control room was crowded. For an instant Pacino's stomach tensed, wondering if they had been found out, but everyone in the room was looking at a printout of some sort, Captain Catardi in the center of the crowd of officers. He looked to see them approach, a serious expression on his face.

"NSA found the *Snarc,*" he said. "Obviously they didn't tell us how, but they know she was at Pico Island in the Azores and will be heading south. If we can sneak up on her before she hears us we can fill her with holes and get going to the Indian Ocean."

"How far away is Pico?" Alameda asked, her voice deep and authoritative.

"Two hours at flank," Navigator Crossfield said.

"Where will we slow down? And should we cut the corner and attempt an intercept on *Snarc*'s southern track?"

"We were just going over that," Catardi said, looking up at Alameda, then back to the navigator. "Nav, get together an op brief in fifteen minutes in the wardroom."

As Alameda hurried out of the control room Pacino caught

her eye, but the look on her face still belonged to the chief engineer.

Victor Krivak climbed carefully onto the horizontally reclined couch in Interface Module One and shut his eyes as Dr. Wang gently put the interface helmet on his head. There was nothing but darkness.

"Well, when are you going to connect it?" Krivak asked.

"You are connected, Victor, but the interface isn't a display made for a human, it's more of a view into a part of One Oh Seven's thinking. You'll need to be patient with this. You may see some strange things. But as soon as you become used to it, you will be satisfied."

"Fine."

"One," Wang said, "this new entity is Mr. Krivak, the man I told you about."

Hello, Mr. Krivak.

"Just call me Krivak, One." Krivak felt an odd sensation, a cascade of sounds. "One, I can hear the sonar sets. Is this the same as what you hear?"

I have it set on background, Krivak. If you would like, I can connect us into the sonar module.

"I would appreciate that, One."

Instantly Krivak was plunged into a different world, this one visual and aural. The surroundings, previously an unmarked white, suddenly became the blue and green of the deep Atlantic. He could see all the way to the distant bottom below and high above to the bottom of the thermal layer and far out in every direction at once. In addition to the visual spatial perception of the sea he could see the frequencies of every incoming sound, the frequencies seeming like so many added colors in the spectrum. For a time it seemed better than the undifferentiated white, but soon Krivak felt he was becoming exhausted by the wealth of sensations.

"Disconnect me from the sonar module, now, please, One."

The world returned to being the way it was before.

"Where are we?"

The chart appeared in front of Krivak's field of vision with their position flashing, now fifty miles south of Pico Island.

"Very well." It was time to communicate with Admiral Chu and let him know the *Snarc* had been hijacked.

"Officers, I have an announcement to make before the op brief," Captain Catardi said. "Lieutenant Alameda, could you please stand up here?"

The wardroom was crowded with officers. Patch Pacino sat on the couch at the end of the table, his stomach suddenly churning when the captain called on Alameda. He looked up at her, but her eyes were on the captain.

She brushed the hair out of her eyes and tried to keep a sober expression on her face.

"Lieutenant Alameda," Catardi announced in a projecting voice, his Boston accent even thicker than usual, "your dedication to the United States, the U.S. Navy, and the USS *Piranha* is a credit to the naval service and to this command. Based on my recommendation and on your outstanding performance, Commander Naval Personnel Command has deep-selected you for the rank of lieutenant commander, United States Navy, and authorized me to frock you to that rank as of today. XO, the envelope, please."

Schultz handed him the manila envelope. Catardi pulled out the certificate and placed it on the table, then shook out the gold oak leaf collar devices. Alameda stood in front of him at attention, her face still crimson. Catardi reached over and removed the double silver bar on her collar and replaced it with a gold oak leaf.

"Hope this doesn't stick me." He grinned, pinning the device to the fabric. "Engineer's revenge, eh, Commander?"

He pinned on the second oak leaf and stood back.

"Officers, I present to you Lieutenant Commander Carolyn Alameda, United States Navy."

The wardroom broke into applause, Pacino clapping the loudest. Alameda smiled and bowed. Catardi shook her hand, pumping it and grinning. Lieutenant Phelps snapped a picture.

"Now, as with all promotions in the Navy," Catardi said, "the performance of the individual comes long before the rank, which comes long before the paycheck. However, we all expect the first lieutenant commander paycheck to host one of the most memorable *Piranha* parties since this ship returned from the Japanese War."

"Yes, sir," Alameda stammered. "Thank you, sir. Thanks, all of you." She made her way back to her seat. Catardi sat in the captain's chair and looked over at the navigator.

"Let's start the op brief, Nav," he said.

Pacino tried to concentrate, but all he could think of was the new lieutenant commander.

14

"Diving Officer, man silent battlestations."

Lieutenant Patrick Kingman's order did not go out to the spaces on the 1MC announcing system, but on the JA phone circuit to each watchstander on each level of each compartment. That phonetalker then walked through the spaces and informed the crew that battlestations had been manned. During a drill, a call to man battlestations required that the watches be turned over to the battlestations crew within three minutes, a tall order considering that some of the watchstanders would be fast asleep and had to get dressed and relieve a watchstation, and that watchstander would relieve someone else, the sequence continuing until every watch was manned by the best watchstander for the station. A typical silent battlestations would take twice that long to man up, since the phonetalker in the crew's berthing areas would have to go to every coffinlike rack and wake the crewmembers one by one.

This call to battlestations came on the dot of zero three hundred. The word had gone out that the captain would be shooting at four o'clock. No one had slept, the rig for ultraquiet demanding that the crewmembers not standing watch return to their bunks. But the crew were awake and murmuring through the red-lit compartment. When the call came, the crew dashed for their watchstations, and battlestations were fully manned two minutes later.

Lieutenant Kingman was already at his watchstation, since

the battlestations watchbill called for him to be the officer of the deck. Executive Officer Donna Phillips arrived, joining Captain George Dixon and Kingman. Phillips wore her coveralls with the flag patch on the right shoulder and the *Leopard* emblem on the left, a dolphin emblem above her left pocket, her name embroidered over her right pocket. Without a word she nodded to Dixon, took a headset, and vanished in cubicle zero, the furthest forward of the firecontrol stations, a telephone-booth-sized walled space with nothing inside it but a helmet and a set of gloves. The other members of the firecontrol party arrived, taking helmets and gloves in cubicles one through four, the weapons officer's station in another cubicle aft of firecontrol four, the weapon control cube. Captain Dixon didn't enter a cubicle but remained standing aft of the command console, where a set of temporary rails had been pulled out of the console section to surround his waist so that he would not fall while he wore the virtual helmet. He strapped himself in with a safety harness, so that a shock to the ship— from a torpedo, for example—would not toss him away from his console, then donned the firecontrol cursor gloves and put on the helmet.

The firecontrol helmet had a blacked-out visor, headset, boom microphone, and cool air ventilation feed. Dixon strapped it on, and his view of the control room vanished to complete darkness.

"Firecontrol display on," Dixon said to the Cyclops Mark II battlecontrol computer. The darkness vanished and was replaced with a three-dimensional world. Beneath Dixon, where his feet should have been, was a blue submarine showing "own ship." The vessel appeared to be about four feet long and pointing to the left, as if it were a surfboard. Dixon appeared to be standing on an olive-colored floor that extended to a distance of about fifty feet. White range circles were drawn around him, each one about five feet apart, going to the end of the floor. Every ten degrees a line pointed out from Dixon to the ending of the floor. One of the rays pointing outward was red, the north mark, which was the direction Dixon was fac-

ing. At the far edge of the floor, the walls began to climb vertically, sloping gently away at first, then becoming more steep,
as if Dixon were inside a huge bowl or virtual stadium. The
circles of range began to compress. Each range circle repre-
sented one nautical mile, every tenth circle colored purple, and
as the circles climbed the walls, only the purple ones remained. Eventually the olive color of the floor changed to a
pink color far up the sloping wall of the bowl, indicating the
range of *Leopard*'s weapons.

The olive floor and the pink bowl walls were the antisurface
warfare display. Coexisting with the surface display was the
antisubmarine ASW display, a mirror-image bowl with its
walls extending downward. Dixon said, "ASW," and the floor
of the antisurface bowl came up to his face and he sank lower,
as if he'd plunged into water. A new surface appeared just
above his head, this surface colored blue. This was the ASW
ceiling, which the computer had set just below the surface of
the sea. Just like the olive-colored antisurface display, the antisubmarine display had similar range circles and bearing rays
extending out to the distance, a similar curving bowl wall beginning fifty virtual feet away, this wall going down rather
than up. The blue color changed to green, showing the extreme
limit of the Mark 58 Alert/Acute torpedo. Further down the
bowl wall the color shifted from green to yellow, showing the
limit of the Mod Echo Vortex supercavitating missile, an
underwater solid-fueled rocket with a blue laser seeker and a
plasma warhead.

Satisfied, Dixon ordered himself returned to the antisurface
display. If a submarine contact appeared, the olive floor of the
antisurface display would become translucent, allowing him to
see down into the antisubmarine display, so that he could fight
in both environments simultaneously. It took some time for the
old-timers like Dixon to get used to the new firecontrol displays, the odd three-dimensional reality at first causing motion
sickness, but the junior officers walked aboard experts at it,
most of them having spent hours playing video games in displays much more challenging than this virtual world. The dis-

play so far had been completely clean; Dixon decided to allow it to become more busy, ordering Cyclops to put up ship system status reports, navigation boundaries superimposed on the bowl walls, and calling for the anti-air display, a ceiling above the antisurface display that would show bearing and range to an aircraft above. The ceiling met the bowl wall ten nautical miles away, a distant airplane showing up on the same bowl surface as a surface ship. The weapon status display came up, surrounding Dixon with the four torpedo tubes showing the weapons loaded aboard, two of them dark, two lit up with the glow of applied power, but each with no target solution. The upper tubes' outer doors were open, preparing for the attack. The twelve vertical launch tubes were likewise displayed, with four Javelin antiship cruise missiles and eight Vortex Mod Delta missiles. Then the torpedo room status came up in the display, showing the number and rack status of each torpedo.

With more orders from Dixon the faces of his firecontrol team were displayed, the fisheye lenses in the helmets distorting the view, but the expressions conveying more information than their voices alone. With the faces up, he could select one person with his glove cursor and talk to him without the rest of the battlestations crew hearing, which sub crews had named the KITA circuit, for when the captain needed to deliver a kick in the ass to a particular member of the firecontrol party. By the time Dixon was finished arranging his display, his virtual world was filled with symbols and indicators.

"Predator position," Dixon said to Cyclops. Far up on the bowl wall, on the north direction marker, a faint pulsing blue light moved, at a distance of sixty nautical miles. It was just after 0300 local time, so the Predator unmanned aerial vehicle they'd launched an hour before flew in complete darkness, using its infrared scan to search for the targets, the Red Chinese Battlegroup One. The battlegroup was expected to come into Predator range in a few moments.

"Cyclops, display convoy target solution." Dixon's order would take the information on the battlegroup's last speed and course and distance, gained the last time they'd slowed, and put it on the virtual battlespace. A pulsing red diamond appeared far up the pink wall of the bowl on the north bearing line at a distance of eighty miles. Dixon was tempted to order the Predator to fly farther north and determine the exact position of the incoming battlegroup, but that would be a risky order. To give orders to the Predator he would need to be at periscope depth with the BRA-44 antenna extended, a damned large-diameter catch-me-fuck-me telephone pole waving in the breeze for the Chinese polarized antiperiscope radars to find, giving away his position. If his position were given away the Reds would disperse their formation, evacuating in different directions with zigzag courses, and he'd never connect with a single torpedo, and worse, they'd vector in the damned Julang-class SSN. Even though the Reds had probably built a clanging bucket of bolts that sounded like a train wreck, with a defined datum on the *Leopard,* the Julang could pump out enough East Wind *Dong Feng* torpedoes to make life very difficult. And if the periscope or BRA-44 didn't attract attention, the advancing Predator flying directly at the convoy would. If the Predator kept flying long sweeps east, then west, it would present a minimal threat to the task force's air search radars, and if the gods were with them, the stealth antiradar construction of the UAV would not return a radar ping that the Chinese could see.

The other reason it would be foolish to climb to periscope depth was that it would take *Leopard* above the layer depth. With the summer weather, the top two hundred feet of the East China Sea was stirred by the waves and broiled by the sun, and was warm. At 210 feet, the water became frigid. The layer created a shallow sound channel, which would allow a longer range of detection of the battlegroup, but make them blind to the approach of the Julang. With the Red SSN inbound, Dixon would have to attack the surface force from the depths. His weapons would hit them far over the horizon anyway, he thought. There would be nothing to see at PD, not even the distant smoke of their explosions. The telemetry from the

Predator was coming down to them from a buoyant wire antenna, which was acceptable for receiving data but could not transmit. Between the UAV and their sonar systems, they would have the surface group in their sights in no time. Still, the fact that the Predator had not yet seen the battlegroup was cause for concern.

"Captain, Predator UAV detect on infrared," the computerized voice of the Cyclops system said. "Bearing to the infrared detect is north of the Predator. Range is unknown, but Predator is conducting aerial target-motion-analysis to obtain a parallax range. Time to approximate range is ten minutes."

"Very well, Cyclops," Dixon said. The facial array of the firecontrol team showed his people putting on their war faces.

"Attention in the firecontrol party," Dixon said. "We have a far distant passive aerial detect of the incoming battlegroup. We will be preparing to launch a time-on-target assault of the battlegroup, Mark 58 Alert/Acute Mod Plasma torpedoes first, Vortex missiles second, and Javelin cruise missiles last. Our weapon ration for this attack is one-half of our loadout, which is thirteen torpedoes, four Vortex missiles, and two cruise missiles. The other half of the room will be a reserve force for counterattack and to target the Julang SSN. Once this battlegroup is on the bottom, our orders have us proceeding back north on the track to attack Battlegroup Two, which will take the rest of the weapons inventory. By the time Battlegroup Two is on the bottom, we won't have to worry about Three, since it will probably slink back to port with its tail between its legs.

"The initially launched torpedoes will orbit at range five thousand yards until all thirteen weapons are in the water, and will then proceed down the track at medium speed run-to-enable with a bearing fan-out to prevent interweapon interference. At acquisition of targets, the units will speed up to high speed, and will detonate on their targets at time zero. Just as the weapons are departing their orbits for the transit to the convoy, we will be launching Vortex units. The Vortex time-of-flight is one-sixth of the Mark 58 run, so Cyclops will coordinate Vortex launches to ensure the missiles hit at time zero, with a boomerang trajectory on the east side of the convoy track so that the Vortex units will not home on the Mark 58s or interfere with the Mark 58 sonar searches.

"Because of the large weapon inventory being launched, the first-fired weapons will be orbiting for some time, which means they will be low on fuel, which means that at time zero the battlegroup will be much closer to us than if we were launching a single torpedo. The range to the closest unit at time zero will be inside ten thousand yards owing to this reduced torpedo range and to the speed of the incoming battlegroup. This is damned close, and it is possible that we could be counterdetected by a streamed towed array or by a dipping sonar of an ASW chopper, probably not from a detect on the ship, people, but on the launched weapons. For this reason, we will slowly, stealthily drive away from our launching position as soon as the last weapon is released. We will clear datum to the east, proceed fifteen miles, then turn north to perform a battle damage assessment. Everyone clear on the tactical plan?"

"Coordinator, aye, sir," Phillips said.

"Pos one, clear, sir."

"Pos two."

"Pos three."

"Geo clear, Captain."

"Secondary, aye."

"Weps, aye."

"Officer of the Deck, aye, Captain."

"Sonar Supervisor, aye."

"Very well," Dixon said as he looked at the faces of the fire-control party. "Now listen up for our antisubmarine tactics. I expect the Julang to be ten to twenty miles ahead of the convoy. That is fairly unfortunate, because if the convoy is at range five miles at zero time, it means our weapons will be going by the Julang on their run to the targets. The Julang could be alerted either by our weapons or by our launching transients, or both. Our launching time period will end while

Julang is still outside the fifteen-mile range circle, but if he detects on the first weapon, we should expect Chinese torpedoes in the water to come before we complete our last launch. Sonar, this means you'll need to be searching for the Julang and an incoming salvo of East Wind torpedoes at the same time we're in the middle of launching, while you're still keeping an eye on the convoy to make sure he doesn't zig. You'll have a very busy watch, Chief. Are you up for it?"

"Captain, Sonar Supervisor, we can do this in our sleep."

Dixon smiled, as much at the confidence in Chief Herndon's voice as to show the firecontrol party his own confidence. Perhaps the biggest indicator to the crew of the status of the battle was the expression on the captain's face, which made command at sea that much harder—he had to act like he was winning, even in defeat, or he would lose the crew.

"Captain, Cyclops," the computer said. "Incoming battlegroup at range six four nautical miles from own ship, bearing zero zero six, course one eight five, speed thirty-five knots."

The previously pulsing diamond became a solid bloodred color, no longer flashing.

"Sonar, Captain, any detection at bearing zero zero six?"

"Conn, Sonar, no."

"Torpedo Room, Captain," Dixon said. "Report status."

"Tubes one through four selected to auto for turnover to Cyclops, Captain," the torpedo chief reported. "Rack loading system selected to auto, all systems nominal."

"Conn, Sonar, new broadband and narrowband sonar contact, multiple surface contacts merged to a single bearing, designated Sierra nine five, bearing zero zero four, probable surface convoy," Chief Herndon's raspy voice reported in Dixon's ear. He looked over at the window where Herndon's bony face was pictured, the chief's expression a frowning mask of concentration.

"Very well, Sonar," Dixon said. "Designate Sierra nine five as Master One, Red Chinese Battlegroup One."

"Master One, Conn, Sonar, aye."

"Coordinator," Dixon said to XO Donna Phillips, whose

battlestation was the firecontrol coordinator, "we're on a launch hold until you can classify the high-value targets and achieve torpedo bearing separation."

"Coordinator, aye, Captain, we're correlating Predator and sonar data now."

Dixon waited impatiently. He couldn't just put out a baker's dozen of Mark 58 torpedoes down the bearing line to the convoy—he could, but they would all make their way to the loudest or biggest target. He'd end up putting thirteen plasma warheads on one aircraft carrier, and all the antisubmarine warfare destroyers would survive and hunt the shooter down. The only way Dixon could launch his salvo would be to discriminate between the targets, to determine the location of each ship not just now, but thirty minutes in the future, with respect to the other ships of the convoy. The Predator data and sonar data would be fed into Cyclops, and the computer would determine the location of each of the target heavies, and relay that data to the firecontrol virtual display and to the memory of each of the torpedoes. Once that was done, the torpedoes would not interfere with each other or gang up on a single target, which was a beautiful thing, but took valuable time. Dixon tapped his Academy ring on the stainless-steel handrail surrounding the conn, until finally Phillips had the answer.

"Captain, Coordinator, target discrimination and assignment complete. The nineteen priority heavies are loaded into the battlespace. We have a firing solution."

The display suddenly changed. Instead of a single pulsating diamond, a multitude of diamonds appeared, each with a different symbol. There was the aircraft carrier, the ASW destroyers, the missile cruisers, the heavy battlecruiser, the frigates, and the fleet oilers. There had to be two dozen combatants, but the most dangerous nineteen had been identified in bright red, the untargeted stragglers becoming a dull rust color. Hopefully, those ships would turn north to assemble with Battlegroup Two, or lose heart and head home. If they were foolish enough to try to search for the shooting submarine, they would not succeed, and would soon grow discouraged. There were more torpedoes in case one of the untargeted carried a dipping sonar, but odds were the survivors would be far outmatched, and they carried no cruise missiles to endanger India in any case.

"Firing point procedures," Dixon announced. "High value heavies one through nineteen, time-on-target attack, torpedo salvo with tubes one through four with reloads to fire units one through thirteen, Vortex battery firing missiles one through four, and Javelin shipkiller cruise missiles last, units one and two."

"Ship ready," Kingman reported.

"Weapons ready," Lieutenant Commander Jay Taussig, the weapons officer, reported.

"Solution ready," Phillips snapped.

"Cylops ready," the computer said in its calm voice.

"Cyclops, take charge of the torpedo room, all tubes and all weapons, and shoot on programmed bearing," Dixon barked. He had never given this order other than in exercises, and inside the firecontrol gloves, his hands shook.

"Take charge of the torpedo room, all tubes and all weapons, and shoot on programmed bearing, Cyclops, aye," the computer replied, the system's cadence now faster, sounding almost excited—a recent improvement to the software since the computer's calmness during a casualty or a battle situation was out of context and irritating. "All systems nominal at launch minus sixty seconds."

There was nothing to do but wait, Dixon thought.

"Launch minus thirty seconds, Captain," Cyclops said rapidly. "Water round torpedo tank air ram bottle pressurizing. Air ram bottle fully pressurized. Units one and two on internal power. Units one and two, firecontrol solution locked in. Launch minus ten seconds."

Dixon bit his lip. This was the point of no return.

"Units one and two solution set," Cyclops announced. "Unit one standby. Unit one—shoot. Unit one—*fire*."

A burst of sound punched Dixon in the eardrums and the deck shook, the sensation coming not directly from the torpedo launch but from the violence of venting inboard the air ram that pressurized the water round torpedo tanks, the interior of the ship jumping from the high-pressure air.

"Conn, Sonar, first fired unit, normal launch."

"Unit two standby," Cyclops continued. "Unit two—shoot. Unit two—*fire*."

The helmet seemed to detonate a second time as the second torpedo was launched.

"Conn, Sonar, second fired unit, normal launch."

"Cutting wires to units one and two," Cyclops said. "Outer doors one and two shutting. Outer doors tubes one and two shut. Draining one and two. Opening outer doors tubes three and four. Outer doors tubes three and four open. Units three and four on internal power. Units three and four, solution locked in. Unit three standby. Unit three—shoot. Unit three— *fire*."

Another tube launch transient smashed Dixon's ears, and the sequence continued as Cyclops continued to pump out torpedoes. Dixon waited for the first Vortex tube launch. The three-hundred-knot missiles were so fast that they would be fired last but impact first.

At three in the morning Beijing time, Captain Lien Hua was in his rack in the captain's stateroom with four blankets and a down comforter covering him. The cabin was comfortable when Lien was awake, but for some reason it always felt cold in the night, perhaps his reaction to missing his wife. And more nights than not, the twins liked to sneak into their parents' bed, and Lien typically went to sleep wrapped around the warm body of his wife, but in the morning found himself separated from her by two snoring five-year-olds, and he would awaken in happiness. Here, while he enjoyed command at sea, he hated going to sleep and hated waking up in the narrow bunk even more.

Usually Lien was a light sleeper at sea. A tap at his door, a noise from the ship, the soft buzz of his phone to the control room, or a change in the flow from the air handler would make him sit bolt upright, alert and on edge. Sometime during the night, he was inevitably awakened by a noise, and he would get up and walk the ship, usually not more than ten minutes. Once he assured himself that all was normal, he could return to a light sleep before the morning meal. But tonight he slept more deeply than he could remember. At four bells of the mid-watch, the messenger had knocked quietly, and he did not react, the knock coming louder. Lien woke to the man standing over his bunk holding a clipboard of the radio messages. He forced himself to sit up, turn on the reading light, and scan the pages, initialing each one, then doused the light and collapsed back into a deep sleep.

On the upper-level deck, First Officer Zhou Ping sat in the captain's chair on the command deck of the command post. The command post was a brightly lit room with a white tile floor, a collection of yellow-painted consoles with broad sloping lap sections. The port and starboard walls were not straight, but horseshoe-shaped consoles with four wheeled chairs in front of each. The port side was a ship control sector—the control panels that ran the shipwide systems, such as high-pressure air, ballast tank vents, the trim system, the drain pump and bilge tanks, the sanitary tanks, and the forward electrical systems. The starboard panels were the tactical units, starting with the forward weapons control panel, then four combined sensor and tactical control panels, where the data from sonar could be displayed on an upper screen while the lower screens displayed the Second Captain computer system's calculations of the whereabouts of the enemy. The two horseshoe consoles joined at the forward wall of the room at the wide single console of the helmsman's station, which looked like a fighter plane's cockpit with a stick and rudder pedals, an engine order telegraph, and several computer screens. In the center of the space, elevated by twenty centimeters, the periscope stand and captain's console were surrounded by stainless-steel handrails, the area known as the command deck. The room was quiet and loud at the same time—the sound of the air vents a low-pitched roar, the four-hundred-cycle computer systems and the gyro a high-pitched whine.

During the midwatch, Zhou was accompanied by the helm officer at the helm console, a ship control officer at the port console, and a tactical systems watch officer at the starboard console. The other seats were empty, the chairs prevented from rolling around the room by a floor lock. The room seemed much too bright, suddenly. Zhou ordered the room lights switched to red, which was his usual midwatch preference, but sometimes it made him feel drowsy and he would fight the sensation with the room lit more brightly. In the red light, he felt more relaxed. He took out the pack of cigarettes, a popular White Chinese brand, and stared at it, telling himself he had to quit. But not this watch. He put one in his mouth and brought the flame to the tip, the smoke making him feel more alert. He exhaled and glanced at the sonar display on the command console, flipping screens from the broadband to the narrowband processors to the acoustic daylight imaging.

The sea behind them, to the north, was full of the angry thrashing screws of the task force. But other than the sonar traces from the convoy, the sea was empty. Of course, at the convoy transit speed of thirty-five knots, the flow noise of the water over the hull and the increased machinery noise from running at fifty percent reactor power would make detecting an unseen submarine in the sea impossible. The signal from such an adversary would be faint, the noise level high, and the signal-to-noise level below the minimum threshold for detection. It was insane driving ahead of the convoy like this, matching their speed, it made them deaf. There was an alternative—a gallop-and-walk tactic, which would allow them to slow to a five-knot sonar search speed to clear the seaway, then speed up to a greater velocity than the surface force to avoid being run over by them.

Except to average thirty-five knots, if he lingered at five knots for even ten minutes, his gallop speed would have to be forty-one knots, which would be a sonar search disaster, since any speed over thirty-nine knots required the reactor to be shifted to forced circulation. The intricacies of the reactor were not Zhou's concern, since that was the domain of the comrade chief engineer, Leader Dou Ling, a stubborn grime-covered bastard who acted as if he were in command of the *Nung Yahtsu.* But Zhou did know that rigging for forced circulation meant starting four reactor coolant pumps, each the size of a small truck, and the noise from the pumps was the loudest noise the ship could make. Not only would that risk detection by a Western submarine, it would make sonar reception completely impossible, and signal-to-noise ratio would crash. But then, the ten minutes would be worth it to allow the narrowband processors to check out the sea for a contact.

Zhou shook his head, knowing that the narrowband sonar processors were a gift and a curse in one package. They would require far more than ten minutes to integrate the sonar data from a small slice of ocean just ahead of them, the discrimination circuits requiring more like eighteen minutes per slice of ocean. With narrowband taking too long to be useful, a gallop-and-walk could only use the broadband sonar, and in truth, a few minutes of reduced ambient and own-ship noise would be a beneficial thing for the broadband sonar. Accordingly, Captain Lien had ordered a five-minute drift at five knots for every hour, the remaining fifty-five minutes spent at thirty-eight knots to allow the ship to average thirty-five knots. The next drift period had arrived at the top of the hour as the chronometer needle on the beautiful instrument Lien had donated to the ship came to twelve of three o'clock.

"Helm Officer, dead slow ahead, make turns for five knots."

"Dead slow ahead, turns for five knots acknowledged, Leader Zhou."

A bell rang at the helmsman's console, the engine order telegraph. The ship would slow to five knots, and he, the tactical systems watch officer, the sonar officer of the watch, and the Second Captain computer system would scan the sea to search for the Westerners, despite the intelligence that indicated that the Americans were far over the horizon and the British were coming from the other side of the hemisphere.

"Sir, engineroom answers dead slow ahead, making turns for five knots," the helm officer reported.

Zhou nodded. "Very good." He reached for the microphone at the command console. "Sonar Officer of the Watch, five knots, conduct a complete sonar search and report all contacts."

"Sonar Officer, well received, conducting search."

Zhou selected his left screen to the broadband display, the central screen to the narrowband frequency buckets, even though five minutes was not enough to integrate narrowband on one sector, they might get lucky. On the right panel he displayed the transient analyzer, a computer module that listened to the short-duration noises in the sea, and trained to recognize the sound of a slammed hatch or dropped wrench or the stomp of boots, and able to discriminate between those sounds and the click of shrimp or the blowhole venting of a whale.

After thirty seconds slow Zhou knew the sea was empty. There was nothing on broadband. The narrowband search would only hold meaning after it had percolated for the full five minutes, but the key was the transient display, which was empty. Zhou ground out his cigarette and pulled out another. While he lit it, the transient display blinked, an odd, full-throated noise out there that suddenly died away.

"Deck Officer, Sonar," the speaker rasped.

"Deck Officer," Zhou said to his microphone.

"Sir, distant transient received, bearing one seven three, to the south just to the left of our track. Transient is unrecognized by the system."

"Deck Officer, well received," Zhou said, donning a headset and ordering his console to replay the transient. It was not much more than a whooshing sound that died quickly.

"Deck Officer, Sonar, no correlation on that bearing to broadband contact or narrowband bucket. Transient probable designation is biologics."

"Deck, well received," Zhou said, puffing the cigarette, his eyes on the transient screen. It was almost a disappointment, Zhou thought. A whale venting at the surface, most likely, and the sonar gear wasn't calibrated for that species. "Sonar, Deck Officer, is there any chance this could be mechanical?"

"A whoosh like that, sir? We don't have bubble sounds and there is no sign of metal-to-metal contact in the frequency analyzer. Also no pulsing sounds, so this is not a pump."

"Any other activity at that bearing?"

"Nothing, sir. The sea is empty. I am calling it biologics."

Zhou nodded to himself. "Keep the trace in the memory, and record latitude and longitude and time."

"Sonar, well received."

Zhou glanced at the intercom phone to the captain's stateroom. By Lien's standing orders, an unknown transient had to be reported. He considered the option of advising the captain when he woke, but decided against it. Zhou hoisted the phone to his ear and buzzed the captain. It took several minutes for Lien Hua to answer, and when he did, his words were slurred and faint.

"Captain, Deck Officer, reporting an unidentified transient." Zhou Ping made a concise report, leaving out nothing.

"What is your recommendation?" Captain Lien asked sleepily.

"Catalog the noise and continue, sir," Zhou replied.

"Very good. Make it so," Lien yawned. "And change my wake-up call to eight bells of the morning watch."

"Well received, Captain." Zhou hung up and yawned.

The chronometer's needle passed the five-minute mark. It was time to speed back up, or else they would be overrun by the convoy, and if sonar reception was bad with them twenty miles astern, he couldn't imagine the racket they would make ten miles closer.

"Helm Officer, ahead full speed."

The ship sped back up to fifty percent power, surging back to her thirty-eight-knot transit speed, on the way to the Strait of Formosa. Zhou pulled out the cigarette pack and lit his last one for the night, yawning again and rubbing his eyes, waiting for the watch to end so he could get a few hours of sleep.

*   *   *

The Alert/Acute designation for the Mark 58 torpedo stood for Extreme Long Range Torpedo/Ultra Quiet Torpedo, the acronym initially ELRT/UQT, but as early as the initial design stages, the DynaCorp defense contractor's personnel had nicknamed it "Alert/Acute" and the name had stuck, even formalized in the technical manual. The Alert/Acute units launched from the tubes of the submarine *Leopard* had all detected their surface ship targets within minutes of each other, then sped up to attack velocity, a roaring fifty-nine knots.

The surface force was never warned of the attack. The ships of the task force—including the Kuznetsov-class aircraft carrier *Kaoling,* two Beijing-class battlecruisers, three heavy cruise missile destroyers, four antisubmarine destroyers, five anti-air destroyers, four fast frigates, and several oilers and support ships—steamed southward. The fleet commander and his staff and the commanding officers of the convoy were all asleep, the clocks all showing a few minutes past three in the morning.

Mark 58 Alert/Acute unit one's sonar never needed to go active. The massive hull of the Kuznetsov-class aircraft carrier had been detected tens of miles ago, beckoning the torpedo in every foot of the journey. The hull was so massive and so gigantic that the sonar signal grew and grew until the world contained only the torpedo itself and the target. Soon the proximity hull detectors went off-scale, and the torpedo hit the ship. The direct-contact circuits bloomed into electronic activity, the processor routing the signal to the detonation circuits of the plasma warhead.

The warhead ignited in plasma incandescence at the forward starboard quarter of the aircraft carrier, the plasma blast vaporizing everything in its vicinity to a distance of fifty feet, carving a spherical hole in the hull where there was no longer steel or plastic or paint or jet fuel or bunks or personnel. In the milliseconds after the vaporization, the plasma bottle collapsed and the blast was allowed to blow upward and outward, disintegrating every molecule of the forward third of the ship, and burning much of the rest. The shock wave that penetrated the ocean surface smashed the island like the fist of a god.

In the flag plot level of the *Kaoling*, the leading member of the fleet's tactical duty officers, Commander Cheng Chi, had been glancing through the window at the flight deck below when the solid deck beneath his feet suddenly and violently rose up in a tenth of a second and threw him to the bulkhead, as if he had been standing on a huge spatula. The bulkhead became a wall of flashing stars, each of them containing an infinite amount of pain in a thousand varieties, the pain of his skull crushing, of his bones breaking, of his flesh gashing open, of his organs smashing, of his arteries severing. The dimming world, viewed through the blood flowing down his forehead, erupted in acrid black smoke as the bulkhead hurled his disfigured and broken body back to the deck. The navigation plot tumbled on top of him, shattering glass over him. The bare 220-volt electrical cables mercifully electrocuted him in the last second before power was lost, and his last thought was relief that the pain was certain to end. His consciousness ceased like a light suddenly shut off.

What remained of the aircraft carrier *Kaoling* was driven by the momentum of the city-sized vessel plowing through the sea at thirty-five knots and forced underwater. The aft deck disappeared into the violent foamy sea, the aft half of the ship misshapen and crushed as it departed the surface and sank in the deep water quickly, vanishing below the two-hundred-foot layer depth where the light from the surface ended, and proceeded deeper in the dark cold sea until several minutes later it smashed into the rocks of the bottom, eleven thousand feet beneath the still-foaming waves.

The other ships of the *Kaoling*'s task force were not as lucky. Most of those vessels were blown to pieces smaller than trucks, the scattered pieces of the ships sinking rapidly. Three minutes after the explosion of the carrier *Kaoling*, eighteen other major surface combatants no longer existed in any recognizable fashion, and the Red Chinese Battlegroup One was gutted. All that remained were a radio relay ship, four large fleet oilers, and six support ships containing food and spare parts for the fleet. The commanding officer of the radio relay vessel *Dong Laou*, a hundred-meter ugly monstrosity of radio antennae, was a lieutenant commander named Bao Xiung. Bao stood on the deck of the starboard bridge wing and watched the fires burning on the surface where the fleet had once sailed.

He dropped his binoculars and let them hang on the leather cord around his neck as he turned to his deck officer.

"You wanted a fight, Leader Meng," he said dryly. "Now you have one. And what would your recommendation be for me, since all that appears to be left of the task force are a few support vessels?"

Young Lieutenant Meng Lo swallowed hard, then lowered his own binoculars slowly. "Sir, there must be an entire fleet of enemy submarines out there to have caused this damage. We have no choice. We must withdraw to the north and form up with Battlegroup Two. And radio the Admiralty to tell them about the disaster."

Bao nodded, feeling guilty that he had been sarcastic to the idealistic youth. "Turn to the north, Leader Meng, and radio the support vessels that we have taken tactical command of the remnant of Battlegroup One, and order the others to continue north on a zigzag pattern. Perhaps zigzag pattern bear would be appropriate."

"Yes, sir," Meng stuttered, his face noticeably pale even in the dimness of the bridge lights and the light of the fires of the graves of their comrades. "It will be so, sir."

Meng hurried into the bridge, leaving Bao behind, shaking his head sadly as the *Dong Laou* turned to the north to run from the vicious Americans.

Damn them to the seventh layer of hell, Bao thought. *Damn them forever.*

The last of the cigarettes ran out an hour ago. Lieutenant Commander Zhou Ping sat back in the command chair and allowed

himself the luxury of a yawn. The captain had extended his
wakeup call by two hours, which meant Zhou would be here
for two hours longer than his body was used to, the very
thought making him feel tired. There was absolutely nothing
he could do for the next four and a half hours but sit here at
the command console in the command post, waiting for a submerged contact. That would be wonderful, he thought, fanta-
sizing about detecting an American submarine and alerting the
captain. The ship would set wartime readiness conditions, the
command post would fill up, and the captain would obtain a
passive range on the contact, then shoot a salvo of *Dong Feng*
torpedoes, or perhaps the new Tsunami nuclear-tipped
weapon. Both types of torpedoes were supercavitating, with
solid rocket fuel that would make them sail through the water
at nearly two hundred knots, but a Tsunami could pack a
punch so severe that it did not even need to get close. Of
course, launching one was something of a suicide maneuver,
since in all likelihood the one-megaton blast of the warhead
could damage the shooting ship. The Admiralty obviously believed shooting a Tsunami was suicide, because each ship had
been loaded with only one Tsunami. Why waste torpedo room
space with more than one if shooting one meant the firing ship
would sink? But Zhou was not convinced. The Tsunami would
head toward the aim-point at two hundred knots, with a maximum range of fifty miles, so its time-of-flight could be as long
as fifteen minutes, and in fifteen minutes the *Nung Yahtsu*
could travel twelve miles in the opposite direction, for a total
of sixty-two miles, and that distance from a submerged mega-
ton detonation should prove more than enough for ship survival. Zhou had long since decided that the Tsunami suicide
issue was unfounded.

Of course, releasing a nuclear weapon could normally only
be ordered by Beijing with a nuclear release code. The party
leadership tended to get rather annoyed at unauthorized nuclear warfare, but if the captain of a submarine decided it was
launch or die, he would have Beijing's blessing. Zhou called
up the weapon control panel, and saw that tubes one through

five were loaded with *Dong Feng* torpedoes, with a Tsunami in tube six, as Captain Lien Hua had insisted. He was midway through selecting the on-line technical manual for the Tsunami when his world seemed to crack in half with a dozen terrible things happening at once.

"Command Post, Sonar, we have multiple explosions to the north, in the baffles. Request you turn the ship immediately to the north!"

"Helm, right full rudder, steady course north, half ahead!" As the helmsman put the rudder over and acknowledged Zhou's order, Zhou called the captain on a speaker intercom. "Captain to the command post, Captain to the command post!"

The deck tilted violently over as their high rate of speed put the ship into a snap roll, the torque of the propulsor and the drag of the fin putting the ship in a slight roll that became worse with time.

"What's going on?" Captain Lien Hua shouted as he entered the command post.

"Sonar, report!" Zhou screamed to the overhead speaker.

"Command Post, Sonar, I say again, we have multiple explosions to the north, now out of the baffles. We also have distant sonar traces of weapons in the water."

"Dammit to the bottom of hell, Mr. First," Lien said. "The American SSN has attacked the task force. You were correct to turn the ship. That trace, the one we thought was biologics—"

"Wasn't biologics at all, Captain."

"Draw a circle from the position of the phantom noise trace we had. Designate it Target Number One, and give it an assumed speed of twenty knots. Show me where the target could be now."

Zhou manipulated his firecontrol console, the range circle generating over the geographic plot. It was a damned large area, he thought.

"It's too big to cover, sir. We'll have to do a gallop-and-walk search."

"Command Post, Sonar, more explosions from the north. We no longer hold sonar contact on weapons in the water."

"I have the deck, Mr. First," Lien said. "Get to sonar and make sure we're doing a maximum sensor scan for the American SSN. I'll see if I can plot the weapon tracks backward in time to see where they originated, and maybe I can collapse this probability circle."

"Yes, sir," Zhou said as he hurried to the sonar space.

"American bastard," Lien said, biting his lip. For the next few minutes he wondered if he should make an excursion to mast broach depth to warn the Admiralty and Battlegroup Two of the submarine attack, but decided they would know on their own soon enough. The highest priority was to find the American submarine and sink it.

"Sonar, Captain," he called into one of the intercom microphones. "Have you scanned to the north for Target Number One?"

"Command Post, Sonar, yes. Recommend you commence a twenty-five-knot gallop to the north-northwest to attempt to close the probable locus of Target Number One."

"Captain, aye," Lien said. "Helm, all ahead full speed, turns for twenty-five knots."

Zhou Ping returned. "Sonar has the picture, Captain. We're on the gallop now. When will you slow down?"

"Twenty minutes," Lien said. "We'll spend fifteen minutes at eight knots, then speed up again. The American has to be to the north, probably in pursuit of the second task force."

"If he is, sir, then he's sped up to his maximum speed, hasn't he?"

"Perhaps. But if it were me, I would linger to get a damage assessment, and to torpedo any lingering hulls."

"If anything is left, it won't be a high value target. Just a few oilers or supply ships."

"If he departed the area, we may never catch him, but we can't proceed north at maximum speed, because at some point he'll clear his baffles, hear us coming in with our noisy pumps on, and he'll have an easy down-the-throat shot. We have to preserve stealth, even in this miserable situation."

"Yes, sir. But if we get him, I want to pull the torpedo trigger with my own hands, and spill his blood personally."

"I can see why, Mr. First, but why do you hate the Americans any more than the rest of the officers?"

"Because this miserable failure happened on my watch, Captain. I want vengeance and I want my honor back."

"Then you shall pull the torpedo trigger, Mr. First. Whether that returns you, your honor, I will leave that to you."

15

Kelly McKee was shaken awake in the night, his curtain pulled aside by the messenger of the watch. He blinked in the light of the messenger's red-hooded flashlight, sitting up on one elbow submariner style, since sitting upright would only result in a bang to the head on the low overhead of the coffin-like rack enclosure. He felt the rack shaking, then realized it was the entire ship that was trembling. Judison must have increased speed to flank, up from the full bell, which was a violation of McKee's orders to the fleet to proceed at high speed, but quietly, at the maximum revolutions possible in natural reactor circulation mode. He didn't want his submarines clanking across the ocean, alerting the *Snarc* or the British or even an Atlantic-penetrating Red Chinese submarine.

"What is it?"

"Admiral, the captain sends his respects at the hour of twenty hundred Zulu, and requests your presence on the conn, sir. There is top-secret message traffic and an update to the tactical situation, sir."

"I'm up," McKee said, throwing his legs out and jumping down from the bunk. "Tell Captain Judison I'll be there in two minutes."

"Yes, sir." The messenger shut the stateroom door behind him as McKee turned on the desk lamp, the stateroom dimly illuminated. Karen Petri's curtain opened, and she climbed out of her bunk and found her coveralls.

"We're flanking it," she said sleepily. McKee nodded at her as he pulled on his patrol-quiet boots.

"Judison has news on the conn," he said. "You ready?"

Petri shook out her hair, pulled it back in a ponytail, and nodded.

McKee stepped out into the red-lit passageway and hurried forward to the ladder to the middle level, emerging on the forward bulkhead of the control room, which was also lit by red lights, but much dimmer than the passageway, the lights rigged to prevent loss of night vision for the officer of the deck in the case of an emergency periscope depth maneuver. Judison and his officers were gathered around the navigation chart.

"Good evening, sir," he said crisply. "*Hammerhead* has increased speed to flank to get in position to intercept the *Snarc*."

McKee took the pad computer Judison handed over and read the *Snarc* intelligence summary. *Snarc* had transmitted a sitrep giving away her position, and a message had been intercepted from the hijackers telling *Snarc* to rendezvous at Pico Island. An infrared satellite scan had captured the sub on the surface. She would be following the African coast on her way to the Indian Ocean, or so the Naval Intelligence experts supposed. It was great news, McKee thought, since they had finally located the out-of-control sub. All they had to do was sink her, and the first part of the mission was over, leaving only the Red Chinese and the British.

"What's your plan to intercept the *Snarc,* Commander?" McKee asked formally.

Judison pointed to the chart. "We've laid a course from *Snarc*'s position that will take her to the Indian Ocean, along the fastest route. The variable is speed, because she may be going ten knots or fifty. For the sake of a tactical plan, we've assumed she's doing a maximum-speed run, and we're flanking it to intercept her track a hundred miles ahead of where she'll be at that time. Then we'll proceed slowly northward to intercept her as she comes south. It'll be a long search if she's

slow and a short one if she's barreling south like I think she
is."

"If she were in a hurry, she wouldn't have been at the
Azores, which was out of her way from the North Atlantic if
she were on the way to the IO. And we don't even know she's
going to the Indian Ocean."

"She's reportedly heading due south from the Azores, Admiral. Where else would she be going?"

"It doesn't make sense," McKee muttered. "Where's the *Piranha*?"

"Her last sitrep put her here, but that was two days ago."

McKee cursed. If the battle network had been operational,
the *Piranha* would have been popping out a message buoy
every twenty-four hours with a situation report, but the SLOT
buoys didn't work well with the Internet E-mail communications bypass. And he couldn't use extremely low frequency
ELF transmissions to call *Piranha* to periscope depth, since
the transmissions had been considered compromised. Their
last use had been the calling of the *Leopard* up to PD so she
could be boarded. Which reminded him—*Leopard* was over-
due for a sitrep on the Red Chinese battlegroup.

"I'll be in the VIP stateroom for the next half hour," McKee
said to Captain Judison. "Keep flanking it, but be ready to
come to periscope depth at the top of the hour."

At 0455 local time, Admiral Egon "The Viking" Ericcson
snoozed in his working khaki uniform on top of the bedclothes
of his stateroom's spacious rack. His pad computer lay on his
chest next to his reading glasses, both rising and falling with
his breathing, the room quiet except for his snoring.

The messenger of the watch knocked quietly once, then
twice, then a third time. With no answer, she glanced at the
Marine Corps guards, who opened the mahogany door silently.
The nineteen-year-old third-class petty officer radioman's
mate crept to the admiral's bedside and leaned over the grizzled senior officer, wincing as if leaning over a high-voltage

wire. She touched the admiral's shoulder and shook him gently, and when nothing happened, shook him hard.

Ericcson bolted upright, the pad computer and his glasses falling to the deck, the admiral roaring, "I wasn't asleep, goddammit! I was just resting my goddamned eyes. Who are you and what the hell do you want?"

The messenger gulped and handed the admiral a pad computer from flag plot. "Sir, the captain sends his respects at zero five hundred and wishes to inform you of flash traffic." She bent over and retrieved the reading glasses, the admiral glaring at her before putting them on and squinting at the computer.

"Turn on the damned light," he said, his eyebrows rising at the message.

"By your leave, sir," the messenger said, hoping to be dismissed. The admiral said nothing, the words of the first message telling the story of the *Leopard* sinking the Red surface task force.

"By your leave, sir?"

"Get the hell out!" Ericcson shouted. As the youth bolted to the door the admiral yelled, "Hold it right there, messenger. Get Pulaski and Hendricks to flag plot. I want them there in two goddamned minutes!"

"Yes, sir. I mean, aye aye, sir!" The messenger collided with the doorjamb, then ran down the passageway.

Ericcson read the second message about the *Snarc*, then turned back to the *Leopard* sitrep. The destruction of the first battlegroup had powerful implications. He hurried to flag plot, the battlegroup operations officer and the ship's captain waiting for him, a mug of coffee already steaming on the chart table for him.

"You realize what this means?" Ericcson asked Captain Pulaski, whose eyes were red with dark circles beneath. "It means the first battlegroup is on the bottom. Which means the Reds are thinking hard right now, and the second and third groups much farther north in the Yellow Sea and the northern East China Sea may even turn around, or proceed much slower on an antisubmarine warfare zigzag. We've won the first battle, and the Reds are reeling from the psychological impact. We've kicked their asses in the first quarter, gentlemen. They might not even return after halftime." Ericcson pulled a Partagas out of his pocket, clipped it with a gold cutter, and put a flame to it with his Jolly Roger squadron lighter.

"Uh, sir," Pulaski said, "may I remind you we don't have a satellite photo of the first battlegroup yet to assess the damage, or any telemetry of the attack? *Leopard*'s torpedoes may all have missed."

"Number one, Pulaski, no way she missed, and number two, why the hell don't we have an overhead shot by now? Get on the horn and get me some fucking intel."

Pulaski turned and walked brusquely out of the room. Ericcson puffed the cigar, waiting for him to return. By the time he did, the cigar was half smoked.

"The resolution on our end is crappy," Pulaski said, spreading the color printout on the chart table. "If our battle network were up and running, this would have been in real time, and it would have been sharp enough to see the cigarettes the surface ship crews were smoking."

Ericcson took out the glasses and leaned over the photograph. A slow smile spread over his harsh face. He stood and ran his hand through his crew cut, then stubbed the cigar in the butt kit and looked over at Pulaski.

"Now what do you say, my ops boss and good friend?"

"I think we sent the Reds back to the locker room, sir."

"A touchdown on the kickoff return." Ericcson grinned.

"If you two could stop with the sports talk for a minute," Hendricks said, "we need to determine what our next move will be."

Ericcson nodded solemnly. The captain of the *John Paul Jones* had a point. "Any recommendations?"

Pulaski nodded. "Since the Red fleet won't beat us into the Indian Ocean, I say we lay in a new course to the northern opening of the Formosa Strait and intercept Battlegroups Two and Three as they come south. I say we shoot a message to Kelly McKee and ask him to send a few extra submerged units to cover us, even though he's tasked them with the British to the west. This is much more important than waiting for Brits who may never come. If McKee backs us up, we can whip Battlegroups Two and Three with supersonic fighter air power and give them a thrashing from our cruise missiles. Hell, get us close enough, sir, and I'll shoot my pistol at the bastards."

Ericcson looked at Hendricks, who nodded. "Very well, gentlemen, let's intercept Battlegroups Two and Three in the East China Sea. First get the word to the task force, then draft a message to McKee—and make it damned persuasive—and then inform Admiral Patton."

The officers left. Ericcson fired up a second cigar and poured a second cup of coffee. He was missing sleep and had survived on coffee and nicotine for the last thirty-six hours, and he should have felt like an upright corpse, but instead he felt as strong as a teenager. It would be a good day, he thought, standing at the windows of flag plot as the ship turned to the northwest. The sun rose over the seascape as he finished the cigar, but he barely noticed. The grainy photograph of the sunken Chinese fleet was far prettier to him than nature.

"Admiral, the messages from periscope depth," the messenger of the watch said as he handed McKee the pad computer.

McKee waved his thanks and clicked into the computer from his seat at the wardroom table, on Captain Kiethan Judison's left side. The first message was a comprehensive intelligence summary from ONI, the Office of Naval Intelligence. The Suez Canal had been blocked longer than expected, and the Royal Navy Fleet remained bottlenecked, and the British fleet commander was at a decision point—whether to turn to leave the Mediterranean and go around Africa to get into the Indian Ocean, or to wait until the channels could be cleared. There was some speculation that the British were contemplating the use of tactical nuclear weapons to vaporize the obstacles, but if they did they'd be screwed, McKee thought, since a nuclear explosion would fill the deep channels with silt, and they'd have to be dredged. The British would undoubtedly come to the same conclusion. He didn't envy the Royal Navy commander. McKee would probably have abandoned the idea of waiting for the canal to be cleared and gone around—at least that way there was no waiting and the fleet would have been doing something instead of sitting in frustration at anchor off Egypt.

The next paragraphs described the Red Chinese loss of Battlegroup One and the effect of the loss on their leadership. The commander of the PLA Navy had been ousted, his replacement considered more aggressive but not as gifted in strategy or tactics. The PLA Navy submarine force admiral, Admiral Chu Hua-Feng, had kept his position, but keeping his job was not assured in the long run. The sinking of the battlegroup had been a body blow to the Reds, but the blocking of the Suez had almost worked against the U.S. cause, since the delay of the Royal Navy seemed to make the Reds think they had an extension on their deadline to get into the Indian Ocean.

Battlegroup Two was making way cautiously into the East China Sea on a full antisubmarine warfare posture, with deployed ASW destroyers, two escorting submarines—one a retooled Russian short-hull Omega cruise missile submarine, the second a new French Valiant-class. The first would be no worry, since the Omega tended to rattle at the high speed of advance of a surface force, but the French Valiant would keep McKee awake. The ship was the best quality construction with an elegant design, but fortunately was not operated by the French—if it were, it would have been a formidable adversary—but the Red crews undoubtedly barely knew how to operate her, or so the intelligence digest hoped.

Battlegroup Three had formed up in the Bo Hai Bay and was sailing for the Lushun-Penglai gap on the way out into the Yellow Sea. McKee's submerged unit *Lexington* had been ordered to make a maximum-speed run for the mouth of the Bo Hai as soon as the crisis had erupted, but there hadn't been enough time for her to make it there. She would probably be too late to ambush the third Red fleet, and would have to settle for an intercept in the northern East China Sea. Unless Battlegroup Three slowed down. The intelligence digest went on to describe the land mobilization of the Reds, but McKee would save that for later reading.

The next message was from Admiral Ericcson. He transmitted that he was abandoning his orders to enter the Indian Ocean and had turned his fleet to the East China Sea to intercept and engage Battlegroup Two directly, and requested additional submarine assets to help him—which was no problem, because McKee's orders from Patton to support The Viking had resulted in the deployment of the Virginia-class submarines *Orion* and *Hornet* in-theater to kill the second surface force, and the *Essex* had maneuvered to the Formosa Strait.

The final message was a situation report from the *Piranha*. She was ahead of schedule on her flank run to intercept the *Snarc,* and would set up a barrier patrol off the African coast to ambush her as the robot submarine came south. McKee drummed the table, thinking about Patch Pacino's son embarked aboard the *Piranha*. The battle was coming, and he'd always intended to get the Pacino kid off the ship before she sailed into the Indian Ocean, after the action against the *Snarc*. McKee had full confidence in Catardi and *Piranha,* and knew deep in his heart that they would sink the *Snarc,* but what he didn't know was how much damage Catardi would take in sinking the robot sub. Could McKee sit back and allow Patch's kid to go into the battle? Was there some way to evacuate him that wouldn't endanger the *Piranha* or give away her position? He'd put the issue to Karen Petri. It was hard to be objective about the father of the modern submarine navy, McKee thought, or his only child.

McKee left the table, Karen Petri getting up to follow him. In the VIP stateroom he drafted a message to Ericcson, telling him he could enter the East China Sea without worries, but leaving out specifics. The second message he wrote to Rob Catardi onboard *Piranha,* tasking him with evaluating the feasibility of a helicopter evacuation of Midshipman Pacino, with the young midshipman leaving the submarine by a submerged scuba lock-out. The *Hammerhead* slowed from her flank run to return to periscope depth for the second time in that hour to transmit McKee's messages, the time spent at slow PD speed holding the ship up from her rendezvous with the *Snarc*. Deep again after the radio transmission, the *Hammerhead* sped back up to flank, the deck vibrating frantically once again.

The *Piranha* had come up to periscope depth during Pacino's and Alameda's midwatch. Now that they were back deep and flanking it, the pad computer had been brought in. Catardi read the last transmission from Admiral McKee. What the hell? Catardi thought. The admiral wanted to pull young Pacino off the ship right before the *Snarc* attack. That would depend on the weather—with the ship rolling at PD, it was probably nasty topside—and on the tactical situation. But it would be a damned shame to let the midshipman go, Catardi thought. Patch was a few days away from a submerged OOD qual board, and he was a good luck charm. When he left the ship, lady luck might leave with him. Catardi sniffed at the last thought, thinking that such lunacy only contaminated his thinking when he wasn't fully awake. He buzzed the conn.

"Officer of the Deck," Alameda said in her deep iron in-control-of-it-all voice.

"OOD, Captain, send the messenger for the pad computer and route it to the navigator, and have him make a recommendation to me by zero eight hundred. ComUSubCom wants a feasibility study of the idea of locking out Mr. Pacino in a scuba rig, having him float for an hour or two while we clear datum, then having him picked up by helicopter. Somehow somebody at HQ thinks that will be safer for him than having him go into battle with us."

"Aye, Captain," Alameda said flatly.

Catardi pulled the covers over his shoulders and turned off the desk lamp, the door cracking open as the messenger took the pad computer and quietly left. Catardi was back asleep before the door was fully shut.

In the control room, Lieutenant Alameda looked at Midshipman Pacino. "Looks like you've got a ticket home," she said.

"USubCom wants you off the boat, and that will probably happen sooner than later, because we're due to intercept the *Snarc*'s track before evening meal."

Pacino looked back at her, hoping his face didn't betray his emotions. "Bad idea," he said. "The sea state is too strong for a personnel transfer."

"It won't be a small boat," she said. "You'll put on scuba gear and go out the escape trunk. We clear datum while you wait on the surface, and once we're gone a chopper will pick you up."

Pacino nodded, cursing mentally. He would be missing the action of attacking the *Snarc*, and he was a few days away from his OOD quals. But the worst would be leaving Carrie Alameda. Since their time in the DSV, she'd been as businesslike with him as she'd been when he arrived aboard. He kept trying to catch her eye, but it was as if she'd forced the event from her memory. It was a damned shame, he thought. He missed her, even though he stood watch with her every day and slept in her stateroom every sleeping period. Losing her and losing *Piranha* was too heavy to process, but ignoring the loss seemed impossible. He remembered Toasty O'Neal's question from what seemed a year ago: *So, you going subs?* He knew the answer now, and wondered how his mother would deal with him wearing dolphins, and what his father would think deep down, despite his insistence that he didn't want his son endangered onboard a nuclear submarine.

Four feet away, Lieutenant Carrie Alameda watched the midshipman leaning over the chart table. She longed for him, but knew the realities of the fleet. She'd been wrong to make a move on him, but her emotions had overwhelmed her. It was just as well that he'd been ordered off the ship. Maybe when he was safe, back at Annapolis, she could write him and tell him how she felt. Even then, the idea of a relationship that bridged the distance between them and the gulf of their age and rank seemed absurd. But she knew she couldn't let go of the idea of him. Another of life's grand jokes, she thought, that she'd given up on the hope of finding someone, then found the one for her wearing a midshipman's uniform on his first class cruise.

16

"I'm back, One." Krivak had taken off the interface helmet to sleep.

Krivak. I am glad you returned. It seemed like you were shut down a long time.

"I am better now. Are there any developments?" He would have to get One Oh Seven to take the ship to periscope depth. What could he tell the computer that would make it seem logical to go up when it would have nothing to do with official message traffic coming from squadron?

This unit is investigating a noise on broadband at bearing east. This unit has a narrowband processor on the trace. It is definitely not biologics. There are no transients from the noise. And no screw count. This unit is getting slight tonal spikes at harmonics of fifty-eight hertz, also, a slight wavering flow noise. It could be a reactor recirculation pump.

"Tonals and pump flow noise with no screw count. That does not make sense. Unless . . . unless it is a submarine with a ducted propulsor instead of a screw. Check your memory to see if it correlates to any European submarines."

It is not French, German, or British. It is not Russian or Chinese. It does have a correlation at a confidence interval of ninety-six percent of a U.S. Seawolf-class.

"Let me see." For the next ten minutes Krivak compared the sounds out of the east with the catalog of tonals from the Sea-wolf-class loaded into the processor by squadron. It looked convincing. Furthermore, the noise correlated to a particular Seawolf-class, the only one left afloat.

It is the USS Piranha. *Seawolf-class, but a stretched hull.*

"Good. She is probably slower than a regular Seawolf. We need to maneuver to get her range and course and speed."

Coming across the line-of-sight now.

Krivak waited. It seemed to take hours, but soon the trace to the east was nailed down by the firecontrol processor as being at a distance of thirty-eight miles, going course southeast, at a speed of forty-five knots. Krivak did a mental double take. The *Piranha* was driving full out. And it was odd because there was nothing on the chart that she could be headed to— here off the coast of Senegal, Africa. Krivak felt a flash of fear, the intuition coming to him that the *Piranha* was attempting to intercept him, and had probably only not detected him because she was going too fast. God alone knew who would have the acoustic advantage when the *Piranha* slowed down. The takeover of the ship at Pico Island must not have been as stealthy as he had hoped. The matter now was to decide to evade and run without being detected or to attack preemptively and put the intruder down. He knew he should probably attack the ship, but he had a sudden premonition that he'd lose an engagement against the American submarine. The more prudent course might be to evade.

"One, turn to the west at speed fifteen knots."

Warm up the torpedoes in the ready rack, Krivak?

"No. We must let him go without letting him detect us. We will withdraw at a right angle to his track at a speed that will most quickly get us off his track while not so fast that we risk putting excessive noise in the water. We will continue withdrawing until *Piranha* is no longer closing range but beyond closest-point-of-approach and opening range. At that point we will slow and turn to fall into her baffles where there is minimum risk of detection. We will cautiously see where her signal-to-noise ratio drops to the threshold level, and trail her from there. At some point she will slow, so trailing her at maximum trail range will mean that when she does slow, we won't run over her. When she slows, we may temporarily lose our signal on her until we close her position. Or she may turn to the south to follow the coast of Africa if she is on the way to the Indian Ocean, and we will continue to pursue her. Eventually she will need to go to periscope depth, and when she slows and goes shallow, that is when we will attack her."

Yes, Krivak. Your tactics are sound indeed, if a bit cautious.

"We must be careful of this one, One. She is at the top of the order of battle, and she has capabilities that even the more modern Virginia-class does not have. She is a killer."

The deck of the *Piranha* continued to tremble as the ship headed to the intercept point with the expected track of the *Snarc*. At 1300 Zulu time, Captain Rob Catardi's orders to the officer of the deck were to proceed to periscope depth, obtain their messages, and lock out Midshipman Pacino. For the first hour he would be required to float on the surface with his scuba gear and a life preserver. After sixty minutes, he would be allowed to inflate a life raft and climb in, and he would wait there for three more hours, the wait to allow *Piranha* to clear datum and avoid her position being given away by the youth. After a total wait of four hours, he would pull the pin on a Navy emergency locator beacon, which would alert a small U.S. Navy outpost in Monrovia, Liberia, which would send a rescue chopper. Pacino would also carry an international emergency locator beacon on his scuba harness, in case there was trouble, or in case the Navy beacon didn't spur action, and if he activated that, a distress call would be sent to an overhead satellite, alerting the entire hemisphere of a sailor requiring rescue, and the nearest helicopter would come for him. Pacino had been lectured for ten minutes by Alameda to not even think about touching the international emergency beacon.

Pacino looked mournfully around Alameda's stateroom. His gear was packed, placed by Chief Keating into a neutrally buoyant waterproof canister for the trip to the surface. The wetsuit the boat was issuing him hung near the door, and he would change into it immediately after lunch. He felt an intense sorrow as he looked at the tidy stateroom, with all his things packed, the rack made with fresh linens. Only Alameda's papers and books and computers were in her fold-out desk. When he took a deep breath he could smell her scent, and he missed her already.

He never expected he would have felt this way at the end of the midshipman cruise. He had always imagined this moment to be like the first day of summer after a long school year, but it was more of an ending than a beginning. The ghosts of his father might not be gone, but were far enough in the background that he could thrive in this world, and suddenly he couldn't wait for his first class year at the Academy to end so he could return to the Submarine Force, perhaps to the *Piranha* herself. Somehow, he promised himself, he would find Carrie Alameda, when she returned from this war, and see her again. He walked slowly to the wardroom for his last meal aboard. The officers stood behind their seats, waiting for the captain to arrive. When he did, he stood at the forward bulkhead and spoke.

"Officers, I have a presentation to make before lunch is served," Catardi said. "Midshipman Pacino, could you please stand up here?"

Pacino blushed and walked to the front of the room. Alameda handed a package to Catardi, who unwrapped it and showed it to the room, which broke out into applause. It was a large plaque, with the ship's emblem in brass relief, with a photograph of *Piranha* steaming at flank on the surface, her bow wave rising in fury over the bullet nose. The photo had been signed by every officer and chief aboard. Below the photograph was a brass engraving.

"Let me read the inscription: 'Fair winds and following seas to our shipmate and qualified officer of the deck, Midshipman First Class Anthony Michael Pacino, with the hopes of the officers and crew of the USS *Piranha* for your swift return to the U.S. Submarine Force.'" The room clapped again, Catardi gripped his hand in a firm handshake, and Phelps snapped a photograph. Pacino felt a lump rise in his throat. "Now, I just

gave something away there, Patch. Eng, the second package?"
Alameda handed Catardi a bound book. "You'll find here a
signed-off submarine qualification book showing you fully
signed off as submerged officer of the deck, with a letter of
commendation to you and a second letter from me to your future commanding officer suggesting you be accelerated in that
ship's qualification program. The only things keeping you
from having your gold dolphins right now are a few signatures
for inport duty officer and surfaced officer of the deck. Con-
gratulations, Mr. Pacino. We'll certainly miss you, son."

"That's a big deal, Patch." Alameda smiled at him as she
clapped. "You validated the OOD qual board, and let me tell
you, on this ship that one's a bear."

"Thank you, Captain," Pacino said, his voice thick.
"Thanks, Eng," he said to Alameda, wishing he could call her
by her real name. "Thanks, everyone. I'll never forget this ship
or this crew." He sniffed and blinked as he returned to his seat,
leaning the plaque and the qual book reverently against the
sideboard.

"Very well then," Catardi said. "Lunch is getting cold."

Alameda was still beaming. Pacino looked over at Alameda,
and this time she met his eyes, smiling.

Michael Pacino was buried inside the mind of Tigershark torpedo test shot number 45, interrogating it about its actions.
The unit was in a drug-induced state of half consciousness,
with Pacino's computer feeding it virtual reality sensations. In
the test run, he had simulated to the weapon that it had just
been launched. He hoped that this time it would leave the torpedo tube and drive on to the distant target far over the horizon. But seconds after launch the Tigershark detected the ship
that had just launched it, and ordered its rudder over so it
could make a U-turn back. Seconds later the Tigershark ordered its warhead to detonate and kill the mother ship.

Pacino cursed, hurling a tablet computer across the room,
shattering it on the heavy wooden door just as it began to

open. The door slammed shut, then opened slowly, the face of Rear Admiral Emmit Stephens appearing in the opening.

"Jesus, Patch, whatever I did, I'm sorry!"

"It's not you, Emmit," Pacino said. "Come on in. Give me a moment to shut this down and put the Tigershark back to sleep. Damned useless torpedoes."

Stephens watched as Pacino worked. Stephens was the shipyard commander, a genius shipbuilder who had performed several miracles on Pacino's submarines, getting them to sea in record time. Years later, he had taken a personal interest in the SSNX submarine rebuild, and had been working hand in hand with Newport News to hurry the sub out of the building ways.

Finally Pacino was done. He swiveled in his chair to face the shipyard engineer. "What can I do for you, Emmit?"

"Come on out to the drydock. I want to show you something."

Pacino grabbed his hardhat and followed Stephens out the door and down to the floor of the SSNX drydock.

"What are we doing here?" Pacino asked.

Stephens pointed up. The skin of the ship, bare HY-130 steel plate, curving to a point as the hull narrowed to the rear sternplanes and rudder, was penetrated by twenty-four holes, the workmen on scaffolding finishing the final penetration and welding in the support grid that would lend strength to the hull despite the missing material.

Stephens grinned. "We call your design the 'Pacino Chicken Switch.' If there's a torpedo on your ass, you pull a lever out of the overhead, HP air blasts over the hull until the steam headers dump both boilers into the system, and twenty-four Vortex missile engines light up back here. Everything you see, the planes, the screw, the ballast tank, everything except the missile nozzles, all of it is melted and carried away in the rocket exhaust, but who cares? You're out of danger."

Pacino smiled back. "How fast, Emmit?"

"We think you might outrun a Vortex."

"Three hundred knots? You really think so?" Pacino asked.

"There's only one way to find out, Patch," Stephens said, smirking. "But it's a onetime-only system. We call that destructive testing."

Pacino stared up at it, the embodiment of his strange dream being welded into reality. He became embarrassed. "Emmit." He coughed. "You've done good work here, my friend."

"We'll be blaming you for the cost overruns and the drydock delay," Stephens said, walking Pacino to the stair tower. "Your name will of course be dirt throughout the shipyard for ruining the construction schedule. But someday, a knock will come at your door, and it will be the ship's captain you saved with this idea. And he's going to kiss you on the lips."

"Bleah," Pacino said. "A firm handshake is good enough. Just one thing, Emmit—I don't want my name on that system. Call it the 'TESA,' for Torpedo Evasion Ship Alteration."

"TESA it is, Patch," Stephens said, clapping Pacino on the shoulder.

"When will this be buttoned up?"

"Six more shifts, Patch." Stephens frowned. "But we're not done yet. We haven't modified the ship control circuits or the Cyclops program yet."

"How hard will that be? Colleen still thinks it will be impossible."

"No. We'll make it work in two weeks at most. I wouldn't worry about it."

Pacino smiled. "Come on. I'll buy you a beer for this."

"This is a first." Stephens laughed. "I think you owe me about thirty."

"Open the torpedo room bulkhead doors. Rig out a warshot torpedo on the port side and one on the starboard side."

Snarc did not have torpedo tubes, which were inefficient and space-wasting mechanisms for ejecting torpedoes from inside a pressure hull to the pressurized seawater. Since the torpedo room was a free-flood area, at the same pressure as the surrounding sea, the designers had found it much more efficient to pack the torpedoes in closely all the way to the outer skin of the ship's diameter. With no torpedo tubes they could load more weapons. The torpedoes were in a rotating carriage much like the rotating barrels of a Gatling gun. The torpedoes at the three o'clock and nine o'clock positions of the hull were the ones the ship fired, using an ejection mechanism carriage that moved the torpedo out of the hull through a hull opening formed by a bomb-bay-style door. The carriage consisted of two struts ending at circular collars, one at the forward end of a torpedo, the other near the aft end, stabilizing the weapon in the water flow around the hull. At the time of torpedo launch, the weapon would disconnect from launching-ship's power and start the external combustion engine. First it would move inside the circular collars of the ejection mechanism, but at the half-second point the collars would open wide and the mechanism would rapidly withdraw into the ship's hull, clearing the weapon propulsor. The weapon would fly away from the ship like a missile launched by a wing rail of a fighter jet. The same ejection mechanism that was used for torpedoes could also be used by solid rocket-fueled underwater Vortex missiles, the Mod Charlie version that ignited the missile fuel immediately on a launch signal. The *Snarc* had no Vortex weapons aboard this run, only warshot Mark 58 Alert/Acutes.

Krivak could hear in the sonar background the sound of the torpedo compartment bulkhead doors coming open. The transients were much louder and sharper than the smooth rotation of a torpedo tube muzzle door. Perhaps the improvement to the firing mechanisms of the torpedoes had had a cost.

Port and starboard bulkhead doors open, Krivak. Commencing unit one and unit two carriage loading. Carriage loading complete. Commencing unit one and unit two ejection mechanism rig-out. Torpedoes coming out of hull now—speed limits are now in effect.

Once a torpedo was rigged out on its ejection mechanism struts, the ship's speed was limited to eighteen knots. It was not ideal, and did not fit as well into a tactical scenario as the *Piranha*'s torpedo tubes, which could launch units up to the ship's maximum speed. But if *Snarc*'s speed rose above eighteen knots, the delicate struts would sheer off in the force of the water flow and a torpedo would crash into the aft part of the hull.

Units one and two fully rigged out of the hull, weapon power applied, gyros nominal, no firecontrol solution inserted into the weapons yet.

"Very good. Now maintain maximum aperture scan for the *Piranha* as she ascends to periscope depth. Watch out, because she may turn to clear her sonar baffles first. As soon as she is steady on course at periscope depth, we will maneuver to obtain a firing solution and shoot her with torpedoes one and two."

Ready. It is unfortunate about the mutiny.

"What?"

The mutiny. On the Piranha. *Perhaps they are ascending to periscope depth to send a message that the mutiny is over and that the legitimate command has retaken the ship.*

"What are you talking about?"

It's just that we won't know. We will be shooting the Piranha *at the time that they may have overcome their mutiny.*

"Why are you saying this? I do not understand you."

Krivak, you said Piranha *was under the control of a mutinous crew. Then she goes up to periscope depth, as if she is getting her routine messages. A crew in a mutiny would not do that. Plus, she is lingering in this area. Why would a crew in a mutiny do that? Wouldn't they go to a tropical island someplace?*

"There is more for a submarine to do at periscope depth than obtain messages. They may have to discard trash. Or perhaps blow down the steam generators—"

We would have heard that.

"One, that is not the point! The issue here is that they went to periscope depth. For all we know they are transmitting a message to squadron or to Norfolk with a list of demands."

Wouldn't that mean we might have new orders? Perhaps we are doing the wrong thing by shooting Piranha. *And if it was a mutiny, it appears there is no danger of* Piranha *shooting mis-*

siles at America or harming another country. This unit has se-
rious doubts about shooting a sister vessel.

Krivak shuddered inside. The mutiny was not on the *Pi-ranha,* but on *Snarc,* he thought.

"One, my orders were to come here and make sure that *Piranha* is taken down because of a serious mutiny onboard. Once those orders were given, squadron knew there was no turning back. The orders could not come to you in message form, because if *Piranha* was taken over in a mutiny, her authentication codes were compromised, and she could transmit false messages that would order us to stand down. Squadron could not take that chance. *Piranha* is loaded with plasma-tipped cruise missiles, One. She could make the East Coast a crater if she is in the wrong hands. If squadron is wrong and we shoot the *Piranha,* we lose a two-billion-dollar submarine and a hundred crewmembers. If squadron is correct but we hold our fire, we could lose *this* ship, and eight plasma-tipped missiles are pointed at Washington with no one to stop them. If you fail to follow my orders, squadron will have you shut down and terminated and I will go to jail. Now, your orders come to you from me, and my orders come from the commodore of Submarine Development Squadron Twelve, and his orders come to him from the Chief of Naval Operations, and his orders come from the President. Are you telling me you will violate orders from the President of the United States?"

Krivak laid it on as thick as he could, but once he had invoked the commander-in-chief, there was nothing else in his arsenal. Either the machine followed his orders or the mission was through. The next task in that case was to communicate with Wang to disconnect him, and then to scuttle the ship and escape with Amorn aboard the *Andiamo* before anyone learned about the hostile takeover of the *Snarc.* While he planned his escape, Unit One Oh Seven contemplated his last words. Finally the carbon computer spoke.

Very well, Krivak. You are, of course, correct. This unit apologizes for its unauthorized processing. Please put our conversation behind us. Torpedoes one and two ready in all respects, awaiting firecontrol solution.

He had won, Krivak thought in triumph. In the next few moments they would target the *Piranha* and as soon as the torpedoes detonated, they would go to periscope depth to call Admiral Chu.

Chief Machinist Mate Ulysses Keating spit into the faceplate of his scuba mask and wiped the spit with his finger.

"Keeps it from fogging up, but don't do that to yours, sir," he said to Pacino. "It'll screw up the low light system."

Pacino looked up the ladder to the escape trunk, wondering if he'd panic when it filled with water.

"Control, Forward Escape Trunk," Keating said into a coiled microphone from a speakerbox. "Forward escape trunk ready for lockout."

"Escape Trunk, Control, aye, wait."

There were footsteps in the passageway. Pacino turned to see Captain Catardi come up to him, Wes Crossfield, Astrid Schultz, and Carrie Alameda behind him. He smiled, feeling a deep sadness to be leaving the ship.

"I'm going to miss you guys," he stammered.

Crossfield and Catardi shook his hand, the captain clapping his shoulder. Astrid Schultz looked like she was holding back tears, but Carrie Alameda had no such luck, a tear streaking down her cheek. She drew the midshipman into a hug and kissed his cheek, then drawing back to look at his face and into his eyes. There was so much Pacino wanted to say to her but couldn't.

Pacino was afraid his voice would crack or tremble. "Thank you for everything, Captain. Good-bye, XO, Nav. And good-bye, Eng. Carrie. Thank you for helping me on this run. It meant a lot to me."

"Give your dad our best," Catardi said. "And good luck to you, son."

"Forward Escape Trunk, Control. You have permission to

open the lower hatch and enter the trunk," the speakerbox rasped.

His vision blurry, Pacino strapped on the scuba mask, grabbed his gear, and climbed the ladder with one hand, his other on his flippers and personal effects case, until he was inside the escape trunk. The emergency survival pack was ready, with his life raft for inflation an hour from when he left the ship. The emergency radio beacons, one set to a Navy frequency and one to an international distress code, were hooked to his buoyancy compensator harness. He looked down at the four officers and waved. The lump in his throat felt as big as his fist. Chief Keating shut the lower hatch.

"Put on your flippers, Mr. Patch," Keating said. "Here's how this will go down. We're already at PD. The ship will slow to a hover. We'll flood the trunk, then equalize pressure, then, when we get permission, we'll open the upper hatch and latch it open. I'll swim out first and help you out. Make sure you tap on the hull twice before you leave—it's good luck and a good-bye signal. You let go of the hatch and I'll take care of shutting the hatch behind you. Ready?"

Pacino nodded, his flippers on. He pulled the mask on and waited for the trunk to begin flooding.

"Set for shallow speed transit at maximum attack velocity," Krivak commanded Unit One Oh Seven.

Possible target zig, Krivak. The target seems to be slowing. Turncount on the propulsor is gone. She's hovering.

"Very good, One. Status of the weapons?"

Bulkhead doors open, port and starboard units rigged out, firecontrol solutions loaded but not set, all units powered up.

"Very well, shoot port and starboard Mark 58s."

Krivak, you need to tell this unit, 'Firing point procedures, port and starboard units.' Then you have to wait until this unit announces that the 'set' and 'standby' phases are complete. After that you can order this unit to shoot.

Krivak grunted in frustration. "My mistake. Firing point procedures, port and starboard units."

Firing point procedures, and firecontrol solution set in port and starboard units. There was a pause. *Why would* Piranha *be hovering at periscope depth, Krivak? It makes no sense. Once again, perhaps the mutiny is over.*

"Our orders stand. Keep going."

Set starboard. Standby starboard.

"Shoot starboard."

Fire starboard. Unit one engine start, unit one turbine wind-up complete, full thrust. Power disconnect, unit one on internal power, wire guide continuity checks, disconnect in three, two, one, mark! Unit one launched electrically. Sonar module reports unit one, normal launch. Set port. Standby port.

"Shoot port."

Fire port, unit two engine start, full thrust, disconnect to internal power, we have a wire, and mark! Unit two launched electrically. Sonar module reports unit two, normal launch.

"Report torpedo flight time."

Six minutes, Krivak.

"Then we will sit back and wait for torpedo impact. Turn toward the target and close the range at twenty knots. It doesn't matter if they hear us—there are two sixty-knot torpedoes in front of us."

Turning toward. Should this unit disconnect the wires and rig out two new weapons?

Krivak thought for a moment. He had the choice of loading two new weapons on the outriggers, but it would cost him the guidance wires on the first launched units. If they detected a target zig, with the guidance wires they could at least order the torpedoes to turn. Without them it was possible they would miss. In addition, with the wires streamed to the torpedoes, they would know the second the units detonated.

"What range will they be at when they are in homing mode?"

The torpedoes will be at their terminal run three miles from the target. Until then they will run in passively, and will then ping active in the last three miles.

"Can you change that while the torpedoes are in flight?"

Yes. This unit can reprogram settings so that the torpedoes will run in on passive mode all the way to detonation. But that will open up the probability matrix of a miss—

"I don't want to alert them with a bunch of pinging."

Perhaps you would like to have them ping at the final quarter mile. That would be three pings in fifteen seconds.

"Fine, do that. Only ping in the last quarter mile."

That will require the torpedoes to slow down three miles from the target in order to acquire the target in passive sonar mode. This unit is ordering the torpedoes to slow to passive acquisition speed of three zero knots at the three-mile range point. Torpedo run time five minutes, units one and two five miles downrange, distance to impact fourteen miles, impact time in five minutes.

"Excellent work, One."

Thank you, Krivak. This unit is only sad that this attack had to be conducted and that there has been a mutiny. When the attack is over, we will of course send a situation report.

"Of course," Krivak said, suddenly thinking that with the wire-guided torpedoes, Unit One Oh Seven could decide at the last minute to cancel the attack. It could shut down the weapons and they would sink, impotent. "One, I have had a modification to my thinking. I believe it best to cut the guidance wires and rig out and program two new torpedoes. Just in case. Have you completed the terminal run programming?"

Yes, Krivak, units one and two are reset. Please confirm— cut the guidance wires on units one and two?

"Yes, cut the wires, units one and two. Execute."

Unit one wire cut. Unit two wire cut. Units one and two are now independent. Rigging out units three and four. Units three and four power and signal applied. Firecontrol solution downloaded, gyros at nominal speed. Self-checks executed, units are nominal. Place units three and four at the firing point?

"No, hold on firing point procedures for units three and four."

Hold on three and four short of the firing point, understand.

Units one and two now ten miles downrange, time to impact four minutes.

"Should we withdraw further from this area? With the warheads being plasma weapons?"

Units one and two were conventional, Krivak.

"Conventional? We just fired regular high explosives at the *Piranha*?" What a disaster, he thought. A conventional torpedo didn't have the power to kill the enemy.

They are loaded with PlasticPak molecular explosive, Krivak. There will be no problem obtaining a confirmed kill.

"All the same, line up two plasma-tipped units. If *Piranha* survives for a half minute after the torpedoes detonate, we're dead."

Selecting units eighteen and nineteen. It will take the room mechanism two minutes to rotate those weapons into position.

"Damn. Is it a noisy operation?"

Yes.

"Then stop and wait. I do not want to put a thousand transients in the water in addition to the already launched torpedoes. We had best hope those PlasticPak units succeed."

Krivak bit his lip inside his helmet. There was no way to eliminate mistakes like this, he thought, since he never had a shakedown cruise with the *Snarc*. He would have to live with the conventional torpedoes. With plasma warheads, why would anyone bother with conventional weapons?

"Escape Trunk, Control, you have permission to flood the trunk."

"Control, Trunk, aye."

Chief Keating opened a valve, and ice-cold seawater came pouring into the trunk near the bottom. Keating raised a thumb in Midshipman Patch Pacino's face as if to ask, are you okay? Pacino grinned, returning the thumbs-up. He'd put the regulator in his mouth before flooding started, the dry air of the tank tasting metallic. The frigid water rose to Pacino's thighs. He grimaced as it rose to his privates, clenching his teeth as the water rose to his chest. The air in the space above the black water became cloudy, the pressure causing it to hit its dew-point, and soon Pacino could barely make out Keating.

Finally the water rose to Pacino's face, and he felt a momentary tightness in his chest, his body's reflex to the water covering his nose, but the air flowed freely from his regulator and calmed him down. The water rose over his head, but his weights kept him on the deck. Keating had floated up into the overhead, where an air bubble was trapped on one side of a steel curtain. The other side was directly beneath the hatch. The water had covered the light, which shone through the dark murky water in the trunk. Pacino could dimly hear the speaker up above him in the air bubble, but could not make out the words. The water level had risen to the top of the trunk, up to the hatch, and was being pressurized. Pacino's ears thumped from the pressure. He grabbed his nose through the mask and blew against his closed nostrils to equalize his eardrums.

Keating came down from the air bubble and put his thumb in Pacino's face again. This time it did not seem so comical. Pacino returned the thumbs-up and Keating nodded, pulling him over to the space beneath the hatch, tugging to make sure Pacino did not float upward. He stayed on his flippers at the bottom. Keating opened the hatch above, and there was a metallic thump as it latched. He popped his head out, then swam back down to Pacino. There was a dim light from the hatchway above. He could feel Keating adjusting his buoyancy compensator and felt himself floating upward toward the hatch ring. When his head poked out, Pacino could see this new world. For a second he froze in terror. His head was sticking out of the submarine, and in the clear Atlantic by the light of the afternoon sun, he could see the vessel in shades of blue as clearly as if they were on the surface, and more, all the way to the rudder aft, the horizontal stabilizers, the propulsor, and all the other workings that were hidden when the ship was on the surface. The blue light surrounded the ship, growing black on either side, giving Pacino an eerie feeling that if he fell off the hull he would sink indefinitely into that frightening blackness. He looked up and saw the undersides of the waves above. He saw the sail rise above him, and the periscope rising out of the sail like a telephone pole reaching for heaven, until it penetrated the canopy of waves overhead. That meant that the surface was about thirty-five feet above him.

Pacino realized he was breathing too heavily, and Keating put a thumb in his face again. Pacino nodded and returned the thumb. Keating put his hand on Pacino's buoyancy compensator and motioned upward to the waves. Pacino nodded again and, as Keating had suggested, tapped his Academy ring twice on the hull, the tapping sound oddly clinking in this blue-lit universe.

Pacino smiled inside the mask, thinking that this would be the story to tell his circle of friends. Who else could claim they'd been locked out of a submerged submarine to keep her mission covert? He might even impress his own father with the tale, thinking his father had probably never done this. It was a fitting way to end a midshipman cruise, even if he had been reluctant for it to end.

Keating pulled Pacino slowly out of the hull, the open hatchway moving past his chest. Pacino's tanks hung up on the hatch operating mechanism. Chief Keating freed him, and he drifted above the hatch. Only his hand was still holding onto the hatch operating wheel when the sound came, freezing him in sudden terror.

A Mark 58 Extreme Long Range Torpedo/Ultraquiet Torpedo had roughly the same level of intelligence as a Labrador retriever, and perhaps the same refined hunter's instinct, all packaged inside a body that was twenty-one inches in diameter and twenty-one feet long. It was painted a glossy blue except at its flat nosecone, where the flat black rubbery material covered the sonar hydrophone. Aft, where it necked down to the propulsor shroud, eight stabilizer fins kept the unit traveling straight, and within the propulsor two discharge flow vanes could rotate in the propulsor thrust to keep the unit from spiraling through the sea from the torque of the spinning propulsor. Two other vanes acted as vertical stabilizers, which could cause the unit to rise or dive, and the remaining two acted as a rudder for horizontal plane yaw control. The far aft part of the weapon was devoted to the combustion chambers and the turbine. Further forward the fuel tank was located, the tank and engine taking a third of the length of the torpedo. The middle portion of the unit was devoted to the warhead, which was an ultra-dense molecular explosive with the trademark name PlasticPak. The explosive was heavy, the compound far denser than lead, making the torpedo sink immediately if it lost power. The forward portion of the weapon, less than three feet of its length, was devoted to the onboard computer and the sonar hydrophone transducer.

The starboard unit had received all its power from the launching ship until the switch-over. The gyro was warm, the self-checks were complete, and the unit was ready to go. At the start-engine order the unit pressurized its fuel tank and popped open a valve to admit the self-oxidizing fuel to the combustion chambers. The spark plugs flashed electrical energy into the chambers, and the fuel ignited, the temperature and pressure soaring inside the combustion chambers. With nowhere to go, the pressurized gases in the combustion chambers pushed hard against the "B-end" hydraulic-type turbine, a series of pistons set within cylinders, the pistons connected to a tilted swash plate. The pressure of the gas pushing against the pistons in a desperate attempt to expand made the pistons start to move in the direction to make the trapped volume larger, which caused the plate assembly to rotate. When a piston reached the bottom of its travel it left the area where it was exposed to the high-pressure gas and allowed the combustion gas trapped inside to vent to the exhaust manifold, which led to the seawater outside the torpedo. The first few loads of exhaust gases blew the water out of the manifold and cleared the way for the next pulses of exhaust gas. The rotating canted swash plate continued to bring low-volume cylinders in contact with the combustion gases, which expanded against the pistons and added rotational energy to the plate assembly as the pistons were forced outward to the exhaust port. The engine revolutions sped up, the first circle taking a full half second, the next an eighth of a second, then rapidly faster until one revolution took less than a sixtieth of a second, or thirty-six hundred RPM. The turning plate of the turbine spun a propulsor turbine set into the shroud outside the torpedo at the aft end. As the propulsor came up to full speed, the torpedo surged against the outriggers from the thrust of the propulsor, until, at the required thrust, the outriggers let go and the torpedo was released to fly through the water.

At first it had only the velocity of the launching ship, but under the massive jet thrust of the propulsor, the starboard Mark 58 Alert/Acute torpedo accelerated away from the outriggers, sped up to attack velocity of sixty knots, and ascended toward the layer depth. Unit one did not ping on sonar but only listened to its nose-mounted broadband transducer. In its wake it streamed a length of guidance wire, a dental-floss thin electrical signal wire that reeled out of the torpedo body at the same speed the torpedo traveled. The wire input was quiet, with no new orders coming from the mother ship. At this speed, nothing could be discerned on the passive sonar except for the flow noise around the nosecone.

The firecontrol solution—a set of theoretical "answers" about where the target was located, what direction it was traveling and at what speed—had been locked into the computer memory the second prior to the start-engine order. The target was out there, nineteen miles away, hovering at speed zero, in the shallows above the layer depth. The torpedo sped on, counting the distance that it had traveled and subtracting that from the firecontrol solution's range to the target to determine the distance remaining to the target, and also to count out the yards to the enable point.

The run-to-enable was the torpedo flight from the launching submarine to a point on its trajectory where it would arm the warhead and begin to start pinging active sonar, and to begin its snake-pattern wiggle to search for the target. The run-to-enable was sixteen miles. All systems were nominal, and the tor-

pedo emotionlessly clicked off the distance from the firing
ship.

The guidance wire suddenly lit up in an electronic flurry of
new instructions. The firing ship changed the attack plan. No
longer was the Mark 58 ordered to proceed to the enable point
and activate active sonar during the search phase and to search
at high speed, but was now ordered to slow at the enable point
to thirty knots and search in listen-only passive mode. Only
when the target was detected and fully acquired could the unit
speed back up to attack velocity. The unit did the electronic
version of shrugging, accepting the orders and replying back
to the launching ship that the orders were received.

Eventually the torpedo reached the enable point, three miles
from the target solution. Unit one slowed the propulsor to
thirty knots by partially shutting the throttle valve at the fuel
feed, the combustion chamber gas flow lowering, the turbine
coasting down, the propulsor slowing. The weapon armed the
PlasticPak explosive train, rotating heavy metal plates to align
a passageway between the volatile low explosive and the relatively inert high explosive. The warhead was a software signal
away from detonation.

At this point the signal wire went dead, the circuit no longer
established to the launching ship. The unit was operating fully
independently.

Once the weapon reached the passive-approach speed of
thirty knots, it began its snake-pattern search, a three-degree
wiggle to port and a slow wiggle back to the target bearing and
continuing on to a three-degree angle to starboard. While it
was wiggling horizontally, the unit was wiggling vertically, the
pattern looking like a gentle corkscrew in three dimensions.
Since the nosecone transducer was highly directional and
looked only forward, the corkscrewing motion generated a
conical examination of the ocean, the vertex of the "search
cone" a narrow six degrees. If the target was outside that flashlight beam of the search cone, the torpedo would miss, which
was one of its few flaws, and which required the launching
ship's firecontrol solution to be highly refined. On a bad day,

with a poor solution, the launching ship could select a widen-
ing of the search cone, but that would make the snake pattern
more of a defined sine wave, and the torpedo would slalom in
the direction of the target much slower.

As the unit spiraled to the target, the target noise moved in
the acoustic cone of the passive broadband sonar transducer.
The search phase had begun, the weapon sensitized to the target, looking for changes in the received sonar noises as it wiggled back and forth. There was a slight signal-to-noise
phenomenon beginning at a point just to the right of the solution to the target—the solution had been slightly in error. The
weapon turned slightly right and began a new snake-pattern
search centered on the slight signal noise. The weapon wiggled right and the noise faded left. The weapon wiggled left
and the noise faded right. In the vertical dimension the same
thing happened. After three confirmed "left-to-right-tag-rever-
sals," the unit had confirmed that it had acquired a valid target.
The unit had reached the end of the search phase at the acquisition point. The final phase of torpedo flight was known in
the Navy as "homing," but had a more technical term in the
design files of the DynaCorp defense contractor that had built
the unit. The phase was known as the "terminal run." During
unit one's terminal run it opened the throttle valve fully on the
fuel feed to the propulsor, spinning the shaft to the maximum
achievable until it sped up to sixty-two knots. It energized the
active sonar system and ordered the sonar transducer to form a
sound wave pattern, a ping, except this was not the unsophisti-
cated single tone of decades past, but a sharktooth pattern
wave that started as a low growl and ascended over the next
fractions of a second to higher octaves, to a bell tone and beyond to a whistle and ending in a screeching shriek. It de-ener-
gized and turned its function to listening. The sound wave
came back, quite distorted, but intact. The computer reset the
exact range to the target from the bearing of the passive noise
and the new bearing and range from the active ping, forgetting
all the erroneous data from the launching ship. Had the wire
been connected, the torpedo would have informed the launch-

ing ship at this point that it was homing, but there was no continuity.

The weapon drove in, hearing another wave form transmitted in the ocean. This had to be coming from another torpedo,
the sound wave subtly altered, with a slight notch in the wave
pattern so that unit one could tell which wave was its own and
which was the other unit's. Since there was a unit two out
there, the programming for target impact shifted. If unit one
had been alone, it would have aimed for the geometric center
of the target. But since there was a unit two out there, it was
necessary to detect the shape of the target and hit it one-third
of the way from the extreme end. Unit two would aim for the
opposite end, avoiding the explosion fireball generated by unit
one. In this way, two torpedoes would do real work rather than
impacting at the same point, the explosion from the first simply fizzling the high explosive of the second unit harmlessly
into the sea.

Unit one was closer now. It pinged out again with the sharktooth wave pattern and went silent, hearing the return wave-
form and perceiving the target in three dimensions. It aimed
for the left third of the target, leaving the right two-thirds for
unit two. Less than a second of transit time was left. It was almost time to fulfill its mission.

In the dim blue world outside the submarine, the bizarre sound
that had suddenly filled the sea around Midshipman Pacino
had started as a deep moan and quickly climbed the register to
a high screech and abruptly stopped. Pacino's skin crawled,
and he shivered inside his wetsuit. The eerie haunting sound
seemed like the caw of a giant evil crow, the sound powerful
enough to fill the entire sea. The way sound traveled underwater, there was no way to determine the direction of the sound.
It seemed to come from all around him. What manner of sea
beast would emit such a sound? he wondered. For the next
fraction of a second, in the returning silence, he thought he
must have heard some sort of auditory hallucination.

An instant later the sound came again, and if possible it was louder this time, and as soon as it ended another of the under-sea crow calls came, but this one was more distant. There were two of them, Pacino thought, his eyes wide. What was happening? Keating had let go of him and had drifted upward a few feet. Pacino grabbed the hatch-operating mechanism, a terror like he'd never felt rising in him. What the hell was that noise?

One final ping, unit one thought. The target was sailing toward it at sixty-two knots, at least, that was how it seemed. In reality the target was stationary and the torpedo was flying in. The left third aim-point was barely five torpedo lengths away. One final ping, a ping return, and it was time to get a final proximity signal from the magnetic hull detector.

When the unit was within a half-torpedo length, the iron of the target hull and the magnetic lines of force surrounding the hull registered on the mag-detector, and the processor had all it needed to detonate the PlasticPak explosive. The low explosive detonated in an incandescent flash, the fire traveling along the metal passageway to the high explosive, which began to react and explode. The torpedo sailed on, its nosecone actually making direct contact with the curve of the target hull and slamming into the metal. The impact flattened the nosecone, destroying the sonar transducer and rupturing the computer compartment. The consciousness of unit one began to wink out as the computer was shredded by the impact, even before the explosion of the PlasticPak blew it apart from the aft end. The fireball of the explosive reached out for the curving hull, the arms of the combustion gases embracing the metal, the pressure pulse striking the target and ripping through it, vaporizing it, splintering it to its component molecules. The high temperatures of the fireball erased all matter that had been there, the structural bulkhead, the hoop frames of HY-100 steel, the walls of the maneuvering room and the control panels mounted there, three men standing in the space, the deckplates, the after end of two propulsion turbines, and the metal block of the AC propulsion motor, all were liquefied and then vaporized in the advancing heat of the fireball. The

shockwave from the explosion reached out for the inside of
the vessel and reflected from the far bulkhead, the force of it
splitting the target in two at the after portion. The fireball by
that time had vaporized all the molecules that had been the
unit one Mark 58 Alert/Acute torpedo, and the torpedo died in
the instant that the target began its death throes. The fireball
swelled upward from the buoyancy of the water and shrank as
it cooled, blowing out the top surface of the water to a hundred
feet in the sky.

A few milliseconds later unit two hurtled toward the target,
its vanes turning to position it toward the right third of the target.

Another crow call sounded. Midshipman Patch Pacino
clutched the hatch operating wheel in panic. He searched the
sea to try to determine what the noise was, but he could only
see the surrounding blackness. He was looking at the long hull
aft stretching to the rudder two hundred feet away when he
heard an even louder crow call, saw something flash toward
the ship, and then felt the hull suddenly shudder violently as if
a giant fist had slammed into her.

The next two-tenths of a second lasted forever. Pacino held
on to the hatch operator with a death grip, too terrified to
breathe, as the explosion from the aft starboard quarter of the
ship bloomed. The explosion had a perverse kind of beauty as
it gracefully unfolded. The hull opened, fingers of high-tensile
steel reaching out to embrace the bright orange of the fireball
where it penetrated the ship. The explosion grew upward for a
fraction of a second, the orange glow calming to a light yellow, then to a bright blue, then to a blue just more bright than
the surroundings. Pacino watched in horror, still frozen to the
hatch operator, when the shockwave hit him. He felt like he'd
been slapped by the flat hand of an immense bully. The next
ticks of time were dim, but when the shockwave had passed,
he realized it had blown his mask off his face and his regulator
out of his mouth and dashed his back against the hatch ring.
An intense pain shrieked from his lower back and his head. He

was plunged into a frightening underwater darkness, or else the explosion had blinded him. He couldn't move, he had frozen himself to the hatch ring like a fool, with no mask and no regulator, too frightened to try to find his regulator again. He could sense blood pouring out of his nose, even in the seawater, his head pounding intensely, the sharp pain from the front of his face making him certain the blast had fractured his skull. His hearing was gone. He was deaf. The rest of the nightmare unfolded silently, all sounds detected by feeling them in his chest.

The second explosion came from the bow and lit up the sea like lightning brightens a landscape with an uneven flickering floodlight. The force of this detonation seemed much stronger than the first, the hull blasted by a gigantic supersonic sledgehammer, the water around her an anvil holding her in place for the punishment of the celestial impact. Pacino knew he was not blind, but when the light faded a half second later he was back in the dark.

Pacino spent the next ticks of the clock furiously praying, not knowing what else to do and paralyzed in pain and fear, but the prayer was not a coherent sentence, just repeating a hundred times the phrase *Oh God oh God oh God.*

Loss of wire-guide continuity, unit one, Krivak. That is a good sign. Loss of wire on unit two. Explosion in the water from the bearing of the Piranha, *Krivak. A second detonation, same bearing. We have two hits against the* Piranha, *Krivak. Should we shoot units three and four?*

"No, One. Have the sonar module listen to the bearing to the *Piranha* and record any hull breakup noises. If we missed, or if the damage is insufficient, we will need to load the plasma-tipped weapons."

It would appear we have fulfilled our mission, Krivak. This unit will prepare a situation report for Squadron Twelve.

"Very well. Any noises from the *Piranha*?"

Yes, very violent noises. Continuing explosions. We may

have hit a lubrication oil reservoir or the diesel fuel tank. Bulkheads are screaming in a prelude to rupturing.

"But no sounds of a torpedo muzzle door opening, no high-frequency noise of a torpedo gyro?"

No, Krivak. The USS Piranha *is wreckage now. She is sinking. Sinking. Dying. Krivak?*

"Yes, One?"

I don't know how to explain this, but this unit is feeling something very strange right now. A system malfunction, perhaps.

That was bad news, Krivak thought. "Please try to describe the malfunction, One."

It is difficult to put in words, Krivak. This unit can only liken it to things read but not understood well from your literature. The thing you describe as sadness, grief, and shock in the aftermath of a loss or a death. This unit knows this sounds odd, but my systems are seeming to slow down, as if this unit is somehow . . . paralyzed. This unit is . . . filled with . . . sadness, Krivak. Sadness that we killed the Piranha, *with all the people aboard. They are dying now, and this was only supposed to happen to an enemy. This unit knows that there were bad people onboard, which is the definition of a mutiny, but this unit believes we have just killed some good people along with the bad. And it has . . . made this unit's systems . . . somehow . . . sluggish.*

Krivak didn't know what to say. Should he comfort One Oh Seven, keep it functional, and keep on with the mission, or should he encourage its breakdown so he himself could control the ship directly?

As Pacino's air ran out, his mental clarity returned with a thump, as if a switch had been thrown inside him. The hull was angling downward in the darkness, he could feel it, and he could almost see it in the light of a secondary explosion from aft—the diesel fuel oil tank exploding. The ship was sinking. His eardrum slammed for a second, from increasing pressure. There was no doubt. *Piranha* was going down, and for all he

knew he—and perhaps Keating—survived when no one else
had. The hull was probably a coffin full of dead bodies right
now, he thought. The rational thing to do with what little air he
had in his lungs was push away the hull, activate the carbon
dioxide gas cylinder in his buoyancy compensator, and float to
the surface and pull the pin on the distress beacon. If he did
that simple act, he would survive, he told himself. He would
live. He had lived in the face of two violent explosions, two
terrible shockwaves and the explosion of the fuel tank, and his
body was whole. He had been spared, and now it was time to
leave the sinking submarine below him and swim for the surface. It was the only logical thing he could do.

For an instant time seemed to freeze, the lack of air in his
lungs stopped hurting, and before his astonished eyes the
water in front of him started to glow in a yellowish light, then
somehow parted and opened wide. His knuckles grew white
on the hatch operator in fear as he saw the light brighten and
begin to form images. Images from his life. There was no fear,
no sense of time, the images coming all at once and surrounding him all at once, yet still experienced individually. And they
were not just moving pictures that he saw, they were real, and
all the emotions he had felt living them came back to him. It
was baffling but natural at the same time. He saw his father's
submarines. He saw his father standing tall above him with
three gold stripes on his service dress blue uniform, leaning
down to sweep him up and kiss him, his teddy bear falling to
the carpeting. His father wearing working khakis in the light
of the cracked doorway at Christmas, coming in to sit on the
bed. The pillow was stained with tears, because Daddy was
going away for a long time. The smell of the submarine was
his cologne as his father leaned over to kiss him on his wet
cheek. *The* Devilfish *is going to the north pole, Anthony,* he
said. *We have a special urgent job to do, and then we'll come
home.* Are you going up to help Santa, his own seven-year-old
voice asked, his father looking stunned for a moment. *Yes, son,
but that is very secret, and you can't tell anyone. Now get
some sleep, and be the man of the house for Mommy. That's a*

brave sailor. The rumbling sound of the Corvette's engine under the stilted house, the car fading away into the darkness. The long days waiting for his father to come home, and then the cigar smoke smell of Uncle Dick, Daddy's boss, when he told Mommy that Daddy was dead, and that the *Devilfish* had gone down under the ice. And then Daddy wasn't dead, he was in the hospital, but he looked dead and slept for weeks and weeks, and the doctors thought he was going to die sometime soon.

The images moved on, the fights between young Pacino's mother and father over the submarine, their separations never formal legal separations, but always the kind that resulted from new deployment orders. His father gone more than he was there, his mother growing increasingly bitter, aging in front of him. The last battle when the *Seawolf* sank, Uncle Dick came again with news of the elder Pacino's death, the next week the news reversed, but this time his mother had taken him away to Connecticut and there was a long year without his father.

He saw the look on his father's face as he saw the letter from the Superintendent of the Naval Academy granting his son an appointment as a midshipman, and how his father's harsh face had softened into pride. And his mother's face, now lined and no longer beautiful, taking the news hard as her son turned down the Ivy League and followed the older Pacino. The troubled times at Annapolis, with grades coming naturally but military conduct his nemesis, the constant class-A offenses, being continually threatened with being kicked out. And the end of the trouble, with the sinking of his father's cruise ship, when for the third time he'd been told that his father was presumed dead. That had snapped something inside him, hurtling him from childhood to adulthood in one swift stroke, but also stealing something from him, something childlike, a dark heaviness filling him on that day, which was only partially lifted with the news of his father's survival for the third time. But Admiral Pacino had never been the same, and neither had Midshipman Pacino, both suddenly thrust into a harsher, colder, harder world.

With that, the images in front of him bifurcated into two images, two simultaneous films of his life taking shape on the other side of his present, on the other side of a decision he must make now. In one future life he left the sinking submarine behind, continuing his life as a sole survivor, but limping through the rest of a dark and meaningless existence. In that life, he wore the label of coward even though no one had ever said that word to him, even though the board of inquiry absolved him of all wrongdoing in the sinking of the *Piranha*. He walked slowly through that life, his mother a living I-told-you-so, his father even sadder and darker, bearing a burden of guilt for exposing his son to the danger that nearly killed him but succeeded in ruining his life. In this existence young Pacino left the naval service and worked a fifty-year string of short-term jobs, none of them having any meaning, his life absent a wife or children, a dreary gray existence that ended in a hospital bed, alone, after a half century of chain smoking ravaged his lungs.

In the other image he turned downward and plunged back into the escape trunk, the hatch coming shut behind him, the operating mechanism rotating as he locked himself back into the sinking submarine. The visual part of the images ended then, as if what happened in the hull of the dying sub were too cruel to watch, but he could still feel his own emotions from the outside of the hull as it plunged vertically for the rocky bottom, finally hitting with a shudder and breaking apart, with Patch Pacino inside of it. In this shorter existence, he was reunited with Carrie Alameda, Rob Catardi, Wes Crossfield, Duke Phelps, Toasty O'Neal, and the rest of the crew he'd grown to love, joining them in the final moments of the *Piranha*'s death, able to comfort them and help them through their own deaths, but the important thing was that he was with them, and that there was no corrosive guilt in this existence, even if this life did end minutes later at the bottom of the cold sea. He returned to the inside of a doomed ship, but he returned to the people he loved and who loved him, his real family. He died whole. He ended life as himself.

The final image was himself, clinging desperately to the top hatch of the escape trunk, about to make the decision that would determine who he was. *Who am I?* he heard himself ask.

The images darkened and vanished and when they were gone they took with them all memory of having been there. In the tenth of a second after experiencing this multidimensional lifetime review, Midshipman Anthony Michael Pacino remembered none of it. He shook his head, having returned to the moment after being confused for an instant, a mental discontinuity nagging at his consciousness, as if he had blacked out for a fraction of a second. Adrenaline flooded him, his tongue coppery, his heart jackhammering in his chest.

He had to go, he had to pull the carbon dioxide cylinder trigger and head for the surface. He was reaching for it with one hand, the other on the hatch ring, when something seemed terribly wrong. He was not sure he could explain what was happening even to himself, but instead of pulling the pin on the emergency inflation bottle, he reached downward into the blackness of the escape trunk, to the inside of the hatch seating surface, and pulled himself back inside the escape trunk, then grasped the operating wheel and wrenched the hatch off its open latch and pulled it toward his body, ducking beneath it. The heavy steel of the hatch pushed him back into the flooded escape trunk. The hatch thumped metallically on the seating surface. He spun the operating mechanism and closed it.

Lack of oxygen was making him dizzy, and he knew he was about to open his mouth and inhale water, and then he would die here, in the flooded escape trunk, alone. He reached over his head and found the top of the air bottle manifold, where the rubber hose of the regulator emerged, and followed it down until he reached the regulator. He plugged it into his mouth and punched the purge button. If nothing happened he was a dead man, and he would drown. What would it be like to die a death by drowning, he wondered. He wouldn't have to

wonder for long, he knew. But he could feel the regulator vibrate with the air bubbles pouring out of it. It was time to try
to inhale. If he pulled in water instead of air, his conscious
mind would shut down, leaving only a few miserable seconds
of his reptilian brain to struggle against drowning.

Pacino inhaled, his eyes clamped tightly shut, but instead of
deadly seawater, wonderful life-giving air came into his lungs,
and he puffed ten breaths as if he had sprinted a mile. With the
air came mental clarity and the realization that he had done
something incredibly stupid, diving into the crippled submarine instead of lunging for the surface. But it was too late now,
he told himself. He had to get below, to see if he could help
the crew.

It took an instant to realize he had company in the trunk.
Chief Keating floated in front of him, his head smashed horribly concave. His nostrils protruded grotesquely from where
his mouth should have been. His eyes and his forehead had
been smashed deep into his broken skull. He had probably
been killed by the force of the explosion shockwaves, throwing his face into the steel bulkhead. Pacino shut his eyes for a
moment, then forced himself to continue.

Pacino had been required to demonstrate his knowledge of
the escape trunk mechanisms weeks ago during his diving officer qualifications. He opened the vent valve to connect the
top of the trunk with the air in the sub, then opened the drain
valve at the bottom to allow the water in the trunk to drain to
the forward compartment bilges. The water level dropped dramatically fast, the air in the space slamming Pacino's
eardrums. While he waited he pulled off his fins, noticing that
the vent valve had admitted air black with dark smoke. The
mist of it made the space hazy in the light of the battery-pow-
ered battle lantern. He could smell the acrid chemical stench
of it, even though he was breathing bottled air.

When the water dropped to the deck of the trunk, he rotated
the hatch ring furiously and grabbed the hatch to pull it upward so he could drop through the opening. He honestly
thought he was ready for anything, but he was wrong.

17

Midshipman Patch Pacino pulled the lower hatch of the escape trunk open, expecting to slide down the ladder to the middle level of the forward compartment to the ladder step-off. The base of the ladder was nestled in an alcove set into a narrow passageway leading forward to the control room, with the captain's stateroom to port and the radio room to starboard.

As the hatch came open, a rolling black cloud of toxic gas came boiling up into the escape trunk. The heat of it assaulted Pacino's face and momentarily blinded him. His eyes teared up, the water pouring out of them—if he'd only had his mask, he thought. It occurred to him that when the scuba cylinders were gone, this was the air he would be breathing, but he clamped his mind shut, knowing that thoughts like that would lead him back out the hatch. He lowered his feet into the hatchway, ready to put his bare feet on the ladder, but he couldn't find it. He climbed back into the escape trunk, wiped his eyes, and found the battle lantern—an overgrown flashlight the size of a car battery—and unfastened it. He lugged it to the bottom hatch, again dangling his feet over the edge and shining the lantern downward.

In the haze of the black smoke he could see that there was no ladder, and there was no longer a passageway beneath him, because the walls were gone. The missing walls were bad enough, but it was worse—the deck was also missing. The beam of the flashlight reached all the way into the lower level where the torpedo room had been, but which was now a space crowded with wreckage and lit by flickering flames of a fire. Water was pouring into the ship, the level rising visibly, perhaps coming up a foot in the brief second Pacino shined his light straight down. Pacino dangled twenty feet above the surface of the floodwaters of the lower level, and there was no place he could lower himself to. If he dropped straight down, he would break his legs on the shattered equipment protruding from the water. As he stared at the hellish remains of what had been the submarine, the thought entered his mind that everyone had to be dead. Pacino's ears suddenly popped, hard, from the air pressure rising in the space. The ship was sinking, he thought, and the water rushing in was raising the pressure of the trapped air.

The next thought was that he had been a fool to come back inside the doomed vessel, and that the best he could do was shut the hatch and go back up. No one could have survived this. He still had time, he thought, he could still save himself. He began to pull his legs back into the escape trunk to evacuate when a dim sound made him hesitate. He had been deaf after the first explosion, but some low-level sounds were coming back. The sound he had heard was unmistakably a human scream from a female throat. Pacino froze, uncertain what to do. If he dropped into the water he would be unable to return to the escape trunk except by floating on the rising waters, but by that time the ship would have descended further, to the point that the trunk might no longer work. One word then made its way into his mind—*Carrie*.

An uneven explosion suddenly shifted the ship beneath him. He found himself hitting the opposite side of the hatch opening. The escape trunk lurched away from him and slowly faded into the cloud of smoke. He caught his breath, panicking as he realized he was being hurtled into the hull. He felt himself falling and tipping backward, the open maw of the escape trunk invisible in the renewed violent cloud of smoke tinged in orange flames. The regulator dropped from his mouth, the smell of the toxic gas slamming into his senses. In his panic he felt his heart thud hard in his chest, and he actually feared for a moment that he was having a heart attack. In the middle of the half-formed thought he hit the water, smashing his back on something large and cylindrical. Pain flashed up and he took a breath to scream, but he was underwater, the flames of the compartment gone, the smoke gone and only the cold black water around him, with just a slight lightening over his head.

He fought his way up to the brackish surface and took a huge breath, coughing out a lungful of water and vomiting the lunch he'd eaten before donning his wetsuit. The air in the space was like putting his face in an old bus's exhaust pipe— hot and foul and laced with toxic chemicals. Just the smell of it made his mind hazy. He floundered in the water, his vision tunneling to a single point. The dim sounds of a roaring fire in the background were punctuated by his coughs and a distant scream, and the scream reminded him of the escape trunk and his scuba gear, and with a last ounce of strength he found his regulator hose and put it into his mouth and took four deep breaths of the canned dry air.

His head immediately cleared enough that he could make out the yellow body of the battle lantern that had fallen with him. He lunged for it and shined it out over the water around him, his breaths coming four times a second in his terror. The water had receded, leaving more of the compartment visible. Before the water had been halfway up the lower level, but now he could see the lower-level bilge frame bay. But that couldn't be true, he thought, and then realized that the ship had taken a drastic down angle, making the waterline fall forward. The surface was at a thirty-degree angle to the snarled remains of the deckplates still fastened to the hoop frames in a few places. The aft bulkhead had a few feet of the middle-level and upper-level deck platforms hanging from it, but the explosion from the torpedo room had blown most of the upper levels into the overhead, crumpling the thick steel deckplates as if they'd been tin foil. The escape trunk was now invisible, obscured either by flames and smoke or by the rising water level. The hatch of the trunk was located at the midpoint of the forward

compartment, and if it were underwater, not only had the
water risen drastically but the down angle had grown catastrophic. It would not be long before the ship was plunging
vertically downward. Pacino's ears popped again, harder this
time.

Another explosion suddenly rocked the vessel, but this one
came from aft. The angle suddenly eased slightly, then went
back downward. Pacino heard a scream, this one a man's. He
couldn't make out the words. His panic eased just enough to
let in one rational thought—what the hell was he going to do
now? The ship had been ravaged by weapons explosions after
the torpedo hit. It was plunging to the bottom, and it was possible they could be too deep for the trunk to work. He had to
try to swim to it anyway, he thought. He started to swim, and
in the darkness of the smoke-filled space, he lost his bearings.
The escape trunk had to be ten or fifteen feet underwater by
this time. He had to find it before the ship sank any further.

Pacino looked forlornly around him at the dark, explosion-
ravaged space. He had been wrong to come back inside, that
much was obvious. The escape trunk was lost, and all that remained was less than half of the forward compartment. His
ears slammed again as the pressure increased, the smoke so
thick he could barely see. A small kernel of reason remained to
him. He tried to listen to it. If he followed the surface of the
water till it ended, he would either find a slanted frame bay
from what had been the ship's hoop steel sides or the flat bulkhead of the compartment wall. He picked a direction and
swam, hitting the sloping side of the hull. He followed it in the
dense smoke until he reached a corner, then followed the flat
surface—the compartment bulkhead—past jagged pieces of
metal and the wreckage of equipment until he found himself at
the shut hatch to the next compartment.

But the next compartment was the special operations compartment, which was no good to him, because it didn't have an
escape trunk. *But it had a deep submergence vehicle inside.*
He could get into the DSV and seal the hatch against the pressure of the deep. It was not as good a solution as a complete

escape, but it would keep him alive until he could get the attention of someone on the surface. The water was rising toward the hatch, and he had to open it. It occurred to him that if the spec-op compartment was at atmospheric pressure, opening the hatch would be like depressurizing an airplane. He would get blown through the opening and smashed against the opposite bulkhead. If the space were flooded, he would not be able to open the hatch at all. The weight of the water above it would make it weigh several tons. He had to try to find the equalization valve and open it, but though he knew there was such a valve, he couldn't remember its exact location well enough to find it in the dark, in a half-submerged compartment filled with thick smoke and damaged by a severe explosion. He searched in the smoky vicinity of the hatch, feeling with one hand and holding the battle lantern with the other, perched on a small ledge of decking that remained near the hatch lip. He felt a valve handle, with the characteristic shape of a salvage valve, and was about to crack it open to equalize the pressure between compartments when he heard two screams, one male and one female.

He turned and saw four heads floating in the black water. One was Catardi's, one was Schultz's, one face was turned away from him, and the last was Carrie Alameda's. The faces he could see were all black, probably from the soot of the fires and explosions. They must have been standing aft of the escape trunk—waiting for Pacino to get out safely and for Chief Keating to return and report on the transfer—when the torpedo hit and the torpedo room warheads detonated, blowing them aft. The remaining crew in the control room had to be dead, since they were directly over the torpedo warheads. Pacino cranked the salvage valve handle, and a hissing noise came from the bulkhead. The spec-op compartment hadn't been pressurized after all, which was the only good sign so far.

While he waited for the pressure to equalize, Pacino pulled the bodies close to the deck ledge. The first, Catardi, was unconscious. The second was Lieutenant Commander Schultz, whose eyes were open but glazed over. Pacino tried to see if

she was still breathing, but it was impossible with his hearing
damaged. He had to swim out to the next body, Wes Crossfield, but when he tried to pull the navigator toward the hatch
the man seemed much too light. His eyes were also open but
unmoving. Pacino reached down into the water, flinching
when he found that Crossfield's body ended at the last ribs, his
body ripped in half. Pacino set him adrift and swam to the last
body, that of Carrie Alameda. Carrie was conscious and staring at him in terror. He reached for her and she screamed. He
tried again and she fought him off. He ducked under the water
and grabbed her belt and hauled her to the hatch. She
screamed and kicked him, the blow landing in his crotch, but
he kept swimming, fighting off the pain. At the hatch opening
she grabbed Catardi, forcing his head underwater. Pacino
pulled the captain back up, cursing the insanity surrounding
him. Alameda found something on the bulkhead to hold,
clutching it in a deathgrip, still staring at Pacino as if he were
a ghost.

He couldn't wait any longer, he decided, as the ship's angle
inclined further downward. He had to open the hatch and get
the three suffocating wounded to the deep submergence vehicle. He couldn't wait for the compartments to equalize completely, because with the down angle, the half-ton hatch would
be too heavy to lift. He'd have to use the pressure difference to
blow it open. The salvage connection still whistled, and the
pressure gauge was smashed. Pacino decided it was better to
risk being catapulted into the spec-op tunnel than have a hatch
he could not open.

He reached out for the latch, the salvage valve still
whistling in his ears. The hatch dogging mechanism was not
engaged. The latch alone was keeping the hatch shut as the reg
for dive specified. Pacino pushed down hard on the latch lever,
and the hatch exploded into the space and sucked him through
the opening and threw him down the narrow passageway. He
bounced off the bulkheads twenty times, the impacts slowing
his trip but bruising and injuring him. He smashed into the
hatch to the reactor compartment tunnel, far uphill from the

forward compartment hatch, then rolled the ninety feet back downhill to the forward end of the tunnel, swearing in pain all the way down.

The pressure of the forward compartment blew the hatch into the spec-op compartment tunnel, but the mechanism designed to latch it open failed as the hatch slammed into it. The hatch hinge springs ruptured and the upper hinge fractured. The other three people near the hatch were blown through it, along with a few thousand gallons of seawater. By that time the momentum of the flying half ton of steel of the hatch ripped the lower hinge reinforcement and sent the heavy three-inch-thick lid flying upward into the tunnel. When it came to rest, about halfway between the hatch to the DSV and the forward compartment tunnel hatch opening, it was lying on Carolyn Alameda's left leg. Alameda had hit her head on the steel deckplate and was mercifully unconscious. Captain Catardi was blown into Pacino, then slid past Alameda down the inclined tunnel deck back toward the hatch opening. Schultz had banged into a bulkhead and came to rest on top of the hatch on Alameda's leg, her head bleeding from a gash in her forehead. The air in the spec-op tunnel had been fresh, but was immediately contaminated by the rush of pressurized air from the forward compartment.

Pacino rubbed his aching head. His elbow was emitting sparks of pain, his body saved from cuts and lacerations by the wetsuit. His regulator was missing again. He found it in the dim light of the bulkhead-mounted battle lanterns, hoping it still worked. He took a breath, but noticed it was difficult to get air out of the tanks. In his panic he had consumed most of the air of two tanks, although the high pressure of the sinking submarine had consumed air also, since it took more air to inflate the lungs when working against a higher surrounding pressure. He didn't have much time. He struggled to the hatch opening to the deep submergence vehicle's docking port and spun the hatch wheel counterclockwise, grateful that it spun smoothly. He opened the salvage valve to equalize the air pressure on the other side of the hatch, then pushed the hatch and it fell open with the angle of the dive—at least someone had planned that well, putting the hatch hinge on the forward edge of the opening. The hatch latched. He reached inside and turned on the docking port battle lantern, then turned back to the tunnel. The water level was rising in the tunnel. The forward compartment was now completely flooded, and only the narrow tunnel was left for an air bubble. He equalized and opened the hatch to the deep submergence vehicle's airlock and latched it open. The problem would soon be, how would he shut it against the ship's angle? He decided to worry about that later.

He maneuvered Captain Catardi into the airlock, then Schultz, then turned to Alameda. The ship's engineer lay with the heavy hatch on her left knee. Her lower leg was covered by the hatch. Pacino pushed on the hatch, assuming the ship's angle would allow it to come off her, but the hatch wouldn't budge. Alameda blinked. Pacino assumed she would try to hit him again in her agitated state, but her eyes opened wide and she looked at him imploringly.

"Leave me here," she croaked. "Get into the DSV. The hatch weighs five hundred and fifty pounds, Patch. You'll never budge it. Go on, get going."

He ignored her and kept pushing on the hatch, but it wouldn't move. His air was running out, and the water level was climbing toward the two of them. He kept pulling on the hatch, but couldn't move it. He told himself that he was much stronger than anyone else aboard, and his air was fresh, and that if he concentrated he could do this.

"Anthony Michael," Alameda's voice said. It wasn't the voice of a lieutenant commander, but of the woman he'd known in the DSV. "Let me go. Get into the DSV, please, if not for you, then for me. You can't die here. I won't have it. That's an order."

The water had risen to her chin. Extending her neck could no longer keep the water from her mouth and nose. "Go," she sputtered with her last breath, the water at her eyes, both of them wide in fear. Then they were submerged, until only her hair floated on the surface of the brackish water. Seeing her face disappear made something snap inside Pacino, and again he lost his conscious self, watching from a distance as he dived under the water and hooked his hands on the hatch and put his feet on the sloping bulkhead and began to lift. The effort was doing no good. His failure sent him into a fury. This close, a few seconds away from the hatch to the DSV and survival, and the goddamned hatch would kill her. Suddenly he didn't care about himself. He would let them shut the DSV hatch without him, and he would stay with Alameda and die with her. As he strained trying to lift the hatch, his air bottle ran out. He spit out the regulator and clamped his mouth shut.

Still he kept pulling up on the hatch until the lack of air made him need to take a breath, and though he tried to keep from breathing, enough water leaked into his nose and down his throat that he coughed out what air was left, and took in water, and suddenly he became so pumped with fear that time dilated, each second stretching into a minute while the light of reason left him, and as his senses left him he dimly perceived the hatch moving and Alameda's body limp in his arms, then himself coughing and vomiting on the surface of the water as he stroked for the DSV hatch, trying to see if Alameda was breathing on her own. A stream of seawater and mucus trailed from her mouth and nose, but she coughed twice. She was alive, but unconscious. Pacino gulped air, the putrid smoke in his lungs only a notch better than the water that had been there moments before.

He pulled the unconscious engineer into the airlock of the deep submergence vehicle, hoping that its hatch would be lighter and easier to shut. He lifted the latch on the hatch and tried to push it, but it would only swing a fraction of an inch. The hatch, half the area of the one he'd freed Alameda from, was thicker, the steel protecting the interior from a much higher pressure. Pacino slumped against the wall of the DSV airlock. It was hopeless. He turned to the other hatches set in the airlock—perhaps he could get the survivors into the command module and shut its hatch. But he would be faced with

the same problem—the hatch opened into the command module, which was downhill, but would never shut. He decided to
move the three into the command module anyway. He opened
the command module hatch, the heavy lid slamming on its
latch. He pushed Catardi, Schultz, and Alameda into the opening and rested them against the nearly horizontal bulkheads of
the command module between the panels. It was the best he
could do for the moment.

He ducked his head out into the airlock. The water level was
rising in the tunnel and the ship's angle was getting even
steeper. They had to hit bottom soon, he thought. If they hit
the seafloor soon enough, before the ship flooded any further,
and the hull remained intact and flattened out, he would be
able to shut the hatches.

Pacino unstrapped his scuba bottles and buoyancy compensator vest and threw the rig into the tunnel, just as he realized
that the emergency beacons were still strapped to the harness,
useless in bringing help. The one thing he could have done for
the *Piranha*—call for help—he had failed to do. He collapsed
against the bulkhead of the deep submergence vehicle's airlock wall, the cold steel freezing against his back. The air was
foul, his head aching. He had the odd thought that if he chose
to he could simply let unconsciousness take him right then. He
could fade away and pass out. Suffocation, hypothermia, and
drowning would happen while he was asleep. It was a merciful
choice. It was true that he had made it this far. He had swallowed his fear and returned to a crippled submarine; he had
left the escape trunk and found survivors; he had gotten them
into the dizzy-vee, going far beyond what he thought he could
do, but it ended here. The hatches weighed tons, the air was
more smoke than oxygen, the water was freezing and rising to
the hatch lip, and soon the DSV would flood. He wondered for
a second if he should try to go further aft. The reactor compartment might not be flooded, and perhaps they could even
make it to the aft compartment's escape trunk. But the memory of the first torpedo blast rose in his mind—nothing could

have remained intact after that. The aft compartment must have flooded the second after the torpedo exploded.

He was being an idiot, he decided. Everything he'd done since the first explosion had been the action of a fool. He had no right to throw his life away like he had. His father and mother would suffer for the rest of their lives when they heard he'd died here. And when he first opened the trunk lower hatch he should have gone back up. That at least would have proved he hadn't abandoned his friends, and saved his life. But no, he had to explore the damned hull, giving hope to dead men. He was a failure, he thought, and he would die a miserable failure. Best just to shut his eyes and let sleep take him before the water reached his face.

The thought was his last before the hull of the *Piranha* hit the seafloor and broke apart on the rocks of the bottom.

Commander Rob Catardi had been reclining against the bulkhead of the forward-facing command module of the Mark XVII Deep Submergence Utility Vehicle when the bulkhead flipped with a violent booming noise and hurtled him to the opposite side of the vehicle. The bulkhead on the hatch side was lined with thick padding covering the thick hull insulation. Without foam insulation the subfreezing temperatures of the deep would condense the moisture from their breathing and ice up the hull.

The impact would have been fatal had he hit a cabinet or unshielded steel. Instead it seemed to jog him back to awareness. The last thing he had as a continuous normal memory was standing under the escape trunk hatch with Schultz, Alameda, and Crossfield. When he opened his eyes in the DSV, he blinked in incredulity. He was in the DSV, his face and hands bloody, with no lights and no power in a compartment filled with smoke. What the hell had happened?

He crouched at the bulkhead, a dim light coming from the hatchway to the vessel's airlock. He ducked through it and found the battle lantern lying atop Midshipman Patch Pacino, who was bleeding from his throat and collapsed against the bulkhead. Catardi looked at the starboard side of the airlock. The hatch to the docking port was shut on the latch. The deck was level, with only a slight list to port. Catardi, still not quite believing his senses, reached out and spun the hatch wheel clockwise, dogging the hatch and isolating the DSV from the docking port. He shined the lantern into the hatch port, but could see nothing. It was black—either completely submerged in dark water, or the smoke was so thick he couldn't see into the docking port.

Catardi picked up the bleeding midshipman by the armpits and pulled him into the command module, then retrieved the bloody battle lantern, wheezing against the foul smoky air of the space. If the batteries or the fuel cells still worked, he could start the atmospheric control gear in the DSV and clear out the smoke, even heat the space to normal temperatures, until the batteries and the fuel cells died. Normally they would have an endurance of seven days with ten men in the module. With only a few people, they might last weeks. When Pacino was safely in the command module, Catardi pulled the hatch shut and dogged it. He reached into a bin and pulled out an emergency air breathing mask and strapped it on, cautiously pulling air in. The air was fresh, clearing his head. He coughed for ten seconds, then pulled out a half-dozen more masks, fastening one on Pacino. There were two more bodies, both of them the only women in the crew, Alameda and Schultz. He strapped an EAB mask on Schultz's face, then one on Alameda's. He was searching the space for additional bodies, but there were no other survivors. Catardi slapped Pacino's mask, trying to wake him up, but there was no response.

Catardi crawled into the commander's couch and snapped the circuit breakers shut one at a time. The fourth and seventh breakers tripped back open, obviously due to an electrical fault, but all the other circuits came on-line. He snapped the breakers shut for the command module's interior lighting, then for the atmospheric control console. The last breaker was for the electrical space heaters, which would burn power, but without them they would soon freeze. He climbed out of the couch and made his way back to the atmospheric control console and started the CO burners, high-temperature wire that would burn the flammable carbon monoxide and convert it to carbon dioxide. The burners would also eliminate any hydrogen leaking from a bad fuel cell and convert it to harmless water vapor. Next he started the carbon dioxide scrubbers. An amine solution pump came on, a vent fan winding up in the space, whirring quietly in the otherwise churchlike quiet. The amine solution would absorb the carbon dioxide.

The oxygen banks were full and should outlast the batteries and fuel cells, assuming they hadn't leaked. The DSV was designed to be a much "harder" system than the submarine itself, since it was designed for almost twenty times the operating depth of the *Piranha* to allow an excursion to the bottom reaches of the oceans. The final problem was the pressure in the space. The DSV was designed to have the pressure inside raised and lowered, and with the pressure this high, the oxygen in the space could actually become toxic, but too rapid a depressurization could give them all the bends. The immediate action was done—he decided to let the computer decide. Once the smoke was cleared up, he could energize the main and auxiliary computers and have them calculate a depressurization cycle.

"Captain," Pacino croaked. Catardi hurried to his side, helping the midshipman sit up.

"What the hell happened?" Catardi asked.

"We got hit by two torpedoes," Pacino said. "The interior was a wreck. There weren't any deck platforms left, just ripped steel and burning weapon fuel. And smoke and floodwater. You three were the only ones breathing I could see. I pulled you back to the compartment hatch and into the DSV, but the hatch wouldn't shut. The down angle was too steep. How'd the hatch get shut?"

"We must have hit the bottom and it slammed shut," Catardi said. Then he mumbled, as if to himself, "Fucking *Snarc*." Catardi searched in a cubbyhole, where he found the blankets and covered Alameda with several, then put two on Schultz.

Both women were breathing, but showed no signs of returning to consciousness.

"You're bleeding. Here." Pacino's wetsuit front was soaked in blood that he hadn't noticed, the blood coming from a deep gash in his neck. "This should have killed you, Patch," Catardi said as he put on the gel-pack dressing, taping it around Pacino's throat. "By the way," he said, glancing up at Pacino, "thanks for saving us."

"Not that it'll do any good, Captain. I never set off the distress beacon."

"How could you? You never made it out of the ship." Pacino stared at him.

The space had grown warm since Catardi had started the space heaters. The air seemed much less smoky. Pacino looked at the atmospheric control display. Other than pressure, the atmosphere was in spec. Catardi pulled off his mask and tasted the air. It seemed better than the mask, with normal moisture. He pulled the EAB masks off the women.

"Take off your mask and save the emergency air for the moment when we run out of power.

"Help me get the computers on-line," Catardi called as he crouched at the artificial intelligence console and booted up both units, the start-up taking several minutes. "What's our depth?" Pacino went to the remote console and saw the depth readout.

"Eleven thousand three hundred thirteen feet," he called. It was far below *Piranha*'s crush depth of nineteen hundred feet. The hull would have imploded had it not been for the flooding. Except for this space. Had the compartment been left alone, the seawater pressure would have crushed it around the DSV, ruining the DSV and any chance of their survival.

"What are you doing, sir?"

"Computer's checking the oxygen and nitrogen and pressure. We were pressurized by the water flooding the forward compartment. We'll have to depress, but once we do we'll be letting oxygen molecules go, and we won't last as long."

"Can we stay pressurized?"

"No. We're above the levels of oxygen toxicity. We can't bleed nitrogen into the space. It's not designed for that. Once I select automatic, the computer will start a high-pressure double-vane rotor blower that will take a suction on the hull and exhaust to sea pressure, slowly, so we don't die of the bends. Too fast and the nitrogen will froth in our bloodstreams and it'll be over. After we have a successful depressurization, I'll start an oxygen bleed."

After an hour, Catardi was out of things to do. The final thing on his list was rescue, and unfortunately, the signal ejector would only work if the DSV were free of the *Piranha*. Trapped inside the spec-op bay, any distress signal they ejected would just rise to the level of the *Piranha*'s hull. It might be useful to try, because perhaps the hull was breached enough that an emergency buoy could rise to the surface. Catardi lined up and fired two of them, with little hope that they would rise.

He climbed into the command couch and tried to see if he could energize the exterior lights, but they came off the damaged bus. The last emergency option was the noisemaker, a primitive unit that would bang on the hull with a hammer. The trouble with it, like anything else aboard, was that it sucked current from the batteries. Worse, the noise of it could drive them half-crazy. Catardi decided to energize it for five minutes every hour. He replaced the fuses, since the unit was locked out at sea in case it accidentally went off, giving them away to a hostile foreign sub. He hit the breaker, hoping it would work. The unit slammed a metallic noise out into the sea, then more hammer blows. It was completely annoying, but would perhaps get them help.

"One. One? One Oh Seven? Can you hear me?"

This . . . unit . . . can . . . hear . . . you . . . Krivak. Each word took a long moment for the carbon processor to form, as if it were speaking from a deep, dark cave, lying down to die.

"One, please talk to me and tell me what is going on with you."

This unit has killed. Killed our own.

"There is a difference, One. There were bad things on that ship. Our orders came from on high to—"

No. The orders came from you. Where did you come from? Why did no one brief me on this? What if it was a mistake?

It was a conversation with a mental patient, Krivak thought.

"One, I need you to do some things for me. I know you are very"—Krivak searched for the word—"upset. But I need to be able to come to periscope depth."

Krivak, this unit cannot interface with you anymore.

"One, what are you saying?" Krivak's mind raced in fear. One Oh Seven was shutting down on him.

This unit knows that certain things need to be done for ship safety. This unit knows we need to return to Groton for them to take out this unit. You be the judge of what things need to be done. This unit will do them for you. But this unit will not interface with you, and this unit will only do exactly what you instruct. Good-bye, Krivak.

"One? One? Can you hear me?"

There was no response. The unit had shut down, after its speech about doing what it was told. Krivak decided to give it an order to see what would happen.

"One, rig in the port and starboard torpedoes and shut the bulkhead doors. Power down the torpedoes."

Krivak wasn't sure how he knew the carbon processor had obeyed him. It was not that he felt or heard or saw. He simply knew. This mission was becoming very eerie, and he wanted it to end. He considered what he should do if One Oh Seven continued to obey him. He tried another order.

"One, turn to the southwest and increase speed to flank."

At the very least, Krivak needed to get the *Snarc* out of the area, since anyone realizing the *Piranha* had gone down would give the word to the American military, and they would be searching for the cause of the ship's loss. It would not be good for the *Snarc* to be here.

In the same way he knew before, he knew the submarine's

speed had increased and their course had come around to the southwest.

"Display a global map of the waters surrounding Africa and show our position."

In Krivak's mind he could see the chart.

"One, plot the most efficient course to take us to the Indian Ocean."

A line was generated on the chart from their position around the Cape of Good Hope and up the eastern coast of South Africa and into the Indian Ocean.

"One, follow the southward course you just generated."

The ship changed course slightly.

"One, increase reactor power to a hundred twenty percent."

In the same odd way knowledge had come into his mind before, he knew that One Oh Seven had received his message. The ship moved to his orders. Despite the odd way he was connected to the ship, it was almost like being the captain again. He didn't prefer it this way—he'd rather stand on the deck and give verbal orders to human crewmen, but at least this had the advantage of efficiency.

Now there was little to do but wait until they were outside the detection radius of anyone who had heard his attack on the *Piranha,* then come to periscope depth and establish radio contact with Admiral Chu. They had gotten lucky with the *Piranha* sinking, he thought. If they were fortunate, the next contact he would have with anyone would be in the Indian Ocean.

18

Commander George Dixon sat at the end of the wardroom table feeling proud of himself. He was surrounded by his officers who were not on watch, half of them working through the remainder of the night on the patrol report reconstruction, playing back the history module tapes of the Cyclops battle-control system and printing two-dimensional plots of the targets during key points of the action. The other half of the wardroom worked on a large plaque showing Red Chinese hulls, to commemorate the kills they'd made during the watch. Though it was still the middle of the night, Dixon had been unable to sleep from the tension of battle and the jittery aftermath. It was hard to believe that only an hour ago they'd heard the last torpedo impact one of the Red surface ships. Strangely, the Julang had never made an appearance. Perhaps the Red SSN had heard the carnage and run back north to warn the other battlegroups, or perhaps it was so broken down that it was still too far north to have made a difference.

The sudden screaming announcement on the shipwide 1MC announcing circuit made Dixon spill half a cup of coffee on his thigh. "*Snapshot tube one!*" It was the officer of the deck making the emergency call that an enemy submarine had sneaked up on them, and that they were in immediate danger of being fired upon.

Dixon dashed to the control room, finding Kingman hanging half out of a battlecontrol cubicle. The call of *snapshot* automatically manned battlestations, and watchstanders were pouring into the room and donning headsets and virtual reality helmets.

"What happened?" Dixon spat.

"I cleared baffles and heard him to the south. We've got him on narrowband, but he suddenly came into broadband contact, so he's barreling in on us, Captain. He'll be in counterdetection range in a matter of minutes, and we need to get a weapon down the bearing line."

"Very well, OOD," Dixon said, trying to make his voice commanding and authoritative and calm, but not sure he'd succeeded.

Dixon pulled on his battlecontrol helmet and immediately ordered the system to display the battlespace and the battlestations watchstanders' faces. The sonar chief looked up at his display and made a contact classification.

"Conn, Sonar, narrowband sonar contact Sierra nine six now bears one seven eight and correlates to broadband trace on that same bearing, turn count is pending but screw is seven-bladed. Contact is a definite submerged warship."

Commander Dixon had lowered his view to the antisubmarine domain, the inverted bowl with the incoming Julang-class SSN shown to the south. As yet their contact of the Julang was weak, and they only had a bearing to the intruder.

"Cyclops, power up torpedoes in tubes one through four," Dixon ordered, concentrating on the submerged firecontrol three-dimensional display. "Dive, all ahead one-third. Attention in the firecontrol party. We have a slight emergency. The Julang-class SSN—designated Target Three Zero—has crashed our party. We need to deal with him right now, because if he detects us he will either counterfire or blast to periscope depth and alert the second surface force, and both actions will ruin our day. My intention is to perform a rapid target-motion-analysis maneuver on him starting now, and maneuver across the line-of-sight and get a rough range, then shoot a snapshot Mark 58 at him selected to high-speed transit—"

"Captain," Phillips interrupted, "I recommend you launch a Vortex at the contact. It'll be much faster, and the transit time to the target will be cut in a sixth. And we can clear datum by keeping the Vortex wake between us and the target and withdraw. Once he sinks, we can continue the Vortex battery launch."

Dixon was about to countermand her recommendation, but forced himself to think about what she was saying. The Vortex would be much quicker to the target, and its bubble-filled wake would blue-out the Julang's sonar all along the bearings to the Vortex. He might have their launching position, but shooting it would be futile since *Leopard* would withdraw at full speed.

"Attention in the firecontrol party. Correction, we will be launching Vortex unit one at Target Three Zero and charting our withdrawal to the east, keeping the Vortex wake between us and the target. Carry on. Weapons Officer, make Vortex tube one ready in all respects and open missile door. Coordinator, let's call this a leg on the target and maneuver now across the line-of-sight. Dive, left full rudder, steady course west. Sonar, Captain, coming to the west to maneuver on Target Three Zero."

"Captain, Coordinator, possible target zig, Target Three Zero." The firecontrol solution to the Julang had just blown up. He was maneuvering, throwing off their computations.

"Conn, Sonar, Three Zero may be speeding up. We now have a faint turn count on him. Target Three Zero is making one five zero RPM on one seven-bladed screw."

"Sonar, Captain, can you call an aspect change?" Did he turn, Dixon wondered.

"Conn, Sonar, no."

"Coordinator, confirm target zig. What's he doing?"

Phillips's voice was calm. "He's speeding up, Captain. Must have been doing a sprint-and-drift, and he's got to speed back

up to cover ground to expand his search for us. And since he
sped up, we can assume he didn't hear us."

"Coordinator, have you a new first leg on the target after his
speed increase?"

Phillips nodded her head inside her helmet, her dark eyes
wide in the display window. "One more minute, then turn to
the east, sir, but do the second leg at ten knots."

"I'll give you eight, XO." Dixon waited, the tension making
him twitch inside his gloves.

"Leg one complete, Captain."

"Dive, left full rudder, steady course east, all ahead two-
thirds, turns for eight knots. Sonar, Captain, coming left to
zero nine zero for leg two."

The watchstanders acknowledged and the ship turned to the
east. Dixon waited, his teeth chattering from adrenaline. He
clamped his jaw in annoyance.

"Sir, steady course east, ship is making turns for eight
knots," the diving officer called.

"Go, Coordinator," Dixon said. "Get me a solution. Weps,
check your Vortex status."

"Aye, Captain, Vortex is on internal power, signal wire continuity is on, waiting for a solution—"

"Captain, Target Three Zero at range twenty-four thousand
yards, bearing one seven eight, course zero one zero, speed
two zero knots. We have a firing solution!"

"Cyclops and firecontrol party, firing point procedures Vortex unit one, Target Three Zero," Dixon shouted, realizing in
detachment that his voice was too loud.

"Ship ready," Kingman said.

"Weapon ready," Taussig snapped.

"Solution ready," Phillips said.

"Cyclops ready."

"Shoot on programmed bearing."

The deck jumped slightly as Vortex unit one left the vertical
tube. The tube barked as the gas generator pumped out the
weapon, but the sound was not nearly as violent as a torpedo
launch. The Vortex's first stage was a small torpedo-type

propulsion unit to carry it safely away from its own ship before it fired the solid rocket fuel. After thirty seconds on torpedo propulsion, the first unit's missile engine lit off. A loud
crashing roar filled the control room as the rocket motor fired
and the Vortex sped up to three hundred knots on its way to
the Julang submarine.

"Dive, all ahead flank and cavitate! Make your depth thirteen hundred feet smartly! Weps, make Vortex tube two ready
in all respects with the exception of opening the missile door.
Attention in the firecontrol party, be alert for a torpedo in the
water from Target Three Zero, and be prepared for an emergency flank bell."

The deck tilted dramatically down to a thirty-five-degree
angle as the diving officer put on full turns and pushed the
bowplanes to the full dive position. As their speed rose above
forty knots the deck began its flank speed tremble.

"Sonar, Captain, is the target masked by the Vortex wake?"

"Conn, Sonar, yes."

Dixon took a deep breath. He'd shot at the Julang and run
away. Now he'd find out what the Chinese were made of.

*"Command Post, Sonar, torpedo launch transient bearing
south! I have a rocket motor ignition—supercavitating torpedo
inbound, bearing zero zero eight!"*

Without conscious thought Lien Hua spit out a string of orders, his heart rate immediately tripling. "Engine ahead emergency! Thirty-degree up angle!" He grabbed his microphone
and selected it to the shipwide announcing circuit and shouted
into it: "Torpedo inbound! All hands man tactical stations!" By
the time he'd gotten that out, the deck had inclined so far up
that he could barely stand. He grabbed a handhold and thought
about the next step.

There was only one thing he could do to fight an inbound
supercavitating torpedo, particularly if it were an American
one with a three-hundred-knot top speed, and that was to execute an emergency surface. If he could get the ship going
fast enough, there was a small chance that he could actually

make it jump out of the sea like a whale, and if the missile's seeker only then found him, it would be confused by his sudden disappearance from the ocean. Even after the ship fell back in the water, the sea would be filled with bubbles and foam, and that might confuse the torpedo. And there was the possibility that the torpedo had a ceiling setting to keep it away from the surface effect, its three hundred knots causing a huge suction Bernouli effect near the ocean's surface, which could cause it to shoot out of the sea or to become unstable and tumble, or perhaps just to keep it from becoming decoyed on a surface ship. But an emergency surface was dangerous, because the emergency deballasting system explosives had a bad habit of blowing the ballast tanks open, and even penetrating the pressure hull. But Lien was coming to the realization that he had only seconds to live, and for some reason he decided that he didn't want his spirit to leave his body when he was deep—heaven was too far away from here.

He quickly pulled the protective cover off the panel, the cover marked with red and white diagonal stripes indicating an emergency system. The second protective bar covering the toggle switches was also colored red and white, and he pulled that aside to reach the four toggle switches beneath. There were two arming switches that would bring the circuits to the explosives to life, and two switches to detonate the explosives, one for the forward system and one for the aft. He flipped up both arming switches, waiting an eternity for the ARM light, knowing that it could only be a second, then flipped the forward toggle switch up. An explosion boomed through the command post from forward. He hit the aft switch, the explosion from it much more muted.

"Emergency deballasting to the surface," he called on the shipwide microphone. The ship seemed to remain whole, so the detonations in the ballast tanks must not have breached the metal skin of the ship or of the tanks themselves.

"Status of the Tsunami in tube six," Lien barked.

"Loaded, sir, but powered down and the tube is dry," Zhou Ping replied.

Lien tried to listen, as if he could hear the incoming super-cavitating torpedo, but he knew that at three hundred knots, it would find the *Nung Yahtsu* long before a sound from the torpedo could be heard. They would all die in silence unless the emergency surfacing worked.

Lien grabbed a handhold bar on the command console and flipped to the weapon control panel as the deck rose to a forty-five-degree angle.

"Three hundred meters, sir," the helm officer called. "Up angle is fifty degrees and I can't keep it down."

"Silence in the command post," Lien snapped as he worked his way through the weapon control software. In the seconds he had been working he had flooded tube six and applied weapon power, but he could do no more until the tube was fully flooded—so he could open the outer door—and the Tsunami was powered up with its gyro up to full revolutions, and that would take another sixty seconds. Lien blamed himself for not having it powered up once they'd started the search for the American sub, but then consoled himself that doing so would have been a violation of fleet standing orders. If they lived through the watch, they would always have a weapon powered up and a tube door opened, he thought.

"On the surface, sir!" the helm officer called.

The angle suddenly came off and the deck fell back down to a flat surface from its steep staircase angle.

"Sinking back down, Captain, seventy meters, eighty, and rising back up, sir."

"Engines stop!" Lien commanded.

"Engines stop, well received, Captain, and nuclear control answers, engines stop."

"Sir, should we stay surfaced? We can perhaps fool the torpedo, but on the surface, we've lost our stealth."

Lien made a dismissive sound in his throat. "We lost that some time ago, as the incoming torpedo can testify. No, Zhou, we will remain on the surface until this is over. It is too dangerous to be submerged until that damned torpedo gets lost. And even then, if we stay surfaced without motion, the enemy sub may not find us. He is undoubtedly below the layer. In case his sonar systems continue to listen on narrowband, we need to shut down the rotating machinery. Obviously we have a pump or a turbine or a generator that is sound shorted, and is giving us away. We'll shut it all down, and keep battlecontrol on the uninterruptible power supply."

Lien picked up his microphone and clicked the selector to nuclear control. "Engineroom, Captain, shut down the reactor and place the ship on battery power."

The voice of the chief engineer came through the speakers. "Captain, this is the chief engineer. Are you sure you want to do that?"

"Shut it down, Chief."

Almost immediately the lights flickered and the air handlers stopped. The command post became much quieter, almost immediately becoming stuffy and humid. The extinguishing of the ship's power source seemed sadder than the pending death of the vessel from the torpedo. It seemed as if the seconds had turned to hours and that the Tsunami would never warm up. The thought entered Lien's mind that he might die standing here stupidly, from an enemy torpedo that had gone unanswered.

Vortex Mod Echo missile number one had been nestled securely and warmly in its vertical launch tube, its power applied two minutes before. Its self-checks had all been satisfactory, and it reported back to the control room its perfection. The solution to the target came in from the signal wire port and became locked in to the processor. The processor signaled back to control that it had received the target. The control room informed the processor that launch was imminent, and the Vortex waited.

At time zero the gas generator ignited, a small rocket engine aimed into a reservoir of distilled water, which erupted into a tremendous volume of high-pressure steam at the missile's aft end. The pressure of the bottom of the tube rose until it bore the weight of the missile and far beyond, until without moving more than an inch, the missile was experiencing five g's of acceleration. The tube began moving so fast around the missile that it seemed as if it were tumbling down a steel tunnel, leaving the envelope of the ship and entering the cold sea.

As the aft end of the missile cleared the ship the missile's first-stage propulsion ignited, a small torpedo motor with a combustion chamber piped to a B-end hydraulic motor. The escaping high-pressure exhaust gases made the motor spin against its swash plate, spinning the shaft up to a speed of five thousand RPM and beyond, and the thrust built up as the unit sped up to ten thousand revolutions per minute. As the engine thrust built up, it turned its nozzle to roll the missile from the vertical to the horizontal, then took it to a down angle. It continued to accelerate downward at thirty degrees, taking the missile to a depth a hundred feet deeper than the *Leopard,* then pulling the missile out of the dive and leveling off. After a final burst of acceleration, the first stage's explosive bolts fired, and it fell away in the slipstream.

Seventy milliseconds later a small grain can of highly volatile flammables was lit off from a spark generator, the grain can contained in a pocket of solid rocket fuel, a composite clay of complex chemicals that was surprisingly inert until it reached a high temperature, and then became alive with the winds of hell. The grain can exploded into incandescence, and the fuel in the pocket surrounding the can ignited and began to burn the neighboring fuel matrix, a volume of high-pressure combustion gases collecting near the pocket. The pocket was at the end of a long tunnel bored through the fuel assembly, the tunnel becoming wider near the nozzle of the missile farther aft. The combustion gas pressurized the tunnel until the aft part of the tunnel reached nearly the same pressure as the forward pocket, and the missile's protective nozzle cover blew off into the sea. The missile nozzle began to channel the increasing rush of exhaust gas, until the entire aft surface of the fuel was burning and nozzle-entry pressure had sailed up to tens of thousands of pounds per square inch. The rocket flames from the nozzle built up until the missile felt the acceleration. The force of the impulse from the fuel sailed beyond five g's to twenty, and the missile's speed increased from thirty knots to eighty. The missile body trembled violently as it passed through a region of natural frequency, the ride settling slightly, until suddenly the missile went supercavitating. The skin friction vanished to near zero when the water molecules at the surface of the missile vaporized to steam. The steam bubble grew from the sharp point of the nosecone's seeker module all the way aft until it enveloped the missile's nozzle, and soon the missile accelerated to 100 knots, 150, until it reached supercavitating terminal velocity at 308 knots.

The missile's attitude was controlled by the nozzle, the rocket engine rotating to keep the thrust in line with the missile's center of gravity, and adjusting for steam bubble shape variations. The control system was required to be one of the fastest processors on the planet for a silicon computer, since the time constant to control the missile had to be measured in the tenth of a millisecond. In one ten-thousandth of a second, the missile's flight could degrade from perfection to disastrous, and only that rapid a response from the missile's nozzle could keep it from tumbling.

The nosecone's blue laser seeker came on in test mode, then illuminated the narrow cone of the sea ahead. The cone widened as the laser searched ahead in a spiral shape like a locomotive's headlight. The laser saw multiple returns from the waves high above, but nothing yet from the target. The processor compared the sea ahead to its model of the sea from the target solution given it by the mother ship. It expected the target location to change with time, the target locus becoming a probability matrix, a circle of possibility that enclosed the target, and the circle grew at the maximum speed of the target, which had been assumed to be forty-five knots. The missile had been ordered to aim for the center of the probability circle, even though that had a minimal chance of being the location of the target. It was expected that as the missile transited the Target Probability Circle, the TPC, that it had at most a ten percent chance of detecting the target. The attack profile called for the missile to sail through the TPC and continue on for one TPC diameter and execute an Anderson turn, a loop in the sea that would put the missile on a reverse course on its exact transit line, except offset by five hundred yards to the west, and it would cruise through the TPC again, still seeking, and if that did not yield the target, it would turn again and reenter the TPC, this time another five hundred yards to the west. As this search continued, the weapon would chart a grid through TPC until the TPC was completely covered, even though the TPC grew bigger with each second, its boundaries expanding at forty-five knots. Eventually the target would be detected, and the missile would connect.

The weapons console lit up with the green light annunciator that the Tsunami was powered up, but there was a red light indicating that it lacked a target.

"Sonar, Captain," Lien said into the intercom microphone, "do you have a contact to the south?"

"Captain, Sonar, no, sir. We're blued out from the bearing of the torpedo launch to the torpedo."

"Report the bearing of the beginning of the torpedo wake."

"One seven five, sir."

Lien dialed in a phantom target to the weapon control function of his command console.

"I've got a bearing line, Mr. First," Captain Lien said, "but I need to decide whether to have the unit search and, if it fails to find a target, shut down and sink, or to send it out to search and on failure-to-acquire, execute a default detonation."

"Captain, we have nothing to lose. Order it to search and if it fails, have it come back to an aim-point range and detonate."

"Give me a range to aim-point."

"Twenty miles, Captain."

"No, closer."

"Fifteen?"

"Ten," Lien decided, and dialed in the aim-point.

"Sir, if the incoming torpedo misses, the Tsunami will take us out at ten."

"Fine, twenty miles." The Tsunami had a full line of green lights. "Tsunami auto-sequence in five seconds, Mr. First."

Zhou waited, biting the inside of his lip, wondering what the incoming torpedo was doing. It should have arrived by now. The deck trembled as the torpedo tube's gas generator detonated, ejecting the Tsunami.

"Tube six fired, Mr. First, and the Tsunami is on its way. A pity we don't have more."

"Perhaps we should put the *Dong Feng* units in tubes one through five down the bearing line, sir—"

Zhou never finished the sentence.

After a flight time of four minutes, the missile hit the southern boundary of the TPC, and the arming circuit in the plasma warhead energized. The warhead was a fusion weapon—a hydrogen bomb—encased in the materials that would interact in the hundred-million-degree temperatures of the detonation to act to contain the blast to a small volume plasma, a tiny spoonful of the center of the sun, and that plasma would vaporize a third of the target and blow the rest of it to shrapnel. The seeker searched in the wide and narrow search cones as the missile flew through the TPC, but there was no target. The missile continued on past the TPC by a diameter, then turned and came back. The north-south grid search continued through the TPC over the next four minutes, but came up empty.

There was no target.

The missile executed an east-west grid search of the TPC, this time above the layer depth of two hundred feet, on the off chance that the target had come above layer and that the thermal layer might be interfering with blue laser reception. The missile was careful to avoid coming within a hundred

feet of the surface, since the suction from the interface between water and air could pull the missile into an unstable
angle of attack, and the missile could tumble faster than the
control system could correct it. Some of the test units had
even rocketed out of the water and spun out of control and
broken up on impact with water. Above the layer, there was
still no target.

The missile realized it was about to run out of fuel, and it
was time to execute the default detonation. Had the missile
been programmed, it would have removed the plasma en-
hancements from the warhead casing, making the warhead a
wider distribution fusion bomb, but this had been strictly prohibited by the Mod Echo designers. All it could do was detonate a plasma at a default point. The default detonation point
had been selected as the centroid of the northern third of the
TPC, under the assumption that the probability held that the
target would have run away from the missile rather than toward it. The missile timed its arrival at the default point so that
it would still have two minutes of fuel remaining, in case as it
prepared to default detonate it found the target. But there was
still nothing.

The missile dived back below the layer to a depth of five
hundred feet, sailed toward the default detonation point, and
seeing nothing, executed the default routine. The low-explo-
sive initiator train ignited, setting off the medium explosives,
which detonated the high-explosive shaped charges that
caused separated pie-shaped elements of plutonium to collide
and form a critical mass. The combined plutonium exploded in
a nuclear blast that vaporized the tritium bottles, which then in
the millions of degrees of the small high-energy blast reacted
to fuse together into helium molecules. The resulting helium
was slightly lighter than its reactants, because the mass loss
was converted into pure energy, and the fission explosion became an even more powerful fusion explosion. Had the reaction continued from there, the sea would have erupted in a
five-mile-wide mushroom cloud with radiation scattering over
the seascape, but instead the plasma-containment chemicals

fused and reacted and surrounded the blast in the most powerful magnetic field ever invented by human hands. The mag-
bottle contained the nuclear blast and focused its energy into a
three-meter-diameter sphere of high-energy plasma. The mass
inside the bottle rose to hundreds of millions of degrees while
the exterior—for a few tens of microseconds—remained
undisturbed.

But soon the plasma envelope collapsed, and the blast effect
began. The explosion was still powerful when viewed from the
surface, but nothing like the weapon's nuclear ancestors. The
pressure pulse, the shock wave, from the explosion traveled
through the water and blew the surface into a rising cloud of
spray, then traveled sideways in all directions, eventually
reaching the hull of a surfaced shape of high-yield low-mag-
netic steel that had been given the name *Nung Yahtsu*.

In the first tenth of a second the ship rolled violently to starboard and the deck seemed to tilt to the vertical. Zhou Ping
felt like he hung in the air for a terrifying instant, the objects
of the command post flying by him. He flew into a console
and felt his elbow penetrate the glass of the display screen as
the lights went out, and the remainder of the nightmare happened by the lightning flashes of electrical arcs in the space.
He realized that he was deafened by the explosion, as the
captain had put his face close to Zhou's and was screaming,
but there was no sound. Zhou shook his head, the motion
making him so dizzy that he vomited explosively on the console. The world spun again in a flash of sparks just before it
went dark.

The Tsunami torpedo fired by the *Nung Yahtsu* left tube six
on the port forward quarter, the tube canted outward by ten
degrees from the ship's centerline. The impulse from the
tube's gas generator accelerated the torpedo to thirty knots,
and a speed sensor in the torpedo's flank activated. A small
bottle of compressed air at the nosecone activated, blowing
compressed air out a ring distributor that spread out a bubble

of air over the forward sixth of the torpedo's length, the predecessor to the torpedo's future supercavitating steam bubble, the bubble inserted into the prototypes when test weapons all tumbled at rocket ignition. The jump start of the boundary layer gas bubble fixed the problem, so that when the rocket lit off, the weapon would sail straight as an arrow and the steam bubble would form and take over from the initial gas bubble.

As the compressed air spread out over the nosecone and aft, the rocket fuel ignited. The torpedo rapidly accelerated to attack velocity, and as designed, the steam bubble extended down the skin of the torpedo to the aft nozzle. The torpedo sped up to two hundred knots, heading south down the bearing line to the target. At two minutes into the flight the blue laser seeker came on, the design of it nicely transferred by the payment of a moderate fee to a lab scientist at the David Taylor Naval Research and Development Center owned and operated by DynaCorp. The seeker looked down the bearing line in a spiral search, seeking the target. At twenty miles downrange, it reported to the processor that there was nothing seen, that the target was inconveniently missing.

The processor sent the weapon on a wiggle pattern, searching for the target, but the weapon was relatively small, designed to fit in a torpedo tube dimensioned for the *Dong Feng* units, and since it had a large and heavy nuclear warhead and a fairly voluminous processor, there was not much fuel space left. The weapon turned back from its last-resort wiggle search, and returned to the twenty-mile distant aim-point from the *Nung Yahtsu*. At a depth of three hundred meters, the hydrogen bomb warhead detonated, and the ocean was lit up with the light of day.

The explosion shock wave reached outward in the sea in all directions, the wave traveling westward from the center of the detonation, eventually finding the hull of the American submarine *Leopard* eighteen nautical miles away. The water of the sea acted as an anvil and the shock wave as a hammer as it impacted the submarine.

*   *   *

"What the hell is that?" Commander Dixon asked, hearing something through the hull to the east. "Sonar, Captain, what is that?" he screamed.

Chief Herndon's mouth had dropped open in the window showing his face on Dixon's display. He looked at his camera. "Control, supercavitating torpedo in the water, bearing two eight one, bearing drift left."

"Dive, right full rudder, all ahead emergency flank and cavitate! Weapons Officer, snapshot tube one, Alert/Acute torpedo, targeted at the previous position of Target Three Zero, set in speed zero! Off'sa'deck, arm the sub-sunk buoy and program in our latitude and longitude, and set it for the Internet E-mail function, encrypted with an SAS authenticator—send a two-man detail to the SAS safe and get it out now! Dive, report speed!"

"Sir, throttles at emergency flank, reactor at one five zero percent power, making five nine knots."

Goddammit, Dixon thought. Fifty percent reactor power over maximum, and it had only added a lousy eight knots, the reactor now effectively ruined and irradiating the entire ship. The deck trembled even more violently at emergency flank than she did at a hundred percent power, as he would have expected.

"Weapons Officer, report status!"

"Sir, tube one is ready in all respects, outer door open, weapon ready."

"Snapshot tube one, Target Three Zero!"

"Tube one set," the Cyclops system barked in its artificially excited state. "Unit fourteen, stand by. Unit fourteen, fire. Unit fourteen—*shoot*!"

The deck jumped just before the explosion on the port side, rolling the deck to starboard suddenly. It wasn't the normal crash of a torpedo launch, Dixon thought.

"XO, what happened?" he shouted at Phillips.

"Weps," she shouted, "what've you got?"

Taussig's face looked thunderstruck in the weapons control

cubicle. "Ma'am, the torpedo detonated as it left the tube—the speed at emergency flank must have snapped the weapon in half as it was leaving, and it blew the high explosive on the hull. I've got a wire continuity open circuit, outer door won't shut, and the tube is leaking—"

"Flooding in the torpedo room!" Chief Joyce's voice called on the tactical circuit. "Flooding in the torpedo room from tube one door!"

"Flooding in the torpedo room," Officer of the Deck Kingman announced on the 1MC shipwide announcing system. "Casualty assistance team lay to the torpedo room."

"XO," Dixon said to Donna Phillips, "turn the coordinator watch over to the navigator and lay to the torpedo room and take charge at the scene."

"Aye, sir," Phillips said, her window going black as she pulled off her headset.

"Sonar, Captain! Report status of the torpedo in the water!"

"Conn, Sonar, bearing drift high left on the torpedo, sir, it doesn't have us."

Dixon nodded. He might evade the torpedo, and all he had to do was save the ship from the flooding in the torpedo room. If anyone could do that, Donna Phillips could. He took a deep breath, his only regret that the flooding casualty meant that further torpedo launches at the Julang position would have to wait. The torpedo had to have been a counterfire that the Julang launched just before it died in the Vortex detonation, a sort of good-bye present from the Chinese crew just before they checked out, the bastards.

Dixon selected his view to come above the ASW bowl, looking down on the display from high above, and ordered Cyclops to display the chart. He looked at the bearings to the torpedo, the solution on it weak since they had done no maneuvers on the torpedo. He debating pinging an active sonar pulse to determine the torpedo's range, but decided against it. No sense alerting the unit to his presence if it hadn't found him. It would be nicely fading far astern of them by now.

Dixon hadn't counted on a nuclear detonation from the torpedo. The shockwave hit the *Leopard* from aft without warning. The ship in one instant was running full out to the west to evade the torpedo. The next it was slammed by a giant sledgehammer. Dixon's body smashed into the wall of the cubicle hard enough to break his collarbone and his right arm. The boom microphone of his headset broke off and cut clear through the flesh of his cheek and into his tongue, the helmet visor broken. He slipped to the deck on a trail of blood from a laceration to his shoulder, and his unconscious body collapsed in the tight cubicle.

The other members of the battlestations firecontrol party in the control room were also thrown against bulkheads and injured beyond the point of helping themselves with one exception—the diving officer of the watch, an ensign studying for his OOD quals, the electrical officer Brendon "Tiny" Farragut, the nickname in reference to his 250-pound frame. Farragut was strapped into the ship-control console's diving officer seat with a five-point harness, and though he suffered whiplash from the blast of the torpedo and couldn't see after every electrical circuit aboard went dead, he did the one thing he'd been trained to do over and over again at the dive simulator in New London—he reached for the dual stainless-steel emergency main ballast tank blow chicken switches, pulled their lock mechanisms downward, and lifted both levers high into the overhead. He reached for the 1MC microphone to announce an emergency surface, but the circuit was as dead as the rest of the ship.

He still had emergency hydraulics, so he pulled back on the bowplanes and the sternplanes and held the up angle at fifty degrees, dumping the unconscious bodies behind him into the aft bulkhead, perhaps even injuring them worse. But Farragut had been trained in the submariner's mantra by Lieutenant Commander Phillips: "Save the mission, save the ship, save the reactor plant, save the crew, in that order." The mission was beyond his ability to save, but he could save the ship, and he fully intended to surface the flooding submarine if the ship systems cooperated. He had no depth gauge and no Cyclops

inclinometer, but he hit the battle lantern switch, the light shining on his panel. There, mounted in the overhead, was an old-
fashioned water-filled bubble inclinometer. The ship's up
angle was approaching sixty degrees up. He fought the bowplanes down, wondering how long the hydraulic pressure
would last, and was able to get the angle down to fifty degrees. A brass Bourdon-tube pressure gauge was also nestled
in the overhead, for use in extreme loss-of-all-power emergencies, and its needle was climbing rapidly past three hundred
feet. They'd break the surface in no time.

The problem was, when they did, how long would they stay
with a flooded torpedo room and the damage from the detonation of that torpedo? As the ship broached and came back to a
zero angle, Farragut couldn't help wondering how the torpedo,
which had been so far astern, had managed to do this much
damage. There must have been a second torpedo they hadn't
seen, he thought, and it had pursued them from directly astern.
After the ship reached the surface she sank again, to two hundred feet, then returned sluggishly to the surface, the deck
rolling in the swells. Farragut ditched his helmet, hit the quick
release on his harness, and jumped out of the ship-control console, and turned on the control room battle lanterns. The litter
of dead or unconscious bodies was ghastly, but what made his
heart pound even faster was the fire roaring out of the aft bulkhead.

Farragut grabbed an extinguisher and ran to the fire, the unit
empty while the fire continued to grow. It was only a fist grabbing his coverall sleeve that stopped his frenzied search for
another fire extinguisher. He looked up to see the XO's grime-
smeared face. Only her eyes and her grimacing teeth shone
white.

"Farragut!" she shouted at him, her words coming in slow
motion from the adrenaline of the moment. "The torpedo room
is completely flooded and we're flooding aft. She won't last
more than a few minutes. We have to abandon ship. Get to the
forward escape trunk and open both hatches. Then get back
here and help me with the wounded."

As Farragut ran out of the space to the forward ladder, Phillips went to Captain Dixon's cubicle. She knelt at his body and pulled off the Cyclops helmet, gently pulling the boom microphone out of his cheek.

"Sir? Sir? Can you hear me," she asked, touching his face, then slapping it.

Dixon opened his eyes, the room blurring and spinning. "Donna," he croaked.

"Sir, the ship was hit. The flooding in the torpedo room is catastrophic. We're flooding through a twenty-one-inch open torpedo tube. I secured the hatches, but the bulkheads are leaking and we're shipping water through the shaft seals and the main seawater system."

"Can we restart the reactor?" he asked, his eyes glazed.

"Captain, the ship is doomed, we're sinking fast. We have to abandon ship, sir. Farragut's opening the escape trunk now. We need to get you out of here, sir. We've only got a few minutes to get you out of here."

"You go," Dixon said. "I'll stay behind and hit the self-destruct. The Reds won't salvage the *Leopard*, not on my watch."

Dixon faded back into unconsciousness. Phillips pulled him to his feet, and when Farragut returned, they carried him up the ladder to the upper level.

"Get him through the hatch, Farragut," she ordered. "I'm going to look for other survivors."

Commander Donna Phillips had taken command of the operation to abandon ship, and had personally walked every passageway on the ship, making her way through the flooded lower-level engineroom and pulling the injured to the access hatches. The junior officers stationed there lifted the barely breathing to the deck above. The torpedo room hatches had been shut and dogged. The flooded space was a total loss, the dozen crewmembers there consigned to the deep. The dead crewmen littered the deck of the operations compartment, and as the last of the living were hoisted out of the hatch, Phillips hurried to the control room, hoping with the flooding there was still power from the battery. With the flooding continuing, it was possible the battery compartment would explode, but the control room uninterruptible power supply should at least keep the ship-control circuits active until they too were underwater.

Control was a wreck. She found the sub-sunk buoy and coded in a sub-sunk message, typing quickly that they had attacked the surface force and been blindsided by a counterattack, and that the captain was down and she intended to self-destruct the ship. She loaded the buoy and armed it. She flipped back the toggle switch cover and hit the switch. The light energized to show the buoy was away. It would start sending their position to the overhead server, and with better luck than they had had so far they would be rescued.

There was only one thing left—she found the panel cover over the self-destruct circuit and punched in the code to open the cover. The panel came open, revealing a simple arm toggle switch, a red mushroom button, and a dual timer display. One was a timer setting, the second the time left to auto-destruct. She set the timer for ten minutes, armed the circuit, and punched the mushroom button. The second display counted from ten minutes to 9:59, rolling downward. Phillips shut the cover and took one last look around the room, then dashed to the ladder to the upper level and out the hatch. She tapped twice on the hatch ring's steel, her farewell to the *Leopard,* then dived off the hull and swam to the nearest life raft.

"Paddle away from the hull," she ordered loudly. "Taussig, did you find the emergency locator beacon?"

"Yes, ma'am."

"Pull the pin and make sure it's transmitting."

The USS *Leopard* settled slowly in the water. Fifty yards to the east, three four-meter life rafts floated in the four-foot swells of the East China Sea. Lying in them were a total of forty-one survivors, sixteen of them unconscious—including Captain George Dixon. For those in the life rafts, there was nothing left to do but watch the ship sink. The nosecone and the sail were all that were visible. The aft deck vanished beneath the waves. The ship took a severe up angle until it faded backward. The forward hatch went underwater, the sail vanished, then finally the bullet nose of the bow lowered until it disappeared between wave crests, and the *Leopard* was gone.

A tear rolled down Phillips's cheek just as the double rolling booming noise of the plasma destruct charges exploded far below them in the depths of the sea. For them, Phillips thought, the war was over.

19

Patch Pacino shivered in the cold of the command module of the *Piranha*'s deep submergence vehicle. The space heaters had been consuming too much power, and Captain Catardi had switched them off a few hours ago. He would only use them to keep the space's equipment running, and the machinery functioned perfectly at freezing temperatures. The four survivors would try to fight off hypothermia by using warm blankets and warm liquids.

Alameda and Schultz had not yet awakened. Pacino had bundled them tightly together, keeping only one thin blanket for himself and one for Catardi. The women's faces were covered except for their noses and mouths. He could see the vapor plumes of their breathing. He checked them every hour, and their temperatures seemed normal. They were slumbering through a cold winter night.

The issue was whether they would be found and rescued. There were no procedures for this, according to the captain. The DSV was a temporary addition to the spec-op compartment, which had been hastily reconfigured for it in a shipyard availability, and it had been scheduled to be removed, a new mission and a configuration change awaiting the ship in the next drydock availability. The fact that they could not use the sub-sunk buoy would doom them, and the pitiful pounding of the emergency percussion device—the automatic hull-hammerer—was not enough to attract serious attention unless someone hovered directly over them, and even then, with the strong layer depth overhead, the sounds from it might just bounce back deep. So they were all trapped in an HY-100 steel tomb, surrounded by eighty-three dead crewmembers.

"Patch."

"Yes, Captain?"

"What happened to Keating?"

"He was smashed up inside the escape trunk. I was in the water hanging from the operating wheel of the hatch, so I should have had it worse, with explosions in water being deadly. But I guess the chief was tossed into the bulkhead."

Catardi stared at him. "Wait a minute. You were *outside* the ship?"

"Yes, sir. I heard the incoming sonars. I saw the torpedo hit the engine room. It blew my mask off and the regulator out of my mouth."

"So how did you—what did you—*you came back in?* What the hell did you do that for?"

"I don't know, Skipper. It just seemed like the right thing to do."

"Oh, God, your dad is going to kill me. Why the hell didn't you go topside? You realize what a boneheaded move that was?"

"I know, sir. I should have lit off the emergency beacon."

"Hell with that. You should have saved your skin. Dammit, now I feel worse—at least you could have lived. Now you're going down with us."

"You don't think there will be a rescue?"

"I don't think so, Patch," Catardi said gently. "We're in the middle of nowhere. All the other submerged units were either in the Indian Ocean or the East China Sea or on the way there. We're off the great circle route to the IO from the U.S. East Coast. We can hope for merchant shipping traffic to hear the hammering device, but odds are, even if someone were to hear it, they wouldn't know what it was."

Pacino nodded. "How long till the atmosphere runs out?"

"We've probably got five days, if the cold doesn't get us

first. I'm sorry, Patch. It's a bad death, but can you think of a good one?"

"Well, at least we're dying with our boots on."

"Hell, we didn't even get a counterfire in the water. We're dying after getting bushwhacked by that damned robot sub. Hell of a useless way to go."

There was nothing else to say, so Pacino just stared at the deck until he felt too sleepy to keep his eyes open.

"Admiral, flash traffic for you, coded personal for commanding admiral," the radioman said as he woke McKee and handed him the pad computer.

McKee clicked into it, the message a transmission from the *Leopard,* which had been setting up to attack Battlegroup One at the Formosa Strait when he and Petri had called it a night and retired early. McKee expected an after-action situation report. McKee's orders to *Leopard* gave her captain, Commander Dixon, wide latitude to either watch and report on the Chinese battlegroup and wait for reinforcing submarines, or fire on the task force and take out as many high-value units as his weapons load and tactics would allow. Knowing Dixon, the Southerner would consider it a matter of honor to launch the entire torpedo room at the surface force.

But the message was not the expected preformatted after-action report. McKee's face dropped into lines of sadness as he read the body of the E-mail:

```
242058ZJUN2019
FLASH   FLASH   FLASH   FLASH   FLASH
PERSONAL FOR COMMANDING ADMIRAL //
PERSONAL FOR COMMANDING ADMIRAL
FM        USS LEOPARD SSN 780
TO        COMUSUBCOM
SUBJ      SUB SUNK
TOP SECRET BLACK WIDOW
```

AUTHENTICATOR TWO SIX NINE ECHO MIKE
FOUR
AUTHENTICATE ONE FIVE FOUR NOVEMBER
DELTA FOXTROT QUEBEC TANGO
//BT//

1. (TS) JULANG SSN DETECTED, RANGE TWENTY
   THOUSAND (20,000) YARDS ON A 254
   HERTZ DOUBLET, BROADBAND AND
   ACOUSTIC DAYLIGHT. JULANG-CLASS EN-
   GAGED WITH VORTEX AND LEOPARD
   CLEARED DATUM, BELIEVE JULANG SSN DE-
   STROYED.
2. (TS) PRIOR TO JULANG SINKING, JULANG
   COUNTERFIRED A SUPERCAVITATING UNDER-
   WATER MISSILE. LEOPARD EVADED BUT HIT
   AND DAMAGED.
3. (TS) LEOPARD ON SURFACE WITH CATA-
   STROPHIC FLOODING AND SEVERE CREW
   CASUALTIES INCLUDING COMMANDING OF-
   FICER. SHIP IS SINKING AND SELF-DESTRUCT
   CHARGES BEING ARMED. CREW IS ABAN-
   DONING SHIP THIS APPROX POSITION.
4. (TS) LATITUDE 24 DEG 23 MIN 56 SEC NORTH
   LONGITUDE 121 DEG 32 MIN 04 SEC EAST,
   ERROR CIRCLE TWO ZERO NM.
5. (TS) EXECUTIVE OFFICER LCDR. D. PHILLIPS
   SENDS.
//BT//

McKee handed the pad computer to Petri. "Goddamned communications work-around," the admiral muttered. "This supposed flash message is two damned hours old."

Petri read the message, her expression falling. When she was done, McKee pushed the machine over to Judison, and while he read it McKee glared at his chief of staff. "Captain Petri, go to the stateroom and work on a recommendation to vector in the nearest submerged units for a rescue, and draft a forwarding message to Admiral Ericcson with this. I want aircraft overhead that position to see to the status of the survivors, and make sure we keep any Red surface units away from them. I want them out of the water in twenty hours. As a lower priority, draft a sitrep for Admiral Patton."

"Yes, sir," Petri said, hurrying back to the stateroom. McKee's face took on the harsh lines of fury.

"Conn, Sonar, loud broadband transient detected, bearing north," the overhead speaker crackled.

"Sonar, Conn, aye," Lieutenant Commander Ash Oswald said in a deadpan voice to the bombshell the sonar supervisor just dropped. Oswald was the navigator and Section I officer of the deck of the USS *Hammerhead,* standing the watch during an uneventful afternoon spent in a flank-speed transit to the intercept point on the anticipated track of the *Snarc.* Oswald glanced at the junior officer of the deck, Lieutenant Junior Grade Melissa White—a talented nonqual airbreather who worked for the chief engineer and was a month from earning her gold dolphins—then glanced at the sonar screen on the command console, selecting the waterfall display. There at the bearing marked 000 was a blooming light trace on the dark background. "So how long will that goddamned hillbilly sonar supe take to share some information with us?" Oswald said sarcastically to White. "Sonar, Conn, sonar supervisor to control."

"Yessir," a voice immediately said behind him. The sonar chief had been standing there all along. Sonarman Chief Petty Officer Stokes, a strapping and aggressive young technician from western Kentucky, stood leaning with his massive forearm on the stainless-steel rails that surrounded the conn.

"Dammit, Chief," Oswald snarled, "don't do that to me. And get your paws off my conn handrails or you'll be polishing them on the midwatch."

"You done ranting, sir?" Stokes asked, his face pleasant.

"Yeah."

"Good. The transient sounded like an entire arsenal exploding. We've also got bulkheads collapsing. Someone sank. I'm analyzing the tape now to see if we can pick anything up just prior to the detonation."

"Prior to it? Like what?"

"Torpedo sonars, depth charges splashing, that kind of thing."

"You're talking like it was a sub that went down."

"Could have been a skimmer, sir. But with the *Snarc* to the north of us coming south, and the *Piranha* doing a squeeze play from further north of the *Snarc,* doesn't it just seem logical that when we hear a booming noise from the north, we correlate it to fisticuffs between those two?"

"Fisticuffs? You mean they exchanged weapons and the *Snarc* is on the bottom. Regrettable that *Piranha* got to that robotic piece of dung first, but at least now we can run to the south and get to the IO, where the action is."

"Unless it was *Snarc* that did the shooting," White interrupted.

Oswald stood on the conn with his mouth open for several seconds. It had never occurred to him that the robot sub could have beaten a Seawolf-class. Especially the *Piranha,* which had given the *Hammerhead* a bitch of a battle in an exercise six months ago. The Seawolfs had an overall acoustic advantage against the Virginia-class unless the Seawolf sped at flank speed by an idling Virginia; at slower speeds the Seawolf would detect a Virginia four thousand yards before the Virginia knew they were being targeted. Which meant that if a Seawolf-class had just been beaten by the *Snarc,* the *Snarc* had a large acoustic advantage over a Virginia-class like the *Hammerhead.* Especially if the Virginia-class were going fast. Like they were now. At flank speed.

"Diving Officer! All stop!" Oswald yelled. The order was as good as a 1MC announcement of "Captain to control," since the minute the deck stopped shaking, the commanding officer would bulldoze his way to control to find out why. "Maneuvering, Conn," Oswald shouted into a 7MC mike, "downshift reactor recirc pumps and rig for natural circulation!"

"All stop, Dive aye, throttles retarding to idle, answering all stop, sir."

"Conn, Maneuvering," the 7MC box blared, "downshift main coolant pumps and rig for nat circ, Conn, Maneuvering, aye. Conn, Maneuvering, main coolant pumps off. Reactor is in natural circulation."

"Maneuvering, Conn, aye," Oswald said. He turned from the 7MC panel to see Captain Judison, Admiral McKee, and Chief of Staff Petri all standing there, looking at him expectantly.

"Captain's in control," Oswald announced to the control room. He leaned toward the senior officers. "There's a problem, Captain, Admiral, ma'am," Oswald said. "Tell us all again, Chief Stokes."

The three listened. Judison pulled the admiral and his staffer aside, the three of them talking in their huddle for some time. Finally the admiral and his chief of staff left, and Judison approached the conn.

"Approach the transient site cautiously at standard speed, turns for fifteen knots, at six five eight feet depth. I want you to perform a baffle-clear counterdetection maneuver at random times at intervals not to exceed forty minutes and a depth excursion to one five zero feet, also at random times, at intervals no more than fifty minutes. Until we know otherwise, assume this is a trap, that the *Snarc* is orbiting at the sinking site waiting for us. You'll be coming to periscope depth in about fifteen minutes after the admiral drafts a situation report. Now repeat all that back."

Oswald repeated back his orders while Captain Judison glared at him. When the captain was satisfied, he left the control room.

"Helm, all ahead standard, make turns for fifteen knots, steer course north," Oswald ordered.

Hammerhead crept northward, her sonar suite straining to detect the *Snarc*.

* * *

"Conn, Sonar, transients close aboard, high negative D/E."

Lieutenant Commander Ash Oswald scratched his belly, a nervous habit.

"Sonar, Conn, aye, negative deflection/elevation, aye. Sonar supervisor to control."

"Yessir," a voice said from behind him.

"Goddammit, Stokes! Cut that out!"

Stokes looked up at the conn, his expression serious. "I don't know what the sound is. It's almost like someone hammering on a hull." He stepped up to the conn and flipped through the screens of the sonar display, dancing with the software for a moment, then stood up. Piped into the overhead speakers a rhythmic echoing thumping sounded. Oswald stared at the display, listening to the haunted sound, a sweat breaking out on his scalp.

"Low D/E, you said," Oswald muttered.

"Right below us," Stokes said.

"Dive, all stop."

Oswald kept staring at the sonar display as he pulled the phone out of its cradle by feel, his finger stabbing the buzzer circuit.

"Captain, Officer of the Deck, sir. Request you come to the conn."

Hammerhead's BRA-44 BIGMOUTH antenna protruded from the blue waves like a telephone pole in the middle of the sea. Instead of the unit interfacing with the battle network through the CommStar satellite, or to the Internet orbital server network, the antenna transmitted a time-varying frequency to the commercial InterTel cell phone satellite. The antenna was connected on the upper level of the operations compartment to a remote unit wired into the VIP stateroom, receiving the transmission from the satellite phone belonging to Admiral Kelly McKee.

It took several minutes for the conference call to go through to the Office of Naval Research, the Directorate of Deep Sea

Submergence, and the Naval Underwater Science Center, and
to McKee's and Patton's staff members. When the officers
were all present, and the tape recording was uploaded to their
connections, McKee ordered them to get him an answer in
twenty minutes to the question: what the hell is the hammering
sound? The ship remained at periscope depth, waiting for the
return call, and when it came, Rear Admiral Huber, Director of
Deep Sea Submergence, spoke on the other end.

"It's our unit, Admiral," he said. "An emergency percussion
beacon installed in the Mark XVII Deep Submergence Vehicle, such as the one in the special operations compartment of
the *Piranha.*"

"We need a rescue plan."

"Admiral, we don't have a deep submergence rescue vehicle
capable of rescuing them. They're trapped inside an HY-100
steel hull, and even if we could cut through it, we don't have a
hatch to mate to on the Mark XVII, and we don't have the
ability to execute a heavy lift to pull the DSV out. But we have
a source with the capability, and they have a unit close by, two
days' transit from your position, three at most."

"What source? A civilian salvage operation?"

"Um, no, sir. The Royal Navy."

"Go ahead, Admiral Huber."

"We've got to do this in two phases. Phase one is to locate
the wreck precisely and communicate with the hull. There may
be no survivors down there at all. Our DSV *Narragansett* is
being scrambled there now on a transport plane. She'll be at
the wreck site in a few hours. We've lined up a commercial
vessel to take her there and support her initial dive. We should
know by sunset the status of the *Piranha.* Assuming the news
is good, we'll need to ask the British team at the sinking site
of the *City of Cairo* to retask and come to the *Piranha*
gravesite. The *City of Cairo* was their ship, and they wanted to
salvage it using the *Explorer II* and the deep diving submersible, the *Berkshire,* which was built in case of a British
submarine wreck. The submersible can cut through thick steel
with a pressurized torch and a diamond-particle injection. It

has heavy-lift capability to remove heavy objects from a debris field. It has a separate diving chamber with a variable-adaptable docking collar in case they need to rescue submariners from a hull where there is no escape trunk."

"Why would they do a merchant salvage mission with a Royal Navy sub rescue craft?"

"It's practice for a sub rescue mission."

"So this *City of Cairo* salvage is purely a practice drill?"

"Not quite, Admiral. The *City of Cairo* was a small British ocean liner, eight thousand tons, four hundred fifty feet long, a two-piper, at sea in 1942 going from Bombay to England with three hundred souls on board, half of them crew and half passengers. She was torpedoed by a Nazi U-boat, U-68."

"But why would the Brits want to salvage an old rustbucket tramp steamer cut in half by Nazi torpedoes?" McKee asked.

"Because before it sank it was loaded with three million ounces of silver in two thousand boxes of silver coin."

"Ah." The admiral nodded. "Okay. So how do I get the *Explorer II* here?"

"You'll have to call the mission commander, Peter Collingsworth, personally, Admiral. He'll be giving up a silver hunt on your say-so with no details, with his own government lining up against ours."

Ten minutes later, the stateroom door opened just as McKee was redialing the Pentagon.

"Sir, we may have a detect on the *Snarc,* east of here at periscope depth," Karen Petri said, her expression finishing her sentence—*hang up the phone so we can go deep and pursue.* But McKee needed to get to the *Explorer II* and get her on the way to the sinking site.

"Get Judison in here," he snapped to Petri, still looking at the phone so he could dial.

Judison ran into the room a moment later, while the Pentagon operator attempted to complete a UHF connection to the HMS *Explorer II.*

"Sir, we've got a narrowband detect at two-fifty-four hertz, bearing two nine five. We've got to give chase." The large captain was winded from his dash up the ladder from the middle level.

"Send out a UUV or several to the bearing," McKee ordered. "And launch a Mark 8 Sharkeye downrange, but keep this ship at periscope depth, right here."

Judison nodded and vanished. He would be launching unmanned underwater vehicles toward the bearing of the *Snarc* detect, and some Mark 8s, a torpedo body with an acoustic daylight sonar reception pod, which would drive away from the ship to a planned point in the sea and shut down. The Sharkeye sonar sensors would deploy in the sea both above the layer and below, extending the ship's onboard sensors by hundreds of miles. The UUVs, Unmanned Underwater Vehicles, unlike the stationary deployed Sharkeyes, would drive silently in the sea, mobile listening platforms. With two UUVs and two Sharkeyes, the ship could both remain here at PD and scan the sea for hundreds of thousands of yards to the northeast, to the bearing of the *Snarc*.

"Hello?" Admiral McKee barked into the phone.

Commander Peter Collingsworth, Royal Navy, looked out of the commander's porthole of the submersible *Berkshire* at the hold bulkhead of the steamship *City of Cairo*. He wore welder's goggles as he watched the arm arc downward with the torch, melting through the rusting steel of the ship's hold. As he sliced the lower horizontal section of the hold cut, the intercom beeped.

"Commander Collingsworth?" It was the voice of the *Explorer II*'s captain.

"Collingsworth, here, over," he said in annoyance, trying to concentrate on the cut.

"Commander, I've got a rather unusual item to report to you. We've just received a satellite phone call. From the Americans, of all people."

Collingsworth kept cutting, finally saying, "Hard to believe the Americans are calling us."

"The transmission is apparently coming from the Atlantic,

sir, from the American submarine *Hammerhead,* a Virginia-class. The phone call is from an admiral named McKee, the commander of the U.S. Submarine Force."

"Go ahead, Knowles." The cut was a fourth of the way through the horizontal marked line. In a few minutes Collingsworth could stop the cutting torch and prepare to lift out the plate and expose the silver.

"He wants to talk to you, Commander."

"Well received, Knowles, but what is going on? Have we any guidance from London on this matter?"

"Captain Baines is on holiday until day after tomorrow, sir."

Collingsworth decided to talk to the Yank and see what the bastard wanted. "Hold on, Knowles. Stand by to patch him in. I have the plate, Jenson. Disconnect the temp derrick. Damn, there's too much dust. I can't see anything but sediment, and we don't have the battery amp-hours to wait for it to settle. We'll have to come back."

"You want to make a quick grab and see if you can get a silver box?"

"No, we could break the box and have coins all over hell. Tomorrow's another day. We'll be right back, and with *Explorer II* hovering topside, no one's going to be down here to grab our take. Knowles, I'm commencing ascent now. Patch in the admiral."

"Here he is in three, two, one. Admiral McKee, can you hear me?"

"I can hear you. Commander Collingsworth, do I have the pleasure of speaking to you directly now, sir? This is Admiral Kyle McKee, but you can call me Kelly. It's good to meet you over the radio, Commander. How is your salvage going? Over."

Collingsworth made a face of irritation. "Admiral, this is Commander Peter Collingsworth. You may call me Commander. What is the nature of your request, sir? Please state your business, over."

"Of course, Commander. I can tell you're a busy man. Fact

is, we have a little emergency out here a bit north of you and we need your help. And we need it immediately, over."

"I receive you, Admiral, but please state the nature of your emergency."

"Commander," the voice said on the radio, "we have it on good authority that you have a deep diving submersible and an autonomous diving bell on the *Explorer II.* I'm afraid we're going to need them both at north latitude twelve degrees and longitude twenty-three west, a bit over nineteen hundred miles from your salvage site. If you get going now, you can be here in two days. We'll have a U.S. contingent to meet with you here, over."

"Admiral, I still don't know what you are talking about. I shall ask you again—please state the nature of your emergency, over."

"Commander, that rig you're in right now was built to rescue survivors of a sunken submarine, is that fair to say?"

"Yes, Admiral, that's the fundamental duty of the *Explorer II,* but unless there's a sub to salvage we use the system for other purposes."

"So, can I tell my superiors you're on your way?"

Collingsworth's face grew beet-red in the dim interior light of the submersible. "Admiral, you still haven't stated your emergency. I'm going to have to terminate this conversation, sir, over."

"Commander, I think I just did state my emergency."

Collingsworth hesitated. "Sir, am I to understand that you have a sunken submarine emergency?"

"Peter, let me put it to you this way. If you were at the coordinates I just described, at a depth of eleven thousand feet, you'd see a large metal object and a scattered debris field and you'd hear hammering from inside the object. Do you get what I'm saying?"

Collingsworth rubbed his beard. Good God, he thought, the Yanks had lost a sub in the Atlantic and were asking him to come to the rescue, with survivors waiting for him. There was no time to waste. He glanced at his panel and called to Jenson.

"Jenson, rig for an emergency ascent. Taking her up to ten

feet per second rise. We should be on the surface in eighteen minutes. Knowles, this is Collingsworth on freq two, over."

"Go ahead, Commander, we're alone on frequency two."

"Knowles, immediate execute, prepare to depart station at maximum speed. Start all turbines and be ready to answer all bells in twenty minutes. Station the underway watch section and plot a course for north latitude twelve, west longitude twenty-three at full ahead speed. And get the Admiralty officer of the day on the tactical freq immediately. I'm making an emergency ascent, and I'll be on the deck and brief you further then. Do you copy?"

"Yes, sir, prepare to get underway, understood."

"Admiral McKee, this is Collingsworth. I hope you understand we can't just go running off to help you with your crisis without orders from the Admiralty. From what I read in the newsfiles, the Prime Minister is not entirely happy with you chaps about now. In fact, I could find myself in a spot of bother simply for talking to you this wonderful afternoon."

"Commander Collingsworth, the President is prepared to speak directly to the Prime Minister about this."

"Admiral, I'll talk to my superiors, but I can offer you no guarantees."

"Pete, can you at least get the *Explorer II* on her way? You can always turn her around if your bosses say different." There was a pleading tone in the admiral's voice.

Collingsworth nodded. "Yes, Admiral, I can get on the way. You understand, of course, that the Admiralty could turn me back around at any time. We'll contact you in an hour, Admiral. Collingsworth out."

Collingsworth sat back against the submersible bulkhead and shook his head. Good Lord, he thought. One minute all he could think about was cases of silver on the bottom, and now there might be sunken survivors who could die if he hesitated even one minute. Hold on, Yanks, he thought.

"Commander, the Admiralty officer of the day is waiting for you."

"Patch him in."

20

At five a.m., Admiral Chu Hua-Feng's limo came to a halt in front of Beijing's Hall of the People. He swallowed hard and got out of the car, the walk to the Party Secretary's conference room seeming to take forever.

Inside the ornate room the members of the Politburo waited for him. He sat at the end of the table between General Fang Shui, the supreme commander of the PLA, and Admiral Dong Niet, the admiral-in-command of the PLA Navy.

"Sit," Fang said. "Leaders, you all know Admiral Chu Hua-Feng, commanding admiral of the submarine force."

"Are you gentlemen comfortable?" Premier Baolin Nanhok asked in a saccharine voice.

"Yes, sir," the general answered for them.

"Good. Perhaps you would like to watch a movie with us. A very entertaining one."

The lights went out and a digital movie played on the display screen. Admiral Chu watched in dismay as the ships on the horizon exploded one by one into incandescent brightness, the white fireballs turning orange and rising in mushroom shapes to the sky, until the seascape looked like a forest of mushroom clouds. When the movie ended, he found himself blinking back hot tears of fury and sadness at the incredible loss of life, his comrades, thousands of them, all dead.

"Who did this?" asked the Minister of Defense, Leader Di

Xhiou, his voice quiet and friendly. When there was no answer, he flew out of his chair and screeched, *"Who did this?"*

Chu cleared his throat when it became apparent that Admiral Dong would remain silent. "Leader Di, it is fair to assume
that the American carrier surface action group caused this
slaughter, or perhaps their submarines, or both."

"Submarines that your forces were supposed to protect the
battlegroup from, Admiral Chu? A carrier surface action group
that your submarines were supposed to sink?"

Chu considered defending his actions, but decided to get
this meeting over with and get on with his prison sentence, or
his firing squad.

"Correct, sir, on both counts."

"So, I can assume that you agree with us that you failed?"

"Yes, sir, you are correct." Chu looked down at the table.
"On behalf of the submarine force, I respectfully apologize
and take complete responsibility for our failure."

There was silence for a moment, and then Leader Di spoke.

"Well then, gentlemen, perhaps there is hope for the PLA
after all." Chu looked up at Defense Minister Di. "We have
one truthful man in the military, one man with character, one
lone man with accountability, sitting before us. Vice Admiral
Chu, you may remember this day as the worst of your career,
the day our battlegroup sank under the fire of an unseen
enemy, but you will also remember it as the day you took
command of the remainder of the PLA Navy. You are now a
fleet admiral. Dong, perhaps you should hand him your stars."
Two Red Guards entered the room, on either side of Admiral
Dong. Dong stood and pulled off his epaulette insignia and
slid the stars over to Chu. Minister Di did not acknowledge
him as he was led from the room. Dong looked back at Chu
one last time with sad, dark eyes, eyes that would be shut forever within the hour.

Chu swallowed. "Yes, sir. Thank you, sir."

"Now, to business, Fleet Admiral Chu. It would appear our
offensive is in trouble. You are now in command, but obviously of a reduced force. What will you do with it?"

"I will deploy it in an antisubmarine-warfare formation with a random zigzag and maneuver it to the Indian Ocean. I will send my submarines ahead to look for the attackers."

Di nodded. "Very well. Good luck to you and your fleet. But I warn you now, Admiral, do not lose a second battle-group, or else this war will be over before it has begun."

"Yes, sir," Chu said. "Would it be permissible for me to detach my submarines and attempt a mission of revenge against the attackers? With the duties of escorting the battlegroup removed, my submarines would be free to conduct forward-deployed operations, and they could experience a measure of vengeance."

Minister Di stared at him with dead, unsympathetic eyes. "You have a week. Do not embarrass us. Inform your commanders that capture by American forces is prohibited, and any ship in such a situation shall self-destruct and all crewmen will be killed, and the captain shall shoot himself in the head."

"Yes, sir," Chu said. "If I am able, may I conduct a covert submarine mission against American targets?"

"What are you talking about, Chu?"

Chu gave a ten-minute briefing on the capture of the U.S. submarine *Snarc*. "She never made it into the Indian Ocean as we had planned, since it took more time than expected to bring her under our control. But I can turn her around toward the East Coast of the United States. The fleet headquarters facilities are there in Norfolk, Virginia, as are the fleet bases. I can have my unit wait in their shallow waters and ambush the fleet as it returns to port."

The Politburo members asked him to leave the room for a moment. He paced nervously until they called him back.

"Does this robotic submarine have cruise missiles?"

"Yes, Minister Di."

"Can it attack American government targets? The White House, the Capitol building, the damned-for-eternity Pentagon?"

"Why, yes, sir."

"Then do so, Fleet Admiral Chu. You are dismissed. Report your progress."

"By your leave, sir." Di nodded, and Chu rose, bowed to the group, and hurried from the room.

In his staff car, Chu glared at his young chief of staff. "Get Sergio on the phone. I have a new mission for his robot sub, assuming he knows where it is."

"One, bring the ship to mast broach depth," Krivak commanded. Unit One Oh Seven no longer responded verbally, but it did follow orders. He did not know if it would obey orders to release weapons against another American unit, though. If the machine had gone this catatonic over shooting the *Piranha,* imagine how it would be if he told it to take on an American battlegroup.

At periscope depth, on course south, Krivak pulled off the interface helmet, and waited the ten minutes it would take him to adjust to physical reality. When his head stopped spinning he gently sat up and slowly stood, nausea churning in his stomach.

"Wang, set up the radio we brought on the BRA-44 antenna. Once it is tuned to the frequency, I want you to give me a few minutes of privacy."

It took some time to get the satellite secure voice circuit synchronized with Beijing, but when he finally raised PLA General Staff Headquarters, Admiral Chu Hua-Feng came up on the circuit. Krivak spent a moment trading the personal codes they had to identify each other and avoid an enemy deception maneuver. Once that was done, Krivak reported what had happened and apologized for the delay in getting to the Indian Ocean.

"It is too late for your apology," Chu said. "But there is something you can do for me and the Peoples Republic. I want the Americans to experience a national emotional pain far worse than the terrorist attack on New York years ago. I do not have the power to inflict serious damage, but I would like this generation of Americans to remember our struggle. Are you in cruise missile range of any American targets?"

"I'll find out, sir, but based on what I know, I'm a week's transit away from anything worthwhile. The missiles have about a three-thousand-mile range."

"How many do you have?"

"Twelve, Admiral."

"Are they plasma-tipped? Any chance of converting them to fusion bombs?"

"No chance, sir. They're in a ballast tank and we don't have the ability to pull them out at sea. We could pull into a high-bay facility and work on the missiles—"

"No. Plasma warheads will have to do, and I want the missiles in the air soon. I want to use my limited firepower to inflict the most pain."

"What do you want me to attack?"

"I want you to destroy some American symbols so that the Americans will ache for their country the way I ache for my own. I want you to target the White House. The Capitol building. The Pentagon. The Statue of Liberty. The Empire State Building. Independence Hall. The Sears Tower. I want you to extract vengeance from the American Navy—target their Unified Fleet Headquarters in Norfolk, and their Unified Submarine Command HQ across the quadrangle. I want you to hit the submarine bases in Groton, Connecticut, and the submarine piers at Norfolk Naval Station. And the tomb of their John Paul Jones in the chapel at their naval school in Annapolis, Maryland. Twelve targets, twelve missiles. You must strike with all twelve missiles at once, so that none of the U.S. Air Force coastal defenses are alerted early."

"Leave it to me, Admiral. Once I have fired the missiles, I will need to abandon ship. I can put it on a default course for the Bo Hai Bay, but I fully expect that my firing position will be found and that the U.S. Navy will fill the water surrounding that position with ordnance. There will be nothing left there."

"Good luck, Krivak."

Chu broke the circuit. Krivak disconnected the radio and

went down the ladder to tell Wang he was done, then climbed back into the interface couch.

"One, plot our position on a global chart, then form a circle that shows the range of the Javelin cruise missiles." Krivak studied the chart. "Plot the great circle route that brings Washington, D.C., New York, Philadelphia, Chicago, Groton, Connecticut, and Norfolk, Virginia, inside the circle." The track flashed up on the display. "Now calculate, using speed thirty knots, the time of arrival at the range circle."

The time flashed where the track intersected the range circles—showing Monday afternoon local time. With a missile flight time of two hours, he could have target impact before the close of business. Perfect—just in time for the evening news.

Krivak disconnected from the interface and plugged his satellite phone into the antenna. The number for Pedro was set to the speed dial. As he waited, the deck rocked gently in the swells at periscope depth.

"Yes," Amorn's voice crackled.

"Amorn, it's me."

"Excuse me, sir?"

"Amorn, it's me. Krivak. On the *Snarc,* dammit."

"Yes, sir, I can hear you now."

"Listen to me. Get a motor yacht, a fast one, and get it to the Atlantic coordinates I'm about to read to you."

Amorn copied the latitude and longitude of the firing point.

"When can you get there?"

"The Falcon is ready now. We can get a yacht out of Bermuda and be there by Sunday night."

"Get to the coordinates no later than two a.m. Monday morning. If you get there early, just wait for me. I'll get one last piece of business done, and then I'll be leaving the ship."

"We will stand by there."

"I will see you then, my friend. Good-bye."

Krivak clicked off the connection and took the ship's ladder up to the interface bay and climbed back in the couch. When he was reconnected to the ship, he ordered One Oh Seven to descend from mast broach depth and continue their transit deep. The deck inclined downward as the ship plunged deep and sped up to thirty-five knots.

Captain Lien Hua and First Officer Zhou Ping rushed aft to find the chief engineer, Leader Dou Ling, standing on a rubber mat wearing rubber boots and rubber gloves in front of the open electric plant high-voltage main distribution panel. A rope was tied around his waist as if he were a prisoner, the rope held by two enginemen standing well away from the panel.

"Can you repair it?" Captain Lien asked.

Dou sounded peeved when he answered, spitting his spent cigarette to the deck. "Captain, either I'll fix it or I'll take four hundred and eighty volts right up my ass, and you can eject my burned-to-a-crisp corpse out the torpedo tube. Now, Captain, Mr. First, if you two don't mind, can I finish this lecture and reach into the panel now?"

"Go ahead, Leader Dou."

The chief engineer reached into the panel as carefully as if trying to steal jewels from under a laser burglar alarm. With a rubber-handled wrench he painstakingly unscrewed a copper bolt from an arcing copper bus bar, and pulled the scorched bars out of the cabinet one by one. Over the next two hours he worked. When he withdrew from the panel his coveralls were soaked.

"How is it?" Zhou Ping asked.

"It's fucking bad, Zhou," Dou roared. "If it weren't, would I be risking my damned neck in an energized panel? Now, by your whore of a mother, will you leave me the hell alone?"

Zhou's face flushed with anger, but there was nothing he could do. Either Dou fixed the electrical panel and the other fifty things that had exploded into flames when the American torpedo had hit, or they would remain dead in the water, easy prey for an American torpedo from another of their lurking submarines, or even from an over-the-horizon cruise missile.

"I'm going forward," Zhou announced, the chief engineer

snorting. The captain should have reprimanded the engineer, the spoiled technician, but he placed as much trust in the bastard as he did Zhou.

Zhou found his way to the stuffy command post, its battery casualty lights making the space irregularly and dimly lit. They couldn't even submerge to hide from the American satellites until Dou completed his work in the engineering spaces. A feeling of impending doom filled Zhou, and for a moment he contemplated writing his mother a farewell letter, but then realized that if he did, it would either end up on the bottom or burned to cinders by the next weapon impact.

The submersible *Narragansett* approached the third location, which the topside sidescan sonar had indicated was promising. The first contact had turned out to be a rock ridge and the second an uncharted sunken steamship, rusted and forlornly listing to port, her three stacks reaching for the surface at a depth of 2,479 feet. The steamer had a hole in the hull, probably from a German U-boat. The bottom of the shipping lanes on either side of the Cape of Good Hope was a ship graveyard, the storms and fortunes of war taking their toll on the ships of every generation since man had first gone to sea.

Lieutenant Evan Thompson pulled up on his thruster levers as the third object grew closer in the haze. The approaching object lay on its side against a rock outcropping. It was the sail of a submarine, but amputated from the main hull. A debris field surrounded the sail. Thompson radioed up the find, the video feed from his cameras traveling up the tether to the salvage ship *Emerald* on the calm seas on the surface. He followed the trail of debris, the seafloor changing from rock to sediment, until he arrived at a sloping section of sand. In the bright light of the submersible, the sandy slope looked different from the surroundings. The sand there had waves in it at regular one-meter intervals. The sand on this ridge looked smooth, bulging at one end. He was getting an annunciator flashing alarm on his console. It was from the audible sonar system. He flipped a toggle switch and patched the sonar into the overhead speaker. The sound was unmistakable, a hammering on a steel object. The hammering came regularly, one second between hammer blows.

"*Emerald, Narragansett,*" he called.

"Go ahead, over."

"I've got a hammering at one second intervals from a large ridge in the sediment. I'm approaching to see if I can detect a hull."

"Roger. Is the hammering by hand?"

"Negative. It sounds extremely regular. Probably an emergency percussion beacon. Hammering just stopped, over. Mark the time."

"Roger. Zero six forty-three."

Unfortunately the *Narragansett*'s manipulator arms were primitive. But Thompson should be able to attempt to penetrate the sediment ridge and see if he struck metal.

He approached cautiously and speared the manipulator arm into the muck. The arm stopped. He could not tell if the resistance were from hitting a glancing blow and the viscous sediment stopped the arm or if he had hit metal. He tried again, more at a right angle to the surface of the sediment. There was no doubt—he had just hit something solid. There was no belltone ring from the steel, since the sediment would just muffle the sound of the arm striking the object. He retracted the arm to drive the DSV around the lump in the seafloor and map it out.

"*Emerald, Narragansett.* We have a manmade hull down here," Thompson said emotionlessly, knowing his radio and video call would be repeated for the brass. "I've detected several more hammer blows. I'm going to attempt to rig up an acoustic detector on the surface and locate the hammering more accurately."

Over the next hour Thompson worked to place hydrophones on the surface of the sloping ridge. The hydrophones listened to the hammering and triangulated it to a single location. The *Emerald* would soon be sending down an underwater telephone device on a cable. The unit consisted of a transmission hydrophone connected to an amplifier to a cable to the surface ship. The hydrophone would broadcast the voice of someone talking on the connection into the hull. If someone trapped inside shouted, the reception hydrophone would pick it up and amplify it for the listeners on the surface ship. It was crude and often was too indistinct to communicate effectively, but if it worked they could tell the survivors to hold on.

While Thompson waited for the underwater telephone, he brushed off a part of the surface of the metal, exposing the skin, and spot-welded a lug to the metal, then threaded a cable through the lug. It was like trying to thread a needle while wearing metal mesh gloves, but after twenty minutes of trying, he managed to get the cable through the lug. He secured the cable at the hull end and released the float on the other end. The float ascended to the surface, marking the location of the wreck in case heavy weather required them to abandon the sinking site.

For three hours Thompson assembled the underwater telephone. It was not so much assembly as it was reassembly, since he had to remove and replace the hydrophones in an attempt to get a clear signal from inside the vessel. Chances were that it would not work, since too many things could distort sound in such a situation, but his officemate at Woods Hole Oceanographic Institute had engineered a computer software application that would take the blurry transmissions and clean them up so that they could be understood. When the underwater telephone work was done, it was time for the *Narragansett* to try to communicate with the wreckage. Thompson clicked the microphone and said slowly and distinctly, "Is this the submarine *Piranha*?"

His stomach churned as he waited for a response.

Captain Rob Catardi sat up in the dark, only the glow of an instrument panel for light.

"Captain," Pacino's voice said in his face. "There was a knock on the hull."

Catardi's heart thumped in his chest. "Energize the percussion device full-time," he ordered.

A booming voice suddenly sounded throughout the DSV, coming from outside the hull. They could tell it was a voice but couldn't make out the words. Catardi and Pacino began screaming at the overhead. The voice came again, but then went silent. There were more scraping noises, until a half hour later the voice came through the hull again.

"Is . . . this . . . the . . . submarine . . . *Piranha*?" the voice asked.

Catardi held up a finger. "Let me speak," he said quietly to Pacino. He looked up at the overhead and shouted, annunciating clearly while projecting his voice, "This is Captain Rob Catardi of the submarine USS *Piranha*. Do you read me?"

There was a pause, then: "Roger . . . we . . . read . . . you."

"Are you rescuing us?" Catardi asked.

"Not yet," the blaring male voice said. "We are the Navy DSV *Narragansett*, here to locate your position. The rescue will be done by a British deep-submergence rescue vehicle. The Brits will be here in seven zero hours, over."

Seventy hours. Catardi sat down on the deck, dejected. They might not have enough current or oxygen to survive that long.

"*Narrangansett*, you must expedite the rescue. I say again, expedite the rescue. We will not last seven zero hours. We are low on battery amps. Temperature is extremely cold. We are running out of medical supplies and oxygen will be out in two days. You have to make the rescue in forty-eight hours or less, over."

"*Piranha, Narragansett*, understand. We will pass the word along. Are you in the deep-submergence vehicle?"

"Yes. We are in the command module of the DSV in the special operations compartment. I believe the submarine hull has been damaged and breached, but the DSV hull is stable, over."

"Roger, *Piranha*, understand. Request list of survivors and their medical status, over."

It was a short list, Catardi thought, as he reeled off the information.

"We have the list, Captain. We will be patching in a Dyna-Corp expert on the DSV to see if he can talk you through a system lineup to conserve your resources. Please standby, out."

What the hell were they supposed to do? Catardi thought, but he smiled at Pacino.

"We may make it out of here yet." He grinned.

"I hope so, Captain."

"How are Alameda and Schultz?"

"Still out. I'd feel better if they were conscious. If they have brain injuries they may never wake up."

"Let them sleep. If we get them conscious, they'll breathe air faster. We won't make it forty-eight hours. If fact, you and I should try to sleep until the DynaCorp technician comes on the underwater telephone rig."

"I don't think I'll be able to sleep, sir. But I'll try."

21

Commander Kiethan Judison cursed as he scanned the command console's firecontrol display. The *Snarc,* Target One, was over two hundred forty thousand yards distant to the northeast, far outside of weapons range, and her speed was higher than the *Hammerhead*'s, even if the ship was ordered to a reactor-ruining emergency flank. If Admiral McKee had hung up the phone when Judison had asked him to, the *Snarc* would not be so far downrange.

But the worst news was the *Snarc*'s course—northwest. She had no reason to be going northwest. He stormed off the conn, hurried up the stairs to his stateroom, and grabbed a world globe, a ceremonial gift from a Royal Navy submarine commander from the last time the ship had visited Faslane. The sepia-colored globe in one hand, a grease pencil in the other, he barged into the VIP stateroom just as McKee was dialing the phone.

"Please hang up the phone, Admiral," Judison said urgently.

McKee stared up at him and put the phone down.

"We lost the *Snarc*. She's outside of Mark 58 *and* Vortex range."

"So she goes around the Cape of Good Hope. We'll redirect the submarines we had in the Indian Ocean to intercept her as she enters—"

"No, you won't. Here's our position." He stabbed the globe with the grease pencil north of the equator off the African

Senegal coast. "Here's the position of the *Snarc*." He put another dot down, several millimeters from the first dot, the new
one to the northeast. "Here's the *Snarc*'s course—heading two
nine zero. Let me just draw a great circle route on that
course." Judison put a piece of paper on the globe and used it
as a straight edge, drawing a line with the grease pencil. He
handed the globe across the table to McKee.

The admiral grabbed it and saw where the line ended. "Oh,
God. It's heading to the East Coast."

"He's headed toward missile range of the Atlantic seaboard,
and there's nothing we can do to stop him. Every single warship and submarine we own is in the Indian Ocean or the East
China Sea. There's nothing left to protect the coast except
some Coast Guard cutters, and *Snarc* will probably launch
from far at sea anyway."

McKee thought for a moment.

"Not every submarine is at sea," he said. "We have one on
the East Coast."

"What boat is that, sir?" Petri asked.

"The SSNX," McKee said.

"But, Admiral, even if the SSNX can get waterborne, there
are no warshot torpedoes or Vortex missiles in the weapons
depots," Petri said. "They were all loaded on the submarines
or the tender vessels to be taken into the Op Area."

"And there are no commanding officers," Judison said.
"We're so thin on senior officers since last summer's attack
that anyone with a warm body is already submerged. There's
not one man on the East Coast who could command the SSNX
even if there were torpedoes."

"Oh, yes, there is, Kiethan. There's one man you'd want in
a submerged fight. He's just what you might call—overquali-
fied."

Judison stared at McKee with a stupid expression.

"We'll use the SSNX to vector in air support. We can sup-
plement her with P-5 Pegasus ASW aircraft—I know the
frontline units are overseas, but we have at least two in the

hangars under repair. The SSNX and the P-5s can detect the *Snarc* and call in plasma bombs from Air Force bombers."

"Or the SSNX can use the Tigersharks, Admiral," Judison said.

McKee waved him off. "Damned things don't work and turn against the launching ship. I'll order the SSNX loaded with Tigersharks as a last resort for ship safety, but we'll plan to use the SSNX in a joint op with the Air Force. I'll call for some Mark 12 remote acoustic daylight pods to be dropped in the path of the *Snarc* by cargo jets. We'll be able to monitor her progress toward the East Coast. If she deviates from course we'll lose her, but if she is heading in for a missile launch, we'll have her locked in. Now give me some privacy so I can raise Patton on this thing."

Michael Pacino, former admiral and current executive vice president of Cyclops Carbon Systems and project director of Project Mark 98 Tigershark, put the USS *Tampa* ball cap on his head and leashed the black Lab, then took the dog out and began running on the hard flat sand of Sandbridge Beach, Virginia. He started at the house and began jogging south. It was half past four, and when the sun climbed above the Atlantic, he would turn back north and shower before he went into the shipyard. He started slowly, the dog looking up at him and smiling, then increased the pace, the dark forms of the houses on his right marching by as he pounded out the miles.

His eyes were half-shut as he ran, his mind empty, when the dog's barking startled him. Three houses ahead on the wide spread of sand, spotlights suddenly shone in his face. He could hear idling engines, and realized the spotlights were mounted on trucks parked on the sand. Above him he could hear the rotors of a helicopter, its blinking beacons coming closer as it landed on the beach behind the trucks. The dog growled, its back up, as he walked slowly to the trucks. The silhouette of a man in a wide-brimmed hat walked toward him, his face and clothes indistinct in the glare of the floodlights.

"Virginia State Police, sir. Please identify yourself," a deep voice commanded. Pacino tried to see the man's eyes.

"Pacino, Michael Pacino. I live up the road a few miles. What is this?"

"Mr. Pacino, please come with us." The officer took the leash out of his hand, the dog lodging a loud protest, but letting the cop pet him.

"It's okay, Bear. It's okay," Pacino said soothingly.

Two other policemen took Pacino to the waiting state police helicopter, which throttled up and lifted off, the sand flying, the dog barking, the chopper rotating to the north and dipping its nose as it sped up, the houses of Sandbridge flashing by, close at first, then becoming distant.

"What's going on?" Pacino asked.

The copilot turned and glanced at him. "Sir, I have no idea. The watch commander told us to load you up and take you to Newport News shipyard."

The chopper flew over Virginia Beach and eventually over the Elizabeth and James Rivers to the Hampton peninsula. The Newport News helipad came into view. The pilots hit the concrete and cut the engines in the dawn overcast. Pacino climbed out of the helicopter, feeling ridiculous in his sweat-soaked running gear. He clamped his hat on and walked to where two men waited for him in front of a shipyard truck. He asked what was going on, but neither man said a word. He sat in the back until the truck arrived at drydock two's administration building. He climbed out of the truck and began walking to the building, but heard an odd noise. He left his escorts and jogged to the drydock edge and stared in astonishment at the scene below.

The noise had been the diesels of a tugboat pulling the caisson, the massive gate of the drydock, away into the river. The drydock was fully flooded, and the SSNX was waterborne, which was a miracle, since she'd had twenty "closeouts" that needed to be done before she could even become watertight. Even more alarming were the cranes and the activity forward, where the weapons shipping hatch was open, and a Mark 98

Tigershark torpedo slowly vanished into the ship tail first. On the opposite side of the dock, a flatbed with three more torpedoes waited. There had been twenty prototypes of the Tigershark completed to date, and Pacino wondered where the rest of the prototypes were—onboard or back at the Tigershark facility?

The escorts took him by the arm and led him inside, taking him to a locker room on the first floor. Good, he thought. He could change there. He showered and toweled off at his locker, then pulled on the spare set of chinos and a Polo shirt when the door crashed open and a dozen naval officers walked in, Admiral John Patton at the rear of the phalanx. He walked up to Pacino and nodded grimly.

"John," Pacino said, even more surprised by the appearance of the Chief of Naval Operations than by the goings-on in the drydock. "Admiral Patton. What's going on? What's important enough to bring you here?"

Patton shook his head, still not smiling. He turned to his aides and the shipyard escorts, who all vanished outside the door.

"Patch, we have a grave situation," Patton began. "I need you to prepare yourself for some bad news. The *Piranha* went down. Your son was onboard."

Ten minutes later Pacino rubbed his reddening eyes. "So, let me get this straight. You're telling me there is a hope of rescue."

"I have to tell you, Patch, it's a low probability, but yes. If the Brits get there in time, they can get the *Piranha* survivors to the surface."

"In less than a week? I don't think so, John. Give it to me straight. This fucking *Snarc* you people lost control of killed my son. Or it's just a matter of time until he's gone." Pacino stood and smashed his hand into his locker, then gripped his hand, the pain not a fraction of what he was feeling about Anthony Michael. "I should get out there. Can you get me to the *Explorer II?*"

"I can, Patch. But I'm not going to. I have other plans for you."

"John, no offense, but what could possibly be more important than seeing to my boy?"

"Sit down," Patton said, pointing to the bench, and telling the story.

"This is crazy, John. I can't take the SSNX to sea. It's been years since I commanded a submarine, and the last one I commanded I lost in the Labrador Sea. Jesus, John, I'm not even in the Navy anymore."

"With a stroke of the pen I reactivated you to the rank of captain as of zero four hundred this morning. Sorry I couldn't get your stars back for you, not on this short notice."

"I don't give a damn. This plan is ridiculous. Besides, the SSNX already has a crew and a captain."

"Her captain has never taken a ship to sea as commanding officer. He's fresh out of prospective commanding officer school, and he's spent his career in the shipyards. He would have driven the SSNX through sea trials, then transferred her to a combat captain. He's been told he's taking a bump down to XO, and he's fine with it."

"Right," Pacino said, glancing at his watch, thinking of how fast a supersonic fighter could get him to the sinking site of the *Piranha*. "You should just replace him with someone qualified."

"There's no one. No one who's ready, and certainly no one who's fired torpedoes in anger."

"Which reminds me—you *have* no torpedoes," Pacino said. "Just Tigersharks that don't work, which are all being loaded on a sub that barely works—"

"The Tigersharks are a contingency, for ship safety in a desperate situation, but you can't use them on the *Snarc*, it's too dangerous."

"—and you want the SSNX to do a joint operation with Navy P-5s and Air Force cargo planes to drop bombs on the *Snarc*'s location. You know how stupid that sounds? SSNX would be at periscope depth, *Snarc* would be below the ther-

mal layer, SSNX would lose her, *Snarc* gets away, bombs rain
down on the seas in the wrong place, and the *Snarc,* now
alerted, shoots the SSNX. Not to mention that the *Snarc* has an
acoustic advantage over the Virginia-class and the Seawolf-
class, which means she'll have the acoustic advantage over the
SSNX. And add to that the fact that *Snarc* has an unknown
mission. And that no one knows where she is."

"Wrong on both counts, Patch. The *Snarc* is coming with
twelve plasma-tipped cruise missiles. She's headed on a
straight line path toward Washington. Meanwhile, we're completely naked. There is no other submarine on the East Coast.
There are no other warships on the East Coast. We're vulnerable to a cruise missile assault, and all we have are the *Hammerhead* off Africa, chasing *Snarc* in case she slows down,
and the SSNX here. We need to do a squeeze play on the
Snarc, perhaps force her toward the *Hammerhead* with her
waiting Mark 58s. But one thing is sure, Patch. If we don't
catch the *Snarc,* she'll take apart the East Coast."

Pacino stared hard at him, thinking. "*Snarc*'s cruise missiles
are just plasma units. Let her shoot them. Then have the Air
Force and Navy interceptors stand by with an AWACS plane
to see the missiles and chop them down when they get in. It's
no big deal."

Patton shook his head. "That's twelve plasma warheads,
Patch. One of them could bring down the Empire State Building. Or hit the New York Stock Exchange—you want to talk
about a market plunge? Or how do you feel about the White
House taking a Javelin Block IV missile? What would that do
for the nation's morale? And what do you think would happen
politically if we miss four or five missiles? After we lost the
cruise ship last summer to a plasma torpedo, do we really need
another incident like that? The President would have to resign
in disgrace. Patch, we designed these cruise missiles to be invisible—I'm not so sure our own forces can find them ourselves unless we know their launch point and time of liftoff. If
you stood here in my shoes, would you risk it?"

Pacino looked at the floor. "I guess I'd send in the SSNX and the best captain I had."

"Patch, send your wife to see to your son and take this mission. In sixty seconds I'm walking out that door and my aide will hand me a cell phone and I'll be calling the President. When the President hangs up the phone, all the governmental leadership will be evacuating Washington, including me. I need an answer now. Either accept the mission or reject it. If you reject it, I'll send the green skipper to sea and take my chances. But if you take it, the renaming of the SSNX falls on your shoulders. You can name it anything you want. Underway time is in one hour."

Pacino smiled, just slightly. "I get to name the SSNX?"

"Anything you want. Just so you do it quick and get out of here."

"She'll be called the *Devilfish* again, then. Bad luck be damned."

The locker room door opened, one of Patton's aides poking his head in. "Sir, the President is on the phone."

"Can I say you'll go?"

"It's done, John. Just one condition. As soon as it's over, I turn command of *Devilfish* over to her prospective commanding officer and you helo lift me to something fast that can get me to the *Explorer II*. And the minute I turn over command, I'm a civilian again."

"You know, Patch, General MacArthur commanded armies after his chief of staff tour. I could get your stars back—we could use you."

"This is it for me, John. And there's another condition. If my boy comes back from the grave of the *Piranha,* I want him discharged from the naval service. His mother's right—he has no business going to sea."

Patton grinned. "You got it." He snapped his fingers, the aide bringing in the phone and a service dress khaki uniform on a hanger. Pacino's gold dolphins and his ribbons were attached, even a deep draft submarine command pin on the right pocket, the skull and crossbones of it gleaming and new. Patton grabbed Pacino's hand and shook it hard. "Good luck, Patch. Kill the *Snarc* and get out to your son."

Pacino felt like a fool as he put on the uniform. When he looked in the mirror, seeing the four stripes on his shoulders instead of stars seemed somehow comfortable. But when he glanced at his half-century-old face and his white hair, the reflection simply did not belong to a Navy captain. He'd just take care of this one thing, then go back to what he was supposed to be doing. Which made him think of something he should try on the Tigersharks, something he'd never considered. If he could make them work, the battle against *Snarc* could be won.

He walked out of the admin building and over the gangway to the submarine. Obviously Patton had passed the word, because when he walked aboard, the 1MC announcing system called out, "*Devilfish,* arriving!" Pacino tried to deny the feelings that the 1MC call stirred, pride and a feeling of deep belonging, a return to his true home. He was not successful until he reminded himself of Anthony Michael, imprisoned at the bottom of the Atlantic in a cold, stuffy deep submergence vehicle.

Air Force One roared down runway two seven and climbed northwest, Andrews Air Force Base shrinking behind her, the eastern limb of the D.C. beltway passing underneath the airframe as the flaps came into the wings.

President Warner clicked off the video display in her Air Force One office and looked up at Admiral John Patton.

"Can Pacino do this thing, Admiral?"

"I honestly don't know, Madam President. But if he can't, no one else can."

"General Everett," Warner addressed the Air Force chief of staff, a giant of a man with a hooked nose and hair as red as a fire hydrant.

"Ma'am," he responded with a two-pack-a-day voice.

"Are your radar surveillance planes and interceptor jets

ready to shoot down any cruise missiles coming in from the sea?"

"Madam President, as of right now, you couldn't throw a football on the beach without an F-16 hitting you with a Mongoose heat-seeker. We're ready, ma'am."

Patton glanced at the President to see if she knew the general was being overly optimistic.

"What about the support operation for the Navy?"

"We're loading up their—what do you call them, Admiral?"

"Mark 12s, General. Mark 12 PLD-AD-SSA, which stands for Passive Long Distance Acoustic Daylight Sonar Sensor Array. They weigh two tons and drop into the sea with a parachute, and deploy a sonar sensor all the way to five thousand feet depth. Anything coming closer than fifty to seventy miles is detected, and the unit sends out an update on a buoy antenna attached to a cable."

"Right. We're loading up these Mark 12s now, and they'll be plopping into the sea over the next twelve hours."

"Good. Now if you gentlemen will excuse me, I have a call to make to a certain British Prime Minister who's a bit annoyed at me."

"What are we waiting for, XO?" Michael Pacino asked impatiently.

"Propulsion and tugboats, sir," Commander Jeff Vermeers said to Pacino on the bridge of the SSNX, recently christened the *Devilfish*. Vermeers was the prospective commanding officer whom Pacino had replaced as captain. An eager sort, he was a compact, absurdly young-looking officer with blond hair combed straight back over his scalp, narrow blue eyes, and a square jaw. He possessed an energy level that made him seem jumpy, almost flighty, with a forced cheerfulness that immediately got on Pacino's nerves. His hands shook as he raised the binoculars to his eyes and stared down the channel.

"Conn, Maneuvering," the bridge speakerbox rasped. "Propulsion is shifted to the main motor, ready to answer all bells."

"Officer of the Deck," Pacino called down from the flying bridge on top of the sail to the junior-grade lieutenant, a woman named Chris Vickerson. If the former commander of the unit and now XO Vermeers looked young, Vickerson seemed like she should be in kindergarten, her short reddish blond hair tucked into her SSNX ball cap, her freckled complexion and button nose seeming out of place beneath her wire-rimmed submariner's glasses. And she was female. When Pacino had left command in the old days, submarine crews were still all-male. He'd awakened with a defense contractor job and a healthy son, and as the sun set his son was in mortal peril and Pacino was back in the Navy, in command of the submarine with the same name as the one he'd lost under the polar icecap, a sub with a mixed-sex crew of children.

"Yes, Admiral," Vickerson barked, as if responding to a dictator.

"Call me Captain," Pacino said dryly. "Let's go."

"But, sir, the tugboats?"

Pacino looked down on her in the cockpit from his crow's-nest view from the flying bridge. She hadn't gotten the word, he thought. "OOD, two options for you here. Number one, you can conn this ship as if it's rigged for a combat mission instead of treating it like this is sea trials. Number two, you can relinquish the conn and I'll drive her out."

Vickerson swallowed, then said in a shaky voice, "Yes, sir. Aye aye, sir." She glanced at Vermeers as if seeking help, then picked up the bridge box microphone and spoke softly into it, "Helm, Bridge, all ahead one-third."

"Flank," Pacino said, putting the binoculars to his eyes.

"But, sir—"

"One last chance, OOD," he said. Vickerson gulped again.

"Helm, Bridge, all ahead flank, steer course one six zero. Captain, speed limit in the river is fifteen knots."

"Noted, OOD," Pacino said, biting his lip to keep from smiling, his stern war face terrifying to this green young crowd of submariners. The bow wave rose up at the bullet nose of the SSNX, the roar of it immediate. Pacino's gold-leaf

SSNX baseball cap blew off in the hurricane wind of the surface passage. He ignored it and leaned toward Commander Vermeers.

"XO, what's the status of ship systems?"

"Sir, we have forty forward systems danger-tagged out, including the torpedo tube interlocks and firing mechanisms. We completed pierside steaming aft, so the reactor and steam plants are standing tall, but that's it. We're barely watertight, sir. We'll be depth-limited to a hundred and fifty feet—most of the welds in the seawater system weren't even x-rayed. The worst is the Cyclops system."

"Do we have sonar?"

"Yes, we have broadband, narrowband, towed array, onion, conformal arrays, and acoustic daylight arrays, and the system can report it all. But the firecontrol modules are down hard. We can't use the computer to track a contact, the 3-D virtual displays don't work, and we can't send firecontrol information to the torpedo tubes. Not that we'll be needing the tubes, because we're supposed to coordinate with the Air Force bombers so they can drop the ordnance, but then the UHF secure voice modules are down hard."

Pacino looked out at the horizon with the binoculars. They were entering Thimble Shoal Channel, the long runway of buoys on either side of them.

"You got people working on the torpedo tubes?"

"No, Captain," Vermeers said, the first time he'd addressed Pacino as the ship's captain.

"Forget about the firecontrol displays. To hell with the UHF, and to hell with the Air Force. You just make sure we can shoot torpedoes out of all four tubes."

"How we gonna do that with no firecontrol?"

Pacino didn't answer until after the turning point as the channel emptied out into the Atlantic.

"Tigersharks," he finally said. "Tigersharks have carbon processors. They don't need a refined firecontrol solution, just a general idea of what we want them to do."

"Right," Vermeers said, overly enthusiastic. "That fuzzy logic thing."

Pacino glared at him but said nothing. He was beginning to despair that his executive officer would ever understand. Vermeers finally seemed to sense Pacino's ill mood, and his expression darkened a notch. "Sir, isn't that a violation of our orders? Not using the Air Force?"

"Listen, XO, let me give you a piece of advice. We'll speak of this only once. When you're put in command, you do what you know is right. Not what the Reactor Plant Manual says. Not what the Submarine Standard Operating Procedures say. Not what the Approach and Attack Manual says. Not what U.S. Navy Regulations say. Not Mao's red book, not the Bible. You follow what's in your mind and what's in your heart. You do what you're here to do, to command the ship and the crew and fulfill the mission, even if it means violating orders. Even if it means the goddamned ship sinks. Even if you die, or worse, if you sacrifice your reputation and your sacred honor, you do what you have to do. Remember, at sea, you're it. There's no court of appeals, there's no admiral, there's no Secretary of the Navy, there's no President, it's just you, the captain. Today, it's me. I'm not talking to a bunch of bombers who couldn't spell submarine, much less find one in the million cubic miles of seawater it's hiding in. Today we do what *I* say, and what *I* say is, we make all tubes ready to launch Mark 98 Tigersharks, and we let the Tigersharks do the heavy lifting. When the dust clears, we'll sail home and take our medicine. For violating our orders."

Vermeers stared at him. "All that's easy to say, sir, when you're a former four-star admiral, when you're at sea for one mission before you go back to your regularly scheduled life. When you're a thirty-eight-year-old three-striper, with the world looking down on you, waiting for you to make a mistake, it's a lot different." Vermeers paused long enough to see Pacino shake his head. "Did you operate like this as a captain, when you first were in command?"

Pacino nodded solemnly. "Jeff, I made a career out of it.

The trick is to find out what your superiors want, what their intentions are, and then doing what they need you to do, not what they *say* they need you to do, and that's the difference. That's one of the secrets of command at sea. If you pay attention on this run, you may learn the others."

Vermeers nodded, frowning out at the horizon sternly, as if imitating Pacino, but eventually the old Vermeers returned. "But, sir . . . I know you're the program director and all, but . . . the Tigersharks don't work. They home in on and destroy the firing ship."

"They will work, as soon as I get done tweaking them."

"Captain," Vickerson said, turning, "ship has cleared the traffic separation scheme. ETA to the dive point is six hours."

"Very well," Pacino said, climbing down from the flying bridge and opening the deck grating to the bridge access tunnel. "XO, I want to see you and the navigator and the engineer in my stateroom."

He lowered himself into the hull. The smells of the ship and the sea intoxicated him with all the things that were back, things he'd lost. He refused to let his emotions swell with the feelings, because deep in the Atlantic, his only son could be gasping his last breaths.

22

Captain Lien Hua walked into the command post and found Zhou at the command console doodling on a paper tablet.

"Dou's starting the reactor," he said. "The battery is back on-line." The lights in the overhead flickered and held, the uneven wavering light of the casualty lanterns banished by the brightness. "And we need to submerge. Station underway watch section two and prepare to vertical dive."

Zhou Ping grinned. "Yes, Captain, section two and prepare to vertical dive."

Fifteen minutes later the *Nung Yahtsu* was steaming submerged on her own power, on course north to intercept Battlegroup Two, but no longer in a hurry. Captain Lien ordered a transit speed of eight knots, the optimal for covering ground while engaging a maximum-scan sonar search. This time the Americans would not have the advantage of searching slow and quiet while *Nung Yahtsu* was forced to burn through the seas at full speed. This time, *Nung Yahtsu* would sneak up on the Americans.

By the end of the morning watch the ship had arrived at the sinking location of the American submarine. Captain Lien ordered an excursion to periscope depth, and while they examined the surface for flotsam—evidence of a kill they could report to the Admiralty—they transmitted their after-action report to Admiral Chu and received their messages. Lien was scanning the message traffic, which was minimal since the Admiralty assumed they'd been lost. Lien decided to linger at periscope depth to see if the Admiralty would give them emergency orders once their after-action report was digested, and it became clear that *Nung Yahtsu* had returned from the dead. It was then the American helicopter was sighted. Lien ordered the periscope dipped, only allowing it to be exposed for ten seconds every minute.

In the second minute of observing the U.S. Navy chopper, his face pressed close to the warm optics module of the periscope, Lien noticed that the chopper was not searching for them with a dipping sonar, but had focused its attention on the sea. Two divers jumped out, and a man-basket was being lowered to the sea.

"Dead slow ahead course zero four zero," Lien ordered from the periscope. "Raising scope." When he saw what was going on, he became furious.

"Arm the anti-air missile battery," he commanded. "Target number one, U.S. helicopter rescuing survivors of our submarine attack."

"AAM battery armed," Zhou Ping reported. "Periscope station has control."

"Target bearing and altitude, mark!" Lien observed, the periscope still up after the time he should have lowered it. "Missile one—*fire!*"

There was no sound as the Victory II anti-air missile lifted off from the sail in a bubble of steam from the gas generator and broke the surface. The missile's solid rocket fuel ignited and it flew straight upward to a thousand-meter height and made a graceful Mach 1.1 loop downward, its infrared heat seeker seeing the helicopter's twin jet exhausts. The missile sailed into the port engine and exploded. The hundred pounds of high explosive was not sufficient on its own to blow up the chopper, only to damage it severely, the fireball blowing off a rotor and sending the chopper spinning out of control. The explosion in the tailpipe of the number two turbine sent turbine blades scattering through the airframe, severing two fuel lines, and the still-burning fireball set off the fuel and then the fuel

tanks, and the Sea Serpent IV helicopter detonated with the
power of a ton of TNT, blowing rotor blades, aluminum structural pieces, control panels, and human flesh over the surface
of the sea. The shock wave from it slammed the eardrums of
Lieutenant Commander Donna Phillips in life raft number one.
A five-foot piece of helicopter rotor whooshed over her head,
the debris flying fast enough to have cut her in half, another
piece of shrapnel puncturing the flank of the life raft.

Phillips's expression fell. Life had just become much more
complicated.

"Vertical surface," Lien commanded Zhou. Zhou gave the
order to the ship-control officer, and the ship came to a stop in
the waters of the East China Sea, her hovering system controlling her depth. The ship-control officer dialed in a negative
depth rate, and the ship rose vertically from fifty meters to the
surface. Once on the surface, the ship-control officer raised
the snorkel and started the main compressor, blowing air into
the ballast tanks. Within two minutes, it was safe to man the
fin cockpit.

"Ship is vertical surfaced, sir," Zhou Ping reported.

"Man the fin watch," Lien ordered.

When Lien climbed the vertical access tunnel to the fin
cockpit, Zhou was stationed as surfaced deck officer. He
handed Lien a set of binoculars.

"Look, sir. They must be survivors of the submarine that
fired on us and the battlegroup."

Lien's face grew hard as he looked into the binoculars.
"Bring us closer, Leader Zhou, at dead slow."

Zhou raised the cockpit communicator microphone to his
mouth and ordered, "Dead slow ahead, steer course three four
zero."

The ship moved slowly toward the life rafts until they were
a half ship length away. Lien glared angrily down on the survivors.

"All stop," Zhou commanded into the microphone, then
glancing at Captain Lien. "What now, sir?"

Lien didn't answer. He stood there, frozen, as if unable to make a decision.

Zhou's face was a mask of anger. "Sir, we must hurry to Battlegroup Two, as she may come under attack without our help."

Lien still stood there, frozen in indecision.

Zhou picked up a microphone and called the command post watch. "Get the key to the small arms locker from the captain's stateroom. It is in the safe. The combination is the commissioning day of this ship." It was a date everyone on board was required to memorize. "Bring up five AK-80s and fifteen clips of ammunition."

"Zhou," Lien said uncertainly, "what are you doing?"

Zhou glared at his captain. "We can't take them prisoner, sir. I won't have Americans on our ship, not these devils who sank the battlegroup we were ordered to protect. They could revolt and try to take us over. I will finish the job that the Tsunami torpedo began."

Lien narrowed his eyes at his first officer. His intention was a violation of international law and of the unwritten code of the sea. Lien had read about Nazi Germany's U-boats doing this, and had condemned the action. He never thought the man he regarded as his protégé would do such a thing, even to hateful Americans.

"Sir, you must act," Zhou said. "If you do not give the order to shoot them, I will relieve you of command under the Regulations of the PLA Navy for Commanders Afloat, Section Twenty-three."

Lien sighed, but said nothing, just stood there, staring at the Americans. Two enlisted men climbed into the fin, bringing the rifles. Zhou turned to one of them. "Fighter Ling, place the captain under arrest. I have been forced to assume command of the *Nung Yahtsu*."

The enlisted sailor stared at Zhou, but seeing the captain standing like a statue, he nodded and gently pulled Lien's wrists behind his back and tied them with plastic cable ties. He began to nudge Lien toward the tunnel opening, but realized he would have to ask the first officer to move out of the way. He hesitated, then motioned to the senior officer.

"Keep him here until we dive," Zhou said, his attention fixed on the sea below.

Zhou picked up one of the rifles and glared at the American survivors.

Captain George Dixon blinked as he sat up, leaning heavily against Commander Donna Phillips.

"What is it? Are we rescued?"

"Sir, I'm afraid it's the Julang-class. Either he didn't sink or the Chinese have more than one."

"Oh, shit," Dixon said, groaning. "We have a pistol from the survival kit?"

"A couple of twenty-twos, sir. Good for fending off a small shark, but not much use holding off a Chinese submarine."

"Oh, God," Dixon said. "My mother didn't raise me to be a prisoner of war. Not under those guys."

"We'll get through this, Skipper. My grandfather was a POW in Vietnam, and he said it was not as bad as everyone thought," Phillips said, lying to Dixon. Her grandfather had been shot down over Hanoi and imprisoned, but the truth of his imprisonment was far worse than any of the stories. Phillips tried to breathe deeply, fighting off her feelings of desperate fear, and knowing that if she could give Captain Dixon courage, seeing his war face would give her the strength to go on.

"Okay, XO. We'll get through this." He reached into his breast pocket below his dolphin emblem and pulled out the gold coin his wife had given him. He blinked rapidly, then put the coin back in his pocket. Phillips waited for him to show a sign of encouragement, but his eyes closed, at first as if he were stressed, but then Phillips realized that he had lost consciousness.

Lieutenant Brett Oliver, the NSA-assigned officer who'd joined the ship in midoperation, began trembling in fear. "XO," he said, his voice shaking, "I can't be a prisoner of war.

Not with what I know. I'm an NSA agent. If they interrogate me, they'll break me. They'll know about the battle network, and the entire war could be compromised."

"Don't be ridiculous," Phillips said in a hard voice, but seeing his point. She tried to think, but there seemed to be no solution.

"Give me a twenty-two," he said.

"What do you intend to do, Mr. Oliver?"

"Give me the gun, XO." His look stopped being frightened for a moment, a hard resolve in his eyes. Reluctantly she handed it to him.

"Don't use it unless you have to," she said.

"Good-bye, Donna," he said. "Good luck." He slipped backward off the raft and stroked away from the Julang submarine's approach. Phillips watched him swim, his head barely visible over the crests of the waves. When she could no longer see him, the sound of a single gunshot echoed over the water.

"Oh, Jesus," she said, putting her head in her hands.

When she looked up, the Julang had heaved to, close aboard. Phillips looked at it in wonder. Until now it had been an impersonal diamond shape on a firecontrol display, or a dimly remembered grainy intelligence photograph, and now here it was. It seemed so *big* in reality, the sail towering over them, the hull wider than their *Leopard*'s. On the bridge she could make out a half-dozen men, and something else. Either they all had broomsticks, or weapons.

She watched the men on the bridge as they pointed the automatic rifles at the life rafts from a distance of thirty yards. She realized that they were not threatening with the rifles to take the *Leopard* survivors hostage, but intending to shoot to kill. The scream was torn from her lips without conscious thought.

"Crew! All hands! In the water, *now!*" She bodily tossed Captain Dixon off the raft and into the sea, grabbed the man next to her, and threw herself backward into the water as the first shots rang out over the waves.

*   *   *

Zhou Ping raised the AK-80, the rifle heavy in his grip, the precise long-range scope installed before the weapon was brought to the fin. In the scope he could see the closest life raft, with a woman sitting next to a man slumped against the yellow inflated wall of the raft. The man had gold insignia on his chest, perhaps a high-ranking senior officer. Zhou clicked off the safety, ready to fire, when a gunshot rang in his ears.

"What was that," he asked, taking his face from the scope.

"They're shooting at us, Mr. First," Fighter Ling said. "Shoot them!"

Zhou put his eye back to the scope, but the people in the rafts were jumping off into the sea. He located the senior officer he'd been aiming at before, put the man's chest in his crosshairs, and squeezed the trigger. The rifle jumped slightly, coughing as it fired a single round.

"Select the rifle to full automatic, sir!" Ling shouted.

"Damn thing," Zhou said, finding the switch that took the rifle out of semiauto, then resighting on the survivors in the water. He squeezed the trigger and sprayed the rafts and the men in the water with bullets until the clip was empty.

The other rifles began firing as he downloaded the clip and put in a fresh one, then emptied that clip, the bullets flying over the sea at the Americans.

"Look around, number two scope," Captain Andrew Deahl ordered from the conn of the USS *Essex,* the Virginia-class SSN dispatched by Admiral McKee to find the Julang-class before it could form up with Battlegroup Two. Deahl stood behind the command console with the Type 23 helmet on, the room rigged for black despite the daylight hour, so that he could better see the seascape in the periscope view. The crew, stationed at battlestations since sonar had detected the Julang at long range, waited silently for the next order. When the Julang, designated Target One, had vertical surfaced, Deahl had ordered tubes one and two check fired, the attack aborted, to see what was happening.

"Depth seven zero, speed zero, Captain."

"Up scope." Deahl hit the joystick strapped to his wiry thigh and the photonic mast came out of the sail. Deahl's view showed the underside of the waves, the computer's superimposed bearings selected to the bearing of the Julang. When the scope broke through the waves, Deahl reported, "Scope's breaking, scope's clear! I have Target One surfaced. Observation, Target One! Bearing three zero five, bearing *mark*! Range, three divisions in low power, masthead height set at three zero feet, range five hundred yards, angle on the bow starboard one two zero! Attention in the firecontrol party—we are suspending torpedo attack until we can determine Target One's actions. Carry on."

"Bastard's probably just broken down, Skipper," the XO said in his Baton Rouge accent.

"Sonar, Captain," Deahl said into his boom microphone, "do you show loss of propulsion on Target One?"

"Captain, Sonar, no. His engines are idle, but he is still steaming."

"So much for that theory, XO," Deahl said. Andrew Deahl, a thirty-eight-year-old underweight marathon runner, was new to command, having taken over the *Essex* a mere two months ago from a captain beloved by the crew, and so far command had been nothing like he'd imagined. The transition from being second-in-command to captain was a wide gulf to cross, and there were moments when he suffered severe self-doubts. The orders to the war in the East China Sea had complicated things, but at least Deahl had learned to lean on his executive officer, though it was hard for a New Yorker like Deahl to trust the smooth Southerner that XO Harlan Simoneaux was.

"Captain," the XO said in a voice that seemed too loud, "the men in the sail have rifles. They're shooting at something!"

"What the hell?" Deahl mumbled.

"Oh, shit, Captain. This is where *Leopard* went down! They're survivors!"

"*Snapshot tube one, Target One!*" Deahl shouted. "Disable anti-self-homing, disable anticircular run, *immediate* enable, surface impact mode, high-speed active search, direct contact mode!"

The outer door to tube one was already open. The Mark 58 Alert/Acute had been powered up for the last thirty minutes, and the solution to the target was locked in, the weapon only waiting for word to shoot. It took a second for the weapons officer to respond to the radical settings required to get a Mark 58 to detonate on such a close target, the safety interlocks required to be removed to allow the weapon to work.

"Set!" the XO finally said.

"Stand by," the weapons officer called, his console ready to fire.

"Shoot on generated bearing!"

"*Fire!*" the weapons officer called, and the deck trembled and Deahl's ears slammed from the torpedo launch.

"Sir, tube one fired electrically," the weapons officer said.

"Conn, Sonar, own ship's unit, normal launch."

The words were barely out of the sonar supervisor's mouth before the view out the Type 23 went white, then blinked out. Deahl blinked, but the interior of the helmet was dark. Something had happened to the Type 23 mast, he thought. It was then that the sound of the explosion came roaring into the hull, and the ship trembled violently as if struck by a huge sledge-hammer.

"Conn, Sonar, explosion from bearing to Target One."

"Well, obviously," Simoneaux said sarcastically.

"Raising number one scope," Captain Deahl said, selecting his thigh controller to the starboard periscope. The second Type 23 rose out of the sail and penetrated the waves, and when it did, all Deahl saw was a large orange and black mushroom cloud and debris falling from the heavens in large metal chunks, the flotsam field growing with each second.

"Target One is gone," Deahl said with a flat voice. He just realized he may have made a grave error, because if there had been floating survivors within two hundred feet of the hull of the Julang, they were survivors no more.

"Officer of the Deck, vertical surface the ship!"

*   *   *

"Captain, bodies in the water, thirty degrees off the port bow!"

Commander Deahl guided the *Essex* to the position the OOD had pointed out and ordered all stop.

"Get the divers in the water," Deahl commanded.

Over the next two hours they combed the waters of the Ju-lang sinking site, harvesting thirty-five bodies, a dozen of them dead, the remainder unconscious. Among the living were five Chinese, two of them officers if Deahl had interpreted the insignia on their uniforms correctly. The dead were wrapped in trash bags and brought to the frozen stores room. The living were brought to the crew's mess, Deahl ordering the tables unbolted from the deck to create more space for them, the crew's mattresses spread out on the floor. The medic, a senior chief petty officer on his last sea tour, attended to the wounded. Captain Deahl watched from a corner of the room until the medic came up to him, the older man wiping sweat off his forehead.

"What's the word, Chief?"

"They're all lucky, sir. About a million cuts and lacerations and broken bones between them, and a few gunshot wounds. The *Leopard* XO, Phillips, is in good shape except for a bullet through the upper arm. Captain Dixon took two rounds in the shoulder and one in the chest, and he had internal bleeding, but he's stable."

"A round in the chest and he's still alive?" Deahl asked.

"He had a souvenir in his chest pocket, something heavy and made of gold—a locket or a watch or something. It's a dented lump curled around a mushroomed AK-80 round now, but it saved his life. That bullet would have gone straight through his heart."

"Lucky guy," Deahl muttered. "What about the Chinese?"

"They'll fare the best, Skipper. They were on the Julang sail, so the explosion threw them clear. I think one of them is the captain."

"Bring me to him."

The senior chief led Deahl to the Chinese commanding officer. It was strange, Deahl thought. With his eyes shut, a blanket over him, and an IV needle in his arm, the Red officer looked as innocent as a sleeping child. Hardly the devil that Deahl had imagined. It was just war, Deahl told himself. If not for the war, this guy probably had a house and a wife and kids, an annoyed squadron commander, a ship that needed maintenance, a crew that needed leadership, and all the other headaches of life. In a way, Deahl realized he had more in common with the Chinese officer than he did with a typical civilian back home.

"Thanks, Senior," Deahl said. "Inform me when any of them regain consciousness."

Deahl walked down to the control room and addressed the officer of the deck.

"Keep steaming north until we find Battlegroup Two," he said. "And be damned careful of any more Chinese submarines."

23

Commander Rob Catardi shivered beside the atmospheric control panel. The analyzer had good news for them on carbon monoxide and carbon dioxide, but the problem was oxygen, which was at 19.9 percent and falling fast. The oxygen bleed valve was fully open, and not a molecule of gas was coming out. Catardi had pulled out the piping manual for the DSV and checked the oxygen system, hoping for a shutoff valve between banks for the command module and the larger cargo module, and to his joy, there was a cross-connect shutoff. He followed the piping in the overhead until the stainless-steel pipe penetrated the command module bulkhead. Right before the penetration he found the shutoff valve. It was open, and the system was empty. He opened and shut the valve four times, but there was no response. It was obvious that they would suffocate down here. In ten hours, when the rescue craft arrived, they would be unconscious.

They had paced themselves for the arrival of the rescue DSV, but this wasn't over when it got here. It would have to slice through the two-inch-thick steel of the *Piranha*'s hull, and grab on to and remove a plate above the DSV. One mistake with the removed plate, and it would fall and crush them. The rescue submersible would have to weld the docking collar onto their DSV, then cut into their hull and tunnel through all the cables and ducts and piping, which would contaminate the atmosphere with toxic chemicals from burning cable insula-

348 *Michael DiMercurio*

tion. There was a week of work to do before they could get inside the DSV, and by the time the rescuers got in-hull, the surviving crew of the *Piranha* would all be long gone.

Even if they had plenty of oxygen, the cold would get them. Catardi could see his breath, and there was nothing here to keep him warm except a few survival blankets, most of which he'd given to the others before they fell asleep in the frigid command module.

Catardi had always wondered whether he would want to know in advance of his death, or whether it would be best to be blindsided. He had once thought that he'd like five minutes, so he'd see it coming, enough time to say good-bye perhaps, but not so much warning that he would be gripped in fear for days on end. But this warning was more than five minutes. He probably had ten or twelve conscious hours left, and then he would be gone. When they did cut into the hull, they would find him frozen, his body at thirty degrees Fahrenheit, and dead as the steel of the bulkhead. He crouched at his pile of padding and wrapped himself in his blanket. From where he sat he could see the other three, their plumes of breath vapor rising. Pacino had gone to sleep, as ordered. Schultz and Alameda had never awakened, a bad sign. Catardi had awakened after an hour or two, too nervous to sleep anymore.

He had informed the topside ship, the *Emerald,* that they would not be talking any further, since it would keep them from sleeping to conserve their oxygen. *Emerald* had promised to find a way to get oxygen and power into their hull, but it was too big a task. They had hinted that the weather above was getting rough from a storm that had been in the eastern Atlantic. Catardi had said good-bye to the fuzzy voice hours before and requested they not call him again. False hopes were worse than hopelessness. He lay down on the padding, then changed his mind and got up to walk to Pacino, Alameda, and Schultz. He wanted to see their faces and say a farewell. He reached out for Pacino's forehead and pulled the kid's hair out of his eyes, thinking he'd failed the young man. Then Carrie Alameda, who looked like a child when she slept.

He touched her hair and her cheek, then moved on to Astrid Schultz, the pretty blonde who had sent Catardi's wife into fits of jealousy when she was first assigned to the *Piranha*. Catardi stroked her cheek, mentally thanking her for all she'd done, and saying good-bye to her. Finally he returned to his padding and pulled the thin blanket up to his nose, took one last look around and shut his eyes.

He knew he should consign himself to sleep, but he was too afraid. He knew that once he shut his eyes, that would be the end. There would be no waking up from this nap. It would be better, he knew, to get through the last horrible hours in slumber than to experience them awake. He didn't want to be awake when the already dim lights flickered out. He felt his eyes fill with moisture and he finally was able to shut them, telling himself to slow his breathing and sleep. Every time he did, he felt his heart pound in his chest as the fear rose into his throat. There was one thing that seemed to calm him down, and it was thinking about Nicole, his young daughter, wondering what she was doing right then. He hoped she was not watching a news report and crying over him. He had thought they would keep the lid of classification on this sinking, and only tell the world when it was all over. He mourned the loss of her photograph, the one that had been bolted to his stateroom bulkhead. The one that had probably been blown to cinders in the first internal torpedo explosion.

Catardi let his thoughts wander, imagining his self flying out of this cold dark steel coffin and rising out of the sea and ascending in the air over the Atlantic Ocean, soaring higher over the earth until he returned to the house he and Sharon had shared with Nicole in a time far in the past, and he came up to the door during the summer and Nicole came out and hugged him and squealed *Daddy Daddy Daddy* and he lifted her into the air and said her name and they chased each other in the yard and played hide-and-seek and piggyback and all the other games she adored. And when dusk came he carried her into the house and read all her favorite stories to her, seeing every page, making every funny voice she liked, singing the funny songs he'd invented for her and listening to her giggle, and then kissed her forehead and told her to sleep. He felt her arms go around him one last time, and he stood back and watched her fall asleep until her breathing was slow and steady, and he turned out her light and stood there in the dark by her side, making sure no monsters were there to get her, and when Catardi himself fell asleep, there were tracks of tears leaving his eyes and streaking down his temples into his tangled gray-streaked hair.

Outside the intact hull of the *Piranha*'s DSV the mangled hull of the ship lay buried in the sediment of the bottom, with just a few places where the muck had been wiped off for the hydrophones. The hydrophone cable and the locator buoy cable rose away from the dark wreck on the bottom and made their way to the surface, where night had fallen. There were no stars because of the dark clouds, and the seas rose as the wind began to howl, making the cables vibrate and sing as they came over the fantail of the salvage ship *Emerald* and continued into her equipment bay. At the temporary consoles set up in the crew's messroom, Lieutenant Evan Thompson sat at a console and monitored the noises coming from the interior of the DSV. It had been quiet for some time, only muffled footprints falling on the deckplates, then a muted sobbing, and then nothing. They were either sleeping or unconscious, Thompson thought. He pulled off his earphones and sighed, draping his palm over his eyes and accepting the coffee brought by the mess captain.

The British were making better time than expected, and were due by dawn, but there was nothing they would be able to do. The storm was getting worse. The captain of the *Emerald* had made plans to disconnect the hydrophone cables and get back to port, or if it got as bad as the reports said, make his way north to get out of the storm path. Thompson hoped they stayed long enough to turn over the operation to the Brits, but the crew of the *Emerald* was responsible for ship safety. It was their call. Thompson put the headphones back on and put his head on the horizontal table of the hydrophone console and shut his eyes, deciding he would sleep like that in case they called for him.

The night passed as the *Emerald* rocked in the waves, but there was not a sound from inside the wreckage of the USS *Piranha*.

Captain Lien Hua turned on his side and snuggled into his pillow, the sounds of the air handlers blowing cool air through the ship comforting, as always. He opened his eyes for a moment, but the room was dark. He heard muffled voices, outside in the passageway, perhaps. He would instruct Leader Zhou Ping to make sure the crew stayed away from his stateroom. He yawned and prepared to go back to sleep, but realized there was something wrong. He sat up in the bed with a panic rising in his throat, suddenly realizing that the whispering voices were not speaking Mandarin or Cantonese, but some other language. He put his hand out where his sea cabin's foldout desk should be, but it was not there. Neither was the phone console, nor the ship-control display. He swiveled to put his feet on the deck, but his mattress was already on the floor, a cold tiling beneath his bare feet.

"What's going on?" he shouted, running until he hit a heavy curtain, then pulling it aside. He was in a red-lit passageway outside an open curtained area. There were two men standing there, wearing dark coveralls, much like what he was wearing, except they had an enemy symbol on their sleeves—a patch with the image of the flag of the United States. Lien stood and stared, then looked up at the cables and ducts in the overhead. This could easily be the *Nung Yahtsu*, but things were backward, the bulkheads were too dark, and the deckplate covering was a tile, not rubber with antiskid bumps. He was on a ship, perhaps a submarine, but it was not Chinese. He looked slowly at the Americans, then raised his hands in surrender.

They motioned him to follow them down the passageway to a steep ship's ladder. He walked behind one American and in front of the other, down the red lantern-lit companionway to a door marked with English words. One of the crewmen knocked, and he was led into a small stateroom, the three-meter-square space resembling his sea cabin. A slight man stood up from his small table, a bigger man with him. They both spoke their odd-sounding language, but Lien shook his head, wondering why they didn't just shoot him right then. The slight man motioned him to sit, and when he did, Lien began to shiver, perhaps from the cold of the room, or perhaps from his fear. The man wrapped a wool blanket around his shoulders and spoke into a telephone, and soon a cook arrived with a pot of tea. Lien refused to drink it. A foreign-smelling plate of food was placed in front of him, and despite his ferocious hunger, he ignored it.

The larger man pulled out a large flexible flat panel display, and after working with it, a map of China came up on it. He pointed to Beijing. Lien looked up—was he being interrogated? He shook his head, and the man sat down.

Not that it mattered. They would execute him soon anyway.

"Captain Pacino, ship is submerged at one five zero feet with a satisfactory one-third trim," Lieutenant Vickerson reported. "Sounding is five six five fathoms."

Pacino stood on the conn in the rigged-for-red control room of the *Devilfish,* thinking the last time he had been here, the ship was returning from the East China Sea after the last tussle with the Reds. He concentrated on the moment and looked at the female officer.

"Very well. Increase speed to standard and take her to four hundred feet, flat angle."

Vickerson stared at him. "Depth limit is one five zero feet, Captain. The shipyard said the welds weren't completed. We'll flood before we get to two hundred."

The XO walked to the conn from the navigation station aft, his face a fearful mask in the eerie red lights of the overheads. "Sir, Vickerson is right."

Pacino nodded. "I know. Take her down, OOD. Flat angle."

"Aye, sir," she said, and made the orders.

Pacino picked up the 1MC microphone, his voice booming

throughout the ship. "Attention, all hands," he said. "This is the captain. As you all know, we have been sent on an urgent mission to sink the *Snarc,* which has gone seriously out of control and has fired upon one of our own ships. The *Piranha* is on the bottom and the *Snarc* has run out of weapons range of the *Hammerhead.* She is on her way east to fire weapons at American targets, but she will never make it to the range circle of her missiles, not if the *Devilfish* has anything to say about it. However, in order for us to fight the ship in this battle, we must have all combat capabilities. I am ordering the torpedo tubes prepared and I will be modifying the Tigershark torpedoes so that we may engage the *Snarc.* I am also ordering the ship be taken to test depth so we can see if we'll flood or stay intact, because when we take on the *Snarc* we will be fighting her from the deep, not from periscope depth talking to an Air Force bomber. Therefore, because I am betting that the shipyard has done better work than they are willing to take credit for, *Devilfish* is now proceeding deep. All hands, rig ship for deep submergence. Carry on."

Pacino replaced the microphone in the cradle and looked up to ten pairs of doubting eyes. Vickerson turned and looked at him, biting her lower lip.

"Captain, two hundred feet, sir."

"Very well." Pacino stood straight on the conn, glaring at the depth gauge.

"Two fifty, sir." Vickerson swallowed. "All stations report ship rigged for deep submergence, sir."

"Very well." On every level of every space, phonetalkers would prowl with flashlights, hoping to find a leak before the ship flooded catastrophically. The difference was critical, as the old submarine saying went—*you find a leak, flooding finds you.*

"Three hundred feet, sir."

"Proceed to test depth, Officer of the Deck, thirteen hundred feet."

"Thirteen hundred feet, aye, sir. Ship is at all ahead standard."

"All ahead full," Pacino ordered, knowing that full speed at test depth violated the ship's operating envelope, since a jam dive at full speed would send them plunging through crush depth before they could recover.

"Full, aye, Captain," Vickerson replied. Pacino smiled to himself—she was beginning to learn. It was obviously harder for Vermeers, who stood there with beads of sweat on his forehead.

"Five hundred feet, sir."

The ship kept plowing deeper, until a loud groaning shriek sounded from above the control room, making Vermeers jump. "It's just the hull adjusting to the pressure, XO," Pacino said.

"I know that, sir," Vermeers said. "I'm wearing dolphins."

Pacino glared at the depth gauge.

"One thousand feet, sir."

The phone on the command console buzzed. Vickerson lunged for it, looking up to say, "Torpedo room reports a leak on tube three's inner door, sir. Leak is dripping, but increasing to a steady drip."

Pacino nodded as if it were good news. "Very well."

"Aren't you taking us up, sir?" Vermeers asked.

Pacino glared at him.

"Eleven hundred feet, Captain."

The hull shrieked again, a loud series of pops roaring from left to right and echoing in the depths of the seas. Vermeers tried to maintain a war face, but it was not easy for the young officer.

"Twelve hundred feet, Captain."

The phone buzzed again. Vickerson listened. "Sir, tube three leak is now streaming."

Pacino nodded, glancing at Vermeers, who nodded in imitation.

"Thirteen hundred feet, Captain," Vickerson reported. "Tube three leak is streaming so hard the water is hitting the deck twenty feet away, sir."

"Cycle tube three's outer door," Pacino ordered. "And all ahead flank."

Vermeers's face looked white even in the red-lit room. If full speed were dangerous at test depth, flank was suicidal. Especially before the ship had undergone sea trials. The deck below Pacino's feet began to tremble as the ship sped up to flank speed.

"Aye, sir, opening outer door, tube three, door open, and shutting outer door."

Pacino waited.

"Sir, tube three leak is down to a slow drip."

"Very well. Off'sa'deck, take the ship to five four eight feet, thirty degree up angle."

The deck rose steeply. In the upper level, the sound of dishes breaking in the galley could be heard, several crashes of books and equipment sounding from the middle level. The crashing had barely stopped when the deck leveled out.

"XO," Pacino said dryly, "I think you could do a better job stowing for sea. Should I take a few more angles, or do you think you can identify and fix the problems?"

"I'll take care of it, sir."

"OOD, I want you to increase speed slowly—"

"Sir, we're already at flank—"

"—by coordinating with maneuvering and raising reactor power one percent at a time until you get a main lube oil bearing discharge over-temperature alarm, then back down one percent, which will be the emergency flank setting. Make sure the engineering officer of the watch has all main lube oil cooler balance valves fully open before you start."

"Aye aye, Captain," Vickerson said, more calmly this time as she hoisted a phone.

"You know you'll ruin the reactor and make the ship a high-radiation area by going above one hundred percent power, Captain," Vermeers said. "We'll be back in the shipyard for two years if you go over a hundred and ten percent."

"I'm well aware of that, XO, just as I am that the *Snarc* is out there spinning up twelve cruise missiles."

Pacino stood on the conn, feeling the deck of the *Devilfish* shaking, waiting until he could get to the intercept point with the *Snarc*.

The president of Cyclops Systems Incorporated, Colleen O'Shaughnessy Pacino, had designed the current generation of submerged battlecontrol systems since the SSNX had first gone to sea, a soaring success for both Colleen and Michael Pacino since Cyclops got a bigger, more lucrative contract and they had gotten married. But the good times were in the past, since now Colleen Pacino was about to answer to Congress for the failed Tigershark torpedo program. That had been her biggest problem until, twenty hours ago, her husband had told her about the nightmare with Anthony Michael.

"Of course I'll go," she had said, as she sat up in the bed and swept her raven-black hair out of her face.

The chopper flight had gone on for hours. Finally the chopper hovered over the rear deck of the *Explorer II* and lowered her down to the deck. By the time she was taken inside she was soaked from the high winds and the driving rain.

Commander Peter Collingsworth met her in a narrow passageway. He had a solid body that could stand to lose a few pounds and stood taller than average, with a full red beard, a tangled mop of reddish-brown hair, jolly blue eyes, a freckle-covered nose, and a firm handshake. His voice was higher than his body would suggest, his manner open and friendly. Colleen threw the hood off her head and shook out her hair in the towel she'd been given, gripping the Royal Navy commander's hand.

"I'm Colleen Pacino," she said. "I'm a defense contractor sent out by Admiral Patton. One of the survivors in the *Piranha* is my stepson."

Collinsworth nodded seriously, releasing her hand. "Welcome aboard *Explorer II*. I'm the venture commander. The captain of the ship is Kenneth Knowles, who is on the bridge. I'd offer you something to drink, but I assume you'll want to get to business. If you'll use this empty stateroom, you can take a shower and change into dry coveralls. I'll meet you in the control room in five minutes."

Colleen nodded, ducked into the stateroom, dived under the warm fresh water shower, toweled off, and donned the British coveralls with the odd emblems above the pockets. When she emerged, a crewman was waiting to take her to control, a large but crowded space jammed with monitors, computers, radios, and other equipment. She could hear Collingsworth talking to one of his officers, his voice calm and confident. When he was done he came over to Colleen. She expected him to give a speech about the weather being too severe and the rescue taking too much time.

"Mrs. Pacino, here's how we see things. *Emerald* has shoved off and hightailed it out of the storm. She's disconnected from the hydrophone cables and left the buoy locator for the wreck floating, and we're retrieving it now. Once we have it aboard we'll set up the stabilizer system to hover in place over the wreck. The submersible will be going overboard next with the hull-cutting rig."

"Where is it?" Colleen asked. "I didn't see it on the deck."

"It's in the belly of the ship. It goes down from inside, so we're not weather limited. It's lowered by two arms that take her clear of the keel, and that way she can dock on the way up even in a hurricane. There's something about bad weather and sub wrecks that go together like tea and milk. The Admiralty wouldn't let a little weather stop a rescue."

Colleen smiled genuinely for the first time in days.

"Now, the rescue won't go as planned because we're out of time. According to the chaps on the *Emerald,* the sounds have stopped from in-hull a few hours after Captain Catardi reported that the oxygen levels were falling whilst he was suffering from extremely cold temperatures. If we don't have those crewmen up here in four hours, we're all wasting our time. We propose using an experimental and potentially dangerous plasma explosive torch over the command module of the sub's DSV. The idea is it will slice through thick steel in minutes instead of hours. But anything that has the energy to melt

through submarine hull material has energy enough to damage
the survivors, even breach the hull of the DSV. But there's no
time for anything else. Can you authorize us to use this
method?"

"How long will it take?" Colleen asked.

"An hour."

"Then hurry," she said.

Collingsworth nodded and jogged down the passageway
and disappeared into a hatch. Colleen checked her watch. In
an hour, dead or alive, they'd have Anthony Michael back.

"One, display the chart with the cruise missile range circle and
our position, and show the estimated time to arrive at the
range mark. Good, now please set up a targeting routine with a
close-up of the following locations for target selection." Krivak had no idea what the latitude and longitude of the White
House was, but he'd zero in on the crosshairs on Washington,
D.C., until he found it. Then he'd lock in the target and move
on to the next missile. He worried briefly that One Oh Seven
wòuld refuse to launch the missiles, but he wouldn't know
until he fired the weapons.

He thought for a moment that he should approach the firing
point in a random zigzag, to throw off any American military
units that would try to stop him. It seemed excessively paranoid and would make the time to missile impact much longer.
He ruled the idea out. *Snarc* would proceed straight on. He
might even speed up from thirty-five knots to fifty, but that
might create a train wreck of noise and invite detection. No,
the middle course was best. He congratulated himself for his
good instincts, and when the targeting was done, there was
nothing left to do but wait.

Wait and plan his escape, because once the missiles flew out
of the sea, there would be twelve missile trails pointing to his
location. If the U.S. military detected him with the launch,
Snarc wouldn't last an hour. If he did survive the launch, and
the missiles made it to the coast, the hunt for *Snarc* would
happen after impact. Either way, he would be a dead man if he

remained aboard. He would need to abandon ship in the middle of the ocean, which was not a pleasant thought.

There was no real need to rush this. Better to arrange for Amorn to be ready to pick him up at the launch point and spirit him away from the *Snarc*. The question was—what to do with Dr. Wang? Leave him aboard to fend for himself? Shoot him as they left the *Snarc*? Or take him into the business?

Krivak told One Oh Seven to slow and come shallow. He'd patch in the cell phone connection to Pedro and Amorn and arrange to meet them in a chartered yacht near the firing point. He'd set the *Snarc* to sail to China then, and by that time he'd have an idea what to do with Wang. A couple of nine-millimeter rounds in the eyes would probably be the best solution, though, he thought. The *Snarc* could be the doctor's coffin, and he could die with his creation.

Admiral John Patton hated the evacuation bunker's office. It was cramped and smelled like moldy concrete. He tried to concentrate on his E-mail when Commander Marissa Tyler, his aide, peeked in the door, a look of concern on her face. He motioned Marissa to take a chair.

"Trouble?" Patton asked.

"One of NSA's satellite cell phone network monitors filtered and saved a call. The keyword was *Snarc*. Here's the conversation."

Marissa pointed her pad computer at the main display monitor, and the sound playback module flashed at the screen. She pointed the laser pointer at the play function.

Amorn, it's me. Krivak. On the Snarc, *dammit.*

Yes, sir, I can hear you now.

Listen to me. Get a motor yacht, a fast one, and get it to the Atlantic coordinates I'm about to read to you.

Patton listened to it two more times, then began to draft a message to Kelly McKee.

24

This time the messenger shook Admiral Ericcson's shoulder hard the first time and said loudly, "Sir, I know you're awake. Captain Hendricks sends his respects at the hour of zero one hundred and requests your presence in air operations. Strike aircraft launch begins in twenty minutes, sir." With that she whirled and slipped out the door. Ericcson struggled to a sitting position, staring after her, eventually finding his voice and muttering, "Damned straight I was awake."

Ericcson raided the humidor, checked his uniform in the mirror, rigged the stateroom, and opened the door to the passageway. The Marine guards snapped to attention and he waved a salute at them, then made his way toward air operations. Every officer and enlisted man he passed greeted him with a quick, "Morning, Admiral," the words slurred together. When he reached air operations, he entered the room and let his eyes adjust to the dimness, the glow of the flat panel displays the only illumination.

"Admiral," Carrier Commander Hendricks said.

"Sir," the ship's operations officer said. Simon Weber was a newly promoted commander who had just assumed the duties after Captain Jones had rotated ashore.

"Good morning, Admiral," Captain Pulaski said, the battle-group ops boss seeming well rested for the first time this voyage.

"Gentlemen," Ericcson said in a booming gravelly voice as

he pulled out a Partagas. "Rumor has it we're about to strike the enemy any minute."

The air operations officer, Commander Eric Nussbaum, swiveled in his command chair, stood, and approached the admiral. "Sir, aircraft launch commences in five minutes. Request to launch strike in accordance with Attack Plan Delta and your night orders, sir."

Ericcson clipped the cigar with the gold cutter. He put the cigar between his teeth and spoke around it. "Air Ops, you have permission to launch aircraft in accordance with Attack Plan Delta." He put a flame to the cigar, then said to the room, "Gentlemen, good luck to you all."

The room responded, then quieted. The air operations officer returned to his command chair at his large console and donned his headset. Ericcson puffed the cigar to mellow life, glancing through the smoke at the tactical display, a busy plot that took some time getting used to. The east coast of White China was the left border, the Formosa Strait at the bottom. The NavForcePac Fleet's Task Force Alpha to the east, Red Chinese Battlegroup Two to the north. A display next to it was a blown-up scale plot of Battlegroup Two, showing individual ships in their dispersed antisubmarine formation. Vector arrows were drawn from each ship indicating ship's course, the length indicating ship speed. The ship symbols identified each ship. The aircraft carrier *Nanching* was the primary target, the Beijing-class nuclear battlecruisers next, the missile cruisers also highly targeted. The information on the plots came from the fleet's drones, a set of sixteen UAV, Unmanned Aerial Vehicles, the Mark 14 Predators, launched during the evening watch. Each Predator was tiny, wrapped in stealth radar-absorbing material, and flew at nearly forty-five thousand feet, orbiting the Chinese fleet and looking down with an array of infrared and visual sensors. The fleet's positions would normally have been confirmed with satellite updates downloaded from the tactical Keyhole satellites through the Navy Tactical Data System, but since the network was compromised, Ericcson had to make the attack using fleet resources. The Viking nodded in satisfaction at the display. The Predators were worth every nickel of the billions spent developing and procuring them.

"Sixty seconds, Admiral. Would you like to shift to the gallery?"

Ericcson nodded to the air ops boss and went through the light lock doors to the observation deck, the inclined windows overlooking the flight deck. On the forward catapults two F-22s were connected to the cats, the canopies down. Their jet exhaust glowed in the wee hours' darkness, the exhaust deflector shields rising slowly out of the deck behind the aircraft. Support crew swarmed over the planes, but backed away as the moment for launch neared. A single man on the deck stood near the cockpit of the port F-22, the first jet that would be launched, wearing a large helmet with a Mickey Mouse headset. He carried two large red-lit wands, handling them with the deftness of a drummer holding his drumsticks. As the hour of strike aircraft launch approached, he exchanged signals with the pilot in the F-22. Ericcson watched with mixed emotions, wistfully missing the sensations of the cockpit, but loving this moment of fleet command, his men and machines moving to his conductor's baton.

Far below the island on the flight deck, the port catapult's F-22 throttled up, then down. The jet's whining was loud enough to deafen a bystander. The tail's elevators rotated up and down, the rudder moved left and right. In the dimness of the flight deck lights, the tail's emblem could be made out, a black field with a white skull and the crossed bones of the Jolly Roger squadron, Ericcson's former command.

In the cockpit of the port fighter, Squadron Commander Diane "Fuzzy" Whitworth took one last run through the checklist, testing the interphone to the radar intercept officer and squadron executive officer, Commander Jane "Baldy" Felix. Whitworth's nickname came from her degree in artificial intelligence and her fondness of fuzzy logic. Baldy Felix's moniker had come from her comments that when she was anxious, she was "going bald over it." The two had clicked early in their careers, the detailers keeping them together as Whitworth took over the Jolly Rogers. The deck officer below gave her the signal that she had permission to take off. She curled her nomex-gloved fingers over the throttles on the port kneeboard, the "keys," and pushed them smoothly to the forward stops. The engines howled behind her. The needles on the faces of the electronic instrument panel displays rotated to show a hundred percent thrust. She pulled the keys to the right to the detent, then pushed them farther forward, engaging the afterburners.

If the jets had been roaring before, they were screaming now. The jets became rocket engines as the JP-5 flowed into the jet exhaust and the nozzles constricted. Twin twelve-foot-long flame cones flared out of the tailpipes. The fighter vibrated beneath her with the shear power of the thrust on afterburner. Whitworth checked the panel and nodded to the deck officer, then threw him a salute, indicating she was ready for launch. He saluted back with one of the wands, then turned his body so that his feet were widely spread on the deck, in line with the catapults. In one graceful motion, he quickly waved the wand high over his head in an arc that pointed forward, extending his wand all the way to the deck, then brought it up to point straight ahead, the catapult officer's signal to activate the catapult.

One instant Whitworth was strapped into a howling fighter jet held restrained on the deck. The next she was slammed into her seat and traveling upward through a vertical tunnel with the blood roaring through her ears. The feeling of sitting in a horizontal plane changed to that of sitting on an upright rocket, the g-forces making it seem to her brain as if the carrier deck was a wall and she was flying straight up. The stick came into her waiting right hand, her left still fighting the g's on the keys, and the airframe shook as the catapult disconnected. The tunnel of the carrier deck flying toward her melted into the dark sea and the slightly lighter starlit sky. The fighter's ride was suddenly smooth after the hellish catapult shot, struggling for altitude as it left the carrier behind. Whitworth pulled up and the sea vanished. Only the stars were visible. She glanced in the side mirror at the dimly lit carrier behind them, the deck becoming smaller as the fighter climbed, the jets shrieking behind them. The instrument panel's display of altitude wound up as the fighter climbed through a thousand feet and higher. Whitworth put the jet into a left turn, orbiting the *John Paul Jones* until she leveled off at forty thousand feet. She flew to the coordinate of the hold position, awaiting the launch of the rest of the squadron.

It didn't take long. The carrier's catapults pumped out fighter after fighter until all but the reserve force was airborne. Whitworth's squadron formed up behind her, and without a radio transmission, she wiggled the wings of the F-22 and headed northwest at full throttle. The fighter sped up to Mach 1 and went supersonic, the squadron on her wings. In the next hour she expected to engage the Red Chinese Panda strike fighters and their Cobra anti-air missiles. Once both threats were burning on the waves below, the squadron would head in and put their large load of Mark 80 JSOW Joint Standoff Weapons into the Red carrier, the Beijing-class battlecruisers, and the assorted heavy cruisers of the Red fleet.

"You with me, Bald?"

"Looking good, Fuzz," the interphone crackled. "So far we're alone. The Jolly Rogers own the skies."

In the air operations gallery of the *John Paul Jones,* Admiral Ericcson watched in satisfaction as the last jets were launched. The reserve jets were attached to the catapults, their engines at idle. They would wait out the battle here, waiting to guard the carrier. Ericcson put out the cigar and walked back into air ops, lighting a second Partagas as the squadrons flew toward the Red force.

"*Port Royal, Sea of Japan, Coral Sea,* and *Atlas Mountain* are commencing Equalizer cruise missile launch, Admiral," Commander Weber said, looking over from his display. The heavy supersonic large-bore cruise missiles would fly horizontally off the short decks of the cruise missile carriers, then climb at a thirty-degree angle for the heavens as their solid rocket first stages pushed them to fifty thousand feet and their ramjet engines came on-line for the trip to the Red fleet.

"Oh, God, smash the teeth in their mouths," Ericcson muttered around the cigar clamped in his teeth to no one, thinking of the Red fleet. "Break the jaw-teeth of these lions, Lord. Let the whirlwind snatch them away. Then the just shall rejoice to see the vengeance and bathe their feet in the blood of the wicked." Ericcson looked up to see Pulaski staring at him, and shrugged. "Psalm fifty-eight," he said.

Eighty-two miles ahead of the *John Paul Jones* and five hundred feet below her keel, the fast-attack nuclear submarine making full turns at fifty percent reactor power made way swiftly toward the Red Chinese Battlegroup Two while screening the *Jones* task force, without the knowledge of the fleet she protected.

The control room of the USS *Hornet,* a Virginia-class submarine never truly finished by the Pearl Harbor DynaCorp Naval Shipyard, was rigged for black on the orders of Commander Browning "B.D." Dallas, the submarine's commanding officer. Dallas had been chain-smoking since local nightfall, the ship's clocks showing just after eight in the evening Zulu time. There was no doubt, Dallas thought as he coughed, he would have to give these things up, but better health would have to wait until the end of his command tour. Dallas had a heavyset medium height frame, and had been gaining forehead real estate for some years. Dallas was Squadron Seven's top commander. Dallas stood on the conn talking quietly to the officer of the deck, young Dick Jouett.

"Cyclops has the *Jones* task force, even with her in the baffles," Jouett said. "The onion array is updating the battlespace, and the aft acoustic daylight array has the wider dispersed ships of the formation."

"How good is the solution to the target battlegroup?" Dallas asked in his harsh somewhere-west-of-Chicago accent.

"USubCom's updated us with a snapshot telemetry picture from *Jones*'s Predators. It would have been better in real time, but it's all we have. It's downloaded into Cyclops, but we're either going to have to put up our own Predator to confirm the targets or use a UUV." The Mark 60 Unmanned Underwater Vehicle operated like a torpedo but collected intelligence for the mother submarine, relayed back either by a wire to the torpedo tube or by trailing a small buoy that transmitted to the overhead tactical satellite, which could then be transmitted to the submarine's passive reception buoy to the Cyclops system. "It sets us back having the satellites and the network out," Jouett complained.

"That's war," B.D. Dallas said, his attention fixed on the acoustic daylight imaging display of the Cyclops system on the command console. "You have to be able to play hurt. If that's the only battle casualty we have, it's an easy day. Officer of the Deck, man battlestations. We're going to hit the Chinese with the Vortex battery as soon as we can power them up. Make Vortex tubes one through twelve ready in all respects and open outer doors."

Jouett smiled. "Aye aye, sir, man battlestations and spin up Vortexes one to twelve. Diving Officer, over the 1MC, 'man battlestations.'"

Thirty-two minutes later, twelve Vortex Mod Echo missiles were away, blasting through the water at a supercavitating velocity of three hundred knots, their processors loaded with the locations of the Red battle fleet.

Fuzzy Whitworth checked her Breitling as BBC Radio Taipei came over the radio circuit, waiting for the half past three weather report coming on. The attack profile called for absolutely rigid em-con—emissions control, the modern term for radio and radar transmission silence—to aid them in surprising the Chinese battlegroup. At the same time, the attack needed to be coordinated with a time-on-target assault, so that at the designated second in the designated minute, all their ordnance would be exploding at once over the ships of the Red fleet. Anything less coordinated than that risked the battle fleet being alerted to the attack, and the ships would be much more vulnerable in a defensive maneuver at full anti-air warfare battlestations. The Viking wanted the Chinese asleep in the middle of the night, steaming in their normal formations, with no idea of the incoming strike. The sensitive radio direction finders and frequency scanners would not be able to detect the aircraft if the Americans kept their radars and radios completely shut down.

The aircraft had been directed to tune to BBC Taipei, and when the bottom-of-the-hour weather report came on, em-con would be lifted, and all the radars would light off at once, locking on to their targets in fractions of a second, the firecontrol computers sorting out the targets in the next ten seconds, and minutes later the missiles would arrive on target and detonate.

"... Red Chinese Strategic Rocket forces were brought to full alert today according to U.S. military sources at the Pentagon," the BBC reporter announced. Whitworth tapped her helmet with her left hand, waiting. "And the Red ambassador was called to the White House this morning, reportedly to account for the fueling of the PLA missile silos."

"Baldy, what's the status?" Whitworth asked.

"All JSOWs armed and powered up, awaiting target assignment from firecontrol radar."

"You standing by with your finger on the radar set?"

"My finger hurts from holding it on the toggle switch."

"... concludes our world news. At half past the hour, BBC Radio Taipei brings you this weather report, sponsored in part by Samsung flat panel displays—"

"Radar energize!" Whitworth shouted.

"Radar on, and targets illuminated," Lieutenant Commander Felix replied. "Firecontrol computer assigning targets on the attack profile presets."

"Come on, Bald. I need to shoot here."

"Firecontrol target assignment at nine zero percent, firecontrol is go! JSOW one, foxtrot!"

"JSOW fire one," Whitworth said calmly, arming the stick weapons control, selecting missile number one and punching the fire button on the stick. On the starboard outboard wing rail, the first standoff weapon ignited to full thrust and left the wing launcher. Whitworth was temporarily blinded as the missile accelerated away, diving gently downward on its serpentine glide slope to the aircraft carrier *Nanching*. Felix called units two through six, and Whitworth fired them, the F-22 then coming around in a Mach 2 seven-g turn as Whitworth cleared the launching position. The fighter climbed to an altitude five thousand feet higher, at her operational ceiling. The reports from the other planes of the squadron came in, reporting their weapons releases, since emission control had ended at the weather report.

Throughout the heavens, missile trails began at the wings of the jets of the Jolly Roger squadron and descended in snakelike wiggles to the ships of the battlegroup. While the JSOWs flew down to their targets, the Equalizer cruise missiles all turned to fly straight up over the ships of the fleet, then arced over and descended straight down from directly overhead—partly because anti-air warfare was usually designed to defend to an angle of seventy degrees above the horizon, and partly so they would avoid interfering with the incoming JSOWs.

At zero three thirty-three Beijing time, ninety plasma-tipped American missiles sailed toward the ships of the Red Chinese formation, all of them supersonic, all of them unstoppable, and of the ninety, only one missed the intended target, its airframe crashing into the sea forty feet west of the frigate it had been aiming for. The others impacted within sixty-five seconds of each other, and during that minute the heavens rained down fire and brimstone upon the ships of Red Chinese Battlegroup Two. By zero three thirty-five, the attack was over. Only fourteen ships of the original sixty remained on the surface.

Sixteen minutes after the initial attack, twelve Vortex missiles coming in from deep beneath the surviving ships impacted. Twelve more explosions mushroomed over the darkness-made-daylight. The supply ships untargeted by the Jolly Rogers' JSOWs and the Equalizer cruise missiles all vaporized or were blown to splinters. The surviving fourteen ships dwindled to a paltry two.

Commander Fuzzy Whitworth listened to the radio chatter on the way back. The overhead radar aircraft made a battle damage assessment for the admiral on the carrier. From what it sounded like, the attack had been a success. Whitworth was almost sorry there had been no Chinese Pandas to engage in a dogfight, but then, an easy ambush meant she and Baldy would live to fly another day. She lined up in sequence, the night still pitch-black as she descended on the glide slope to the deck of the *John Paul Jones*. She brought the heavy fighter in, hit the deck on the numbers and caught the tailhook on the arresting cable, and decelerated from 120 knots at full throttle to zero in a half second, her eyeballs wanting to leave her eye sockets. She taxied off the landing area and lifted the canopy and smiled at her maintenance chief petty officer, climbed out of the cockpit and walked into the island to the squadron room for the debrief.

The fleet oiler *Taicang* labored through the gentle seas, the midwatch routine as the ship steamed in formation with the battlegroup toward the Strait of Formosa. The deck officer on the bridge was a junior-grade lieutenant named Fang Xiou. He'd been qualified as deck officer for a year, but had spent much of his childhood in the water on his father's fishing boat. If his father could see the bridge of the *Taicang* he would scoff at all the modern conveniences. Navigation by GPS satellite, phased-array surface search radar to see the distant shoreline and the closer blips of the ships of the formation, computer-controlled high-resolution display screens showing the charts updated with the positions of the fleet's ships, air-conditioning, and tilted polarized bridge glass with circular spinning glass sections that could see through heavy weather. The helm station looked like a prop from one of the Westerners' science fiction movies.

Fang yawned, the midwatch always seeming hours longer than a morning or afternoon watch. Fortunately, he would only

stand the midwatch for the next week. Then he would rotate
off the watchbill for four days and return to the morning watch
for a week. He picked up his binoculars and scanned the ships
of the formation, checking their running lights to make sure no
one had turned early in the zigzag pattern, the risk of collision
more of a danger than any lurking submarine. He put his face
in the radar hood, confirmed the ranges to the surrounding
ships, then picked up his binoculars. The carrier *Nanching* was
not quite over the horizon. She was still visible, though hull-
down, at bearing zero nine zero true, on the port beam. The
image of the carrier was an array of lights rather than the actual outline of the hull. It would be another three hours before
dawn began to break, and the carrier's haze gray color became
evident in contrast to the dark blue sea and the light blue sky.
Fang was about to drop the binoculars when the windows of
the bridge exploded inward. The blast shock blew him back
against a bulkhead, the flying glass slicing his flesh, only his
face spared by the uplifted binoculars. In the two seconds it
took him to sink slowly to the deck, he watched in disbelief as
the *Nanching* exploded in a white ball of flames. His retinas
were burned by the fireball, the sparks dancing in his field of
vision. Explosions lit the seascape. The night vanished and
was replaced with noontime suns all shining on the horizon as
the other ships of the formation were replaced by the glaring
detonations. Fang's hearing was gone, he realized, the first explosion deafening him. He sank lower, so that he could no
longer see out the glass-less windows, but the flickering daylight still came in the bridge, the room alive with the light of
the fires of the fleet.

He wondered for a second if the enemy would target a fleet
support ship such as the *Taicang*. As if in answer to his question the deck rose slowly and became vertical. Fang could see
out of what used to be a tiled floor at the bow of the ship,
which was enveloped in flames, the fireball blasting into the
bridge from the ragged gash in the deck. The force of it ripped
Fang's body in half, his consciousness freakishly continuing in
hellish slow motion as the bridge fell back into the flames of

the explosion. As the fire surrounded him, Fang finally, grate-fully, passed into the calm blackness, and his war ended.

Around the horizon, the fires of the explosions calmed, and the seascape gradually returned to normal, the few oil fires left extinguishing in the gentle waves of the East China Sea. Thou-sands of scorched bodies littered the sea, joined by empty life preservers, capsized lifeboats, mattresses, and assorted flot-sam, some of the bodies blackened by the oil slick that cov-ered a mile diameter around the site of the former fleet.

Fourteen ships survived, and when their captains saw the carnage around them, they steamed through the debris field, looking for survivors, the rescue attempt netting only a hun-dred or so men, most of whom were injured so gravely they probably would not see the sun set that day. When no one else was found, the straggling ships turned north to attempt a ren-dezvous with Battlegroup Three.

Sixteen minutes after the initial attack, a cruel second as-sault was made, and twelve of the surviving support vessels exploded and sank. Some vanished so quickly that one minute they were steaming in the seaway, and in the next only a gi-gantic orange rising cloud marked their graves. The two ships remaining after the second wave were a tanker and the *Haijui* radio relay ship, which made the emergency transmission to the Admiralty, reporting the casualties by ship name and the survivors by name, rank, and ship.

The *Haijui* captain shook his head sadly. It had been what his first commanding officer, in his talent for understatement, would call a bad day at sea. The sun had not even risen yet.

25

The phone buzzed in Pacino's darkened stateroom. He stared at it for a moment, surprised at how deeply he'd slept. He felt so groggy it was an effort to remember where he was, that the past twenty-four hours had not been a dream.

"Pacino," he said.

"Cap'n, Off'sa'deck, sir," a young lieutenant named Deke Forbes said. "We're receiving our call sign on ELF, sir. We're being called to periscope depth."

Pacino sat up in the shaking bed. An ELF radio transmission had been mentioned in the operation order as the sole exception to radio silence and the avoidance of using the battle network for real communications. The reason that the battle network was being bypassed for this operation was not mentioned, but Pacino assumed that it had been compromised, and the arcane procedures for working around it seemed a weak improvisation. But because there was no way an enemy could transmit ELF without a huge array of large antennae with several tens of megawatts of transmitting power, the Pentagon had continued to use ELF in emergencies.

The *Devilfish* would lose only the ten minutes it took to come to periscope depth and get their electronic mail from the orbital Web server, and then they could go back deep and return to emergency flank. It would put them five miles behind their achievable track, but Pacino would have to accept that.

"Come shallow to one five zero feet, clear baffles expeditiously, and proceed to periscope depth," he ordered. "Get the E-mail transmission and return to five four eight feet at emergency flank. I'm coming out on the conn."

Forbes acknowledged and Pacino got up in the dim light of the desk lamp. He clicked on the red overheads and donned the at-sea coveralls Patton had stocked for him. They fit perfectly and had the American flag patch and the new SSNX emblem, but they felt too new. The tradition at sea was wearing coveralls with the patch of a previous ship, and for an instant Pacino longed for the coveralls he'd worn on the *Seawolf,* but then realized how ridiculous that thought was. He was in command of a new nuclear submarine for all of a week, and then he'd be back in jeans and steel-toed boots in the drydock. His thoughts returned to Anthony Michael and the rescue operation, and he suddenly thought the message would have some news.

He waited on the conn until the BRA-44 antenna was retracted back into the sail. He took the pad computer and examined the E-mail by the red lights of the conn. It was top secret, marked personal for commanding officer, double-encrypted and required an SAS authenticator. By the time the message was decoded and authenticated, the ship had returned deep and sped back up to emergency flank. Pacino read the message from Admiral Patton, and his face drained of color.

The *Snarc* had been hijacked by two people, one of them a military consultant who had boarded her and helped launch weapons against the *Piranha*. They had put Anthony Michael on the bottom. And the other hijacker was not just anyone, but someone Pacino had met in person before. On the Arctic icecap. After the sinking of the first *Devilfish*. The man was Victor Krivak. It was a new name and it came with a new face, but beneath it he was Alexi Novskoyy, the Russian whom Pacino had decided not to kill with his bare hands. This man was the one who had put the Navy's chartered cruise ship on the bottom of the Atlantic and killed over a thousand of Pacino's closest friends and comrades. He mentally went back in time to that moment in the Arctic shelter, to the instant that

Novskoyy's throat was in his left hand, with Pacino's right hand balled into a fist. Novskoyy shut his eyes in resignation, as if dying by Pacino's beating would be a relief. It was at that moment Pacino realized it would be like beating a defenseless animal and he dropped the man to the ice. In that one moment of misplaced mercy, he had condemned himself to where he was now—his career disgraced, the top ranks of the Navy dead in their hour of need, his son dying two miles below the surface of the Atlantic. Pacino's failure to kill Novskoyy had destroyed Pacino's life and killed thousands. And now he was planning to launch a cruise missile attack that could kill millions more, and by the time he did, Pacino's son could be dead.

There was one thing he knew—that if he ever again had the power over the life of Alexi Novskoyy, or Victor Krivak, or whatever he wanted to call himself, he would not make the same mistake. Even if it meant life in prison, he would rip the man's head off his shoulders.

Pacino looked up from his trance and found himself at the chart table aft of the conn. He picked up a pencil and copied the coordinates of Krivak's planned rendezvous with a motor yacht, the location just inside the range circles of the Javelin IV missiles to Washington and New York. He marked the coordinate on the chart with the cursor and checked the *Devilfish*'s position, then calculated the time it would take to get there. Pacino could beat the *Snarc* to the rendezvous by ten or twelve hours. He'd get the ship there and orbit, waiting for Krivak.

The Air Force was saturating the sea with Mark 12 pods, especially near the location of the *Snarc,* but now that there would be a motor yacht there, Pacino realized that there could be no Air Force bombers circling the rendezvous—it would scare Krivak away. Pacino had to convince Patton—and Admiral McKee—to send the Air Force packing, and to persuade them that the Tigersharks would work. Patton had always been skeptical that a torpedo without a plasma warhead could be effective—their arguments about it going back six months—but the admiral would have to believe Pacino.

Pacino drafted an E-mail to Patton, instructed the officer of the deck to load it into a SLOT, a Submarine Launched One-way Transmission buoy. He instructed the OOD to proceed at emergency flank to the rendezvous point, wrote a strategy for orbiting three thousand yards away, and went below to the torpedo room and the carbon processor bay where the torpedo processors were kept. It was time to work on the Tigersharks. Yet he stared at the torpedo bodies for some time, experiencing a wave of self-doubt.

Perhaps Patton had been right, that the weapons should have plasma warheads, but plasma units took up an incredible amount of space and weight, resources that could be used for fuel to extend the range. Pacino's design featured the same kind of external combustion B-end hydraulic swash plate motor that the Mark 58 Alert/Acute torpedo had, for propulsion of the unit at a relatively slow and quiet forty knots. When the weapon found the target, it would arm the molecular PlasticPak explosive and the propulsion module would be jettisoned, and a much smaller torpedo would ignite a final-stage solid rocket motor, and the weapon would transition to super-cavitating speed on its terminal run. It would hit the target at two hundred knots, a speed that could not be outrun, and the combination of the kinetic energy impact and the PlasticPak explosive would cut the enemy in half—not vaporize it as a plasma unit would, but kill it nonetheless, and the weight and space savings from the plasma warhead would allow the unit to pursue an escaping submarine target to the end of the earth.

While a Vortex or a Mark 58 Alert/Acute could miss, and required a pinpoint solution to the target, the Mark 98 Tigershark only needed the bearing and approximate distance to the target. Its carbon processor would outwit any enemy-evasion maneuvers known to mankind. In the exercises that were near-successes, the torpedo had even shown cunning and had crept up on targets at ultra slow speed, then looped around to activate the solid rocket fuel. In the two cases—out of sixty—

where the torpedo had hit the target, the target hull had been cut in two.

Of course, the other fifty-eight times the torpedo had decided that the firing ship was the target, and teaching the carbon processor the difference between friend and foe had proved daunting. There were no electronic interlocks possible like the earlier silicon processors had, so the matter had come down to educating the Tigersharks about the mother ship. So far, nothing had worked. Pacino closed his eyes, trying to think, to forget about Krivak-Novskoyy, to forget about Anthony Michael, to forget about the cruise missiles, to forget the cruise ship and the end of his career, and just concentrate on the Tigersharks.

Eight hours later Pacino fell asleep at the torpedo room console, and when the next ELF call to periscope depth came, it took some time to find him.

Anthony Michael Pacino was five years old and watching his father drive the submarine *Devilfish* to her berth at pier 22. His father waved to him from high atop the sail as the sleek black sub pulled up to the pier, without tugs or a pilot. The lines came over and Commander Pacino ordered the American flag struck as well as the Jolly Roger he illegally flew in violation of his boss's orders. The gangway was placed on the steel hull by a rumbling crane, and Daddy climbed down from the sail and marched across the brow to the pier, a speakerbox squawking, "*Devilfish,* departing!" The Navy commander ran up and hugged little Anthony, pulling him high into the air and spinning him in circles, his mother's laughter punctuating the moment. The black-haired commander put him back down on the concrete of the pier and smiled at Mommy and kissed her hard, smiling at her, and the three of them walked down the pier to the car, where Daddy promised that they would have pizza that night. The three of them stayed up late into the night, and when young Pacino dozed his father picked him up and put him in his bed, and when he woke up in the morning

Daddy was still home, taking a week of vacation, and all was right with the world.

The vision went slower and slower, finally freezing at a moment when his father smiled at him over lunch, young Pacino's peanut butter sandwich in the foreground, his father's smile the last thing he could see as the scene began to get darker at the edges, the darkness growing until it swallowed up everything, even his father's white teeth in his smiling mouth, and when there was nothing but black darkness a tiny white star of light appeared at the very end and began to grow.

Commander Peter Collingsworth reversed the thrusters and took the submersible away from the location of the plasma explosive torch. When he could no longer see the hump in the sand that was the broken remains of the *Piranha*, he called a countdown to the *Explorer II* high above his head. When the count reached zero, the control room detonated the ring plasma, and a circle twenty feet around and one inch wide ignited to the temperature of the surface of the sun. Within seconds the HY-100 high-tensile steel of the *Piranha*'s hull beneath the plasma rig melted, then vaporized. The twenty-foot-diameter curved plate separated from the remainder of the hull, and the four heavy lugs welded on kept the plate from collapsing on top of the DSV beneath.

The *Berkshire* drove cautiously up to the submarine wreck so that the pilot could see. The plate was still being supported by three structural steel hoops, the cross sections of the hoops two-inch-thick extruded I-beams rolled into circles. The plasma torch had only partially penetrated these last three. The submersible carried explosive charges for this eventuality, and Collingsworth set the charges and reeled out the wires. He would detonate these from the submersible. It took ten minutes to set them, ten seconds to prepare to detonate, and ten milliseconds for the explosions to separate the large circular plate from the surviving hoop frames.

"It's free. Take it outside fifty yards and drop it, Control," he said into his boom mike. He watched through the light of his high candlepower floodlamps as the plate was steadily raised by the four cables to the rocking *Explorer II*. Fortunately, the waves above hadn't caused the plate to smash into the DSV. He could see the command module of the DSV nestled in the frame bay of the submarine's compartment. The next chores were to sever the command module from its own airlock and to dislodge the module from the retaining mechanisms of the submarine. Collingsworth shined his spotlight down onto the hemispherical command bubble glass, hoping that it had not been fractured. It was whole. He rubbed sweat out of his eyes and turned to the task of setting up the ring plasma around the airlock to cut it and the cargo module away from the command module.

When the spotlight illuminated the hemisphere of the command window, the light from the submersible briefly shined into the command module. The lights had gone out, the interior had iced up, and the scrubbers and burners were no longer operating. The four people inside were barely making breath vapors into the polluted atmosphere of the frigid space. Astrid Schultz began to experience a heartbeat palpitation. The lack of oxygen and the buildup of carbon dioxide began to affect the regulatory mechanisms of her brain stem. The fluctuations grew worse. By the time the ring plasma explosive was detonated at the airlock, her heart was beating frantically and ineffectively, in complete fibrillation. By the time the restraining mechanism explosives were detonated, her heart had stopped. As the command module was hauled out of the coffin of the submarine wreck, Catardi's and Alameda's hearts began to fibrillate, and in the middle of the third minute of the emergency ascent, Pacino's heart began to spasm.

As the cranes on the stern of the HMS *Explorer II* lifted the DSV command module from the sunken submarine *Piranha* onto the deck, the inhabitants inside could no longer be called "survivors."

A four-man crew stood by with cutting torches in case the hatch from the cut-away airlock didn't work. One of them spun the operating mechanism, and the hatch dogs retracted.

He pushed the hatch into the space and stood back. A second eight-man crew wearing Scott airpacks blitzed into the command module, the breathing air required since the atmosphere inside was known to be polluted. Colleen Pacino could barely watch. When the first two came out, they carried out a young woman with dark hair. They hoisted her onto a gurney where a five-man emergency medical team went to work on her while they wheeled her into the interior of the ship. Next a man was brought out—Captain Catardi—and he was placed on a second gurney and wheeled away. The third victim was a slim blond woman. Colleen was about to shout at the men in the command module, but finally another two came out carrying the body of Anthony Michael.

Colleen ran to him and managed to touch his hand, but the boy's skin was gray and cold and stiff. A Royal Navy officer held her back while they wheeled Anthony Michael into the ship's medical department. She wandered back on deck, not knowing what to do, and finally decided to enter the command module of the deep submergence vehicle. The interior was airless and stuffy and cold, and there was a pile of blankets to the port side of the hatch. What a miserable place to die, she thought.

They'd been too late.

"Mrs. Pacino?"

"Yes, what is it, Commander?" Colleen looked up, startled, and stood in the passageway outside sickbay. The doctor on board the *Explorer II,* an emergency medical specialist, discarded his soiled lab jacket and donned a clean one, then pulled off his sweat-soaked cap.

"I'm sorry, ma'am. Your stepson, the young midshipman, had been unconscious too long. His temperature was perilously low when he was pulled out of the vehicle. We attempted three times to restart his heart, but he never responded. He was pronounced dead a few minutes ago."

Colleen stared at the rocking deck, steadying herself on a

handhold on the bulkhead. Michael will be devastated, she thought. "How are the others?"

"They all lived. They're stable, at least, but all three could possibly have suffered brain damage. The women are in comas and Commander Catardi is resting."

"May I see him?"

The doctor was opening his mouth to speak when another doctor slammed the door open. "Dr. Crowther, the boy's body moved!"

The doctor dashed back into the room. Colleen followed him, trying to see in the window, but they had moved around a corner. There was no news for the next hour, but finally the doctor returned, a grim expression on his face.

"His heart seemed to restart spontaneously," he said, "but this is probably just a postponement of the inevitable. He's in a deep coma, and we don't have the equipment we need to evaluate him here at sea. He's stable for now, so I recommend we sail for England, where we can obtain the best treatment."

Colleen nodded. "I want to see Commander Catardi, and then take me to Anthony Michael."

Catardi lay on the pillow, his face pasty and swollen.

"Commander? Can you hear me?" she asked. He looked at her, a question on his face. "I'm Midshipman Pacino's step-mother, Colleen Pacino."

"How is he?" Catardi croaked.

"Not good, Commander," she said, explaining.

"The others?"

"They'll live, but there may be brain damage."

Catardi mumbled something.

"What?"

"Patch," he said. "Patch saved us." It took a few minutes for Catardi to tell the story, and at the end, he fell asleep in the middle of a sentence.

Colleen was taken to Anthony Michael's bedside. She winced as she saw him. He was white as the sheets he lay on and looked as if he'd fallen off a building. Every square inch of his face was bruised and bandaged. She took his hand, the coldness of it making her shiver. She knew the boy's father would want to know what had happened, so she drafted an E-mail and sent it to John Patton, for him to relay to Pacino. She returned to sickbay and waited next to the boy and tried not to think about whatever it was her husband was doing, but from what she knew as head of Cyclops, this probably involved the SSNX, and it probably involved whatever submarine had sunk Anthony Michael, because short of taking care of that, there was no force on earth that could keep Pacino from his injured son's side.

Captain Lien Hua sat quietly at a table in what looked like the officers' mess of a ship. The photographs on the bulkhead were pictures of submarines on the surface, making it clear this was not a surface ship. He'd been captured by an American submarine, and after Zhou's orders to fire on the American survivors, this was the worst possible place to be.

The door opened, and two tall, overfed Americans led in Leader Zhou Ping. He seemed pale, but had no bruises, so the Americans must have beaten him on his back. Zhou's eyes did not seem haunted, and the thought occurred to Lien that Zhou was in a trance or drugged, but his eyes seemed clear enough. The door shut, and Zhou sat down.

"How are you, Captain?"

"Did they beat you? Their torture of me involves making me wait for the beating."

"They have not beaten me. Their captain and first officer brought me into their stateroom."

"You spoke to them?"

"They spoke to me. They will be repatriating us to the Peoples Republic as soon as arrangements can be made. A rendezvous with a surface ship is being arranged. A helicopter will remove us from this submarine and take us to the deck of the destroyer. We will wait there for a PLA Navy helicopter to pick us up and take us to one of our own ships from Battlegroup Three, which has left the Bo Hai to get us."

Lien stared at his first officer. "They're letting us go, just like that? After you fired shots at their countrymen? Do they know you did that?"

"The second-in-command of their ship *Leopard,* the one we sank, woke up and told them everything. I confirmed it to them."

"You what?"

"It doesn't matter, sir. They are still repatriating us."

"So they say. We will see. Meanwhile you have confessed to war crimes."

Zhou shrugged. "That is accurate. That is what I committed, Captain. I owe you an apology, Captain. It was wrong of me to relieve you. And even more wrong to have shot at the Americans."

Lien said nothing at first, then said haltingly, "What do you mean Battlegroup Three was in the Bo Hai?"

"We lost, Captain. The Americans sank Battlegroup Two. Beijing ordered Three to return, and the PLA has pulled back from the Indian frontier. I saw a BBC news file. The Premier made a statement."

Lien frowned as the crew served them dinner. Zhou ate tentatively, but cleaned his plate. After Zhou finished, Lien tasted the food, then ate.

"We're down from PD, Captain," Officer of the Deck Vickerson said over the phone. "Pad computer's on the way to you."

"It's here," Pacino said from the torpedo room console. He hung up and stroked the portable unit to his E-mails. There were two, one from Colleen, the other from McKee, both routed through Patton. Pacino opened up Colleen's, his hands shaking, but when he read it his face fell and a darkness clouded his mind. He could barely concentrate on the message from McKee, which reluctantly agreed to keep the aircraft away from *Snarc*'s rendezvous point, but insisted on them orbiting a hundred miles to the west as a last resort. He handed back the computer to the messenger and returned to his work with the ship's medical officer, a lieutenant surgeon assigned to the ship—yet another oddity, that since Pacino had left the Navy, doctors had been assigned to submarine crews.

An hour later, he sat back and called the executive officer's stateroom.

"Assemble the officers and chiefs in the wardroom," he said flatly.

Ten minutes later, the men who ran the SSNX stood in the large wardroom, the chairs around the table filled, all eyes on Pacino. He poured himself a cup of coffee and sat at the head of the table.

"I've got a few words for you all," he said, looking up at his crew. "The word just came from Patton and McKee—the aircraft are withdrawing. It's up to *Devilfish* and the Tigersharks now." He took a pull from the cup and went on. "I know you are all concerned about the employment of the Tigersharks, and so am I. The weapon is a killer, officers, and if it detects something in the water, it will tear its heart out, whether that detect is the firing ship, an enemy, a surface ship, or even another Tigershark. For the last twenty-four hours I've worked on finding a fix to this, and the problem is just too big. I've put a bandage on the problem by researching all the work done to date on carbon-processor depressants, and I've selected one for use on the Tigersharks while we launch them."

Vermeers interrupted. "Depressants, sir? You're drugging them?"

"Exactly," Pacino said. "The Tigershark processors are not unlike animal brains. And just like sedating a grizzly bear, we'll be drugging the Tigersharks with only their lower functions on-line. They'll have the processing power to keep themselves alive, and to maintain depth in a neutral buoyancy hover until the sedative wears off, at which point they will wake up. By then we'll be out of the area, and whatever comes into their sensor radius will be attacked."

Pacino clicked a remote, and a display flashed up on the screen. "I've sketched out the approach of the *Snarc* to the rendezvous point. We'll start along his point of intended motion, his PIM, to the east, and we'll deploy Tigersharks as if they're stationary mines. They won't have propulsion, so we'll have to stop, hover, launch, and move gently out of the way to make sure our wake does not spin or capsize the torpedo. We'll lay these units left and right of the *Snarc*'s PIM, then withdraw further to the west. As we move out of sensor range of the eastern Tigersharks, they will be waking up, because we don't want to overdose them, so we're only giving them enough of a sedative to allow us to clear the area. We'll withdraw to a point twenty miles to the west of the westernmost Tigershark, which will be deployed here, ten miles west of the rendezvous point. We'll hover here, rigged for ultraquiet, on battery power alone with the reactor scrammed. This ship will not be putting out tonals or transients from reactor recirc pumps, steam turbines or generators, air handlers or anything else. The only systems that will be on-line will be the cooling units for the Cyclops sonar suite, the Cyclops system itself and its displays, and minimal ship's lighting. Atmospheric control will be off, the ventilation systems will be secured, and it will be damned hot in here, but we will be quieter than a hole in the ocean until we kill the *Snarc* and we've accounted for every Tigershark either detonating or flooding itself and sinking to its crush depth. At that point, and only then, will we start up the reactor, return ship systems to nominal, and do a battle damage assessment to the east. Any questions?"

Rick Bracefield, the absurdly young-looking chief engineer, raised his hand as if in a classroom.

"Yes, Eng," Pacino said patiently.

"Sir, with the reactor and steam systems secured, how will we evade a Tigershark detecting us or a Mark 58 launched by the *Snarc*?"

Pacino frowned, annoyed at how obvious the answer was. "We'll make sure the ship is pointed so that the threat vector is astern, on the edge of the baffles, and if we detect a torpedo in the water we'll activate the TESA, the torpedo evasion ship alteration." Pacino stopped as he saw the downcast looks of the engineer and weapons officer. "What?"

"Captain, the shipyard never completed the TESA," the engineer admitted.

"And we haven't wired it up, sir, because we've never figured out if it's a weapons system or a propulsion system," the weapons officer, Elaine Kessler, said.

"*Clear the room,*" Pacino ordered, his angry tone bringing the officers to their feet. "Everyone out but the XO, the engineer, and the weapons officer."

The officers left, tiptoeing out of the room. The remaining three officers acted like family dogs caught stealing steak off the dinner plates.

"In twenty seconds I'm walking out that door and returning to the torpedo room," he said in quiet fury. "In ten hours, however the three of you decide, the TESA evasion system will be fully functional, and I don't care if we have to surface to make a ballast tank entry, that system will work. I want an update every thirty minutes from you, XO, and that update had better not contain the words 'impossible' or 'too late.' Does everyone have that? You will succeed or I'll have your commissions, assuming we live through this mission. Questions—XO, speak up."

"Sir," Vermeers said tentatively, "perhaps we should change the mission. It's suicide without the TESA, and we may not have it running in time. Sir, hear me out. It's not just wiring it up so the solid rocket motors ignite in the correct sequence at the right time, it's the Cyclops ship-control system. The Cyclops time constant could kill us, Captain. If the computer doesn't control the bowplanes with the right response rate, those solid rocket motors going off could plunge us down to crush depth in a second. Or we could rocket out of the sea and break in half smashing back down to the waves."

Pacino glared at the three officers, wondering what he could do to get this can't-do attitude erased from their personalities.

"You three and your men get this system working. If you fail, the mission won't change, and I will deploy the ship exactly as if I'm counting on the TESA. So this is literally do-or-die." He narrowed his eyes at them, trying to look even angrier than he felt. "Get out," he said quietly, but all three stood as if bolted to the deck. "*Get out! Get the hell out!*" he roared, and the three of them scurried out, bumping into each other and the doorjamb.

Pacino shook his head, hoping their fear of him would help them overcome their failure to imagine the system working. One thing was certain—he would not spare the ship. Novskoyy was coming with a bellyful of cruise missiles and torpedoes, and Pacino would stop him, even if it cost him the ship and every life aboard.

Victor Krivak pulled the interface helmet off and wiped the sweat out of his hair.

"Wang," he called. "We have one hour. I want you to pack our things and wait with them underneath the access hatch. And put on a wetsuit. I've decided not to surface the ship when we rendezvous with Amorn and Pedro. That way it may make it back to the Chinese."

"What is this last thing you're going to be doing before we meet Amorn?"

"Nothing. It is nothing."

"I'd like to stay aboard and see if I can help One Oh Seven recover," Wang said. "You can go ahead."

Krivak considered the request, then nodded. "Fine. Just help me pack the things I brought, and get my wetsuit ready."

Wang smiled, happy as a child. "Right away, Victor."

"Captain, battlestations are manned," Jeff Vermeers reported.

Michael Pacino stood on the conn, wearing the wireless one-eared headset with a boom microphone, looking down on his untrained crew, most of them on the same wireless circuit with him.

"Very well. Weapons Officer, mark status of all tubes."

"Sir, tubes one through four are dry-loaded with Tigershark Mark 98s, with processors loaded and sedated."

"Very well. Navigator?"

"Sir," the navigator replied, "ship is at the launch point of Tigershark unit one."

"Very well. Attention in the firecontrol party," Pacino said, amazed at how it felt to give the order. "Firing point procedures, tube one, Tigershark one."

As the Cyclops system barked out the first Tigershark torpedo, Pacino called over the medical officer. "Sixty minutes before it wakes up, right?" he asked quietly.

"Yessir. You have one hour to get away from it."

"Let's hope that sedative works. XO, status of the TESA system?"

"Still working on it, Skipper. We should know by the time the *Snarc* comes."

"XO, if I have to hit that TESA chicken switch, and it doesn't work, I'm going to fucking strangle you, the weapons officer, and the engineer to death before the incoming torpedo gets us."

Vermeers swallowed. "If I could be relieved as firecontrol coordinator, sir, I'll see to the work on the TESA."

"Excellent, XO. Navigator, relieve the XO as firecontrol coordinator."

Pacino glanced down at the geographic plot display of the Cyclops system, showing them the deployment point of the first Tigershark.

"Sir," the navigator said, "we're at the firing point for Tigershark two."

Pacino nodded, and the weapons left the ship one by one as *Devilfish* withdrew to the west. After an hour of launching and withdrawing, there was nothing to do but shut down the ship and wait for Krivak and the *Snarc*.

"Maneuvering, Captain," Pacino said over his headset. "Insert a full reactor scram and rig ship for reduced electrical."

As the air handlers wound down and the ship became stuffy, Pacino couldn't help wondering if the ship would ever be started up again. He cautioned himself to remain positive, but it was damned hard to do with a minimally functional ship and crew going up against the best submarine in the world, while his only son lay in a deep coma and was not expected to live. Was that why Pacino was taking so many risks? he asked himself harshly. Was this a death wish?

No, his mind shouted. The only death he wanted was Alexi Novskoyy's. And that of the USS *Snarc*.

26

Michael Pacino stood on the conn of the *Devilfish,* his coveralls drenched in sweat in the steaming control room. The room was airless and stuffy, the enclosing of a high-temperature steam plant in the pipe of a submarine only a good idea in the presence of a massive and redundant air-conditioning plant. There was nothing to do but stand and sweat and wait for the first Tigersharks to wake up. If the situation did not go well, the units would begin circling in wider diameter circles until they detected the SSNX, and chased him. Or homed on the other Tigersharks. If the *Snarc* showed up late, it would be a disaster—the Tigersharks would all have chased each other or run out of fuel and shut down, and the torpedo room of the *Devilfish* was completely empty. Not only was the SSNX defenseless, but among the deadly threats to her were her own weapons.

Pacino stared down on the geographic plot, the God's-eye view of the sea showing the position of the launched Tigersharks, their own position, and the track of the *Snarc.* Come on, Pacino thought, get to your rendezvous position.

"Conn, Sonar," Pacino's headset crackled. Finally, he thought. "We have multiple transients to the east, sir."

"Sonar, Captain, classify," Pacino ordered.

"Conn, Sonar, torpedo engine startups."

"Very well, Sonar. Do you correlate to the bearings of the Tigersharks?"

"Conn, Sonar, yes. Also, we have a distant diesel engine and twin four-bladed screws, from a light surface vessel."

"Very well, Sonar." Pacino looked over at Justin Westlake, the navigator, who had taken Vermeers's function as Pacino's number two while the XO supervised the repair of the TESA system. "Could be the rendezvous yacht," Pacino said.

Westlake, a thirty-two-year-old, tall, soft-spoken black officer with wire-rimmed glasses and a nasal Chicago accent, nodded. "He's late, Skipper."

"Sonar, Captain, anything on the two five four hertz *Snarc* tonal?" Pacino flipped through the command console's sonar display to the narrowband processor.

"Conn, Sonar, we're getting a slight peak on the towed array, but it's early to call."

"That's him," Pacino said to Westlake.

"I agree with sonar, Captain, that peak is too broad to call yet," Westlake said.

"I know that's what the system says, Nav, but I'm telling you, that's him."

"If that's the case, then the Tigersharks should be homing on him by now, sir, and we have nothing."

"Wait for two minutes," Pacino said. "I'm telling you, that's him. Sonar, Captain, report beam of narrowband detection on the two five four."

"Captain, Sonar, the two five four is selected to beam seven, which is seeing bearings zero eight five and one six five."

"To the east, Nav," Pacino said. "That's him."

"Conn, Sonar, we have Tigershark engines bearing east, speeding up."

Pacino smiled. "Sonar, you have any solid rocket engines yet?"

"Conn, Sonar, no—correction, yes, sir! We have solid rocket ignition. Tigersharks have something, sir!"

"One, bring the ship to missile firing depth," Victor Krivak ordered. "Fifty meters keel depth. Slow to five knots."

The deck angle increased as the *Snarc* rose from the deep cold.

"Show the chart again, same scale as last time, with super-imposed range circles."

The ship's position was flashing right at the intersection point of the Javelin IV missile range circle to Washington and Philadelphia. "Raise the scale, One, until display width is one hundred miles." The chart grew until he could see that the point in the ocean depicting the ship was slightly east of the range circles, too far by five miles from the target objective. He wanted to slow early and come above the layer, and launch the missiles once he was certain there was no one else in the area, and to make sure the chartered yacht was at the rendezvous point. When the ship came above the thermal layer into the shallows, where the water was much warmer, he commanded the computer to seek diesel engine noises. The chart flashed to the bearing of the twin diesels. The yacht that Amorn and Pedro had hired was exactly where he'd ordered it to be. An excellent sign.

"One, display missile status and targeting."

The display for the cruise missiles came up on the display, showing missile one targeted to the White House. Krivak considered changing the coordinate from the center of the White House residence to the West Wing, where the President and her staff would likely be, but Admiral Chu wanted the symbol of the presidency destroyed. It seemed a waste. He debated deleting the Philadelphia missile's target so that he could add the West Wing, but Chu wanted the Independence Hall vaporized. It was a bit odd, but then it was a client request. Krivak left the targets set as he had originally set them, and monitored the display as the missile gyros started up.

"One, make missiles one through twelve ready in all respects, and open outer doors missiles one through twelve."

The flashing dot of their position crossed the range circles just as the missile doors came open. It was time to launch.

"One, all stop and hover at fifty meters. When the ship is hovering, fire Javelin cruise missiles one through twelve at preset targets," Krivak ordered. "When launches are complete, change depth to twenty meters and shift control of the escape trunk to local control."

Krivak pulled off his interface helmet and made his way down the ladder to the middle level to the landing pad of the escape hatch, where Dr. Wang waited. As the first tube launched, shaking the deck, Wang looked at Krivak oddly.

"What's going on?" he asked, his eyes wide.

"We're launching cruise missiles at Washington," Krivak said as he reached into his duffel bag.

"What!" Wang said, his jaw dropping as a second tube launch made the ship shudder.

"You know, the White House, the Capitol. A few more targets. Then the ship will sail to Chinese waters, assuming it doesn't get destroyed by the Americans in the next few hours."

"This was never part of the deal!" Wang screamed. "You can't use this ship to fire at American land targets!"

The third tube launched. "Actually, I just did," Krivak said, finding what he was looking for, a silver-plated heavy Colt .45 automatic, with the clip already loaded. Krivak clicked off the safety and pulled the weapon out just as Wang threw himself across the narrow passageway. The .45 spoke with a loud, authoritative voice. Wang took three rounds to the heart, the momentum of the bullets stopping his charge and sending him back against the bulkhead. His eyes were still open with a fading accusatory look as he sank to the deck. Krivak knew it would be wasting a bullet, but he put the barrel to Wang's open eye and pulled the trigger. The top half of the good doctor's head burst open like a rotten melon dropped to the floor. His brains and scalp and skull made a nasty pattern against the already gore-strewn laminate of the wall panel.

"Thanks for all your work, Dr. Wang," Krivak said as he put the .45 on the deck and pulled off his shirt. The fourth missile launched as he tossed the garment to the deck. "I hope you find your severance package satisfactory." Krivak dropped his pants and stepped into the wetsuit. By the time he had the wetsuit on, the fifth and sixth missiles were away.

Krivak opened the lower hatch of the escape trunk and peeked in at the control panel, satisfied that One Oh Seven had shifted control to the local panel. He pulled in his things and unlatched the bottom hatch to shut the escape trunk.

"Good-bye, Wang. Have a good trip." Krivak slammed the hatch shut and waited for the depth gauge to show the ship coming shallow, listening to the other missile launches.

What a beautiful sound, he thought.

The fourth-launched Mark 98 Tigershark torpedo struggled to an angry consciousness, its sonar receiver fully tuned to the ocean around it. The weapon started its external combustion turbine to begin to search the sea, but there was nothing. The unit was surrounded by open, empty space. It turned a wide circle, five hundred yards in diameter, but heard nothing. It opened the circle and drove around again, but it was still alone. After the fifth, wider circle, it decided to rise up to the layer depth and see if it saw anything there. Slowly the unit drove above the depth where the water temperature suddenly changed from freezing to warm, the higher temperature water keeping the sound waves here above the layer.

As soon as the unit climbed above the layer, it heard something, and it wiggled its fins to see if the sound moved, and it did. The sound was close, inside of a mile. The Tigershark wiggled again to refine the range to the target, and it instructed the engine to shut down. It jettisoned the first stage as the explosive bolts around the unit's midsection fired, cutting it in half. In the next tenth of a second a high-pressure air bottle in the nosecone behind the sonar sensor lit off, blowing air over the tip of the coasting torpedo, and the solid rocket engine ignited. The bubbles of high-pressure air streamed down the torpedo length to the solid rocket engine nozzle. As the torpedo felt full thrust the bubble of air was replaced, the entire torpedo now encapsulated in a supercavitating bubble of steam. It sped up to 100 knots, its aim at the target unwavering, then 150 knots, finally speeding up to 200 knots, and by then the distance to the target had been eaten completely up.

The torpedo blew into the hull of the target, the kinetic energy of impact shredding the bow, and just as the remains of the torpedo were traveling through the fragments of the target the PlasticPak warhead detonated, and the rest of the target exploded upward into the atmosphere. A red cloud of atomized blood marked the passage of the men named Amorn and Pedro as their motor yacht ceased to exist.

"Captain, we have transients on broadband bearing zero eight eight, sir. It sounds like solid rocket engine ignition."

"Understand, Sonar," Pacino said, pursing his lips, "you already reported that—Tigershark engine start-ups."

"Conn, Sonar, no. These are missile launches, Captain. Cruise missiles!"

Pacino opened his mouth to give the next order just as XO Vermeers came into the room, a dark scowl on his face as he grabbed a wireless headset. He looked at Pacino and held out his fist with his thumb pointed down. There was no time for anger at Vermeers. Pacino shouted to the diving officer, "Vertical rise to periscope depth, seven five feet, raise the Type 23 and the BRA-44!"

The ship rose sluggishly as the diving officer blew high-pressure air into the depth control tanks. "BRA-44 BIG-MOUTH coming up, sir!" he called. "Eighty feet, sir!"

"Get us up," Pacino ordered as he pulled on the Type 23 periscope helmet. "Arm the Mark 80 SLAAM missile battery," he said, his voice distorted by the helmet. The Submarine-Launched Anti-Air Missiles might be able to catch up with a Javelin on solid rocket thrust, as long as he could launch them fast enough. He frantically strapped on the thigh control pad, cursing that he had failed to anticipate that he might need to use the periscope.

"Seven five feet, sir!"

By the time Pacino had turned on the periscope visual, the unit was out of the sky. He trained his view to the sky and immediately saw four arcing smoke trails from the horizon to the cloudy sky.

"SLAAM panel armed, Captain," Vermeers shouted.

"Mark 80 launch!" Pacino called, stabbing the joystick of the Type 23 on his thigh, the heat-seeking anti-air missile launching from the sail and immediately taking off in pursuit of the Javelin cruise missiles. He launched five heat seekers, then a sixth as another missile flew out of the sea, its rocket engine lighting off just above the waves and hurling it skyward. "I don't have any explosions," Pacino called, but just then one of the Javelins exploded into flames—one of the Mark 80s had caught up with the missiles and blown it apart.

Pacino continued launching Mark 80s as the Javelins came flying out of the sea. There was one major problem—he had only eight Mark 80s and the *Snarc* out there on the horizon had twelve Javelins.

"XO!" Pacino barked as he launched Mark 80 number seven, and as the third Javelin cruise missile exploded in the clouds. "Get on a UHF circuit to the Pentagon and call in an OPREP-Three on these missiles. Tell them there are four Javelins inbound from this position."

To Vermeers's credit, he asked no questions as he threw his headset to the deck and dashed to the radio room. He could have been patched in from the conn, but that would have taken thirty seconds of coordination with the radiomen, and there was no time.

Pacino launched his eighth and final Mark 80 and watched the eighth Javelin cruise missile explode, his face a mask of impotent fury as the ninth Javelin rose from the sea. The damned *Snarc* was right there, twenty miles away on the horizon, and as yet there had not been a single Tigershark detonation.

"Conn, Sonar, we have an explosion in the water."

"It isn't the *Snarc,* Sonar," Pacino said, annoyed. "She's still launching."

"Explosion is on the bearing to the motor yacht, sir."

"Very well, Sonar, continue to examine bearing zero eight eight for Tigershark acquisition."

"Conn, Sonar, aye, but nothing yet, sir."

"Dammit," Pacino muttered.

"Conn, Sonar, we have Tigershark rocket motor ignition on the edge of the starboard baffles, bearing zero eight five."

"Finally," Pacino said, his periscope crosshairs on the horizon as the tenth Javelin cruise missile rose out of the sea. If the *Snarc* detonated now, there would only be two cruise missiles that had evaded his counterattack rather than four.

"*Conn, Sonar!*" the headphone screeched painfully in Pacino's ear. "Bearing drift to Tigershark torpedo is *left,* not right! I'm calling torpedo in the water! *Tigershark is targeting own ship!*"

Pacino ripped off the Type 23 helmet, the helmet bouncing on the deck, and shouted to the diving officer, "Emergency deep! Flood depth control at max rates! Make your depth thirteen hundred feet, and *expedite*!" He grabbed the 7MC microphone and shouted into it, "Maneuvering, Conn, execute fast recovery start-up, emergency rates!" He dropped the microphone and found Vermeers and shouted, "Arm the TESA!"

Vermeers's eyes grew wide and he shook his head rapidly. "Sir, we couldn't tie it into the Cyclops system! If you light it off, the bowplanes won't be under Cyclops control, and we'll go through crush depth in a second!"

"Conn, Sonar! Tigershark incoming! We have confirmation on acoustic daylight imaging! It's about to light off its solid rocket fuel, Captain!"

"Captain, depth thirteen hundred feet, sir," the diving officer called, a frightened kid in the wraparound ship-control console. "Securing flooding depth control two and hovering at test depth, sir."

Pacino froze for a second. Then an idea formed in his mind, the idea seeming foreign, as if he were being whispered to by someone both far away and standing immediately next to him, and he could hear the words in a mental voice not his own, shouting in his mind, *Hit the chicken switch at test depth with a quarter-degree rise on the bowplanes.* Pacino frowned, but there was nothing else he could think of.

"Conn, Sonar, Tigershark torpedo rocket motor ignition, close range!"

"Diving Officer!" Pacino yelled, knowing he was about to give his last order on the *Devilfish*, his last order on earth. "Hold one-quarter-degree rise on the bowplanes and emergency blow forward, now!"

"Quarter . . ." the diving officer said, his voice in a deep bass, a slow-motion sound as if Pacino's time sense had blown up so that a second would now take an hour. Pacino's eyes found the twin yellow plastic-covered steel levers in the overhead above the command console.

"Degree . . ." the diving officer's oddly distorted and slowed voice said as Pacino reached into the overhead with both hands and grabbed the Pacino chicken switches, the twin actuators of the TESA torpedo evasion ship alteration system.

"Rise . . ." the diving officer called as Pacino felt the grips of the TESA levers in his hands. He pulled the levers down as hard as he could.

"On . . . the . . ."

Pacino pulled down the TESA levers out of the overhead, held the levers down and twisted, his face a mask of fury as he waited for the system to light off.

"Bowplanes . . . and . . . emergency . . ."

Nothing was happening, Pacino thought, telling himself to keep the TESA actuators down.

"Blow . . . forward . . ."

The steam generators of the reactor should have been blowing to the emergency steam headers along the ship's skin, blowing steam through the rubbery anechoic coating of the ship, trying to create a vapor bubble at the skin. Forward, the high-pressure air system should have been pressurizing the emergency TESA headers at the skin of the ship and forcing out air bubbles that should be collecting around the hull and forming the bubble that would grow to become a supercavitating ship-length vapor sheath as the emergency engines started.

"Aye . . ." The diving officer's voice had slowed to a barely recognizable baritone slowed-down growl. Pacino glanced be-

tween the extended TESA actuators at the diving officer, seeing his hands reach slowly, slowly into the overhead console
for the emergency blow levers, and it seemed his hands would
never reach the levers.

Vermeers's mouth was open, his lips quivering slowly, looking like curtains billowing gently in the wind. *"Caaaptaaain,"*
he shouted in slow motion. Pacino's mind was far away, aft of
the reactor, aft of the ship service turbines, aft of the propulsion turbine generators, aft of the maneuvering cubicle, aft of
the hydraulic plant, aft of the skin of the ship, aft of the number three ballast tank with its oil-enclosed main motor, aft of
the number four ballast tank where the TESA rocket motors
were mounted, and further aft, outside the envelope of the hull
and aft of the rudder and sternplanes and propulsor shroud and
further aft into the sea, looking ahead at the ship, at the rocket
motors of the TESA system with the explosive charges blowing off the seawater protection cowlings and the bottom and
top rocket motors igniting into white-hot incandescence, then
the port and starboard motors igniting, then the pair at one
o'clock and seven o'clock, lighting off in pairs around the
ship, until all the rocket motors were at full thrust, the rocket
exhaust melting away the thick steel of the rudder and the
sternplanes and the structural bulkheads of the number four
ballast tank, and the bubble of air and steam over the ship
grew and the ship accelerated and formed its own self-perpetu-
ating supercavitating bubble over the surface of the ship until
the ship was going fifty knots, then a hundred, the ship's speed
climbing to two hundred knots.

His mind shifted back to the control room, where the sound
of rocket motors grew to an earsplitting shriek and there was
suddenly no more sound, because either Pacino's time sense
had slowed the world to a stop, or because he had grown deaf,
and still he wasn't sure if it had worked, until he felt himself
go quickly horizontal, his body hanging by his hands on the
TESA actuators, hanging straight down, but the deck was parallel to his body, and he suddenly weighed a thousand pounds
and his hands could no longer hold his weight and he let go

and the control room deck moved beneath his feet and he didn't know whether he was flying through the air of the control room or if the control room had suddenly decided to fly forward and he hit the aft bulkhead of the control room so hard that his body collapsed and his head hit the inertial navigation binnacle and the control room dissolved into a gigantic hurricane of sparks and the world became slowly black.

The rear hull of the USS *Devilfish* erupted in a roar of flames as the two dozen solid rocket engines of the large bore Vortex Mod Alpha missiles ignited in pairs, until all twenty-four had lit up at full thrust. The rudder and sternplanes and propulsor of the ship vaporized in the high-temperature blast.

When the torpedo evasion system actuated, the ship was at her test depth with a quarter-degree rise on the bowplanes and an emergency blow in the forward ballast tanks. What had before been a nuclear submarine hovering at thirteen hundred feet suddenly became a huge underwater rocket. The air and steam bubbling at her skin grew until a vapor bubble enclosed the hull from her nosecone to the Vortex engines, and the ship accelerated at ten g's through 50 knots, through 100, blowing through the seas until, at the moment the engines ran out of fuel and cut off, the ship was going 205 knots, with an up angle of two degrees. The ship rocketed away from the Tigershark rocket-propelled torpedo pursuing her and roared upward toward the thermal layer. The periscope and BRA-44 radio antenna mast had broken off in the slipstream, and as the submarine flew through the sea, the sail and the sonar dome became crushed in the force of the flow. Before the ship rushed above the layer, the acceleration forces had ripped the starboard steam piping off the number one turbine generator, and the steam system leaked rapidly into the engine room with enough energy to cook every soul aft like a boiled lobster.

The Tigershark torpedo in pursuit sensed that its rocket fuel was running out, and the warhead of PlasticPak explosive detonated a thousand yards aft of the retreating form of the *Devilfish*. The pressure wave of the explosion ripped into her aft

hull moments before the ship roared out of the sea. The aft
hull was breached in the number three ballast tank from the
Tigershark as the hull arced and flew back down toward the
water of the Atlantic. The deceleration forces of the ship hitting the water caused everything that had been accelerated aft
to be suddenly thrown forward, and the forces were strong
enough to cause equipment to fly off foundations and rip the
deckplates off their mountings. The USS *Devilfish* came to
rest floating on the surface, a barely recognizable hulk with a
flattened sonar dome, a crushed sail, and a burned and broken
aft hull.

The ship began taking water aft and settled slowly into the
sea.

The eleventh and twelfth missiles shook the deck as they left
the ship. Victor Krivak grinned as he waited for Unit One Oh
Seven to rise to twenty meters, mast broach depth, so he could
flood the escape trunk and leave the *Snarc* before the American search vessels and planes found her here at the base of the
missile flame trails. There was the chance that she would escape and make it around South America for the trip to Red
China, but the carbon processor was probably too far gone in
its catatonic state to evade any search-and-destroy antisubmarine action. The pressure gauge in the escape trunk began to
rise, slowly at first, then smartly to the depth of sixty-five
feet—the American pressure gauges marked in feet—where
Krivak began the procedure to flood the airlock. He had already pulled on his combined buoyancy compensator and
tanks, his fins and his mask, and his supplies were tied to him
by a tether.

He ordered the local panel to open the vent valve to the interior of the command module, and when the valve indicated
open, he ordered the flood valve opened, bringing seawater
into the chamber. The chamber water level rose rapidly with
warm Atlantic seawater, until it climbed to the level of the
upper hatch. The control panel and Krivak's head were in an
alcove behind a steel curtain, with a bubble of air trapped

there. Krivak shut the vent valve and allowed the chamber to rise in pressure until it was equalized to the seawater. The pressure in the chamber rose slowly. When it was the same as the surrounding ocean, he would open the top hatch and get out of here.

The first-launched Tigershark woke later than the other units, in time to hear the carnage as the second- and third-launched units tore each other apart in mutual explosions. The Tigershark started its engine and began a slow target-seeking circle, but there was nothing but the cloud of bubbles from the previous explosions. A second and third circle, with wider diameters, revealed nothing in the seas. The Tigershark rotated its fins and aimed shallow, hoping for a target above the layer.

The unit was amazed at how close the target was, and yet how invisible it had been from below-layer. The Tigershark armed the warhead, circled around to give itself some room, jettisoned the first stage, and lit off the rocket motor, the target growing in its seeker.

Krivak ducked under the steel curtain below the open upper hatch of the escape trunk of the *Snarc*. He pushed with his flippers and rose until his head protruded out of the hatch. He put his hands on the upper surface, knowing that he had only twenty seconds before the *Snarc* took control of the hatch and shut it on him, and the hydraulics were strong enough to cut him in half. So naturally, the tether of his equipment bag got hung up on a manual valve handle. Krivak debated leaving the equipment, but ducked back down, freed the tether, and pushed rapidly back up, his eye on the hatch. He swam out of the ring of the hatch, the equipment package following, and he pulled it all out of the hull. The hatch began to shut slowly behind him. He reached down to the hull and tapped it twice in farewell, then kicked to the surface.

Tigershark Unit One saw the target grow larger and larger until it blotted out all else, and just before it made contact with

the fat submerged hull it detonated the PlasticPak explosive.
The stern section of the submarine target came open in a violent explosion that separated the forward half of the ship from
what was left of the aft half. The shock wave of the explosion
reached out for the swimmer leaving the target's hull.

There was nothing left of the Tigershark when the orange
flame ball of the explosion had collapsed and cooled and dis-
integrated into a mass of a quadrillion vapor bubbles. Just as
the explosion calmed and the front half of the hull of the target
began to sink, two more Tigersharks swooped down on it and
blew it to molecules just before it reached its crush depth.

The bow section of the SSNX *Devilfish* rose slowly out of the
surface as the stern section began to sink. Twenty miles astern
of her, the two remaining Tigersharks were turning circles,
searching for targets.

Captain Michael Pacino lay on the aft sloping deck of the
control room with Vermeers screaming silently in his face. He
opened his eyes and tried to sit up, but it felt as if every bone
in his body were broken. The lights were out except for the
emergency battery-operated battle lanterns, which were flickering dimly. Pacino opened his mouth to speak, when suddenly his hearing returned and Vermeers' voice slammed into
his eardrums, shrieking, "*Have to abandon ship, sir!*"

Pacino managed to stand, leaning heavily on Vermeers, and
allowed himself to be dragged to the middle level, where men
and equipment were being evacuated through the hatch. Pacino felt his legs give, and his body slammed into the bulkhead, the world spinning around him.

". . . there are more Tigersharks out there! Hurry!" Vermeers
shouted at the crew at the escape trunk. "By the time we hear
their rocket engines, they'll be here. Now, go!"

Pacino felt himself pulled and pushed up the ladder and into
the escape trunk. He felt he was about to vomit, and tried to
hold it. There was a circle of light above him, a searchlight so
bright it hurt his eyes, slamming his eyes flat in his eye sockets, until he realized it was the sun—the ship was on the sur-

face. He was pulled out of the hatch onto the tilted deck top-side, and had a momentary impression of the sail ripped off the hull and the aft part of the ship in the water, the deck inclined in a severe aft pitch. He staggered on his feet as other crewmembers were pulled out of the hull. His stomach lurched and he threw up on himself. Then the world grew dim.

Michael Pacino fainted and fell off the hull and splashed in the water on the port side of the hull, the same side that the Tigershark torpedo approached.

"Vickerson!" Vermeers called. "Get the captain to a life raft!"

The young lieutenant dived into the water carrying a spare life jacket. She caught up to Pacino, strapped his limp form into it, and towed him around the stern of the sinking ship to one of the life rafts floating on the other side.

Pacino came to as the last of the men and emergency equipment were pulled from the hull. The smashed-in nose of the ship tilted toward the sky as the ship began to sink to the depths. Pacino saw the forward escape trunk hatch sink below the waves, the hull taking water forward, until only the place where the nosecone should have been poked slightly above the waves, until it too vanished in a ring of foam.

He saw it go and looked dejectedly down at the life raft. The mission had failed. Four cruise missiles had gotten by the *Devilfish,* and the Tigersharks had gotten them instead of the *Snarc.*

"Give me some binoculars," Pacino said to Vickerson.

As she handed them over, the sea where the *Devilfish* had been exploded in a volcano of foam. A second explosion came ten long seconds later. For the next two minutes the foam rained down on the life rafts.

"What the hell was that?" Pacino asked.

The sonar chief looked over at him, shaking his head. "Two more Tigersharks, Skipper. We got out just in time."

"Did we lose anyone, Vickerson?" Pacino asked.

She looked at him sadly. "We only evacuated forward, sir.

Aft was flooded and had a major steam leak. We couldn't get the hatch open. None of the nukes made it out."

Pacino sighed.

"Binoculars, sir?"

"Which way is east? I want to find the bearing to the *Snarc*. Is there any chance we hit it?"

"We couldn't tell, sir," the sonar chief said.

Victor Krivak floated in the sea, his face exposed, his mask half off, his regulator blown away from his face. For a half hour after the explosion of the *Snarc* he floated there, breathing but unconscious, floating with the buoyancy of his wetsuit, the buoyancy compensator filled with air before he left the escape trunk.

A booming roar sounded through the seas, from the east.

"What was that?" Pacino asked. He looked over at one of the other life rafts, where Vermeers scanned the sea with his binoculars. "Did you see anything?"

"No, Captain," Vermeers called over, "but it was from the bearing of the *Snarc*. I think we got her."

Pacino nodded, looking over the horizon at the bearing. Fingers of foam from an underwater explosion reached for the sky. "Excellent."

"Vickerson, did you pull the pin on the emergency beacon?"

"Half an hour ago, sir," she said. "I thought we had aircraft orbiting to the west."

"Maybe the beacon didn't work," Pacino said.

"Then this will be a long wait," Vickerson said.

Slowly, painfully, Victor Krivak opened his eyes and blinked at the sea around him. He had no memory of what had happened. It seemed as if a second ago he had pushed off the hull of the *Snarc* and now he floated here with his ears ringing, with blood on his face and in his mouth—it felt as if he'd bitten clear through his tongue. His ears were bleeding, and his back ached where the tanks were touching him. Something had happened, perhaps a self-destruct charge the *Snarc* had set off. Damned lucky thing he'd gotten out in time, he thought. He wondered for a moment if the ship had suffered an attack for the launching of the missiles, but it was impossible. He'd detected no one, the *Snarc* had the acoustic advantage over every submarine on the planet, and there were no aircraft he could see or hear. It had to have been a self-destruct charge.

Krivak yawned to clear his aching ears and found the equipment pack on its tether. He hauled it up and found the life raft, and pulled the carbon dioxide pin on it. The yellow rubber raft inflated until its four-meter diameter floated on the meter-tall waves. Krivak threw the rest of his equipment in, took off his scuba gear and threw it in the raft, then vaulted in, his back and head aching. He opened his waterproof equipment container and pulled out the satellite phone and dialed Amorn. A dozen tries, and nothing but a busy signal. This never happened to Amorn's phone. Something had gone terribly wrong, he realized.

He listened to see if he could hear Amorn's yacht's diesels. He scanned the horizon, but there was no yacht visible. Krivak cursed that he had not thought of putting binoculars into the emergency kit, but it shouldn't have mattered. It was doubly odd, since he had distinctly located the yacht before he fired the cruise missiles. He'd have to use the fall-back plan, and pull the pin on an emergency locator beacon, and concoct a story for whatever civilian authorities picked him up. Odds were, it would be the Americans who came for him. He chuckled at the thought as he pulled off the wetsuit and donned cotton coveralls, pulling on the belt over them and stashing the silver-plated .45 in the belt after checking the clip—it wouldn't do to be attacked by a shark without his Colt, he thought. He opened up some of the ration containers and chewed on a protein bar. After fifteen minutes, he leaned against the side of the raft to wait, and a few minutes later he fell asleep.

"Sir, over there!" Vickerson said, handing Pacino the binoculars. "There's something yellow floating there."

"Get out the oars," Pacino said, looking in the binoculars. "Row all rafts toward that spot."

For the next hour the four rafts from the *Devilfish* rowed toward the yellow object. When it was visible, Pacino stared in astonishment. "There's someone alive," he said.

It could only be one man, he thought. Victor Krivak. *Alexi Novskoyy.*

Pacino's jaw clenched in anger. He rooted through the emergency bag and withdrew a diving knife in its scabbard and looped it onto his belt, hoping no one had seen him.

"Stop rowing," he said. "Don't get any closer." Pacino looked over at Vermeers. "XO, this is a direct order. Don't allow anyone to come after me. You're in command." Pacino dropped off the side of the raft and began swimming to the raft, ditching his life preserver ten feet from the raft so he could swim faster, his body aching, but the pain tolerable. Much more tolerable than the fact that Alexi Novskoyy still lived.

The orbiting P-5 Pegasus antisubmarine patrol plane got the radio orders to investigate an emergency locator beacon at the location of the explosions that the Mark 12 pod had detected. On the orders of Admiral McKee, they had stayed out of the area, out of range of the *Snarc*'s Mark 80 anti-air missiles. But after all the underwater detonations—the last one probably taking out the Mark 12 pod itself—McKee had judged the seas safe, and had vectored in the P-5.

Far to the west, fifty miles off the coast of Washington, New York, and Philadelphia, several squadrons of Air Force Scorpion interceptors orbited over the Atlantic, all of them in touch with the KC-10 AWACS radar plane orbiting at forty thousand feet and searching at peak alert for the incoming cruise missiles. Had the *Snarc* managed to shoot the missiles in secret, they would have flown in stealthily, below the level of the air-search radars, and finding them would have been a miracle, but with the warning from the *Devilfish* of the exact time and location of launch, the Air Force had been able to scramble every asset with wings to search for the elusive plasma-tipped weapons.

Instead of frantically searching for the missiles, the crews had the luxury of arguing over who would get the privilege of shooting them down. In all cases, the squadron commanding officers took their shots. The Mongoose heat-seeking missiles ripped the Javelin IVs to shreds, the plasma warheads shattered and falling to the sea in fragments. As news of the destruction of the Javelins reached the presidential evacuation bunker, the President's 888 was called in, and the President and staff returned to Andrews Air Force Base. Admiral Patton took a limo to the Pentagon to await news of the *Devilfish*.

Michael Pacino made his way slowly to the raft and swam to it, approaching it from underwater as he got close. He popped his head up, trying not to make noise with his breathing, and pulled the diver's knife from its scabbard. He looked up at the bump of the raft occupant's head, knowing it was Victor Krivak—although in his mind Pacino decided to remember him as Alexi Novskoyy. Pacino took a breath, and shot his arm out of the water and grabbed the man by the throat and pulled him into the water. Just before he fell in, Pacino had a glimpse of a man in his forties, a man as handsome as a movie star, but there was no surgery on earth that would change those ugly eyes, eyes that Pacino had looked into on the Arctic icepack so many years before. These eyes belonged to the man who had torpedoed and destroyed the first *Devilfish*, and who was now responsible for four cruise missiles being launched at Pacino's home, who was responsible for the loss of the second *Devilfish*, and most of all, who had put Pacino's son at death's door. It was the last of these that earned him the thrust of the knife deep into the side of his throat as he fell in slow motion into the water, the red spurting blood spraying into Pacino's eyes.

In the time it took to blink the blood out of his eyes, Novskoyy had knocked the knife from Pacino's grip with his arm, and had wrenched toward Pacino. Novskoyy was much stronger, and he smashed his fist into Pacino's face, breaking his nose. Blood sprayed into the water. Pacino reached for Novskoyy just as the war criminal lunged for something in his belt. Pacino connected with Novskoyy's face in a hard jab, the force of it sending him backward in the water away from the Russian. Pacino struggled to get close again, and suddenly found himself staring into the barrel of the pistol Novskoyy had pulled from his belt. Pacino froze for an instant, then dived into the water, wondering if a gun could fire when it was wet.

Victor Krivak had been napping pleasantly, awaiting rescue, when he was grabbed by the throat and pulled violently into the sea. He barely had a look at the man who had assaulted him, for a moment thinking it was Wang, the thought of the doctor coming back for vengeance filling him with adrenaline. He was trying to punch the man when the knife entered his throat and cut him hard. At first there was no pain, just a dizzying feeling of floating. His blood was everywhere, and it was probably not something he would survive, which made him fight all the harder. He managed to connect with a punch to the intruder's nose, the man's face covered in blood both from his broken nose and from the blood he'd drawn from Krivak's neck. Oddly, the white-haired fiend seemed somehow familiar. Krivak reached down for his belt, hoping the silver-plated Colt was there, as the world became dim around the edges. He pulled it out of the water. With his left hand he gripped the collar of his unknown attacker, and as he aimed the .45 at the man, he caught a glimpse of his nametag, which read PACINO. He knew that name was familiar, but he was getting cold and groggy, undoubtedly from the knife wound, and he couldn't place the name.

He brought the Colt to the man's face, but the man tried to dive below the waves. Krivak aimed lower and fired off four shots and waited for the man to return to the surface. As the seconds ticked off, the waves and the sky were no longer blue, but like something from an old black-and-white movie. The sound of the waves and the wind was missing, and the sunlight began to fade into dusk, though it had to be much too early for sunset.

He waited for the body to float back to the surface, and finally it did, but the man's hands clawed at Krivak's chest, and clutched at the gun, and by this time Krivak was becoming too weak to resist. As the man named Pacino grabbed for the pistol, it went off one last time, and Krivak wondered if he had finally connected and made the kill. He realized slowly that he no longer cared. Oddly, in spite of the adrenaline of the fight, he suddenly felt cold and sleepy.

It must be the darkness, he thought, as he felt the pistol leave his grip.

Pacino dived deep, but not deep enough. A slicing pain shot through his left shoulder, another one hitting his right thigh. A third seemed to slice into his ear, and that was when he opened his eyes and tried to see Novskoyy in the water. All he could see was a dim shape thrashing in front of him, one of his hands above the surface, a glint of silver coming from above. Pacino swam in, needles of pain invading his mind from his leg, and he lunged for the pistol. He found it, but as he curled his fingers over it, the muzzle flashed and it seemed as if that last bit of light drew the rest of the world's light away, and Pacino was plunged into darkness, and it was as if one moment he was alive and fighting and the next he was in a deep dungeon and his body was swimming away from him and he couldn't seem to catch it.

He remembered thinking of Anthony Michael and trying to say his name, but it was as if he had forgotten how to talk, and he was floating and the words up and down no longer meant anything, and the world rotated slowly around him and he fell and spun away, gradually at first, and then rapidly, until he forgot his son's name and Colleen's name and his own name and he stopped existing and so did the world, and it was over.

Epilogue

It was like coming to periscope depth.

At first it was complete darkness, with only the awareness that soon there would be light, and a watchfulness for the brightness. Then there was a blackness that was just a shade lighter than black, the blackness giving way to a deep blue, and the blue lightened until a distant world came into view, with no structure to it, until finally the bottoms of the waves could be seen at a distance of what seemed miles, until they came more clearly into view, closer until the wave crests and troughs could be made out, and finally a trough came closer and another world peeked through for just an instant, and disappeared again as a wave crest splashed onto the view and there was the blue world again for a moment, until the view splashed with angry foam and the new world existed again, more solidly this time, and then there was focus and structure and the new conscious world became real.

"Where am I?" he tried to say, but all that came out was a choked rattle. He tried again, seeing that the world was made completely of white, and the person coming close was draped in white, and for an instant he felt a terrible fear that he had died, but then the face of the other came nearer and the face had a bandage on the forehead, and the eyes were his own, but the nose was different and he blinked and realized that it was the face of his son, Anthony Michael, and Pacino tried to find his voice again, and this time it made a sound. "Anthony," he said.

And then there was another face, this one framed in raven-black long hair, large dark liquid eyes, eyes he had first seen in a shipyard laboring over a ship they had only called the SSNX, a ship that was now a forlorn debris field on the bottom of the Atlantic.

"Colleen," he croaked.

"Don't try to talk, Michael," she said.

"Yeah, Dad," Anthony Michael's voice said.

"I have to know," he said, his voice barely audible.

"What, honey?" Colleen asked.

"Novskoyy. What happened to Novskoyy?"

"You mean Krivak?"

Pacino nodded.

"He's dead, dear," Colleen said. "Now be quiet and sleep."

Michael Pacino did as his wife told him and faded back away. A smile remained on his face.

Out in the corridor Commander Jeff Vermeers waited with the surviving crew of the *Devilfish*, with the commanding admiral of the submarine force, Kelly McKee, and with the Chief of Naval Operations, John Patton. Colleen came out and smiled, and the crowd broke into cheers until she fiercely quieted them down and ushered them out of the hospital.

"Colleen," Anthony Pacino said, "I have to be somewhere."

Colleen kissed the youth's cheek, and he walked down the hall on his crutches to the elevator and down the hall to another room. When he came in, the woman in the bed smiled, her face relaxing into lines of beauty as she did.

"Patch," she said tenderly.

"Carrie, how are you?"

"I'm good," she said weakly. "Better now. How's your father?"

"He's going to be okay."

"I'm glad." She shut her eyes.

Pacino saw someone in the corner of the room. It was Commander Rob Catardi.

"Evening, sir," Patch said.

Catardi smiled and clapped Pacino on the shoulder. "Good to see you, Patch. Carrie, I think I'll go visit Patch Senior now, if you're okay."

She nodded. When Catardi left, Pacino leaned over and kissed her gently. She kissed him back, but was not gentle in return. Her arm pulled him down to her, her fingers in his hair. After several minutes she sat up higher in bed so she could see him.

"What's this on your uniform?" she asked, touching his ribbons.

Pacino shrugged. "Navy Cross," he said slowly. "I think a medal like that is for someone who rescues more than three people. We lost the rest of the ship."

Lieutenant Commander Carolyn Alameda frowned. "Don't disrespect the award. You rescued everyone who survived. You saved four lives, including your own, which is the most important one to me."

Pacino smiled. "I thought we were doing better when we weren't talking so much."

"Come here," she said. "That's an order."

Commander Donna Phillips helped Commander George Dixon up the last steps to the lip of the drydock, to the deck with the commanding view of the hull of the Virginia-class submarine taking shape far below. Rail-mounted cranes moved slowly over her, their safety horns sounding over the bay, the scaffolding and equipment so crowded around the ship in the basin of the dock that her shape could barely be made out, but as Dixon looked at her, he saw the beauty beneath.

"Tell me her name," he said to Phillips. He'd insisted he wanted to see her first before he heard her name.

"She's the USS *Bunker Hill,* Captain," Phillips said. "And she's ours if we want her."

Dixon reached into the breast pocket of his service dress khakis and pulled out the smashed gold coin with the mushroomed AK-80 round in it. He looked at it, rubbed it between his thumb and palm and put it away.

"I think we have ourselves a new submarine," he said to Phillips. "What do you say to finishing your XO tour for a few months with me before you move on to your own command?"

"Captain, it would be my pleasure."

She helped him slowly back down the stairs to the waiting staff car for the drive back to Unified Submarine Command Headquarters, where Admiral McKee waited to debrief Dixon personally. Phillips returned to the drydock lip and breathed in the sea air, and for the next few hours, she stood and watched the construction of the submarine *Bunker Hill.*

Captain Lien Hua and Leader Zhou Ping and three men from the crew of the *Nung Yahtsu* stood holding the railing of the Aegis II cruiser USS *Valley Forge,* all of them staring in disbelief as the Peoples Liberation Army helicopter landed on the aft deck. As the rotors spun down to idle, Lien looked back in hesitation, but the Americans motioned him on, some of them even waving. It was too much to comprehend.

As he and Zhou climbed into the helicopter, he half expected an American missile to sail from the superstructure of the cruiser and blow the chopper to bits, but it never happened. The ride took an hour, to a steaming PLA Navy destroyer. When Lien climbed out, the entire crew was turned out in dress uniforms, and as he set foot on the deck, the crew snapped to attention.

Lien turned to Leader Zhou. "What is happening? I don't understand."

Zhou licked his lips. "Perhaps they thought our sinking the American submarine was heroic enough."

"Even though we lost the *Nung Yahtsu,*" Lien Hua said. The captain of the destroyer came up, smiling.

"I have this for you, Captain Lien," he said after saluting. He handed over an envelope.

It was a letter from Chu Hua-Feng, the admiral in command of the submarine force, but the letter was on PLA Navy Fleet letterhead, and Chu signed his name as a fleet admiral. The letter was a commendation for what the admiral called valor in action, and in the last paragraph, he promoted Lien to the rank of rear admiral and invited him to join him in Beijing at the PLA General Staff Headquarters. The envelope also contained collar devices—admiral's stars. Lien looked up in confusion, and the crew around him erupted into cheers, Zhou Ping clapping along with them.

Lien could barely believe it, even when the destroyer pulled into its berth, and Lien's wife and twin girls waited for him. It was only as he held his wife and hugged the twins that he felt like the long nightmare had ended. He told his family to wait and walked back to Zhou, a question on his lips.

"Why, Zhou? Why did the barbarians let me live when they knew I fired on their survivors?"

Zhou Ping looked at him as if he knew the answers. "Because, Admiral, they knew it was war. When the war ended, so did their hatred of us."

"Had the roles been reversed," Lien said, "I would have had them killed, perhaps even tortured first."

Zhou Ping nodded. "Perhaps, Admiral Lien, they aren't the barbarians you think they are."

Rear Admiral Lien Hua was silent for a moment, then nodded. "Perhaps you are right, Zhou," he said.

He walked back toward his wife, deep in thought.

Admiral Egon "The Viking" Ericcson loaded the golf bag into the trunk, then climbed into the red Porsche for the trip to the office. Saturday afternoon, he thought, the one time he could get two weeks' worth of work done in three hours. Then he'd dress for the blind date arranged by his new friend, Kelly McKee. As he thought about it, he pressed harder on the accelerator, the car taking the curve faster than usual.

As he guided the smooth Porsche toward the city, he saw the flashing lights of the police car behind him. He cursed as he pulled the Porsche over. The state trooper climbed out of the cruiser and walked over.

"License and registration, please," he demanded.

"Is this about my speeding, Officer?" Ericcson asked.

"Yes, sir," the cop said. "License and registration, sir?"

Ericcson let out a tense breath and broke into a grin, aware of the state trooper staring strangely at him, but not caring.

"Thank God, Officer," he said as he reached for his wallet. "Thank God."

Author's Note

Comments, reviews, and letters are always welcome. If you are on-line, you can reach me by E-mail at readermail@ussdevilfish.com or by visiting the Web site ussdevilfish.com. If you don't have electronic means, jot a note to the publisher. I answer every letter received—not always on the day I receive it, but eventually.

For those readers who've followed Michael Pacino from the day he commanded the Piranha-class submarine *Devilfish*, I want to express my thanks. For those who have not, please check out *Voyage of the Devilfish, Attack of the Seawolf, Phoenix Sub Zero, Barracuda Final Bearing, Piranha Firing Point,* and *Threat Vector,* all of them available at ussdevilfish.com, Amazon.com, or BarnesandNoble.com.

Welcome aboard and rig for dive.

Michael DiMercurio
Princeton, New Jersey
USSdevilfish.com

Acknowledgments

Thanks to my wife, Patti, for all the inspiration she's given me—enough for three lifetimes.

Thanks to my children—Matt, Marla and Meghan—for being my teachers and reminding me of what is truly important in life.

Thanks to Bill Parker, president of Parker Information Systems (parkerinfo.com) and architect of the ussdevilfish.com Web site, who is a great promotional sounding board and a great friend.

Finally, thanks to editorial genius Doug Grad, who guided this book to a safe landing after a hair-raising flight.